Publisher
Crime Time
7a King Henry's Walk
Islington
London N1 4NX
Fax: 020 7249 5940
e-mail: editor@crimetime.co.uk
Website:www.crimetime.co.uk

Distribution
Turnaround

Printing
Omnia, Glasgow

Editor
Barry Forshaw

Production editor
Paul Brazier

Film editor
Michael Carlson

TV & music editor
Charles Waring

Advertising
Philomena Muinzer
Tel: 0208 964 9106
Fax: 0208 881 5088

Subscriptions
£20 for 4 issues to
Crime Time Subscriptions,
18 Coleswood Road, Harpenden,
Herts AL5 1EQ
www.crimetime.co.uk

Legal

CT Publishing ISBN 1-84243-020-3

CRIME TIME ON THE WEB

Looking for that particular review or feature? Visit our website on www.crimetime.co.uk: up-dated weekly, and easier than looking in your cherished back issues!

CONTENTS

CRIME TIME

2001 Nº 23

ARTICLES

WOMEN IN CRIME:

FICTION

INTERVIEWS

REGULAR FEATURES

COLUMNS

EDITORIAL

THE DESK

The response to our Pulps issue has, I'm glad to say, been enthusiastic. When choosing the theme, I reasoned that few of us read vintage pulp material except in its reprint form (and then with the cachet of respectability that the years have granted, i.e. Chandler, Hammett), but I knew that we were all fascinated by the more garish and lurid aspects of the era – not to mention a sheer professionalism that accompanied much of the unadulterated drek.

But a *Women in Crime* issue: had I thought about what I was taking on, you might now be starting an issue on Edgar Wallace, or forgotten authors, or....anything. The most difficult aspect of the issue to co-ordinate was a massive questionnaire on women in crime. Just selecting the most apposite questions was tricky enough (even with input from CT's Natasha Cooper, Judith Gray and Eve Tan Gee). Little did I realise the astonishing diversity of answers we'd get. Or, for that matter the ease with which the answers were attained. Compared to obtaining authors' literary guilty pleasures a few issues back (which was like drawing teeth), this was the proverbial doddle. Editing the whole thing was another matter. You can decide for yourself whether it was worthwhile or not.

The thorny question of theme issues is something I'd like to throw into readers' laps: it becomes more and more difficult to come up with something fresh. So before you start reading an issue devoted to William Hague's favourite crime novels, I'd welcome a few suggestions...

Next issue's theme, though, is settled: US vs. UK crime writing. Oh, and if you're wondering where Mike Ashley's Collecting Crime column is this issue, pressure of work on Mike's own books has necessitated a one-issue hiatus. Carlson on Film and Waring on TV and Music as usual, though.

Barry Forshaw

WOMEN AND VIOLENCE

Natasha Cooper

The expression on Tony Blair's face at the Women's Institute last summer said it all. Angry women terrify men. And men still can't understand what all the fuss is about.

Any woman could tell them that it's about the male assumption that women have smaller, less significant lives than theirs. It's about the habit of mind that allows gynaecologists to think, "A few unnecessary hysterectomies here, a missed diagnosis or a slipped scalpel there, but so what? A chap can't get it right all the time." And it's about the phenomenon recorded in Angela Browning's *The Trouble with Boys* (HarperCollins, 1993) that men whose wives work outside the home establish their superior status by ensuring that their own working days are at least an hour longer than their wives'. Even now, men's experience, work and tastes are perceived to be more important than women's. That's what makes publishers advise women authors to take a unisex name for their latest pseudonym, or, like J. K. Rowling, use their initials. Unambiguously female names – as well as book titles that sound too girlie – lead to lower sales. Few men buy or read what they perceive as 'women's fiction'.

And yet when women writers move

into territory assumed to be male they are rebuked. Women are still supposed to be gentler, more restrained, than men, which is presumably why they are also considered to be somehow less. When Mo Hayder published her first crime novel, *Birdman*, last January, she was attacked for the extreme nastiness of the violence in it. Much of the criticism was centred on the fact that she, a woman, was writing scenes in which other women were tortured and mutilated. In one, for example, the killer removes a woman's breast implants while she is conscious because he likes smaller tits. I hated the violence in *Birdman*. I wouldn't have read the relevant passages if I hadn't been asked to discuss the novel with the author and Jenni Murray on Woman's Hour. But I wouldn't have hated them any less if they had been written by a man. Would anyone condemn a man in the same terms that were used for Mo Hayder if he had written about a female character castrating men? I don't think so. Nor do I think he would have received so much attention. Even though Hayder's novel was criticised, it was also widely publicised by the media. Any mixture of women and violence is sexy. Sexiest of all is violence done, or imagined, by a woman. But any woman who provides such a frisson must expect to be condemned for the very excitement she arouses. Of all the double standards that still exist, this is the oddest.

Chris Tchaikowski of the pressure group Women in Prison says that on the rare occasions when a woman is convicted of serious violent crime, journalists besiege her office. They quote Kipling's "the female of the species is more deadly than the male" and long to hear about the growth in girl gangs and unrestrained female violence; and they nearly always ask whether feminism has led to an increase in crime. To Tchaikowski, that question exposes the full depths of misogyny that still exist in this country. In fact, she says, last year there was a fall in the number of indictable crimes committed by women, although there was an increase in the number of women in prison. She also points out that there are at the moment around 2,670 men in prison for killing – and 120 women. Unlike men, women rarely murder for sexual or pecuniary motives, and she has never yet come across a woman who abused and killed a child unless there was a man involved. But those few women who do kill are given quite disproportionate attention by the media

No one has suggested that Ian Brady was less culpable than Myra Hindley, but the world is far less interested in him. If you put together the press cuttings about Brady, Peter Sutcliffe and any other notorious male killer, the pile wouldn't be nearly as large as hers. It used to be said that only two women could raise the circulation of a newspaper by twenty or thirty thousand on the day their photographs appeared on the front page: Diana Spencer and Myra Hindley, the idealised woman and the demonised. Interestingly Rosemary West no longer arouses quite the same frenzied attention. According to Tchaikowski, this may be because many people who are around her 'for twenty-four/seven' believe that she is innocent. Whether or not that is true – and I have no idea – accounts of her case have added to the assumption that women are as violent as men. Lawyers' gossip implies that Myra Hindley is still in prison only because of the press, and that other women who have

committed similar – or worse – crimes have been released long since. In fact, again according to Tchaikowski, only one other woman has ever been convicted of the same sort of crime, and she died in prison, drowned in the bath.

The Home Office could not provide me with any figures to show whether women lifers spend longer in prison than men; but men move through the system to open prisons more easily than women and it is therefore logical to assume that they may also move on to release more quickly. Some attitudes within the legal system are beginning to change. During the 1980s women were generally given longer sentences than men for similar offences, but that is no longer the case. And it is becoming accepted that the definition of provocation as a defence, which entails a momentary lapse into irrationality akin to temporary insanity, discriminates against women. In the past a man who hit out at a nagging wife on the spur of the moment and killed her tended to get off. But a woman who had been subjected to appalling physical cruelty for years would be jailed for murder if she had waited until her abuser was asleep or drunk before taking premeditated action. My own belief is that no killing is acceptable and that the sex of the killer is irrelevant.

As a crime writer I am often asked about my views of violence on the page, whether it encourages real crime, and where the line should be drawn between legitimate realism and pornographic wallowing in cruelty. Every writer has to choose for him- or herself. While I think that treating fictional murder as not much worse than a slap in the face can be dangerous, I also loathe graphic violence. The idea that lavish descriptions of brutality can make an otherwise insignificant book important appals me. And I am sure that writers of explicitly violent novels, who up the ante with each book, contribute to the perception that our society is a lot more dangerous than it actually is. Most stranger violence is committed by men on other men. (What happens in domestic settings is different. There are conflicting reports, at least one of which suggests that equal numbers of men and women are assaulted in their own homes and that more men suffer wounds that need medical care.) But women fear it more than men and alter their behaviour because of it. Virtually no children are allowed to play or walk alone in the streets during the day for fear of paedophiles, even though we are told that abduction of children is no more common now than it was sixty years ago. At night even peaceful suburban streets are empty of women walking alone, and few women would willingly approach a posse of young men at night or in full daylight.

Crime writers, like journalists, must take their share of responsibility for that. If we exaggerate violence against women, we make them feel more vulnerable and therefore constrain their lives by making them avoid danger that may not exist. If we overstate violence by women, we risk feeding the myth that they are deadlier than men and possibly add to the difficulties of real women in the courts and in prison. Women are angry, but we are nothing like as violent as men. Pretending we are, whether for excitement or in an attempt to be taken seriously, is a dangerous game.

MINETTE WALTERS: MY GLITTERING CAREER

As a crime writer, Minette Walters began at the top and has stayed there for the eight years of her creativity in the genre. Her first book, The Ice House, *won the John Creasey Best First Crime Novel Award, and her subsequent books,* The Sculptress *and* The Scold's Bridle, *similarly gleaned prizes. This critical acclaim has been matched by an enthusiastic following among readers, with her new book* The Shape of Snakes *looking set to achieve the same. CT's Eve Tan Gee talked to her in the penthouse suite of her Marble Arch hotel.*

Your first three books all won awards – did this hat trick have an intimidating effect on you?

I found the John Creasey Award for *The Ice House* the most intimidating, because I wasn't writing a series. I started to get really worried when I thought, "My second book is nothing like this: totally different theme, different people – how will it be received?"

Had you been told to avoid 'one-offs'?
Absolutely. I was told Ruth Rendell could only do it because she was so well known, and she had to use the Barbara Vine name. But even that early, I found myself very reluctant to write a series. So I was envisioning the possibility of a glittering – but very short – career.

A shooting star seen all too briefly?
That was my fear. That's why it was so gratifying when *The Sculptress* won the American Edgar Award. It was a huge relief – and then, when *The Scold's Bridle* won the Gold Dagger, I felt that my 'right to be different' was confirmed.

It seems that writers tire of series characters before readers do.
I knew I would. Look at any author who has done a series (starting with Conan Doyle and Holmes): you're in this syndrome where the writer wants to kill off the character, while the readers cry, "More, more!" Agatha Christie wanted to strangle Hercule Poirot (and I can't say I blame her).

So is your principal objection to a continuing character the difficulty of keeping him or her fresh?
There's another reason. One of the most often repeated criticisms of the crime genre is that it is formulaic writing: you use the same place, the same characters, but with a different death each time. In other words, you don't have to think too hard about the next book. In one way I can see that this is a criticism that can be levelled, and I felt that I really wanted to change direction with each book.

Which you've done very successfully – readers are never quite sure what to expect from a new Minette Walters novel.
I'm really pleased that so many people now are writing one-off crime novels – I'm not saying I instigated a trend, but it would be nice to feel I had just a little to do with this.

The other side of the coin is that you have no shorthand recognition for your characters with each book – no violin or cocaine, no vodka martinis.
I have been asked if I felt I would sell more books if I had a series, and this is one of those imponderables. But the answer is probably yes. But would I be pleased with the books I was writing? Probably not.

But would you sell more books? Your

sales are pretty phenomenal – which suggests that many readers respond to the deeper psychological profile you can give to characters who only appear in one novel – along with the closure.

Well, I live in hope that those sales continue, because this is one issue on which I don't really want to compromise.

I'm going to put an idea to you: one-off crime novels with a strong psychological bias are always the ones which are taken more seriously in literary terms. Could this have been a factor with you, however unconscious? Is being taken seriously in this regard important to you?

Not really. I have to say that I set out with very few ambitions, simply because I knew how competitive the field was. I didn't want to say to myself something like, "I want to be published in thirty-six countries", or, to answer your question, "I want to be taken seriously as a writer". This was mainly because I didn't want to be disappointed if I failed. My one ambition was to write the kind of crime novel that I wanted to read.

How do you keep your response to the genre fresh?

I like to dip my toe into the traditions of the genre, and do something creative with them. The new book, *The Shape of Snakes*, is a good example of this. Looking at the history of the crime novel, there was a certain gritty realism with writers like Wilkie Collins and Dickens, however extravagant the plots. In the so-called Golden Age, despite the often wonderful writing, these social issues were sidelined, and now they're back with a bang. But even Christie, often criticised for the cloistered world she deals with, brought about a change in Miss Marple's lifestyle in the later books, reflecting social change.

So you're saying crime novels can sometimes be snapshots of their era?

There's no doubt. And I like to utilise social elements, which I've tried to do here, while never forgetting the demands of the narrative.

It's the death of a black woman, a woman living on the edge of society, who sets the plot in motion in *The Shape of Snakes*.

The Stephen Lawrence Report was fresh in my mind, and this was a way of transmuting that into this book. And by having a

middle-class woman become obsessed with the case of a black woman who dies (which no-one else believes is murder), I was able to deal with such issues as commitment. But I was careful not to make my heroine some kind of saintly crusader – there's nothing more boring than that. She has her own agenda for doing what she does, however laudable the final result.

Through your character, you could be said to be dealing with white middle-class guilt.

That's one element, but by no means the most important one. And telling a story remains the first imperative. If I can sharpen the narrative with this kind of theme, fine. But the end result has to be the total involvement of the reader.

SUE GRAFTON TALKS TO TOM NOLAN

How could we have a Women in Crime issue without the singular Ms. Grafton?

When you began writing the Kinsey Millhone books, did you expect the series to be so popular?

No. I didn't even expect the first one to get published. Though when you come up with a title like *'A' is for Alibi*, obviously you have some hopes for the future. But I didn't expect it to take hold in particular. Because that was something I couldn't control. So it's been sort of astonishing, for me. And often I don't know how to relate to it. In fact I work very hard to just stay as disconnected from it as possible. Because I think what's fatal for a writer is becoming self-conscious. You know, "Here I am, Sue Grafton, writing yet another lofty best-seller": that's like, bullshit! So it's better just to mind my business, and sit at my machine and do the best job I can. When I think about a dozen more books, I about go grey. So I don't think about it. You know, I've become like Scarlett O'Hara: "I'm just not gonna *think* about it, right now!"

You're over halfway through the series.

I think I always thought I could do the first half. The second half of the alphabet is just virgin territory. So it's gonna be really interesting to see what those titles are.

You've talked of how changing plots in the middle of *'K' is for Killer*, which was going to be *'K' is for Kidnap*, interrupted your schedule of a book a year. Did that also relieve the yearly strain?

Yes, I wrote with a light heart. I didn't write with a sense of the clock ticking. So I intend to do that from here on out. Part of my reasoning was, I thought to myself, I can keep trying to work at this one-book-a-year pace; but eventually a book is gonna come along, and some little piece of my psyche is gonna go: "No way, it is over, you've pushed me beyond endurance." So I thought it's probably smarter to pace myself a little bit differently, and then go the distance. In a way it's like running a marathon: You can start out strong, but you can't maintain a killing pace and expect to get to the end without being dead. It was just a new sort of attitude.

See I'm torn, because there's a part of me – I love closure; I love to get to the end, to finish things. And certainly when it comes to the end of the alphabet – I don't wanna be 102, you know, feebly on oxygen and uppers, writing my last few lines. So on one hand, I wanna finish while I have forty years to enjoy. On the other hand, if I try to push myself too hard, I'm not gonna get there at all. I'm imagining it might be fifteen months between books, or eighteen months. I don't wanna do three years between books; everybody I know would be dead. But it seems to me a book should dictate its life span to a writer, instead of the other way around.

Was *'K'* your first false start?

No, it happened to me with *'H' is for Homicide*. I had intended with *'H'* to do a continuation of *'C' is for Corpse*. What happened was, the story kept disappearing like a trail in the jungle. I would say to myself, "Well let's just write up to the point where we can see; maybe the bushes will part, and we'll see where the story goes." But I realised after a while that the story had no chemistry; it refused to generate scenes or suggestions about how the story line might proceed. And in the end, I couldn't solve the problem, so I just threw it in the wastebasket. Which is one of life's most horrible moments. Those are sometimes the longest days of your life: waiting to see what else will be generated. And in that case, I realised I had an entire file full of articles about automobile insurance fraud; so I thought, well, having nothing else, I better go for that.

Did that throw you off schedule?

No. Miraculously I pulled that off, but *'H'* was a very stressful book because I felt so much pressure.

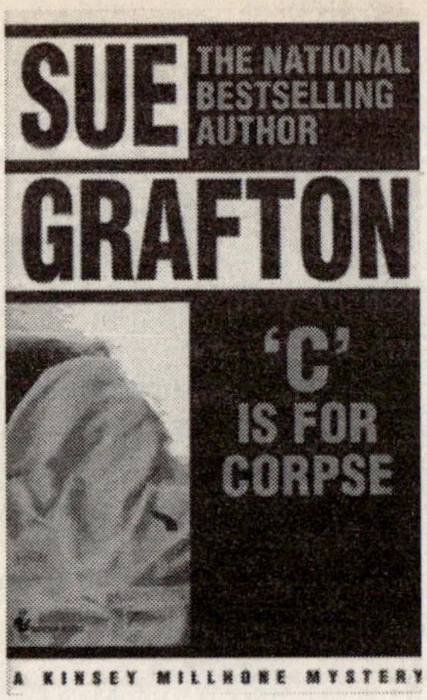

You've reminded readers that Kinsey's fictional life is taking place about a dozen years earlier than today. As you write these books set in Santa Teresa, your fictional version of Santa Barbara, do you keep the geography and architecture of the town true to how things really were in Santa Barbara back then?

Sometimes I pay attention to that. Then I think to myself, "You know, actually I'm writing about Santa Teresa. And in Santa Teresa, it happens exactly the way I say." I am like a complete and total expert. So I do not welcome letters that tell me I've done it wrong when it comes to that town, because I invented it – on behalf of Ken Millar (Ross Macdonald), who *actually* invented it.

Do people write to point out mistakes you've made?

Oh yeah, absolutely. Sometimes they tell me about errors with a kind of 'gotcha' attitude: Ha ha, you blew it! Other times I think my readers just want me to know they're paying attention and that they notice, and they have a piece of expertise they want to share; I think it's meant to be a loving gesture. If I know I don't know something, I go out and do the research. If I need help, I can just call people up. The police captain here's a fan, his wife's a fan; so I get police help. I get legal help. I go talk to the coroner, and it's just great fun. So I do a certain amount of local stuff: I did a talk with the legal secretaries; I thought, "Shoot – these are the people with power!" You call somebody up and if you've pissed her off, hon, you don't git where you wanna go. Every year my connections get better and better. Where I get into trouble – sometimes in passing you think, "Oh I *know* that"; you put it in, and it looks right to you. And later they write you the letters. For instance, in *'K'* I made a reference to the bare citrus trees in someone's backyard. Well! The letters poured in from people who assured me that citrus trees do not lose their leaves; citrus trees are evergreen. And once they said it, I realised: I've got a yard full of citrus trees, and they never lose their leaves. But you can't catch everything. I keep trying to write a perfect book, and I just can't seem to pull it off.

Do readers ever make

mistakes – see things in the books that aren't intended?

One of my readers said to me at a signing, "Oh," wink wink, "I got the little anagram" (or whatever) "you made of that character's name in *'H' is for Homicide.*" I said, "What?" "Oh, 'Bibianna Diaz.' 'Bibi': a book, as in 'bibliophile.' 'Anna': a year. From: 'Di.' 'Az': A to Z." I went, "I never did that!" But it was, wink nudge, your secret is safe with me. They thought I had come up with this name as a veiled reference to doing a book a year, from a to z. I went, "No." I felt I had disappointed the lad something terrible.

But it is the case that the clients in the books do have the same initial as the letter in a given title?

Yeah, I generally do that. For a while, I was thinking that I would write about a town that also began with the same letter. So in *'B' is for Burglar*, I wrote about Boca Raton. I got to a point where I thought, "How far are we gonna take this, dear?" You know, it's gotta get ludicrous, around *'Q'*. I just felt I was gonna get carried away with myself, if I wasn't careful.

How else have readers gotten things confused?

When I was still listed in the phone book, people would call me up who wanted to go to Rosie's restaurant, and they wondered where it was. I went, "Sweetheart, I made that up; I write fiction." Actually, it used to be a restaurant in Columbus, Ohio; but it shut down.

Do people expect you to be like Kinsey? How much do you think you resemble her? Is she more outspoken than you, or not?

Not that much more outspoken. I certainly cuss just as much as she does.

Are you as courageous?

I have cleverly set up my life so I never have to worry about that issue. I try not to put myself in any position where there will be any threat to my personal safety. And when I'm talking about her bravery, I try to keep her sensible. 'Cause I personally hate those books where women do stupid things in the interest of bravery. I always think you should call the police. That's my notion of how to stay safe: call the police. Like one night here I had a prowler on the property. And it was sort of amusing, 'cause it was so interesting how you cope with that sort of thing. I kept telling myself stories about what was happening; I couldn't believe it was actually a prowler. So I would tell myself, "Oh, here's somebody cutting across my property." I go, "Well why is he doing that?" "Oh here's somebody..." So I made up all these stories. Finally I thought, "Shit! I don't care what his story is, he's getting off here." So I go upstairs, I lick my trusty finger and I dial 911; and the county sheriff picked up the phone, and I told him what was going on. He said, "All right you stay on the line, I'm sending a car." I said, "I'm not getting off the line!" I mean my heart was pounding so hard, I was having flop sweat! So we're chatting away, and he says to me: "So how's the new book coming along?" "Just fine, thanks; what's your name?" He says, "Doug." "Doug, it's doing good." So I'm looking out my lawn, and here comes the county sheriff with guns drawn and a dog – and they got this sucker, hiding down in my bushes. Now it turned out later he was a schizophrenic who was off his meds, and he had known the people who lived here before – which is one of the stories I had told myself. But I was fascinated by the fact that I could behave in a sensible manner; my brain was rattling away at a quick clip, but in the end I did what I needed to do. But it did affect me for days: I kept looking out the window waiting to see somebody cross my property. So it's good once in a while to be exposed to the sort of thing Kinsey goes through book after book.

Do other people think *they* resemble Kinsey?

Yes; even though I try to make her as specific as possible, and actually the reader has a lot of information about her, I notice everybody projects on her what they want and who they are. I know many women who look in the mirror and see Kinsey Millhone. Guys'll write me letters and say, I'm married to this Millhone woman. So it is a curious fact about her that she has a certain chameleon quality. And that's why I never want to sell the series to ollywood. They would spoil that.

Did you ever think though about who might be able to play her?

I used to picture Sigourney Weaver, though she's way too tall. I used to picture Debra Winger. But in the end I thought, "No, better to leave Ms Millhone in the imagination of the reader, 'cause they know better than we do; they know better than Hollywood." It's better to let her live that life in the imagination of the reader. That's what reading is about.

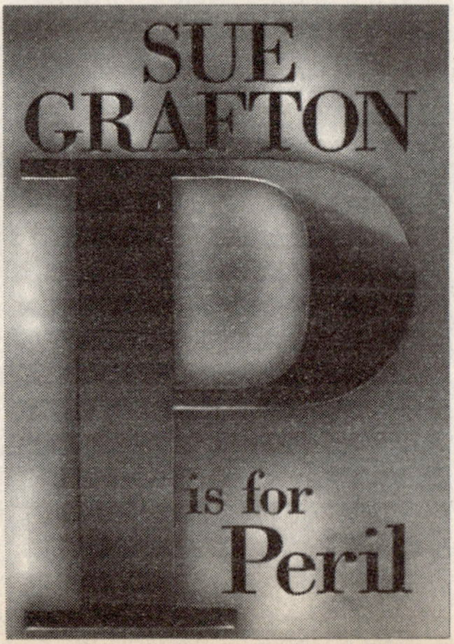

WOMEN IN CRIME

Here it is...the largest survey of women crime writers ever conducted. Questions devised by Forshaw, Cooper, Gray and Tan Gee elicited some surprising responses...

The Questions

Do you consider that male and female crime writing possess different identities?

Why do you think women writers have enjoyed such conspicuous success in the genre?

How comfortable are you writing a male protagonist (first person or otherwise)?

Do you read a mix of male and female crime writers?

Sara Paretsky

Not necessarily: that's such a complex area, I can't believe that there are any simple answers. The finest writers, in whatever genre, transcend gender.

I'm not sure that there is a genetic (or for that matter culturally received) reason: one of nature's inexplicables.

One of my very favourite writers is Peter Dickinson, who I think is a quite superb novelist. He's particularly good at women characters, and if I felt that I could write a male protagonist as well as he writes female protagonists, I'd be immensely proud. I'd feel that I'd moved to a whole new level of skill. I did tackle this new area for myself in Ghost Country with a young male protagonist.

I'm a particular fan of male English writers such as Reginald Hill, and I have a real taste for Michael Gilbert. When I met him and mentioned my enthusiasm, he was initially grumpy and uncommunicative, but seemed to warm after he became aware that I really knew his work.

Sara Paretsky's latest book is Hard Time *(Penguin)*

Minette Walters

I don't think so. Before I knew anything about P D James, I read her books thinking she was a man. I really think the writer's personality can be androgynous. And in my own book *The Echo*, I had some welcome compliments on my use of the male protagonists. But then, I live with a husband and two sons, so male thinking is very much a part in my life – and shouldn't a good writer be constantly observing people, whatever their sex?

In America, people often say to me it's amazing how well women are doing in the British crime novel, so this is seen to be a geographical thing as much as anything else. It should also be remembered that there was a time when male writers couldn't get published in Britain, so great was the grip of the female Holy Trinity of crime writers: Christie, Marsh and Sayers. So whichever sex is doing well, the success of crime writers is both a temporal and a geographical thing.

Very comfortable!

I read everybody, whatever sex. I really don't see how any serious reader could only read one gender. Of course, it's true that (as a generalisation) women tend to mine the psychological area a little more than men, who are generally more concerned with the police procedural side of crime novels. Women are sharp observers of character, and also, of course they are generally more critical than men. And this can pay dividends in the novel.

Minette Walters' latest book is The Shape of Snakes *(Macmillan)*

Denise Ryan

I never think about that, and frankly it's not a road I want to go down: I'm interested in the writing, not the author's gender.

Conspicuous? Hey, this is radical, but... maybe some women writers might just be good writers who the punters enjoy reading!

Never done it in the first person, but otherwise I felt reasonably comfortable. My partner, various relatives and some of my best friends are in fact male, so I was able to do the appropriate research.

Yes, but recently it's been mostly female (purely by chance, honestly!).

Denise Ryan's latest book is Dead Keen *(Piatkus)*

Lindsey Davis

No. All writers with any character possess different identities from all others. Women who can write write just as competently and strongly as men – though men who can't write are worse than incompetent women, because they can't do (and usually omit) female characters.

They can write well. (This is a daft question; it's based on a misconception. Success is spread quite evenly. Come to that, boring books are spread quite evenly as well...)

Perfectly. It's no worse than doing dogs, cats, kids, old folk. You just have to know a few men and watch how they work. Observation is supposed to be part of the writer's craft.

Yes.

Lindsey Davis' latest book is Ode to a Banker *(Century)*

Rhys Bowen

There are stereotypes: males lone sleuths lurking in the dark and fog, violence, lack of emotion, while females tend towards tea parties, quilts, cats – but these don't hold up any longer. Female writers have shown they are capable of writing tense and brutal stories. The only difference is in the level of emotion. Male writers usually keep themselves more detached.

Maybe because their stories are more emotionally charged. And we females are great observers of the trivial details which make up reality. And, of course, we are more lethal than the male!

I enjoy the challenge, although I've (wisely) kept away from first person. After five books, I feel that I know Constable Evans pretty well. He has some of my traits, as do all protagonists, and I like him. However, I do run my work past several male friends to check whether I've said anything a man wouldn't say.

Absolutely. And a mix of cosy to hard-boiled. Any good writing.

Rhys Bowen's latest books are Evan Help Us *(Allison and Busby, UK) and* Evan and Elle *(St. Martin's, US)*

Isabelle Grey

Yes. I find female writers more absorbing, but I admire the style, the edge, the edginess of male writers.

Women have a better grasp of basic psychology (maybe from having kids), are better at interpreting, understanding, explaining – and often excusing – behaviour, which is why they are more often victims of crime than perpetrators – to me, a much more interesting POV, particularly the interplay between victim and perpetrator.

Completely – for me, crime writing is about the emotions and relationships that lead to crime, both within the causal psychology of the aggressor and within the relationships between aggressor and victim, so one always needs both sides anyway. In any case, the primacy of the protagonist in scriptwriting is somewhat different to prose fiction.

Yes, but I do prefer female.

Isabelle Grey has recently written TV scripts for The Bill, Wycliffe *and* Silent Witness

Cynthia Harrod-Eagles

Yes, of course, and it's part of the rich fabric of crime fiction. But it's hard to pin down what the difference is. It's a platitude to say men are more cerebral and women more intuitive, but there's something of that in it. Men perhaps have more straight action and less explanation, but there will be a thousand exceptions to that rule, too. Let's just say there is an essential difference in the way men and women write, and leave it at that. If a stranger emailed you anonymously, you would probably know whether it was a man or woman, wouldn't you?

Perhaps because women spend so much of their real-time lives analysing people's behaviour and assigning motives to it, it comes naturally to do the same for fictional characters. I think women like a puzzle too, and the delicate dissection thereof. A woman will unravel a badly tangled ball of string and rewind it, where a man will throw it away and buy another!

Yes, very much so. I never contemplated for a moment having a female detective. I've spent a lot of time with men over the years, in business before I became a full-time writer, travelling with symphony orchestras, and researching with policemen. I enjoy their company and the way they interact with each other and with their jobs. In fact, I have probably observed more men in action than women, so I don't find it hard writing about them. It's refreshing, too, to look at everyday problems which are all too familiar through the eyes

Joolz Denby

of the other half for a change.

Yes.

Cynthia Harrod-Eagles' latest crime novel in the Bill Slider series is Blood Sinister *(Little, Brown)*

Joolz Denby

I think male and female writers of any genre have different responses to both writing and, very often, life. Not a 'better or worse' situation, more in terms of the old song by the Au Pairs, Equal but Different. Both genders bring valuable insights and interesting reactions to both the depiction of crime and the criminal. Problems only occur when the writer's 'gender agenda' interferes with the pursuit of their craft; too much testosterone can spoil the broth as quickly as too much bitchiness. We should celebrate difference of any sort as variety is the life-blood of writing; any sort of writing.

A fascinating phenomenon, isn't it? Maybe they're just good writers who have mass appeal... Though I once sat through an interesting lecture which posited the idea that as women make up the majority of murder victims, they are simply trying to understand/define/disempower their 'predators' by exploring the nature of such crimes through fictionalisation. Now, that's an idea...

As I have spent most of my working life in a male dominated environment – before being a novelist, I worked in rock 'n' roll and spoken-word performance – I don't feel I'd have a problem with writing about a male protagonist, if I thought it appropriate to the story: in fact in short stories I've often done so very successfully.

As an obsessive bookaholic, I read both genders and all genres equally – my favourite authors, for example, are Edith Wharton and James Lee Burke. What a fabulous combo...

Joolz Denby's latest book is Stone Baby *(HarperCollins)*

Rosemary Aitken
(writing as Rosemary Rowe)

Not really. Perhaps on balance women tend to be marginally more interested in feelings – most of the cosy writers are women – and men more interested in action and the motivation for that action – most violently graphic crime thrillers seem to be written by men: but – like all sweeping generalisations – this is both unfair and over-simplistic. Perhaps, also, it was more true in the past when gender stereotypes were more culturally binding. I think most of the best modern crime novels could probably have been written by either sex, although I do think women aren't on the whole very convincingly accurate about guns.

Perhaps, also for the reasons outlined above. Both women and men have always been interested in feelings or in puzzles – women have traditionally been more squeamish about the details of fights, murders, corpses et al., and for a long time it was not 'womanly' to be interested in that side of the genre. Perhaps, simply, writers like Sayers and Christie appealed to both halves of the audience – or perhaps for a long time it was women (once their children were old enough) who had no job and therefore the time to buy and read crime fiction. We also now know that, scientifically, men are better at spatial things and mathematical reasoning, whereas women excel at verbal puzzles and thinking about several things at once. This is, of course, a great help in creating red herrings!

My first person protagonist is male, and I have always felt comfortable about this. There are, however, one or two special features here – the novels are set in Roman Britain and women would have found it pretty difficult to act as detectives then, since their lives were fairly restricted outside of the home. He needed to be a person with a trade who was capable of being legally independent, and that was not possible for a woman at the time. My protagonist is also older than the average – so I am not obliged to write about physical feats of strength, or about youthful male sexual urges – which I can only know about by deduction! I also wanted him to be an outsider, and hence comment on Roman ways. He can have qualities like loyalty and affection, and he has been a victim of the system in the past, which might make him sympathetic in a fairly brutal authoritarian world where might was right and all culture relative. Besides, he doesn't have to be a modern man – he is already different from all of us in lots of important ways, so my being a woman doesn't – I hope – affect it much.

Yes. Decidedly.

Rosemary Rowe's latest book is A Pattern of Blood *(Headline)*

Sparkle Hayter

I think all writers have different identities: some have many identities. In fact, most writers have mild disassociative personality disorders they deal with by writing different characters. Today, for example, I am feeling like Sally the psychic from the Robin Hudson books, who predicts that by tonight I will be feeling much more like Lola, wanton playgirl. But as far as male-female goes, men and women do tend to write different kinds of books generally speaking. Whether this is due to chromosomes or society is something scientists continue to argue in great food-hurling debates. Personally, I think it's a bit of both. But more and more men are writing cosies and women writing hard-boiled novels, so the lines are increasingly blurred. Still, when a woman writes a hard-boiled novel, it's different. It's often more textured, more deeply shaded, and with an emotional undertow I don't find in most male hard-boiled fiction. At the same time, there's some unnameable quality missing I only find in men's fiction, just as there's some unnameable quality missing in male-written cosies. If you can name that quality, I'll give you a dollar.

If we didn't read and write murder mysteries, there would be far more of us in prison. The pressure to be good girls makes us sublimate more hostility and crap, and murder mysteries are a great way to do this and make it moderately profitable to boot. Maybe if we played rugby or had more outlets to exercise our power (and more experience in exercising it), it would be different.

Not very, and I am not the most feminine of women. I can understand men up to a point, but there are some things that baffle me, like many men's willingness to copulate with any willing female. Even the wildest women I know are somewhat discriminating about who they have sex with, though they're often just as shallow as men. Of course, lots of women baffle me too. I've heard it said that it's easier for a woman to write a male protagonist than the other way around. I disagree. I know men who write credible females (Walter Satterthwait and Dick Belsky spring to mind) but can't think of any women who write fully-rounded male protagonists I believe in. Odd.

Yes, about 50-50. I like darker things, so I find myself reading a lot of male writers, though there are more and more hard-boiled women to read: Carol O'Connell, Val McDermid, Vicki Hendricks… I like funny books, and I think women are writing funnier stuff at the moment. Occasionally, I do like a good cosy, as long as it's funny, like a Joan Hess or a Simon Brett.

Sparkle Hayter's latest book is Chelsea Girl Murders *(No Exit Press). She is one of the founders of Tartcity.com*

Manda Scott

You mean male or female crime writers? If you do then I would say that they only possess different identities to the extent that men and women in general possess different identities – as a massive generalisation, our outlook on life is different, our preoccupations are different, our emotional baselines are different. This, I think, spills over into crime writing, but possibly to a lesser extent than in, say, literary novels. Crime novelists of both genders have a tendency to objectify death – so that a murder becomes a puzzle to solve rather than a life-shattering event that affects all those touched by it.

Have they? I'm not an expert, I tend not to read much crime, but I wouldn't have said that women predominated. Some women have been enormously successful (Patricia Cornwell springs to mind – whatever one thinks of the standard of literacy, plot and characterisation, she sells in vast numbers) but then so have some men. There are equal numbers of both lurking in the shadows of the few at the top. Therefore, some people have been conspicuous by their success, but that's the case in all fields. One could ask why crime writing is such a successful genre, but that's a different question.

More comfortable than I used to be, although, to date, all my male protagonists have been of an era at least one thousand years in the past (pre-1000 AD) which perhaps makes them rather more accessible – or less liable to show the cracks in my understanding of the male psyche. Cross-gender writing is fraught with difficulty. There are very, very few male writers who write convincing female characters. Andrew Greig (not a crime writer) is one of the few that springs to mind. Then again, a fair few women writers write women who are equally unconvincing, so some of that is down to an inability to write character. On the other side of the coin, I think that Mary Renault's writing of Alexander was exceptional and I know that a lot of her male readers believed her to be a man writing under a pseudonym, but I have male friends who find her characterisation entirely unreal. It's all a question of perspective and the spread of 'reality' within each gender is so wide that almost any character, of either gender, is going to reach the boundaries of what individual readers find acceptable (to do otherwise would render them so bland as to be worthless). Good characterisation is one of the hardest elements in the creation of good literature. To write the opposite gender is to make the task at least an order of magnitude more difficult – but not impossible. As far as first versus third person – good writing in either person gives one access to the protagonist's soul. First person simply limits one's perspectives in time and space.

Yes. Good crime is not defined by the gender of the author. Nor is the dross.

Manda Scott's latest book is Stronger Than Death *(Headline)*

Barbara Nadel

Not as much, I believe, as they did in the past. Having said that however, I am not one of those who subscribe to the belief that women were gentler and men more manly in days gone by. The fact that male and female crime is more homogenous now has far more to do with societal changes. Women are now permitted, for want of a better word, to explore violence without attracting negative comments. Men, similarly, may tackle romantic issues. I still believe however, that we (women) have the edge where psychological issues are concerned. We are just that little bit more subtle. But then I would say that, wouldn't I? (I'm a psychology graduate!)

Perhaps because, from a very young age, women are primed to expect fear. How many young men, for instance, are advised to be careful in case their girlfriends 'knock them about'? Some, yes. But in the quantities that women are? I think not. We are told to be careful if we are going out alone and if we wander at night we are told that it is better we do so either in a group or with a man. So maybe it is this intimate relationship we have with the prospect of danger that allows us to write about it so well. That and, of course, the thrill of straying into the previously forbidden and traditionally male

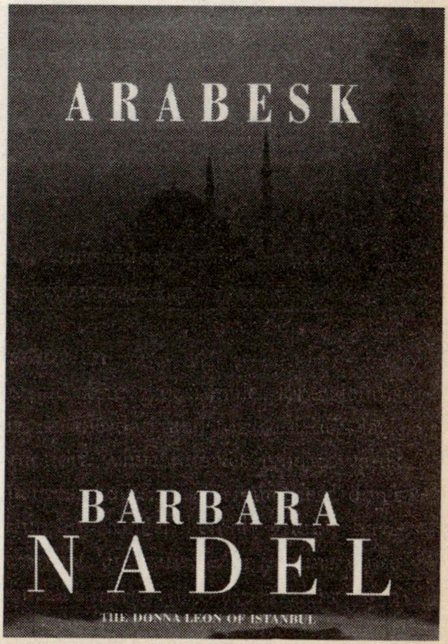

dominated terrain of violence. Possibly people even buy our books simply in order to see how we, odd creatures that we are, tackle that.

I have no problem with my male protagonists, Ikmen and Suleyman. Although written by a woman, they are, I believe, very masculine. Perhaps that says something about me? But that aside, the fact that I do like them is, I think, even more important than that. If you like your men, as I do, you'll portray them as they want to be portrayed.

Yes. At present I am enjoying a book called Blood-Red Rivers by the Frenchman, Jean-Christophe Grange.

Barbara Nadel's latest book is A Chemical Prison *(Headline)*

Janet Laurence

There is a vast range of differences between crime writers. Does gender make a difference and produce a different identity? I don't think so – except in one instance. There are male writers such as Andrew Taylor and the American Charles Todd who have as much subtlety as the most subtle of female writers. There are female writers such as Val McDermid and Denise Danks who can write with as much punch and thrilling effects as male writers. Sara Paretsky, Ruth Rendell and Sue Grafton write as complex, interesting and character-based crime novels with a series protagonist as Ian Rankin and James Lee Burke. The main differences in the crime field are those of writer rather than gender. The one area where I cannot think of male writers who score as highly as females is in the psychological suspense field where writers such as Ruth Rendell (in particular) and the much newer Margaret Murphy and Denise Mina score such hits. This may be because my memory isn't good enough or my reading wide enough to produce male writers who can compete. But I think that perhaps female subtlety and understanding of how people can be manipulated and their fears preyed upon does make a difference. In every other crime area I can think of, it's not whether you are male or female that singles you out but the quality of your writing and understanding of human nature.

It is exceedingly difficult to make a good living out of writing crime novels (or most other novels, come to that). Apart from a few exceptions, now becoming more numerous, most male writers have not been able to concentrate on crime writing if they have needed to pay the grocery bills, raise a family, have holidays, or indulge in new clothes. Only when retirement came along could they settle down at the typewriter to the exclusion of all else. Women, though, found that writing could be fitted in around raising a family and could lead to a useful second income. And women discovered a talent for discerning the nastier sides of human nature that underlie murder, plus the ingenuity to deploy the traditional trappings of deception that lead the reader everywhere but to the murderer. This has led to women writers in many instances dominating the field from the thirties to perhaps the seventies and early eighties. Crime writing, too, tended only to publish novels in a traditional form. However, over the last ten or fifteen years, the scope of the crime novel has widened enormously, its popularity has increased and many new writers have recognised that it offers them opportunities not available in other fiction areas. Earnings for some have increased and all this has meant more male writers are exploring the field. I don't think that women have a greater talent for crime, but they have been quicker and better placed to explore the possibilities it offers.

I have found myself very comfortable writing with Canaletto, the eighteenth century Italian painter, as a male protagonist. I think writing in the skin of any other person requires imagination and observation. Some women characters are as alien to me personally as any male character.

Yes! I look for interesting writers, unaffected by whether they are male or female. At the moment I have on the TBR pile (To Be Read): Killing the Shadows by Val McDermid; Prey to All, Natasha Cooper; The Empty Chair, Jeffery Deaver; Exile, Denise Mina; The Vault, Peter Lovesey; A Small Death in Lisbon, Robert Wilson (I know, I should have read it last year but I didn't!) – all writers I admire. However, they will all have to wait until I've finished the third Canaletto I'm currently working on.

Janet Laurence's latest book is The Mermaid's Feast *(Macmillan), the tenth in the Darina Lisle series*

Francis Fyfield

I don't think male and female crime writers possess different identities, simply different personalities. There are plenty of women writers who follow the hunt / shoot / kill type of narrative beloved by boys, and plenty of men who write books appreciated by women. I think the only real difference is that women write more about fear.

Women haven't enjoyed success in the genre more than men if you look at it historically. They are perceived to be more successful because of the role models (Christie, Sayers, P D James, Rendell, etc.) and because of the titles. There's always been a Queen of Crime, but never a King, and recently there seems to be a backlash against women's success supported by critics. The men are whinging at the moment, without reason, I think.

I'm perfectly comfortable writing male protagonists. I like men and sympathise with them.

I read anything I can get my hands on, and don't take any notice of the sex of the author – as long as they can write.

Francis Fyfield's latest book is Undercurrents *(Little, Brown)*

Ann Granger

There may be a fundamental difference between male and female crime writing. However, over the years we have learned from one another. We now choose similar themes and approaches. I think there's less of a distinction now than there might have been before.

Success breeds success. Some women crime writers have had a lot of publicity, and young writers are inspired to follow. I believe that still – even if there is a frisson of shock at the idea of women writing about crime of violence.

I would not write in the first person as a male character. Too many pitfalls – I wouldn't feel at ease.

Yes I do. I'm a big admirer of Peter Lovesey's detective Diamond.

Ann Granger's latest book is Shades of Murder *(Headline)*

Lisa Appignanesi

Back in the last century, I would, with a few caveats, have said that yes, male and female crime writing did possess somewhat different identities. Paretsky's V I and Dunant's Hannah Wolfe, to name only two examples, were taking women out of classic crime's femme fatale role and casting them into the lead as the white knight of the mean streets. Women's issues, such as domestic violence, surrogacy, plastic surgery, became part of the crime scene. Violence and its depiction became problems to be addressed. The casual, sometimes pornographic slashing or cutting up of women was not something to be treated as a crime novel trope, but as something for which the raison d'être needed to be explored. Violence was felt by the sufferer, toughness an uneasy virtue. Generalisations are always difficult: no sooner made than the exceptions pop up. A shorthand might attest to the tougher, more brutal world of much, particularly American, crime writing by men; the greater interest in the gangster underworld; the machinery of death and so on. Women's crime writing, on the other hand, more often focuses on the violence which erupts from within (from Patricia Highsmith to Ruth Rendell); the relations and emotions of the characters; moral stratagems. But I can think of numerous exceptions to such generalisations.

Women are successful in all fictional genres, so it's hardly surprising that they might be good at crime – and have been since the genre's origins. Broad brushstroke psychologising might say that women are good at secrets and their revelation, which is one of the core plot moves of crime writing. We're also keen observers of everyday pettiness, not unimportant in delineating aberrant character. Personally – and I guess my fictions are proof of that – I'm fascinated by the way in which the ordinary can tip over into the transgressive: women novelists are good at rendering the excesses of passion. Finally, bodily fear or its sister, anxiety – core to the atmosphere of crime writing – is something every woman has experienced.

I enjoy writing male protagonists. It's an adventure, even more so when done in the first person as I did in The Dead of Winter. Part of the novelist's craft is imagining yourself into another person's skin – and there's a certain freedom in being embodied male, particularly within the crime novel. Men's responses to danger – to dark streets, sudden movement, physical attack – are largely different from women's; so if that's your intent, you can take men into places (physical and psychological) women might not go without a great many questions having to be addressed. It also lets you explore women's impact on men, something I'm interested in. When I'm writing a first person male, I sometimes think the key sexual difference lies not in the great anatomical divisions, but in the mundane act of shaving. The particular look and posture of a man taking a razor to his face is something I've never seen in a woman.

I read a mix of male and female crime (and other) writers. Amongst the male Brits, I love Dibdin and Rankin. I also like the dual-sex partnership of Nicci French. Amongst the women, P D James still conveys a sense of polluted Englishness like no-one else and Rendell is brilliant on fear and prickles down the spine. I also like Sarah Dunant's genre-breakers and the sexual banter Minette Walters adds to her pacy thrillers; and the way Frances Fyfield builds an atmosphere of menace through jotted impressions and cumulative detail.

Lisa Appignanesi's latest book is Sanctuary *(Bantam)*

Susanna Gregory / Simon Beaufort

Probably, although I'm not sure I could say why. I think that personal experience is probably the most important factor, and I suppose that this may be determined or influenced by a person's gender. I'm sure my experiences in a sexist police force of the 1980s were very different from those of my male colleagues.

Because they write conspicuously successful books? Seriously, I doubt many readers select a book on the basis of the writer's sex, and I think that household names like Ruth Rendell, Agatha Christie and P D James would be equally well received if they were men. Or perhaps I'm wrong. It's tempting to say that women have an aptitude for crime writing, but I don't know that that's right. Perhaps it's all down to publishers – that they believe women crime writers sell more books than men crime writers, and so more of them are published. To be honest, publishing is quite a mystery to me. Often a book that isn't well written and that has a weak or unconvincing plot will be on the bestseller lists, while books that are brilliantly written and have imaginative and unusual plots barely break even. On reflection, perhaps the whole thing is down to marketing.

OK, I think. Hopefully, my husband will tell me if my main male characters think too much like women. However, my writing period (14th century) is a hard one where women are concerned. They really did have limited freedom, and it wasn't easy to transgress social barriers and be successful. Practically speaking, it would have been almost impossible for a woman to investigate a crime, because there would have been a limit to the places she could go. I think we have a tendency to idealise past times, and even to overlay them with our own liberal ideals, but the reality was that women were certainly not considered equal to men in medieval society. They had a certain degree of power within their household – perhaps even more than a husband in some cases – but not in the world at large. Even powerful and intelligent women like Isabella of France were limited in what they could do and achieve. My problem in writing about the 14th century is trying to find ways in which women can be included at all.

Yes. I buy books purely and completely on whether I like the sound of the summary on the back cover. I often do not even know the title or the name of the book I'm reading. It's a strange feeling at conferences when writers tell me their names, and they mean nothing, but then they tell me the name of their character and I realise I've read all their books!

Susanna Gregory's latest book is A Masterly Murder *(Little, Brown)*

Denise Danks

All writers are different but there are clones everywhere. My manuscripts have had "was this written by a man?" or "can't believe this was written by a woman" scribbled on them by copy editors so I don't know what that says about me. I asked someone once and they said it was the dialogue. Search me. I think male crime writing is vastly more sentimental. I've noticed it in the new batch of post-Leonard American crime writers.

I don't know the figures for crime, but I would say that women writers are conspicuously successful everywhere. Isn't the top Western writer a little old lady from Yorkshire?

Very.

I tend to read more male crime writing than female, and more American than British.

Denise Danks' latest books are Phreak *and* Torso

Ann Prospero

Yes. I've thought a lot about the differences between male and female kinds of writing, and I've come to the conclusion that females write about feelings, relationships, and the depth of personality and soul. Men get into philosophising, or believing that what they have defined as their worldview is worth writing about. The world is as they say it is. And they tell us about it. I know. This is a generalisation and, as with all generalisations, there are exceptions. But I wish someone would study the differences in prosody, prose, poetry: the vocabulary, the rhythm, and subject matter between male and female writers.

The best women writers show off the intelligence, strength, and competence of the female, characteristics needed in solving a crime. These characteristics can be found in the book's characters or by implication within the writer. And those characteristics are very appealing, especially to women readers who make up a large part of the market.

I haven't tried, though I have tried to get deeply into the persona of my male characters. Fascinating!

Yes. I read good writers whether male or female. We need more excellent female writers who can tell a story, reveal a character, and write very good prose. Good prose is the result not only of putting words together in an appealing way, but also of the ability to think well, clearly, and deeply.

Ann Prospero's latest book is Almost Night *(Penguin)*

Rebecca Tope

To a very limited extent, and in an almost meaninglessly general way, perhaps they do. But every time I tried to pin this down to specifics, there were so many exceptions, it lost almost all sense. I think men can be funnier than women. That is, when they set out to be funny, men succeed better. It's mainly in the dialogue – Reginald Hill, Colin Dexter and Petter Guttridge are all funnier than any woman writer I can think of. With women, even the very good ones, humour usually has a laboured tang to it. Another aspect of this is that men very often have a flippancy about death. Their corpses can be wooden and pain-free – like TV cowboys. Death comes swift and bloodless. Woman can convey the reality of it more effectively. Another, perhaps obvious, difference, seems to me to be that women stick more closely to the whodunnit formula. Here there are innumerable exceptions, granted. But the exceptions mostly fall into a formula of their own. Whydunnit, for example. I would say that women keep a closer eye on the plot, and use the personal failings and weaknesses of the characters as integral elements of the story to a greater extent than men do. I generally find the motivation more convincing in novels by women. With men, it often matters less, and can be two-dimensional. But in answer to the question, I'd have to say – not really.

I think there's something in the theory that the writing of crime fiction is a release of pent-up anger, resentment, hostility, aggression, all of which women are discouraged from expressing in Western society. (And Eastern, even more so, come to think of it). It's a sweet revenge to write a story in which someone you dislike becomes victim to a foul murder. Even greater revenge, I find, to make him the perpetrator, or prime suspect. Belonging to the less powerful gender (arguable these days, I know) ensures that playing God, in the form of storyteller, is a deeply pleasurable exercise. The tendency for education systems to push women away from disciplines reliant on logic, concentration, attention to detail, has perhaps repressed such natural abilities – and the devising of intricate plots and puzzles is one outlet for them. This probably applies to older women – and causes me to wonder whether there'll be crime writers in the same form in the younger generation now coming up. But most importantly, I think woman are a lot better than men at death, secrets, betrayal, grief, pain, fear, blood, guilt. These are the staples of our daily existence, and the natural ingredients of crime fiction. We know how to do them, we experience them but seldom admit it. There is a level of gut knowledge – derived partly from the experience of childbirth, but by no means only that – that is more or less exclusive to the female. Women know how

Rebecca Tope

frightening it is to be alive, from all sorts of angles. They know how to be frightening, too. They know how easy it would be to kill, and they routinely betray everyone around them, in matters of sex, money, emotion and desire. They are excellent liars and strategists. The surprise, really, is that more of them aren't writing stories about murder, transgression and treachery.

Perfectly comfortable. Both my protagonists are male. One a police detective and one an undertaker. But they do both have a female sidekick...

Yes, in a ratio of approximately three women to one man. Favourites are Reginald Hill, Laurie R King, Frances Fyfield, Barbara Vine, Minette Walters.

Rebecca Tope's latest book is Death of a Friend *(Piatkus)*

Patricia Hall

I definitely think that male and female crime writers have different identities – although it's a spectrum. At its crudest it's the traditional divide which says women are good at people and men are good at things: women seem to want to read and write about characterisation and motivation, men are fascinated by the nature of violence and the means used to perpetrate it. At it's most extreme it's the cosy / noir, security / danger divide. In the best novels there is a synthesis between the two and the gender of the author becomes irrelevant.

I am not sure that the weight of critical acclaim should come down as heavily in favour of women crime writers as is often assumed, in spite of the regular appearance of James, Rendell, Cornwell etc. in the bestseller lists. But then I never much liked Agatha Christie and think that Gaudy Night is deeply flawed! What I think may be true is that women writers took the crime novel into a more demanding mode, exploring character in depth, probing motivation, looking at the causes and effects of crime on individuals and society, treating women characters as serious people instead of sex objects. What I do appreciate is the introduction of active women protagonists – that's what I missed when I was a kid. The classic feminine cosy and masculine noir novels are fairly simplistic approaches to the genre: the new crime novel is not, and men are very well represented amongst the best British authors.

I'm perfectly comfortable writing a male protagonist. I don't see it's any more difficult to get inside the head of another gender than to attempt to understand the motivation of a violent criminal – it's all a demanding exercise.

Yes, I read male and female writers. As must be clear from the above, I'm looking for a challenging read rather than escapism – which doesn't mean that a good novelist can dodge the obligation to be entertaining. It seems to me that the best men are just as good at providing that as the best women.

Patricia Hall's latest book Skeleton at the Feast *(Allison and Busby)*

Alison Joseph

I suppose it would be true to say that writing a female detective, as I do, lends a different kind of dynamic to the story. But then the fact she's amateur rather than a copper also changes the dynamic, and that's not specific to gender. My detective, Sister Agnes, also has a best (female) friend, which means there's lots of discussions about clothes and boys and make-up. But then that's just her. Apart from the detail, I suppose one could start a debate about male and female narrative – do men expect different things from a novel than women, etc. But I'm not sure it would get you anywhere. I know that women prefer women characters to be well thought out, fully developed characters, rather than just being there to advance the story in a two-dimensional way, but then I'm sure men feel the same. Oh dear, are we all post-feminists now?

There are all sorts of theories about this, ranging from there are more women readers for all kinds of fiction, to women respond to strong, orderly narrative, and the classic crime fiction plot where order is restored is therefore somehow 'female'. Personally, I hesitate to draw conclusions.

Up to now, I've only written a female protagonist. But I've written male characters. It's all about imagination. I'm not a nun either, after all.

I like good writing and strong stories. We all aim for that.

Alison Joseph's latest book is The Night Watch, *the sixth Sister Agnes story (Headline)*

Carol Anne Davis

Writing identity needn't relate to gender. I suspect it's more about which class you're born into and whether your home is violent or peaceful. Those writers who almost didn't survive their first sixteen years on the planet are probably going to write harder books than the person who was safe and loved.

Maybe we women write better begging letters. (Davis pauses to plead with a passer-by to purchase one of her novels.) Seriously, there are more women than men buying books so maybe they gravitate towards writers of their own gender. Despite this interest, most women don't know more about real life crime than men do – with the exception of Crime Time readers, of course. The women I meet tend to believe, wrongly, that they are the most likely victims of violent attacks in darkened streets by total strangers. In reality, most opportunistic violence is meted out by young men against other men. The statistical exception is that women are more likely to become the victims of a serial killer. Again, Mrs Average doesn't know much about this. I attended a Women Against Crime course where we were all asked what the worst thing we could imagine happening in crime terms was. A couple of the women said having their house broken into and others said

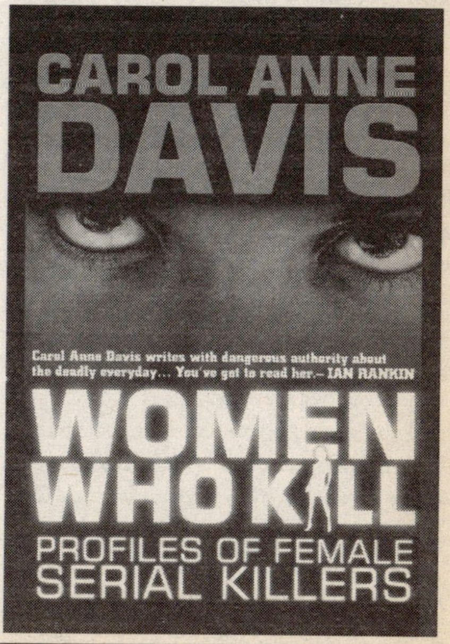

being raped. I refused to tell them the worst thing I could think of because it would only have caused fear transference and the likelihood of any of these women meeting a serial killer was very rare. But it surprised me that, with so many books on the subject, none of them seemed to know the barbarity that such killers were capable of.

It involves the same amount of work (and biscuit eating) for me to create a male or female character, possibly because I'm not traditionally feminine. I chose not to have children, don't care about what length this year's skirts should be, and don't have a clue about polenta or the latest must-have recipe ingredient. People's first words to me are usually, "Have you been out berry-picking?" or "Oh dear, has your iron broken again?" I wrote much of Shrouded from the perspective of Douglas, the necrophile, and one editor said that my work was so dark that I should use a male pseudonym. Safe as Houses also had a male protagonist in David, the sexually sadistic sociopath. As a teenager, I'd felt the level of hatred and rage that he feels against his abusers. The desire for revenge isn't a male-only phenomenon. The new novel, Noise Abatement, contains scenes from the viewpoint of a normal man who is driven to increasing violence through extraordinary circumstances. Again, it was partly autobiographical as I watched a real man go through a similar prolonged hell on earth.

I mainly read true crime texts, and the American murder rate is such that many of these books are by American writers. One of the most successful in sales terms is a female, former policewoman Ann Rule – but the best book I've read in the past couple of years was Howard Sounes' biography of the Wests, called simply Fred & Rose. That said, I don't mind if the writer is male, female or a martian as long as they understand their subject, write with clarity and insight and tell me something that I didn't already know.

Carol Anne Davis' latest novel is Noise Abatement *(Do-Not Press)*

Olivia Dwight

It seems to me that there used to be a greater difference between male and female crime writing than there is now. Men – except for a few English writers like Michael Innes – concentrated on action and general toughness, while women paid more attention to style and characterisation. It's different these days, since the introduction of female private eyes and coroners who try to be at least as hard-boiled as the men.

Women enjoy success if they're good writers, of straight novels as well as crime fiction.

My mystery novels are told in the first person, from the point of view of a male protagonist. I'm quite comfortable using his voice, although I tend to avoid love scenes.

I read both male and female crime writers.

Olivia Dwight's latest book is Close His Eyes

Lynda LaPlante

Yes, I do.

Women writers are successful in every genre! With regard to crime, I think the success of female novelists such as Agatha Christie, Ruth Rendell and Patricia Cornwell is partly due to the many years women were forced to write under a male pseudonym in order to get published (hawking back to famous Restoration playwrights). As a result, I think many women turned to crime fiction not to prove any specific point but simply because they were more difficult to 'detect'! Crime writing requires a complex structure which involves establishing both the police inquiry and the details of the victim whilst developing many plot twists, to hook the readers and keep them guessing. It is a complicated structure to keep on the boil, and requires strong character development as well as (in some cases) an ability to portray horror and the deviousness of the killer. The crime novel therefore has many interesting avenues for research, from the psychological aspect to the forensic science developments that are constantly advancing. To my mind, many of the great romance novelists such as Jane Austin and the Brontes were skilled writers of the thriller element, whether it was attached to Rochester and his wife or to Catherine and Heathcliff. It is the choice of the author to write what fascinates and interest him/her, and, given the choice, I would choose crime fiction every time.

It is rare for a male author to be asked how he feels writing a female protagonist, yet women writers are constantly asked this question. It is as comfortable for me to write a male protagonist as a female. The only criteria is that they are realistic and totally believable characters and therefore acceptable to both male and female readers.

I read a cross-section of male and female crime writers, but enjoy every type of novel, biography and autobiography. It is the content that I am most interested in, and I will read it regardless of the sex of the writer.

Lynda LaPlante's latest novel is Sleeping Cruelty *(Macmillan)*

Kate Ellis

There is such a rich variety in crime writing today. I think that each individual writer has his or her own strengths, style and interests which have nothing much to do with gender. But having said that, I do think that women tend to excel at psychological crime novels and men at the more 'mean streets' end of the genre.

The first reason is probably quite mundane: in the golden age of crime writing women like Agatha Christie had more leisure time than men to indulge their talents and imagination. Secondly, women generally have more instinct than men for psychological insight, what makes people tick... and what might drive them to murder.

I've no problem writing my two male detectives. In fact Wesley Peterson and Gerry Heffernan have become like old friends. Perhaps I feel so at home with male characters because I live in an all male household (apart from the cat), I don't know.

Definitely. I'd say my reading splits roughly 50:50.

Kate Ellis's latest book is The Funeral Boat *(Piatkus)*

Ann Prospero

Absolutely. Women have more fun, don't they? We can be just as serious as the men, but we get down into the feelings, the emotions, and we make them real. I know male writers are writing about female sleuths more and more often, but think about it. Don't the women writers create protagonists who aren't afraid of being afraid? Suze

Cannon, my protagonist, works hard to be a no-nonsense, professional homicide detective, and she succeeds most of the time. She's also a vulnerable and needy woman with a past that sears her with pain. She wants to be loved, and lordy, she's scared to death that she will be. And that's the story!

Smart, cocky, assertive, and aggressive sleuths are the kinds of women most female readers identify with. I consciously chose to make my protagonist, Suze Cannon, a Miami Homicide Detective because I know the city so well and I like to read about women like her. Suze has a past, she has her problems, and she deals with them while making a forceful present. And this generation of women writers is out there and not afraid to tell the world who they are and what they want. Makes for good reading.

I have males in my book and each is an individual. I enjoyed writing them, or actually letting them come forth and people

Margaret Yorke

my book. That goes for Suze's partners (especially Rafael, whom any woman would like to hug) as well as for the killer. I won't say anything more about him.

I sure do: P. D. James, Ian McEwen, Patricia Cornwell, James Connelly. And on and on.

Ann Prospero's latest book is Almost Night *(Penguin)*

Margaret Yorke

How do you define identities in this context? Different characteristics, certainly. As a generalisation, male writers are strong on action, female writers are often stronger on character.

Plenty of male writers are very successful at the moment: Colin Dexter (who owes a lot to the wonderful TV adaptations of his Morse books), Ian Rankin, Reginald Hill, Peter Lovesey, Andrew Taylor – mentioning British writers only. I think the ability of women writers to develop believable characters is one reason for their success – the reader can identify with them.

I was very comfortable writing my Patrick Grant novels with a male protagonist, and I often write from 'inside' male characters, but not in the first person: except for rare sections, as in, for instance, A Small Deceit; my characters are people first, male or female second.

Yes.

Margaret Yorke's latest book is A Case To Answer *(Little, Brown)*

Janet Evanovich

I think in the past men have been more plot oriented and women who are writing now are more character oriented.

Readers are constantly looking for a

new experience. So when women writers brought the character-driven crime novel featuring female protagonists onto the scene, they brought welcome diversity to crime writing.

Not comfortable at all.

I read mostly male crime writers: Bob Crais, Elmore Leonard, Michael Connely, Robert B. Parker are currently on my nightstand.

Janet Evanovich's latest book is Hot Six *(Macmillan)*

Susan Kelly

I'm not sure that I do. Crime is such a broad field these days and there are male 'cosy' writers just as there are women writing brutal serial killer novels. The women seem to have a more bleak view of the world though (can you imagine Patricia Cornwell letting Kay Scarpetta be happy?); while, with some honourable exceptions (Cynthia Harrod Eagles springs to mind), men are generally better at the comic caper.

You know, I have no idea, unless they have more patience in working out the details of a plot.

Both my crime series have a male central character, though written in the third person. I once published a short story with a male first person narrator; I didn't think twice about it.

I read both. My favourite crime writer is a man, Reginald Hill. I also read pretty much anything by Dick Francis, Lawrence Block, Michael Dibdin, Jonathan Kellerman and Robert B. Parker. There do seem to be more novels by women on my crime shelves, though, perhaps because I'm not fond of the noir end of the genre where the 'hero' (an unfrocked policeman) has to step over the bodies of drug addicts as he leaves his boarded-up flat on some sink housing estate in 'sarf' London. I mean, in what way is that more 'realistic' than a country village?

Susan Kelly's latest book is The Lone Traveller *(Allison & Busby)*

Sarah Smith

Different perceptions, certainly. In America at least, female crime writing is seen as more perceptive of character and more concerned with female protagonists, amateur sleuths and family. Male writing is more oriented toward the thriller. A distinction without a difference, I think; so many of the really good crime writers, male and female, care deeply about character, and the best use character as a source of terror. The distinction that really interests me is that between the novel that is only about private concerns and the one that perceives a wider community, which is the community where we all live and have our moral being, and has something to say about the world. I like the people who, even if they're not obviously writing about a big picture, have the big picture in the corner of their eye. I'm very interested in the work of African-American women such as Barbara Neely and Terris McMahan Grimes, explicit feminists and radicals, and in the work of political writers like Philip Kerr or, in the TV genre, Barry Levinson, who explore and usually dismiss the idea that justice is always best served by the discovery of a murderer and the application of a law. Crime is more mysterious than that, more general, more fearsome.

Because we have made ourselves conspicuous, my dear! It may not be so in England, but in America, until about twelve years ago, women mystery writers received a disproportionately low share of the reviews – we were writing about 40% of the books in the field but getting about 25% of the attention. Then Sue Grafton and a handful of other women founded Sisters in Crime, dedicated to advancing the commercial interests of women mystery writers. Sisters in Crime advocate professionalism, shameless self-promotion, and collective action. We write to editors of book reviews that don't review women. We are mad bitches, and it works. I would like to say that women's success is simply due to women's conspicuous talent: P. D. James, Amanda Cross, Ruth Rendell, Laurie King, Sue Grafton, Margaret Maron, Sharyn McCrumb, Janet Evanovich – the list of women writers one must read could go on

and on. But it's not only talent; it's the will to be visible. Bless the Internet, which has made all of us much more visible to each other. Sisters in Crime has a Web site at www.sistersincrime.org and an Internet chapter (as well as many local chapters – none yet in England, who would like to start one?). In science fiction, my other field, the FEM-SF invitational list is doing some of the same work, as is the cross-genre Interstitial Arts movement (see their self-definition at http://www.endicott-studio.com/ia.html).

I actually write two protagonists, one male and one female. Alexander von Reisden has been a leading citizen of the town inside my head for years. I have a lot of fun writing him because I get to explore the particular maleness of one man, who would be very amused at the idea that he is representative of any species. Like me, he comes from a family that was marked by madness; like me, he's had to deal with that, and he's dared to be married and a parent. Unlike me, he went mad himself; he committed crimes. I'm a mother; he's a father. It's fun to speculate on the differences between a mother's experiences and a father's, to write them out as part of Reisden's experiences, and to have them vetted by my male readers who are fathers of small boys. What one learns: Reisden isn't a perfect husband or father, in part because of his past. But I delight to see him work at love and trust. And I love to play him off against my other protagonist, Perdita Halley, who is a very feminine woman who wants love and family and all the feminine things – but needs to play concert piano. This will take her away from home and family for months at a time – which will require her to find a quite exceptional man, and be a quite exceptional woman. But the man she has is Reisden. Even more fun are male secondary characters, told from their points of view. I had the most splendid fun with Leonard, the murderer in The Knowledge of Water. Leonard has been trained to be chivalrous toward women – to the point of having killed one. Spending some time in Leonard's head let me play with the contradictions of male protectiveness and chivalry. Leonard hates the women he adores; he doesn't know what to do without love but he is about to explode from self-disgust and frustration. In the same book, Roy Daugherty, ex-Maine logger and retired lawyer, finds himself in a situation familiar to retired people; he doesn't know what to do with the rest of his life. And then, to his surprise, he finds himself beginning to sketch everyone he sees. In other words, men are not men, they are individuals, and so are women. And though their maleness and femaleness fascinate me, so does everything else, from their religious lives to their families and their work.

Yes (with a slight bias toward the female). But, like many crime writers, I don't read as many writers as I'd like because much of my reading time is spent in research. At the moment I am reading Elizabethan diplomatic history!

Sarah Smith's latest book is The Knowledge of Water *(Arrow)*

Jessica Mann

Differences between male and female crime writing? I see it as a long line, most feminine at one end, most masculine at the other, shading together in the middle. But even where they overlap, I'm sure the differences are there and readers can recognise them.

And that is part of the answer to women's success; because during much of the last century, women were the majority of novel buyers and borrowers, using crime novels for distraction, comfort and consolation; remember that what people wanted to read during air-raids was a cosy Agatha Christie. Now neither sex is writing novels that imply everything will turn out all right in the end, we're all much more realistic and morbid, and I'm not sure it is still true that women are more conspicuously successful. So the real question has to be left for posterity to answer – will crime novels now being written by women survive, as Sayers, Christie etc. have, while those by their male contemporaries disappear?

I prefer writing about female protagonists because I think I understand them better. I enjoy inventing dynamic, ingenious, sensible women and following their adventures and predicaments – to the extent that even as late as the 1980s, my publisher was still accusing me of being too feminist, although I'm not in the gay or political statement category. I do occasionally use a male point of view but never as the main protagonist and not very often.

I read crime novels by men and women alike; I believe I could tell which was which in a blind tasting – and rather regret having to say that my current favourites (an ever changing list) are nearly all men.

Jessica Mann's latest book is Under A Dark Sun *(Constable)*

Joanna Hines

My books have been called psychological thrillers, but the emphasis is probably more psychological than thriller. So I really haven't read widely enough to be able to say whether male and female crime writers have different identities. Since there is a clear split in mainstream fiction writing between a male and female voice, it is most probable that the same is true in crime fiction, although there does seem to be quite a lot of deliberately masculine writing from female crime writers.

Women crime writers are probably successful because they do it well. That they are seen to do it well might be thanks to the very high profile of the early successes, Agatha Christie and Dorothy Sayers, so there is a general expectation that women will hold their own in this field. And they do.

I find writing from a male point of view surprisingly refreshing. This might be because there is less of a tendency for my own voice to start making itself heard, so the proportion of straightforward imagination and invention increases. I find it entertaining to put myself in a man's shoes, just as I enjoy entering the imaginary world of historical characters; if writing is a way of escaping from self, then the less like myself the character is, the better, at least for this author.

Yes, I do try to read both male and female writers, but usually can't get through either in crime fiction. The few exceptions are both male and female, though in mainstream fiction I definitely prefer women writers. Not sure why it should be different in crime fiction.

Joanna Hines' latest book is Improvising Carla *(Simon and Schuster)*

Danuta Reah

That's a difficult one to answer. Excluding the 'splatter' range of the market, I think that women tend to write books that convey the dread of violence and the way this works on the mind. They are very good at the psychology of fear. As a broad generalisation, I think male crime writers write about fear rather than induce it. Also, I think that women often employ more ingenuity in thinking up truly horrible things to happen to their victims (which might explain something about certain notable female politicians. I find as a reader that women tend to draw me more into the total world of their characters. Some male crime writers (and male crime readers) can be a bit geeky about business or technology or espionage, and the people in the books and the world of the books get rather lost. This is, of course, a massive generalisation.

Maybe it's centuries of repressed nastiness. Our society spent a lot of time keeping the lid firmly on women whilst paying lip service to some kind of idealised stereotype. So the occasional woman who got a

chance tended to let rip – for example, Bloody Mary, Elizabeth I, Catherine the Great, and one or two memorable recent examples. It's probably better to get it out of your system via writing – it's deeply felt, it's convincing, it's scary. On the whole, I think that women tend not to be optimists, and this gives their writing – or at least that of the writers I enjoy reading – a core of realism in a genre that must, by its very nature, require a 'suspension of disbelief' from its readers. That core of realism gives a believable context to narratives that might otherwise border on the fantastic.

I don't like writing first person narrative, but I do use point of view. I'm happy writing from both a male and a female perspective. It's interesting – and a challenge – to try and get into the minds of my male characters, and to look at the events of a novel from both perspectives. In fact, it's essential, because I can't work out the plot unless I can work out how the characters are reacting in given circumstances. There are some male characters I might find hard to write. I've never tried to write, for example, a very laddish male. It's a mindset I don't really understand. It might be interesting to try. I'm an academic linguist by training, and I have studied male and female speech patterns, which has been very useful.

Yes. I read Laurie King, Val McDermid, Minette Walters, Denise Mina, John Harvey, Reginald Hill, Stuart Pawson, Stephen Booth. There is a range of 'genres within the genre' in that selection, but the important thing is that these are writers who can make the worlds they create believable to me.

Danuta Reah's latest books are Silent Playgrounds *and* Only Darkness *(both HarperCollins)*

Gemma O'Connor

I sometimes wonder if this male / female thing is overplayed. You get it all the time; the internal (female) versus action (male), yet for every example supporting such a claim I bet I could name you a counterbalance. Writers are magpies and hoarders – everything goes into the pot: gender, experience and background. I don't feel comfortable with the idea of genderification of imagination. I've no idea whether I write the way I do because I'm a woman or because I'm Gemma O'Connor, but I wouldn't like to think that I'm somehow preprogrammed by genital grouping alone. Yeah, it probably has some bearing but then so had nationality, height, hair colour and whether or not you have sex appeal. Or like animals. The imagination is the thing, surely? And the quality of the writing; the power of the storyteller, man or woman. At base, we've all got the same ambition, which is simply to write something with universal appeal.

Compared to what? Romantic fiction? Literary novels? Aren't women equally successful in other genres? That aside, I sometimes wonder if early women crime writers had a second agenda? Since professional policing and detection were barred to them, they could, and did, prove they could handle detailed investigation? Or maybe they simply liked, and were good at, solving puzzles and putting order on chaos?

Quite comfortable. The real challenge is inventing a believable character, once that's achieved, the rest follows.

Yes, all the time.

Gemma O'Connor's latest book is Walking on Water *(Bantam Press)*

Cath Staincliffe

I can't decide. I can make some generalisations: women are more likely to detail the effects of violence in a realistic way; men write more shoot-em-up / car chase / gadgets and dynamite / my dick's bigger than yours type stuff; there don't seem to be many women writing noir (but then is that because only men get landed with that label? And that a gritty, contemporary, realistic book by a woman with a less than happy ending wouldn't be called noir?). Women are probably better on the whole at getting inside women's heads, and the same goes for men, but these are all sweeping generalisations and there are loads of exceptions. My favourite writers are those who can tell a good story and bring some emotion and poetry to it, those who have an acute perception for the details of life, the nuances of relationships, the rhythm of dialogue, the mood of a place, the smell and taste of things. That's not a male or female thing.

Well, I'd say our success is on a par with male writers. And that's unusual because women don't generally achieve conspicuous success in other fields or professions due to all the cultural / political / economic constraints on women; all the glass ceilings and old boy networks and babies and ageing parents etc. Maybe writing is different because it is an individual pursuit and we can structure our work time and methods however we like. It would be interesting to know whether women who have done well are rewarded as handsomely as their male counterparts; do marketing budgets, review column inches, film deals and media features reflect the seeming equality of success of male and female writers. Or is it like the tennis and the acting profession?

Feels fine, though it's only recently that I've tried it – in a book where the story is told from several points of view. Initially I felt on firmer ground with a female protagonist. I was much more interested in exploring a woman as my main character because part of what I wanted to write about was being a woman in this day and age, putting a woman who is also a working mother into the traditionally male role of a private eye. Having written four novels with that main character I was eager to try out other voices and there was no problem at all with writing male protagonists.

Yes.

Cath Staincliffe's latest book is Stone Cold Red Hot *(Allison and Busby)*

Gwendoline Butler

No, since I write under two names and originally planned for the Melvilles to have a masculine name, I do not feel that female writers are different. We are just writers!

Have we had such a conspicuous success? It seems to me that the men have done well too. I think that crime writing is doing well because we are entertainers and know it. People like to read about a problem but they want an answer which we give them.

I enjoy writing about John Coffin. I admit he has elements of my husband and more than a soupçon of me.

I just love crime fiction, always have since I read The Mystery of the Yellow Room aged about eight (I was an early reader). I love all crime fiction, American and French. I read all I can get and belong to every library I have access to. And I buy too, of course.

Gwendoline Butler's latest books are Dead Again *and* Coffin's Ghost *(HarperCollins)*

Jane Adams

Yes, though I feel that the differences are being eroded and suspect that they are now more cultural than gender based. It seems to me that more female American writers have female protagonists than do UK writers, where the split seems to be more even. Maybe this is because the female private eye, bail bondswoman, etc. is more prevalent in America and we don't have the counterpart. I do feel that where graphic violence is concerned, editors are still rather more reluctant to allow female writers to indulge than their male counterparts – there are exceptions of course. I've had experience of an editor being very reluctant to allow certain scenes and I have cut them. I've spoken to other writers who have had similar experiences whereas men on the same list express violence much more graphically. I have to say that my editor was probably right in these instances but I do think that it's interesting.

I think women crime writers have been very fortunate in that they've had such strong women as trailblazers. The likes of Agatha Christie and Dorothy L. Sayers and then later powerful and more psychological writers like Patricia Highsmith have given recent authors a terrific tradition to follow – or subvert according to their own mind. I have to cite Dorothy Sayers as an early influence. Long before I ever thought of writing – or consciously thought of writing – I read Sayers and watched the dramatisations on TV. I loved the puzzle elements and the glimpse into such a romantic – and in some ways quite absurd – world. Sayers was published in the famous yellow covers back when I first read her and this led me to read many other crime writers published in the same format, notably people like Cornell Woolrich whose brooding, edgy vision of the world influenced me heavily when I eventually did start to write.

This is a question I have often been asked and one that still puzzles me. It never occurred to me that I should feel anything less than comfortable in writing from a male POV. It's pretty fundamental after all to the art of the storyteller than you can think yourself into any role. I feel that if I start anticipating problems simply in changing sex – and, after all, I'm fairly familiar with the male species – then how can I possibly hope to think myself into more unfamiliar territory, such as the mind of a killer? I do, anyway, suspect that most writers are frustrated actors and actively enjoy the challenge, and the adventure, in being able to adopt as many different identities as they please.

Yes. I like variety and tend to read different writers for very different reasons. I love the poetry of James Lee Burke and Walter Moseley. The feisty style of Sue Grafton, the realistic feel of Val McDermid and the pure escapism of Peter O'Donnell's Modesty Blaise books – getting harder to find now.

Jane Adams' latest book is The Angel Gateway *(Macmillan)*

Amy Myers

Yes I do, but I can't think quite how I'd define it. Moreover it seems to me that their identities are growing closer together than they were, for example, in the Golden Age.

My first thought was that women tend to have a closer eye for detail but then I remembered Monsignor Ronald Knox and The Three Taps which told me far more about gas taps than I wished to know. My second thought was that when detective stories were chiefly escapist entertainment, women were better placed to write about charismatic male detectives than men about female protagonists.

I'm very comfortable writing both in the third and first person with a male protagonist, with the qualification that, apart from short stories, my crime writing has hitherto all been historical. Now that I'm considering contemporary novels, I am pausing for thought over a male protagonist.

Yes.

Amy Myers' latest crime novel is Murder in the Queen's Boudoir *(Severn House)*

Margaret Murphy

There does seem to be a predominance of women writing psychological crime, which partly answers the next question, since statistics show that fiction readers are, in the main, women readers.

Have they really, or is it just that women are more likely to get a fair crack of the whip in the crime genre? If you look at the balance of big earners over here and in the States, there is still a healthy male presence – in fact, setting aside Patricia Cornwell (and how many of us secretly do?), the American megasellers are all male. I know – there's Sue Grafton, Laurie King and Janet Evanovitch, but how do their bank balances match, say, Elmore Leonard or Michael Connelly? Over here, it seems to me that for every Minette Walters, there's a Reginald Hill… and Ian Rankin has dominated the bestsellers list this year. I'd like to see a statistical analysis of sales and earnings for the lads and the lasses – as it stands, I don't think there's any real evidence to support the original statement.

I've never been any good in an argument because I can always see the other person's point of view – a dead loss if what you need is a damn good gloves off, dingdong row, but a definite advantage when writing from different perspectives. Whether the experience is comfortable or uncomfortable depends on the personality of the character in question.

I like to read good crime fiction and I'm less interested in the gender of writer than in the quality of the writing.

Margaret Murphy's latest books are Dying Embers *(Macmillan) and* Past Reason *(Pan)*

Laurie R. King

Traditionally, to blatantly oversimplify, women wrote relationships, men wrote action. Even that great wordsmith Dorothy L. Sayers began her final Wimsey novel with a note apologizing for mixing up love into a detective story – as if love isn't the biggest mystery of them all. Traditions, however, are meant to be broken, and in recent decades they have been shattered indeed. Jagged bits still litter the ground around our feet. Male writers now happily craft three-dimensional men (and women!) who not only have feelings, but actually talk about them, while women writers are free to revel in tough-girl tales with characters every bit as two-dimensional as a forties pulp novel. Personally, this question reminds me of that teenage test of one's sexual identity, the command: look at your fingernails. A girl (the theory had it) will automatically spread her hand out flat and drop it, the better to study the whole from wrist to fingertip; in contrast, a boy would cup his fingers and bring the hand up so as to inspect the nails for dirt. Looking at your fingernails the wrong way made a person immediately suspect. Me? I looked for the dirt. Still do.

I loved the study Jim Huang of the Drood Review did a few years ago, which concluded that women now accounted for roughly half of all mysteries published. Taken in conjunction with the common perception that these days crime writing is a woman's game, the only possible conclusion one can reach is that when it comes to women writers, equality amounts to domination. If we women are conspicuous in our success, it probably indicates less about modern times than it does about the previous era, when we were inconspicuous in our lack of success.

I tend to write about women because women's minds and lives interest me more: when I write men, they are generally in a supporting role. However, I have a much-nominated short story narrated by a male, and I am thinking about a book with a male central character. Whether or not I could maintain the intimate voice of a first-person male character for 400 pages remains to be seen; the book I'm thinking of will probably be in the more objective third person, where it isn't so immediately apparent if the author doesn't know precisely how a man moves inside his skin.

Absolutely. In fact, I've been asked several times recently to do articles on my favorite three / six / ten authors and have been surprised to find my list weighted somewhat toward male writers. No doubt a close analysis would reveal outside influences on my choices: the phase of the moon, perhaps, or the size of my most recent royalty cheques.

Laurie R. King's latest book is Folly *(HarperCollins)*

Hilary Norman

I started out thinking yes, of course, but then, taking a closer look at those I read frequently (strictly speaking, thrillers and suspense rather than crime for the most part), I find that male / female doesn't seem to be what makes the difference for me. I find that I tend to read more female British writers and more American male thriller / crime writers, though that's only a generalisation, and I have to say there are scores of writers I'm obviously missing out. British women – Rendell / Vine and Walters especially – seem to face up to warped psyches and the ugliness of murder in a more matter-of-fact way than many of the male writers I read, with much less need for sensationalism – but then again, glancing at my shelves, I appear not to read British male-written crime, so this has to be a limited 'snapshot' impression. I like the calm, the comparative cool approach of the female Brits, enjoy the quirks of their characters, the endless variety of nightmares on familiar territory, the sometimes hugely civilised backgrounds (Joan Smith, Jill Paton Walsh, Clare Francis) that spawn horrors. Family units and close 'normal' relationships appear to be, on the whole, what attract me to my favourite group of American crime / thriller writers. Patterson gives me the lovely Alex Cross, Nana-Mama and the kids; Kellerman brings me Alex

Delaware, Robin and Spike, the dog; Peter Blauner's Intruder drew me in with that old winner (for me, within and outside my own writings): the contented family lethally disrupted; and my favourite Grisham hero remains, I think, Jake Brigance – I suppose I'm still a sucker for a 'decent' guy. I loved the originality of David Hunt's Magician's Tale – I respected, if not exactly empathised with, Kay Farrow. I'm fond of Scarpetta, too, like her strength – and I like Tempe Brennan (though too many maggots tend to put me off). So where does that leave me with this question? I'm still not sure – I read constantly, but clearly not enough to answer thoroughly. I believe gender alone may not play that great a role, that the nationality and background, for example, of any writer is equally significant. (Though what does this say about me, since I'm a female Brit who writes largely US-located thrillers?) The American male suspense writers I favour are somewhat romantic, I suppose, with warmth mixed in with their brands of brutality. For sheer, cool intelligence, plus readability and realistic, intriguing characters, British women rule.

Because they're so damned good at it, particularly at the psychology of evil. Their originality comes through individuality, I think, rather than an attempt to find new ways to shock. Quality will out.

I've written a number of male protagonists, and feel peculiarly at ease inside them. I wrote a male first person lead for the very first time in Too Close, and can honestly say I felt more comfortable with his thought processes than many I've created. I'm doing that again with my current thriller, and the same applies. I expect, though, that when the time comes for me to write a first person female lead, I'll be just as comfortable, if not more.

I do, but I think I've answered that in my rather overweight first answer.

Hilary Norman's latest book is Blind Fear *(Piatkus)*

Judith Cutler

Do you remember the time when all women of my generation had to live up to (down to?) D. H. Lawrence's vision of women, because Leavis said that D. H. Lawrence was the expert on women? Then it became de rigueur to deny any differences between male and female anything. At least it's now safe to generalise a little, even if you don't quite believe that the sexes come from different planets. So I'd have thought – and there are notable exceptions, of course – that you could say that men tend to write more about violence, including all the gory details, while maybe women are more interested in putting crime in the context of relationships in particular and society in general. Take Natasha Cooper, for example, and Sara Paretsky.

If writing crime involves juggling different characters, weaving multiple plots, and generally doing several things at one, of course women should make good crime writers. After all, we're used to soothing toddlers, feeding babies, preparing four course meals for six, dealing with tomorrow's paperwork and reminding partners to open the wine – and reading a book at the same time. That's what women do. Maybe new men do the same things. Maybe I'm so busy juggling I don't notice.

I've used male protagonists quite happily in romantic fiction, so when I get a chance I shall enjoy trying to do the same in crime fiction. Watch this space.

Of course. At the moment Edward Marston rubs shoulders on my bedside table with Georgette Heyer. What I'd really like to do is read one by every member of the CWA. Unfortunately if I read other people while I'm actually writing a book I tend to pick up their style – it was an excess of late Henry James that gave me a very nasty attack of writers' block some years ago. The other thing is that you can't avoid comparing yourself with other writers, so if you happen to be writing contemporary crime and to be reading Val McDermid or Reg Hill at the same time, you know you might as well switch off the computer and go and dig in the garden. So if I'm not reading one of your books at the moment, dear reader, please forgive me!

Judith Cutler's latest book is Dying by Degrees *(Headline)*

Priscilla Masters

Do I consider male and female crime writers possess different identities? Sometimes – not always. Some male writers fool me into thinking they're women. And vice versa.

A love of detail, an interest in the minutiae of people's lives and relationships, The 'gossip' factor.

Not quite. I've had a go but never feel quite as comfortable wearing the boxer shorts as in high heels and skirts.

I certainly do read a complete mix of male and female crime writers.

Priscilla Masters' latest book is A Fatal Cut *(Macmillan)*

Ellen Crosby

I don't believe that male and female crime writing necessarily possess different identities; actually I think there is more of a difference between British and American crime writing – a matter of nationality, rather than gender. Obviously there are women writers whose work is generally considered to have more appeal to women than men (no such distinction exists for male writers and a predominantly male audience, though!) but men read Agatha Christie, Ruth Rendell, P. D. James, Patricia Cornwell and Sue Grafton... to name but a few.

I think the women who have enjoyed conspicuous success as crime writers have done so because they are, first and foremost, good writers. As Maxim Jakubowski pointed out last year in his monthly column for The Guardian called 'A Beginner's Guide to Crime Fiction', women have been equally and well represented in every major 'era' of crime writing (cozy, hard-boiled, police procedural, historical, psychological, etc.) once Agatha Christie paved the way.

Since I write in the first person and my fiction is considered 'women's crime / thriller', I prefer to stay on my own turf and write as a woman. Although I thought Donna Tartt did an excellent job in The Secret History writing in the first person as Richard Papen, a number of male friends told me they knew a woman wrote the book. When I asked them to elaborate, no one was able to explain specifically what he meant... they just said, "there's a difference."

Absolutely.

Ellen Crosby's first novel is Moscow Nights *(Piatkus)*

Kate Charles

There are exceptions, of course, but I do feel that women are better at observing detail, and this is reflected in their writing. This can take the form of psychological insight, as well as the more obvious area of description.

Women are often skilled at conveying the subtleties of human nature and psychology, and readers find this satisfying.

I have written a male protagonist, in my David Middleton-Brown series. David's gender doesn't really seem to matter that much, in a way, because he's a strong reflection of my own interests and preoccupations. I don't think of him as a man, but as an alter-ego.

I do read more female than male crime writers, but there are notable exceptions. Andrew Taylor ranks as one of my all-time favourites, and I enjoy other male writers as well.

Kate Charles's latest book is Cruel Habitations *(Little Brown)*

Liz Evans

Yes – although I don't think that it is confined to crime novels. Male and female writing of any genre has a different identity. It has to: with the best will in the world, you can never truly know how the opposite sex is seeing the world.

Beats me. In fact I'm not entirely sure that this is accurate. It is, after all, male writers who are enjoying the success on TV (Colin Dexter, R. Delderfield, Reg Hill, etc.) over the past few years. I know there are a lot of successful female writers in the genre, but they're balanced out by the male ones surely?

Okay, I think. Before the current series of Grace Smith novels, I'd written a series set in the early forties where my chief protagonist was a male detective and I think he came out of them with a fair degree of integrity (although I must admit I gave him a female sidekick and her chapters always came easiest). I've also written a lot of short stories and quite often when I sat down to start I didn't know whether my main character was going to be male or female until I typed the first line. (Cometh the plot, cometh the man (or woman), so to speak!).

Absolutely. Reg Hill, Minette Walters, Colin Dexter, Patricia Cornwell, Robert Goddard, Ruth Rendell, etc. I am, in fact, a total crime reading tart.

Liz Evans latest book is Don't Mess with Mrs In-Between *(Orion)*

June Thomson

Yes. Men tend to put more emphasis on plot and action, whereas women concentrate on character and relationships.

Because of their ability to understand the character and relationships, along with descriptive ability, ingenuity and attention to detail.

Fairly comfortable.

Yes.

JuneThomson's latest book is Holmes & Watson *(Allison and Busby)*

Denise Mina

Because men tend to write about men and women tend to write about women, the nature of the plots reflect the different world of male and female detectives. It's pretty rare to read about a female detective who completely lacks self-reflection, or about a male detective who hides from the baddies in a cupboard and cries, wishing he were at home with his cat, Cuddles. Still, there are always those writers who transcend any rules. I think there are sensibilities that are uniquely male and female though. Few female writers, I think, would have a central female character raped in the present plot because realistically that can't be tidied up before the end of one book. Fewer female writers would resolve rape or child sexual abuse by giving the victim a nice boyfriend at the end, which I've seen some male writers do. Gaffs aside, cross-gender writing can open up possibilities: I suspect few male writers would happily have an impotent protagonist like Val McDermid's Tony Hill.

The 1970s, 80s and 90s should rightfully have seen women breaking through in all genres. Crime writing is one of the few areas where that did happen, largely because it is more democratic and less precious than mainstream fiction. I think this is because it is plot led and because of the speed and eagerness with which it's read. The rigidity and discipline of crime fiction easily lends itself to subversion and female writers can be seen as part of that. Because the parameters of the genre are so set – the loner, the problem, the mucking about and the failure, the final success and resolution of the loner's personals – minor and major variations such as the protagonist's gender can become central to the plot.

I'd quite happily write with a male protagonist. I don't think we're all that different on the inside and a male protagonist can go places and explore social pockets a woman can't.

I do. Heaven forfend that I should discriminate and miss out on a good read.

Denise Mina's latest book is Exile *(Transworld)*

Natasha Cooper

This is a little like asking whether the ability to strip down an engine is an inherently masculine trait and whether the maternal instinct is innate. I would answer no to all such questions. Some male writers produce novels that are so plotty, so violent, or so devoid of interesting characters that I can't be bothered to read them. On the other hand some men, e.g. Reginald Hill, write novels so full of character development, wit, understated violence and emotional complexity that I devour them. And some female writers put so much absolutely revolting physical cruelty in their novels that I cannot bear them. It's the writer – not the writer's gender – that matters to me.

Women writers have enjoyed conspicuous success in most genres. I think some women find crime writing liberating because it allows them to escape the sexist straitjacket that forces them to behave as though anger doesn't exist.

Fairly comfortable. Novelists have to have the kind of imagination that allows them inside the minds of characters quite different from themselves. But my main interest lies in the way women respond to fear, violence, emotion, bullying and so on, which means that I will always create more female characters than male. And there is always the danger that imagination and observation can lead a writer to produce a character unrecognisable to real people of the same gender. I am thinking here mainly of female characters created by male writers. There seems to be a lot of wish fulfilment and a lot of bizarre misapprehension in many of them. I suspect the same is true of many male characters created by female writers.

Definitely. And a lot of my best friends are male, too...

Natasha Cooper's latest book is Prey to All *(Simon & Schuster)*

Laura Lipman

Yes, and that's a good thing. I think female writers are apt to fail when they try to make their private eyes female versions of male prototypes – there has to be a clear delineation. Women excel at the medium-boiled crime novel – the really hard-boiled novel is a male province.

Largely speaking, the relative popularity of male and female crime writers is both a geographical and historical thing, always in flux.

In my next book I'm tackling a male protagonist in a far more thorough fashion than I've ever done before, so this question comes a little early for me.

What writer worth their salt wouldn't read a healthy mix of male and female writers?

Laura Lipman's latest book is The Sugar House *(Orion)*

J. Wallis Martin

I do in fact believe that male and female crime writers possess different identities. I attribute this to the fact that, whilst women tend to be rather more in touch with their emotions, men tend to be rather more in touch with their souls.

Male and female writers have always

J. Wallis Martin

enjoyed equal success in the genre, but not necessarily at the same time. There have been, and always will be, periods when success seems to favour one sex more than the other. At times, we find ourselves with an abundance of exceptionally good male authors. At other times, women have been (excuse the pun) top-heavy. I feel there is currently a good balance.

I am comfortable whether writing male or female protagonists, but my muse is most definitely male.

Like most people, I am drawn to a particular type of story, or genre, or prose style, or subject – the sex of the author is completely irrelevant to me.

J. Wallis Martin's latest book is Dancing with the Uninvited Guest

Molly Brown

Molly Brown

That may have been true once, but these days I think differences in writing style, approach and choice of subject matter tend to have more to do with the writer's background and age than his or her gender.

I think crime fiction has a history of being more open to women writers than any other genre except romance, possibly because of the early success of Agatha Christie. If you started asking strangers in the street to name a famous mystery writer, I bet the first name to come out of most people's mouths would be hers.

I feel quite comfortable writing from a male point of view, but before I became a fiction writer I spent several years as a stand-up comic and actress, and one thing I remember from those days of trudging around from audition to audition was that there were always many more parts for men than for women. When I started writing I made a conscious decision to feature female protagonists in my fiction whenever possible, with the idea that if they ever make the movie (I can dream!), the least I can do is make sure there will be some good parts in it for women. Then guess what happens? A Hollywood film company decides to option one of the few stories I've written with a male protagonist. And they've hired a male scriptwriter. (Sigh.)

Yes, definitely. My only concern as a reader is the quality of the writing, not the gender of the writer.

Molly Brown's latest book is Bad Timing and Other Stories *(Big Engine)*

Joyce Holms

My answers to your questionnaire are:

No.

Can't imagine.

Fine 'cos I do lots of research.

Male.

Not wildly interesting copy, I agree, so the following rant might fill a gap.

Joyce Holms on a Bad Day

I could be drummed out of the CWA for saying this, but it's a long long time since I read a crime story – by either sex – that I really really enjoyed. This is probably down to the fact that if it's better than mine, I hate it, and if it's worse than mine I wouldn't waste my time reading it. That said, I still feel that the reader is, in too many instances, being short-changed. For eighteen quid I expect originality, lively writing, well paced plot development, two-dimensional characters, plentiful incident, interesting backgrounds, realistic and idiosyncratic dialogue, conscientious and invisible research, and, most importantly, a strong and surprising ending – not necessarily who-dunnit but at least why or how. Eliminate any one of these ingredients and I'd like a refund.

Okay, somebody's going to say, "Yes, but I give something else instead, like atmosphere or insight." Well, thanks mate, but, I'm sorry, I want that as well. I've already learned as much as I need to know about horse racing, drug dealing, cosy villages etc. God help me, but if I have to suffer yet another hard drinking, heavy smoking, divorced police detective with a swinish boss breathing down his neck for a quick arrest, I could turn nasty.

The latest trend is to pad out a weak plot with buckets of blood, dismembered body parts, gouged eyes etc., which is simply an insult to the intelligence. Just as you can be sure that a film showing the sex act in the first five minutes will turn out to be total rubbish, so gratuitous gore advertises contempt for the reader and a deliberate attempt to pass shoddy goods.

You can't get away with sub-standard work forever. Individual writers will lose sales and, what is infinitely more scary, when the percentage of rubbish vastly exceeds the percentage of good writing the genre will lose credibility. I watched it happen to romance and I'm watching it happen to crime. When I see writers like Ed McBain (who wrote three of the worst crime novels I've ever read, and God knows how many others I've cut dead in the bookshop) awarded the Diamond Dagger, I'm tempted to comment, "Never mind the quality feel the width". Okay, so he invented the police procedural but I've yet to be convinced that that was such a boon. (So, sue me!) To my mind, a reader sampling the genre for the first time and choosing, McBain's Mary Mary Quite Contrary as an example of honoured crime writing would be put off for life. Not good news for the rest of us crime writers, right?

There has to be some significance in the fact that UK publishers churn out twice as many books per annum as do American publishers. No, not per capita – in total. Does this mean that American readers are more selective or that UK readers read more? Or what? Answers on a post card, please. Put them in the box down the hall. And flush.

Joyce Holms' latest book is Mr Big *(Headline)*

SKELETON AT THE FEAST: PATRICIA HALL

The ever-reliable Hall talks to CT about Thackeray & co....

Skeleton at the Feast is the seventh in my series about DCI Thackeray and the local newspaper reporter Laura Ackroyd with whom he has a somewhat on-off relationship. Normally my books are set in West Yorkshire which is where I was born and brought up, but as I live in Oxford now I've always had a yen to set something down here. What's put me off is the thoroughness with which Colin Dexter has explored the territory, but in this one I've been brave enough to bring Thackeray back to the college where he was a very unhappy northern undergraduate. Quite topical as it's turned out, but I didn't know that when I was writing it. There is still a strong Yorkshire element to the plot but the Oxford college strand also allows me to explore some issues around class and regional conflicts and the Establishment's timeless and utterly ruthless ability to obscure what's really going on. Thackeray is not popular when he starts uncovering what the college mandarins would rather stayed well hidden. Another theme is the damage that the older generation routinely does to the younger – both in a privileged setting and also in the 'other' Oxford,

where the tourist buses don't go – and against my more usual backdrop of grimy Bradfield and its sink estates.

I'm not sure who has influenced my style of writing. I guess I write like a journalist and, like Alice, I like lots of conversation. As far as content is concerned, you assimilate ideas over years. I started reading crime fiction as a child at the Agatha Christie end of the spectrum, and have worked steadily deeper and darker. But what I always demand as a reader – having a butterfly's attention span, like most journalists – is a plot which moves along at a cracking pace. In that department I don't think you can beat Dick Francis, who I gobbled up in his early career, although I know he's not fashionable now. But plot is just the bones of a novel and I think that what I needed as a fairly late starter in the field was some feeling that the crime novel could actually accommodate what I wanted to say. I think the two people who gave me the confidence to have a go myself were Reginald Hill and Sara Paretsky. Hill because of his humanity and humour (how I wish I could do that!) and his ability to explore complex issues with enormous subtlety within the confines of the genre, and Paretsky because she gives us strong, active women who make things happen and play a full part in the action. And both writers share the ability to present a society which seems to me totally real, full of fallible people and moral dilemmas and astonishing gulfs between the privileged and unprivileged living cheek by jowl. I came to other writers I admire like Val McDermid and Ian Rankin too late for them to be an influence. But you'll gather from all this that I aspire to being a humble member of the 'realist' school of crime fiction – no country houses and no fantasy mean streets either.

It would be difficult, I think, for a crime writer not to be aware of the genre on film and TV, particularly as in this country so much of the latter's output comes from novels anyway. I'm waiting with all fingers crossed to see what will happen to an option on my own series which has got as far as a script. Cross-fertilisation is inevitable, I think, though I guess that how creative that is varies from one writer to another. Personally I use *The Bill* to check up on the latest police procedure because the experts tell me it's pretty accurate. But there's no way I want to write a police soap. I don't think I'm particularly influenced by film but that's because my books are in the British tradition not the American, which tends to dominate film. I'm as fond of *The Big Sleep* as anyone and can get my mind round Tarantino, but I don't think either says much about policing the multiracial mean streets of West Yorkshire. They are more relevant perhaps to the men who write 'noir' – and it is usually men, isn't it? I love music, from jazz to opera, but apart from making my DCI a Billie Holiday fan, I don't think there's much connection with my fiction.

Though I started late as an adult novelist, my first effort at a crime story, with which I attempted to enliven one rainy and very boring holiday when I was about sixteen, went in the bin soon after. For the next twenty odd years I wrote fact not fiction as a journalist (don't laugh), and didn't have another go at fiction until the late eighties when I produced a novel which was just as ruthlessly disposed of on the grounds of

 COVER FEATURE: WOMEN IN CRIME

sheer embarrassment. The next (*The Poison Pool*, 1991) was accepted by the first publisher I sent it to. Which astonished me because, although I'd always earned my living by writing, I discovered when I'd completed *The Poison Pool* that I really had no idea whether it was any good or not. If I write an article for the Independent I know whether or not I've done the right research and put the argument together logically. With fiction I was too emotionally involved to make any judgement and I couldn't bring myself to let anyone I knew read it. My family had no idea – if mother was glued to the word processor no-one ever bothered to look at what was on the screen! So off it went under plain wrapper. But once I had the letter back accepting it, of course, I was hooked. I started the next one the very next day. I was hooked, and still am, though the money's a joke.

I still read a lot of crime fiction, which I think is a bit like a bran tub – you never know what you're going to pull out next. When I meet or listen to someone new at Dead on Deansgate or Bouchercon I always try to give their work a whirl. On this basis I've been bored too often, revolted occasionally by vomit on the pavement excesses, made hopping mad by the snobbery of the English middle classes who still haunt the genre, and sometimes made some very good new fictional friends. Musts for me are Reg Hill, Val McDermid, Ian Rankin and Sara Paretsky and I've enjoyed all the John Harvey books. Before I got involved myself, I was never a fan of historical fiction but I've been converted by Lindsey Davis and Gillian Linscott, who was a former colleague at The Guardian. I like Judith Cutler's books very much. We write about the same sort of multicultural urban landscape and I always think our heroines would get on well together. I do try to keep up with so-called literary fiction too, although I think the standard of writing in crime is superior far more often than the critics are willing to admit. I hate Martin Amis, like Graham Swift and Roddie Doyle, and over the years have taken in the major women writers like Fay Weldon, Penelope Lively, Angela Carter, Toni Morrison and Alice Walker. I have a go at the Booker shortlist every year and am often disappointed.

People you meet often ask how you can be so hooked on reading violence and writing about crime. I dislike censorship of any kind, except where children are concerned, but as a writer I am fairly pragmatic on

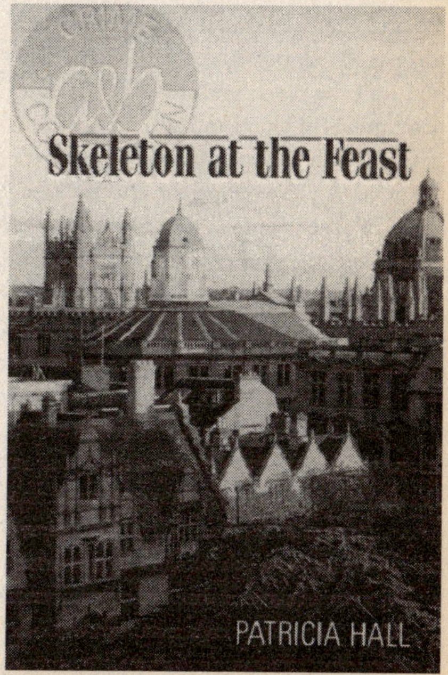

these issues. If we are writing about murder we are writing about violence. That is a given. How you approach its description depends on what sort of crime novel you are trying to write – it is a very broad church and what is appropriate in a comic novel may be very different from what is appropriate in something heavily 'noir'. You need to be aware of who your audience is likely to be. Personally I take a middle course. I want to be realistic but I don't want the reader so repelled by the detail that s/he stops reading. I take my family as a barometer: my mother in her eighties reads my books without getting too upset, though she hates some of the language, and my streetwise sons in their twenties seem to like them too, so I reckon I'm getting it about right for the sort of audience I'm likely to have. But this is not just a pragmatic question, is it? The Greeks produced moving drama without any violence on stage at all. For my taste, the best crime fiction isn't the novel with the most graphic descriptions of blood and guts on the street or post mortem examinations in the lab, it's the novel which explores the effects of violence on the victims, the criminals, the police and everyone else caught up in events. On other words, I'm a character rather than a plot or sensation person.

The same arguments apply to the treatment of sex – and to 'bad' language for that matter. If it's essential to the story, then fine: if it's gratuitous, then not. But you tread a particularly fine line with sexually explicit description anyway, to avoid tipping over into soft porn. I expect there's a market for soft porn crime but it's not what I want to read or write. My two main characters – and others – have a fairly energetic sex life, but when they get down to it I tend to leave it to the reader's imagination.

Then there are the other taboos of polite dinner party society – politics and religion. I am a 'personal is the political' woman. I find it almost alarming how clearly people's political attitudes jump off the page when they write fiction, even if their opinions are never overtly expressed. England is still a class ridden society, whatever Tony Blair thinks, and the way characters are portrayed, the way lifestyles are taken for granted, the part women or ethnic minorities or gays play in the story, speaks volumes. I'm sure my views are as obvious as anyone else's: I don't see how you can avoid it, especially if you are writing about crime, the police, law and order, punishment and the rest. All these are highly emotive issues and your characters must stand somewhere on the political spectrum. There are some overt political threads running through my books anyway. Laura Ackroyd is the granddaughter of a very Old Labour campaigner who lives in hope of Nye Bevan's resurrection. Laura is more sceptical than her gran but still more liberal than her lover, the somewhat puritanical copper, and that occasionally leads to tension. Then there's the inevitable conflict between openness and secrecy with a journalist involved in the stories and ethical issues about methods and corruption within the police force. I don't think there's any such thing as apolitical.

Religion, morality, ethics, they are all in there, inevitably. I was brought up in the Church of England, my husband as a Catholic, so we have that background though neither of us is a churchgoer now. I

COVER FEATURE: WOMEN IN CRIME

think when you are writing about crime and punishment, right and wrong, you need to be aware of the fact that people have been debating these issues for millennia and that what may appear morally abhorrent to one person may not bother another. So I suppose for a crime writer a sense of a moral dimension rather than of the trappings of religion is important. That doesn't mean being crudely judgmental and there are excellent writers who seem to offer a totally amoral perspective, but I find that a bit unnerving.

I genuinely don't believe crime novelists are any different from any other sort of novelist. I refuse to get uptight about the borderline between genres or between 'mere' entertainment and 'art'. A good novel is a good novel and should expand the mind, but if it's not enjoyable to the reader it won't expand anything except the box of junk going to Oxfam. This obsession with genres is quite a modern phenomenon. No-one told Dickens that because *Our Mutual Friend* is a mystery story it could only have a five line review six months after publication. So on the whole I think the appeal of what I write is the same as the appeal of any other kind of fiction: the creation of an imaginary world where the reader is entertained and hopefully learns something new about life. Whether it's any good or not is an entirely different question.

Place is very important to me. I do get out and about – to Oxford in the new novel, to Docklands in London in the one before that, *Dead on Arrival* – but essentially I write about the part of Yorkshire where the old industrial towns surrounded by the glorious Pennines are pulling themselves up by their boot-straps. People ask whether my fictional Bradfield is in fact Bradford and the answer is not quite. Because I haven't lived there for a while – though I still visit regularly – I don't want the hassle of readers writing to tell me that the pub Thackeray visits on page sixty-seven closed three years ago. And I wanted somewhere a little bit smaller and more incestuous than Bradford, which is a city not a town. But a lot of the places I describe are real – just transposed a bit. I love the wild moorland countryside and the old stone towns and villages which are struggling to find a new role now the traditional industries have almost gone. And the tensions inherent in industrial decline and regeneration and a multiracial population, are, as Bob Barnard once said about one of my books, fresh out of yesterday's newspaper

How do I work? In purely practical terms, I am devoted to my word processor. In fact I don't think I would ever have written a novel at all without it. As a journalist I was using the technology anyway, but for nothing much longer than 2000 words. 70,000 or more seemed really daunting and I'd never have made it on a typewriter. Once under way I aim to write a chapter a week – though that's not always possible as I'm still a working freelance journalist. When the first draft is complete I revise and revise until I'm happy, and then do a last check to make sure the logic of the actual mystery is sound and all the loose ends are tied up. The whole process usually takes about nine or ten months, leaving me two months a year to mull over the next. In terms of constructing the novel, I start with the plot because that, for me, is the most difficult. I can't begin

Chapter One without at least a sketch of where the novel is going and how it is going to end. For ideas I rely on what's going on around us. I quite often pick up the germ of an idea from a newspaper story. So successfully at times that it's almost creepy. My last book had a group of illegal immigrants found dead in a lorry. The current one deals with northern kids going to Oxford. Both were written long before either issue hit the headlines. The plot outline is not sacred. Very often it gets changed during the actual writing and sub-plots or digressions get added, often character led. But the characterisation is what I really enjoy. A group of the characters go with the series, and I feel now that I know them very well. But creating the one-off characters (which usually includes the main villain) is interesting too. I don't think you can easily sideline plot in this genre. I'm not against an ambivalent ending. I don't need every last sub-plot tidied up or villain clapped in jail. But on the whole I think resolution is the name of the last chapter and this is a genre mercifully free of post-modernists more interested in style than substance.

I write essentially because I have to. I've been doing it since I was about eight. But since I was eighteen and went to work on a newspaper for the first time, almost every word I have written has been published, so I can't really imagine not having readers. So, although I don't consciously write *for* the readers, the whole process for me is very much about communication. There are things I want to say, stories I want to tell, and I want someone to read them – the more the better. I don't know what happens when you get older and maybe the publishers give up on you. Perhaps the urge to write becomes less acute. I hope so because I would hate to be left talking to myself.

A bit of monastic solitude is essential for the actual writing process for me. I hate to be interrupted in mid-flow. But for the content of my books I really want to be in touch with what's going on in the world, so my journalistic work comes in useful, and I read a lot of newspapers and magazines and watch TV to try to keep in touch with the zeitgeist, and I visit Yorkshire and other places for the local colour.

In spite of new technology, I'm optimistic about books so there may be hope for me in my dotage. I think fiction will survive in book form. Factual stuff will transfer to the Internet or CD Rom or the mobile phone. But none of that technology is any good in bed, or in the bath, or on the beach or the plane, or any of the other places people choose to read fiction. I am even fairly optimistic about the younger generation. The twenty-somethings I know do still read. I share books with one of my sons, although the other is much more a film and video person. And Harry Potter has to be a good thing, doesn't he?

I'm well into the next book now. It's the next in the series and takes the characters back to Yorkshire where a series of demonstrations outside an abortion clinic ends in violence. Again I started writing some time before anti-abortion campaigners announced this summer that they were importing more militant methods into Britain from the US and Ireland. With guns, you wonder? Premonition plays a part in the story too. There are plenty of moral dilemmas and a nasty shock for DCI Thackeray.

MURDER, TORTURE AND DEPRAVITY WITH INGRID PITT

Vic Buckner

If actors and actresses are lucky, they can enjoy a second life as a writer after the glory days of their primary profession are over. Dirk Bogarde accomplished this, and so, in her way, has Ingrid Pitt. Pitt is unquestionably the Queen of British horror, even though her actual body of work is small. But such was her huge impact in a few short years, that she has become a much-loved feature of the film festival circuit and (with an entertaining series of books) is now a writer who may not ever be reviewed in the serious press, but is assured a healthy readership. Pitt (her real name is Ingoushka Petrov) was born in Poland, and is certainly best remembered in the blood-boltered Hammer epic Countess Dracula *(1970). Her actual genre debut was in the* Spanish Sound of Horror *(1964), but the real impact came with her performance as the highly sensuous, lesbian vampire in* The Vampire Lovers *(1970). It's difficult after so many years to remember the amazing impact this movie made in its day. The film upset the more fastidious critics as well as the moral guardians of the day, and Hammer movies (which now look models of restraint, full of the cream of the British acting profession) had many critics reaching for their most vituperative adjectives. However, by the 1970s Hammer realised that it was losing its capacity to shock – and that was bad news for them. With* The Vampire Lovers *they upped the ante in terms of sex and violence, with the bloody mayhem of the movie matched by the statuesque, sultry Pitt providing a sensuousness which had previously been relegated to the bosom-heaving victims of Christopher Lee's Dracula. Her nude scenes inaugurated a new frankness in the genre, and transformed the British horror film until* The Exorcist *which (to all intents and purposes) drove a stake into the heart of the industry. With* Countess Dracula, *Pitt took on the role of Countess Elizabeth Bathory, a real-life female monster who believed that bathing in the blood of virgins would keep her young. After the up-front horrors of* The Vampire Lovers, Countess Dracula *(while stylish enough) seemed a tad restrained (a subject which Pitt feels strongly about), and, despite her blood-drenched nude scenes, the film did not make the expected impact. Nevertheless, her career continued with appearances in the cult classic* The Wicker Man *and a notable turn as a ruthless terrorist in* Who Dares Wins.

Since those heady days, she has been a familiar figure at film festivals celebrating horror and the macabre, with her vampire associations much to the fore. And a new book has appeared: The Ingrid Pitt Book of Murder, Torture and Depravity *(Batsford), an intelligently written history of such monsters as the demented Roman Emperor Caligula, the ruthless Torquemada and the murderer of Ten Rillington Place, Christie. The grisly cover is Caravaggio's study of Judith and Holofernes: a close-up of a detail showing Holofernes having his head hacked off by Judith's sword as blood spouts onto the pillow. This classical reference is gorily echoed inside by illustrations that are redolent of the most unbuttoned excesses of mid-1950s horror comics. Countess Dracula herself, Elizabeth Bathory, is the subject of the first chapter, accompanied by a picture of the naked Countess ecstatically rubbing over herself the blood dripping from the screaming young woman (also naked) in the spiked cage directly above. While these images may help to sell the book, it's actually well written – and as a concise history of some of most memorable monsters of the past, it takes some beating. But getting the ebullient Pitt to discuss the book is initially a little difficult: she's talking about Christopher Lee, whom she regards as a 'gorgeous' man, and mentions that he is related to both Rasputin and Ian Fleming (admittedly, a pretty interesting genealogy).*

Can we talk about the book now? No, Pitt has moved onto a new Constable anthology to which she has contributed, called (at present) *Vampires*, along with such luminaries as Anne Rice.

It's going to be a very fat book, and I'm glad to say that they seem to be really happy with my contribution – they said it's really unusual.

But back to *Murder Torture and Depravity:* was this book Pitt's idea, or did the publishers come to her with the concept?

Oh, the books are always my idea. Good or bad, the concepts are mine. I had seen nothing quite like this book (although, of course there are similar volumes), and I'm happy with the way it's turned out.

Why so few female monsters?

Well, I begin with a lady with whom I have a certain association (having played her in the Hammer movie), Elizabeth Bathory. But a woman who kills on this scale is unusual. After all, the epic killers are usually men – because they have the power which makes it possible to commit mayhem on a massive scale. Caligula, for instance. And (in any case) don't you think that men have pretty well cornered the market in monsters? Nevertheless, Bathory was a serial killer on the epic scale, and she really did bathe in the blood of young girls, which she believed would restore her youth. In a remake of the film, I could play her again – but this time as the older Countess. I wouldn't need the latex any more!

It's a well-known fact that the crime genre has a very large female following. Why does she think that is?
Actually, I think it's fear. We are (unless trained in martial arts) less equipped to deal with the threat of violence, and women can certainly relate to that. But as for enjoying that frisson of fear – well in books and films, it's safe. The reader or viewer is never in any real danger. Ironically, when I lived in Hollywood, I spent a lot of time living in fear of being mugged. In fact, I actually learnt karate! But fear is an interesting thing. After my success in the vampire movies, I used to be asked at children's parties to play a vampire and pretend to frighten the kids. While a lot of the children had great fun with this, I quickly realised that some of them were not able to perceive that this was play-acting and were genuinely scared, so I quickly started refusing to do it.

Pitt, of course changed the course of British horror films by doing the central female character in a movie, instead of screaming at the sidelines.
Yes. I was the first female predator. It's interesting that now most of those films are regarded affectionately, but they were criticised as beyond the pale in their day. Even the beheading in *The Vampire Lovers* was cut, and most TV prints don't have it. Look at all the beheadings in Tim Burton's *Sleepy Hollow* today! I'm glad to say that the new DVD issue will restore the film.

Had she ever seen the quote about her own career in Kim Newman's *BFI Companion to Horror:* 'the British cinema was no longer able to accommodate her predatory beauty'?
No, I hadn't seen that... that's really interesting! But it wasn't just me the British cinema couldn't accommodate any more. When American movies like *The Exorcist* and *A Nightmare on Elm Street* came along, the writing was on the wall for the British period horror film. Now horror had to be very much set in the present day, and those Hammer trappings began to seem old-fashioned. Ironically, that's the very thing that has made the films more and more fondly remembered as the years passed by. But those movies were considered very strong stuff in their day. Except that I always felt that *Countess Dracula* (for censorship and other reasons) pulled its

punches somewhat. On the set, I tried to insist they made more of her bathing in blood, but the director Peter Sasdy mentioned censorship, and I think it would have been a far more powerful film if we'd been able to show just how depraved Bathory was. That's actually the case with most real-life monsters and their equivalents in film. Ed Gein (who is in my book) inspired both *Psycho* and *The Texas Chainsaw Massacre,* and did far more horrible things than either of those films showed, but I suppose that it's inevitable such changes will occur.

In *Countess Dracula*, she was supported by one of the very finest British character actors, the late Nigel Green. What were her memories of him?

Nigel was wonderful, but he wouldn't take my advice. At the time they were making the film of *Nicholas and Alexandra*, and I suggested that he would be perfect for the part of Rasputin. I told him he should speak to Sam Spiegel, but he said, "If he wants me, he can come to me." And he never really got the parts he deserved, although he's wonderful in *The Ipcress File* and *Zulu*. As well as in *Countess Dracula*, of course.

Had Pitt ever suffered from the obsessed, stalker type of fan, as Janet Leigh did after *Psycho*?

No, I've been very lucky – that's never happened to me. Thank God! Look at what happened to Jodie Foster... it's really worrying that people like her stalker are out there.

So what led Pitt to undertake the literary career she's carved for herself?

Desperation! The parts weren't there any more, and I was a survivor.

But although the vampire industry may have been what made her successful, hasn't it been something of an albatross?

No – I don't think so. After all, I find vampires great fun, and the genre has been kind to me.

Before she began making her films for Hammer, vampirism had always been something that happened instead of sex. But Pitt ushered in an era in which both could take place. How did she feel about being in the vanguard of this innovation?

Well, when Jimmy Carreras offered me the part in *The Vampire Lovers*, I really did my homework about the phenomenon. And in Le Fanu's story *Carmilla*, there is this strong sexual element. I think the director, Roy Ward Baker, really made it work – although the producers were two lascivious little chaps. On the way to do my nude scene with Madeleine Smith, I came out of the trailer with my dressing gown on and nothing underneath, and I saw these guys walking towards me with their heads down. I thought, what the hell, I'll make their day and just flung open the dressing gown. Their reaction was priceless!

Time for a final question: if there is a connection between the sexual and bloodthirsty aspect of those films, is that healthy?

Why not? Sexuality is a complicated thing, and films should reflect that.

KATE CHARLES

talks to ***Dean James***

You couldn't tell it by reading one of her books, but Kate Charles grew up in the American Midwest. She and her husband, both librarians by training, decided they wanted to live in England, and since they had the necessary skills in hand, they figured out how to accomplish their goal. For the past fifteen years, they've been living happily in Bedfordshire, an hour north of London. Charles worked for a period as a parish administrator, while her husband is in publishing. In recent years, however, Charles has concentrated on her writing and a stint as Chair of the Crime Writers Association.

Kate Charles' first novel, A Drink of Deadly Wine *(Headline, 1991), introduced solicitor David Middleton-Brown whose avocation is ecclesiastical history and architecture. These interests draw him, over and over again, into the mysterious goings-on in the Church of England, and church politics and policies provide ample fodder for Kate Charles' fascinating stories. To date there have been five books in the series, with a sixth still in the writing stages. Most recently Charles has published* Unruly Passions *(Little, Brown, 1998) and* Strange Children *(Little, Brown, 1999), both of which are non-series books. These new books present*

something of a shift in style for Charles. Though the themes of these books are similar to the series novels and make use, in some ways, of her trademark ecclesiastical connections, they are crime novels, rather than "whodunits."

You once upon a time had a job with the parish in which you live. Did that inspire you to write clerical mysteries? Or had you wanted to do that before you took the job?

I had always wanted to write mysteries, but the 'clerical' part came along with the job, following the old maxim 'write what you know'. My job with the church, along with providing inside information, opened my eyes to the possibilities of mysteries set against this backdrop. I find the church a fascinating setting for mysteries – it has something to do with the gap between the ideal and the actual, the holiness of the institution itself versus the all-too-human imperfections of the people who constitute it. I sometimes think it's true that the Church brings out the very worst in people rather than the best, or at least magnifies the bad that is already there.

What happened when they found out you were publishing mystery novels involving the church?

My boss, the Vicar, took a very dim view of it! He and I shortly came to a parting of the ways. I make light of that, but I must admit that it was very traumatic at the time. I enjoyed my job as Parish Administrator, and hated giving it up. But the Vicar seemed to think that I was incapable of imagination and that every person and event in my book was drawn from someone or something in the parish. Incidentally, he hadn't read the book when he made that assumption, and I don't think he's read one to this day. All of the hurt associated with this was redeemed though (to use a theological term!) when I met the former Archbishop of Canterbury, Robert Runcie, who confided that he loved my books and had read every one. My fans now include several Bishops, to my certain knowledge, some Deans, a number of Canons, and Vicars innumerable.

How do your friends in the church react to your books? Do they all imagine that various characters are modelled upon them?

Most of the people in the church have no idea that I write books at all – that is why I use a name that is not my own. My friends know that I wouldn't be crazy enough to use them as characters, and my enemies don't even know about my books. But that said, there have been some very odd goings-on at our church lately – things far too outrageous to put in a novel, and several people who have in the past rather looked down on my books have now admitted that they're not so far-fetched as they once might have seemed. 'This parish is turning into a Kate Charles novel' is a phrase I've heard more than once in the past few weeks.

What drew you to writing mysteries in particular? Are there any writers who have influenced you in important ways as to the type of fiction you write?

As I've already said, I've always loved reading mysteries, especially English ones – something I learned at my mother's knee.

From Nancy Drew I moved on to Agatha Christie. As a teenager I discovered Josephine Tey, whose books I still adore, as well as Sayers, Marsh, Allingham and Crispin. About that same time, P D James began to be billed as 'the crown princess of crime', and I read everything of hers as it came out. Though I loved Alan Grant, I suppose it was P D James who turned me on to the potential of characters to define and enrich a crime novel, in contrast to the plot-driven books of Christie. I can still remember how knocked out I was by Cordelia Grey in *An Unsuitable Job for a Woman* and *The Skull Beneath the Skin*. Apart from mysteries – and I still read them in great numbers – the writer who has undoubtedly had the most influence on me is Barbara Pym. The sheer Englishness of her books captivated me from the first, then I came to appreciate her ironic humour and her wonderful observing eye. When I wrote my first book I described it to myself as 'P D James meets Barbara Pym', and indeed my writing has been described in that very way by more than one reviewer. I'm quite proud of that! Barbara Pym also had a great love for the Anglo-Catholic branch of the Church of England, and she wove it into her books in a way which has influenced me.

What is the most difficult part of the process for you?

The middle bit is the most difficult, always. I don't write from an outline, and that means that the middle is the most fluid part of a book. The beginning is easy – introducing characters, setting up relationships and situations, laying the ground-work of the plot. And the end, by the time I get there, writes itself, as the momentum carries me through to the last page. But the middle is tough. Usually I have a number of elements in my mind which will fit somewhere in the middle – scenes, plot twists, clues – but I don't have a clear idea of their place in the structure of the novel. Sometimes they have to be in a particular order, and other times not, so this is when I usually get bogged down, trying to sort out the shape of the middle. And each time, when I get that far, I'm afraid that I'll never be able to make it to the end. In fact, I'm just about at that point right now in the novel I'm writing: the murder has been committed, leaving me teetering on the brink and staring over into the abyss. What comes next, I ask myself?

What do you worry about the most?

I suppose I worry that things which are out of my control – the dire state of the publishing trade, changing trends and reading habits – may mean, one day, that either I'll be forced into writing books that are not the books I want to write, or that I will write books that no one will want to publish or read.

In the first book, *A Drink of Deadly Wine*, your main character, David Middleton-Brown, turns out to have had an unusual 'romantic' history. Did you worry at all that readers would be troubled by David's seeming bisexuality?

Because I wrote *A Drink of Deadly Wine* under a strong inner compulsion to tell David's story, and to understand for myself what made him tick, it never occurred to me to worry in the least about what readers would think of him. In fact, I didn't write the book with an eye to publication. That was an unexpected bonus. And it surprised me no end when people began to write to me with strong opinions about David's sexuality. Funnily enough, in the time since I wrote that book, bisexuality has become the in thing, according to the media. So I was there first.

David develops a very important relationship in the books with the artist Lucy Kingsley, who's very strong-minded and independent. How important is their ongoing relationship to the texture of the books?

Lucia's role in *A Drink of Deadly Wine* was intended to be a small one, but to my amazement she asserted herself and refused to go away. Her relationship with David has become an integral part of the series, and is the element that engenders the most interest and comment from my readers. She has grown through the series, and sometimes seems to take over from David as the main protagonist and detective, though I try to keep them roughly equal. It's difficult now to imagine David without Lucy – even more difficult than imagining Lucy without David.

Will Lucy ever say "yes" to David's proposals of marriage?

That is the question I am most often asked! Or more accurately, I'm asked, "Are David and Lucy ever going to get married?", which is not the same question at all, really. I don't want to give anything away, but there may be an answer in the next book, *Free Among the Dead* – to one question, if not the other.

Do you ever fear that you might lose readers because of some of the subject matter of the books?

Because most of my books deal in some way with homosexuality – the next really big issue facing the Church, I'm convinced – I do fear that some people might be put off. But mystery readers are, by and large, an open-minded bunch, so I'm not too worried!

You've recently written a non-series book that was published in England recently. What can you tell us about it?

It's a suspense novel rather than a detective novel, but is still very much within the context of my previous books. It's called *Unruly Passions* and deals with the intertwined lives of three women: a Vicar's wife, a woman Archdeacon, and a famous novelist. They are tied together through a catalyst character, the Archdeacon's husband. There *is* a murder, but I won't say more than that.

Fifty years ago, most writers could stay at home and write, concentrating on their art. Nowadays, they have to get out and travel – promote, promote, promote. How does this affect you and your writing? How does this much contact with your reading public affect you as a writer?

Things are a bit different, living in the UK, where promotion is more low-key and distances smaller. I can confine my heavy-duty travel to one or two trips to the US each year, centred around the conferences, so that isn't too onerous. I travel with my laptop, so I'm able to write even when I'm on the move. And it must be said that I love meeting my readers – there are times when the validation that they give makes all the difference between elation and despair.

You have been Chair of the Crime Writers Association of Great Britain, and you've been an active participant in many of the mystery conventions in the United States. What are the important differences you've observed in the mystery publishing business on both sides of the Atlantic? Are mid-list mystery writers in Great Britain having as much difficulty these days getting published as their American counterparts?

I believe that British publishers are still a bit more willing to take a chance on a writer who may not be a big blockbuster, but who will have steady sales (ie the mid-list writer). They do, however, pay notoriously poorly for non-blockbusters. Until recently, it was much easier for a British writer to be published in the US than for an American to be published in the UK, but that has changed as many US publishing houses are dropping English writers from their lists, and some UK publishers are bulking up their lists with Americans. There are big differences in mystery readers on the two sides of the Atlantic. In keeping with the national character, British readers are more reserved and low-key, so the 'fan' convention doesn't really exist here. Even book signing sessions are quite different: the diffident British reader hesitates to 'bother' the writer, though he will hover in the background and buy a signed book as soon as the writer leaves! I must say that I prefer the forthright American approach!

***Unruly Passions* is a crime novel, whereas your series novels fall more into the 'whodunit' tradition. Do you find devising the plot of one type easier than the other? Are crime novels more flexible in terms of plotting?**

Writing crime novels like *Unruly Passions* or *Strange Children* has proved to be an interesting departure for me. While I hesitate to use the word 'formulaic' in describing traditional whodunits, there are undeniably certain conventions which must be observed, and more of a framework already in place. So I've enjoyed stretching myself beyond those conventions. It's certainly true to say that I've found the plotting of the crime novels to be more organic than the whodunits – I can more or less sit back and let them take me where they will, without the necessity for intensive advance plotting.

This book was sparked by an article I read a few years ago – I don't want to give too much away, but something about it piqued my interest and seemed ready-made for a crime novel. I'd thought of it originally in terms of a David-and-Lucy book, but realised that it would work very well as a one-off. This is, I think, because Tessa is the primary focus of the book, and almost everything is either seen through her eyes or relates directly to her.

Now that you've been writing in a somewhat different vein for a while, do you think you'll approach further series books any differently?

Probably. I'd like to use the skills I've been developing in these recent books to 'push the envelope' of the series novel.

FRANCES FYFIELD: THE ENGLISH ARE NOT WHAT THEY SEEM

Eve Tan Gee

It took some time, but there are clear signs that Frances Fyfield has acquired the literary gravitas of the two British Queens of Crime (and habitués of the House of Lords), mesdames Rendell and James. Fyfield is now regularly identified as part of a formidable triumvirate, and books such as Staring at the Light *and* Without Consent *have mined the same vein of psychological acuity and dark menace as her more famous fellow authors. Fyfield's manner is appropriately dark and intense, but a wry self-deprecation makes her a beguiling conversationalist. What is more dear to her – the actual writing of her books, or the dangerous world they usher the reader into?*

I can answer that by talking about my latest book, *Undercurrents* (published by Little, Brown) if you like, because it's dear to my heart. I love books which grow out of their own scenery and this one did – it just rose up and hit me as a result of living in the place where it is (loosely) set. The place has a pier and a castle and a history: what more could I want? The ideal setting for a story is a small community where everyone thinks they know everything about one another, while really they miss the obvious. It carries forward a central theme in all my books: nothing is quite what it seems. The book features an American coming to a small coastal town of a very English kind, and finding that the English are not what they seem either: they are devious and decent.

Choosing titles is a bugger. They never occur to me until near the end, which is about the time I begin to know what the whole thing is about. I wanted to call *Undercurrents* by the title of *I Can't Talk Now*, but that was a bit unwieldy. Unfortunately, when I start to think of titles, my sense of the ridiculous comes into play, usually because I'm having the seventeenth crisis of confidence by that stage anyway. Since *Undercurrents* is a moody book, full of English winter climate, I did think of calling it *Under the Weather*, which is where a good editor with a sense of humour is a great asset. One of my worst editorial experiences in the past was telling an editor that my working title for a book was *Death by Blow Job* (*Without Consent*) and she didn't even laugh. I didn't mean it: it's awful to be taken literally. Sometimes it's awful to be taken seriously. Because you take writing seriously, it doesn't follow that you take yourself seriously. The worst thing about being edited is finding that someone is afraid to point out the inevitable mistakes in case you get a fit of the vapours.

Undercurrents is dear to my heart because I enjoyed writing it, or at least part of it. Writing is hell, let's face it. A bad day is one when I can't even spell 'and'. Those kind of days are always made worse by remembering what it was I meant to do in the first place, all those books ago, and what a high aspiration it still is. I wanted to write the kind of novel which keeps the reader glued to the page, not effortlessly, but with real attention. I wanted to write the kind of novel which had given *me* great pleasure, as well as insight, entertainment, relief. I mean the sort of novel which when you read it, you identify with it and get taken out of your own world into the world of the novel, and when you get to the end, there's a kind of benign grief because you have to come back.

You always learn something from a good novel, because good novels, whatever their genre, are truthful about the human condition, however fantastical the fiction. Reading is a primary source of education: it refines concentration, understanding and compassion, and it underlines all the knowledge gained in so-called real life. You can read a novel about people living at the extreme edge, or about people who live next door, and you'll still absorb more about humanity than someone who does not read. Which is why writing is such a high and frightening aspiration, whatever you write, because an author is a gateway to the world, giving another view of it. The thought of reading becoming a peripheral activity, indulged in by few, is frightening. There simply isn't enough time to learn about life without reading being part of the process.

There are no issues that an author should be afraid to tackle in the context of telling a story. There's a sneaking political correctness which suggests it is somehow morally wrong to dwell on violence and sex and all the other taboos which are part of daily life. The only limitation an author should feel about subject matter is their own ability to illuminate and explain it. The novelist's imperative is to turn the subject matter into as good and convincing a story as he or she can make it. If violence and sex, raped women and torture in the dental chair are integral to that story, so be it. If it is a well told story, it will not outrage because it has a human context and it is explaining human impulses as well as exploiting them. What outrages is bad writing, like the sort you might get in a porn mag. All an author should do is write to their own strengths and acknowledge their weaknesses. I'd be glad to include scenes of frank and erotic sex if I could, but it always makes me laugh. I know I can write violence and I do. For no other reason than that it belongs to a lesser or greater extent in my stories and I think I understand the impact of it better than most. I want the reader to share the horror of it, not to celebrate it.

FROM FLAPPERS TO FILM NOIR

Michael Carlson

The sexual essence of film noir is the image of the woman as black widow, poisonous destroyer of a man trapped helplessly in her sensual web. Black widows are often counterbalanced by a 'good' woman, whose love is often squandered by the man who has been seduced by the deadly allure of the world of the darkside. It helps that this man is usually a broad-shouldered bozo, with a one-track mind and half-track brain. Think of Dana Andrews, or Glenn Ford, or Cornell Wilde.

Many commentators have seen the obsession with woman as destroyer in classic film noir of the late 1940s as a reaction to the increased liberation of women, fresh from the wartime workforce, and in the post-war era needing to be reconditioned to their traditional role as homemakers, to open up jobs for the returning war veterans. But the roots of the film noir heroine can be traced back further, all the way to the America's Roaring Twenties, when flappers ruled the swinging roost. Last summer's series of flapper films shown at Nottingham's Out Of Sight film festival (followed by a larger season at the National Film Theatre) celebrated an earlier liberation of American women, one that was just as threatening, in its own way, to the status quo

Professor Laura Mulvey of Birkbeck College, who programmed the flappers series, sees the 'new woman' of the 1920s as a product of increasing urbanisation and economic boom which provided new opportunities for employment and new consumer power for women. Joining the workforce created 'leisure time', and chief among the things American women consumed was the Hollywood film. "It was a period of almost utopianism for working women in America," she says, "and issues of equality at work and voting rights were subsumed into those of sexual liberation. Hollywood wove folk tales defining self-expression through sexuality fuelled by a consumer boom. These had a huge impact around the world, and while selling a sort of democracy of glamour, also helped Hollywood sell itself overseas."

The generational rebellion implicit in the flappers' lifestyle is made evident in *It*, the film which launched the 'It Girl' Clara Bow. Elinor Glyn, who defined the concept of 'It' in Cosmopolitan (some things just never change!) appears as herself in the film. Looking exactly like Margaret Dumont in a Marx Brothers movie, Glyn explains her theory of 'It' in a speech which amounts to the longest title card ever seen in silent cinema. There is an astounding contrast between her own image as a society matron, wrapped in the fashions of the Edwardian era, and Bow's sleek vivacity, shimmering in an improvised homemade flapper gown.

In a stroke of programming genius, Out Of Sight's Laraine Potter ran their flapper films alongside an impressive series of German silent horror. Relatively familiar works such as *The Cabinet of Dr Caligari*

and *Nosferatu* were joined by new restorations of *Waxworks, The Student of Prague* and *The Hands of Dr Orlac,* all starring Conrad Veidt, and *The Golem,* the forerunner of the Frankenstein series. In *The Golem,* Rabbi Loew constructs the titular monster out of clay to save the Jewish population of Prague, but there are eerie undercurrents of the Nazi future in the way the film presents Loew as a satanic sorcerer, and in the way the Golem soon is made to do the physical labour for the Jewish community. Expressionistic photography in these films projects a modernity of dislocated vision and sharp, threatening angles onto traditional horror motifs: a style which would continue to develop through more contemporary tales.

The juxtaposition of American flappers and German horror suggests the way the two strands would eventually intersect in film history. These horror films grew out of an era of new violence following World War I. Weimar Germany was to serial killers what Renaissance Florence was to artists, and German Expressionism reflects that pathology. Professor Maria Tatar, in her study *Lustmord*, suggests that German men sexualised murder in reaction to feelings of disempowerment stemming from the loss of the Great War and the new emancipation of women. This idea of serial killing as gender vengeance would be more attractive were it not for the fact that Weimar's most feared serial killer, Fritz Haarmann, who inspired frightening children's rhymes, sought out only male victims. Similarly, the greatest serial killer of German cinema is the effeminate Peter Lorre in Fritz Lang's *M*, but his victims are children, not women. Serial murder may well be a generic response to emasculation, but the liberated flapper can be seen to have created a new kind of male hero as well. "In the Twenties there is a rise of effeminate masculinity in matinee idols like Valentino", says Professor Mulvey, "which disappears in the sound era." Certainly, when Clara Bow aims 'It' at Antonio Moreno, a Latino playing the WASP department store heir Cyrus Waltham, his suave veneer turns to jelly in the face of her sexuality. It is a sort of melting the traditional strong silent type would find impossible.

It was director G. W. Pabst who brought together the liberated modern woman and the emasculated post-war man. Pabst sensed the insecurity at the core of the ultimate flapper, the incredible Louise Brooks, and brought her to Germany to play, in *Pandora's Box*, a woman who served as both alluring destroyer and helpless victim. The insecurity comes primarily from an instinctive recognition of the limits of sexual energy, something which eventually would be transferred to the victims / men of film noir. But in the context of Weimar, it was the fatal weakness that would see Pandora eventually destroyed by an out-of-control rage which has grown out a chaotic society.

It is from Pabst's brilliant collision of American flappers and German horror that film noir grew. He took the driving modern woman and trapped her in a classic expressionist landscape. Here, the female's energy is a force that ultimately is revealed to be powerless in the face of a threatening world it not only cannot control, but which uses that energy against her: the more 'liberated' Brooks becomes, the more she exposes herself to danger and isolates herself from society's traditional protections. Brooks brought with her all the drive of the New World, a relentless libido which can best be described as 'consuming', in both the classic romantic sense and in the Hollywood sense implied by American business. But where Clara Bow represents American society, Louise Brooks transcends it. She incorporates both the 'good' woman and the 'bad' in one creature.

The classic femme fatales of film noir brought Brooks' character back to the American mainstream, although to accomplish this the good and bad sides had to be re-divided into their classic archetypes. If one sees the roots of film noir in that early reaction to female liberation, then surely the classic films noirs of the post-war era are a reaction, at least in part, to the increased liberation of women into the work force during World War II. In *The Big Heat*, the safety society promises the 'good' woman in a suburban home is abruptly shattered when a bomb intended for Glenn Ford which kills Jocelyn Brando. And the 'bad' woman, Gloria Grahame (surely Louise Brooks' hedonistic spirit incarnate), dies to prove to the dumbo hero that she really isn't Louise Brooks after all.

The reaction to the next wave of women's lib, in the late 1960s and 70s, is best seen in films like *Jackson County Jail*, where 'liberated' women run afoul of traditional male prerogatives. Not only have the protections of society been withdrawn from women who decide that society's rules are too confining, but they are used against the women as a means of revenge. Who needs serial killers when you have redneck sheriffs? Those looking to the cycle of 'slasher' horror films which come at this time should also remember that, although precocious sexuality is inevitably punished in these films, there is usually at least one woman who triumphs in the end over a killer who is often a representation of sheer repressed male sexuality.

In the 1980s, as feminism took another turn into the 'you can have it all' idea of women as both workplace dominatrices and traditionally glamorous seductresses, another wave of films sprang up, launched perhaps by *Thelma and Louise*. Did no-one else think of Thelma Ritter and Louise Brooks as the inspiration for those roles? In films like *Basic Instinct* and *The Last Seduction*, the 'bad' woman no longer needs the approval of the dumbo man, nor does she secretly yearn for a happy home. He has become a figure to be manipulated, led by his stupidity and his dick, which are often seen to be the same thing. Finally, in *Bound* we dispose of the men altogether, literally and figuratively, although we can't help but feel it's as much to provide the audience a voyeuristic glimpse of Gina Gershon and Jennifer Tilley doing things Robert Mitchum and Jane Greer were never allowed to do on screen.

And when Uma Thurman dons a Louise Brooks wig in *Pulp Fiction*, playing a character as close to Brooks' as we've seen in decades, and then needs to be brought back to life with a stake (well, a syringe, but the motion is the same) through the heart, the link between flappers and horror, and thus to film noir, is not only recalled, but chiselled in celluloid reference for generations who have no idea who Brooks, or Bow, or Murnau were.

FEMALE PRIVATE EYES

Laura Lipman

Her Tess Monaghan series has won considerable acclaim (not to mention a bushel of awards) is her native USA, and in the UK, where Lipman is published by Orion, her titles are already gleaning good reviews. Here she talks to Crime Time *about writing as a female crime writer with a female protagonist.*

I have been faulted for not having enough violence in my books. I just met a professor who has written paper on female detectives in popular culture – he showed me an early draft which made the point that the violence was underdeveloped in my series. So I suppose I have to do something about that, although I am always aware that it's unrealistic when one has a super-tough female private eye, able to mix it with the men on the most violent terms. I feel that my heroine has to have a way to survive in a tough universe. I exercise a lot, I lift weights and can probably take care myself – but I'm fully aware that up against some broken nose thug, I wouldn't stand much of a chance, and I extrapolate this for Tess. Tess is pretty fanatical about fitness, and I think that gives her a more realistic chance of dealing with the rigours of the job.

Problem-solving has to remain the main agenda for the female private eye. In the latest book, *The Sugar House*, Tess realises that she's put everyone around her in extreme jeopardy, and it's imperative that she solves the problem very quickly. Many a male writer will solve things with a wonderfully glorious shoot-out: I'm a fan of such things, and, after all, it often makes for a cathartic denouement. But I've always felt that there has to be another way – certainly for my characters.

I don't know how it is in the UK, but in the United States women are the book buyers, and certainly there is a strong female response to women private eyes. I suppose there must be a wish fulfilment element, but these heroines hardly lead truly admirable lives. However they usually arrive at a certain closure- and we'd all like to do that in our lives.

Something else that I've been able to draw on as a writer is the fact that for many years I've been a journalist, often assigned to stories that I've really had no sympathy for. I learnt quickly that a degree of flexibility is needed to get results – I've seen many a tough reporter try to bully the subject and fail. That's not my approach – I'm a listener. And a listener can often get the best results. There is unquestionably an element of that in Tess, and this is one of the most authentic things about the series.

WOMEN WHO KILL

Crime Time *talks to* ***Carol Anne Davis***
about her new study of female serial killers

Prior to writing this book, I knew that women weren't always selfless and nurturing individuals. I had first hand experience of a mother who had watched her offspring being battered throughout their childhood and I was familiar with many of the cases in which women have killed their burdensome babies to start a new relationship with a man. But researching *Women Who Kill: Profiles of Female Serial Killers* took me into territory in which women killed total strangers. And these homicides weren't due to a moment of uncontrolled rage. Instead, the woman fantasised for weeks or months about each crime.

Take power-motivated Charlene Gallego (now released) who planned her abductions carefully. She approached one girl at a fair, hoping to kidnap her and make her the perfect sex slave – but the girl mentioned that her uncle was the fair's security guard. Charlene immediately left her and approached other teenagers who didn't have a similar protector. She offered them money to distribute leaflets for her – but when they got into her van they found Charlene's husband, Gerald, pointing a gun at their heads. Charlene then stripped the girls, tied them up and drove them to remote locations where her husband repeatedly sexually abused them. Forensic evidence suggests that Charlene herself bit the breasts of at least one teenager. She also forced most of the victims to give her sexual satisfaction before Gerald murdered them. As well as selecting her many captives carefully, the bisexual Charlene took great care to scrub her van free of forensic clues afterwards. And when one man dared to intervene during an abduction, she punched him hard in the face and told him to fuck off. He did, and the couple she was holding at gunpoint were later found dead, the female having been raped and beaten prior to being shot.

Karla Homolka, who sexually assaulted several teenagers and helped murder three of them, also used malice aforethought. She began her crime spree by stealing powerful drugs from the vet's surgery where she worked. She used these initially to sedate her female victims. Then she stripped them and held them captive for up to three days, videotaping each assault and telling them how to perform sexually for herself and for her man. Karla acted rationally throughout, hiding the phones in her house so that the teenagers couldn't call for assistance. After one of the deaths she even cut off the corpse's hair in case it contained fibres from her beautiful upmarket home.

Carol Bundy similarly took great care to cover up her crimes, sending her sons to live with relatives in another state before she embarked on her killing spree. She offered to perform analingus on one of her lovers, so he eagerly undressed in his van and lay down on his stomach. Carol promptly shot him in the head. Then she realized that his skull would contain bullets that might be traced to her gun, so she cut his head off and removed it from the scene of the crime. Carol's co-killer, the necrophiliac Doug Clark, also cut off one female victim's head and Carol obligingly went out and bought a special box in which to dump the head. Again, she acted rationally, concealing her fingerprints whilst buying the box by wearing gloves.

Aileen Wuornos – wrongly described by the media as America's first serial killer – was a highway prostitute who took care to choose victims she could control. She targeted older men and made sure that she got them to drive to a remote location. She often told them to strip for sex, then shot them when they were nakedly defenceless. She also used various aliases when pawning their property. Society likes to suggest that the female serial killer is always acting on behalf of her male partner but Aileen Wuornos was a sole operator. So was Genene Jones, who may have killed dozens of babies. (Like most serial killers she was charged with far fewer deaths than she was actually implicated in.) Similarly, Rose West physically and emotionally abused her first child and stepchildren whilst Fred West was in prison – and Martha Ann Johnson used her immense weight to suffocate her own offspring in the hope of winning her absent bisexual husband back.

Judith Neelley, at nineteen the youngest woman on Death Row, did sometimes act in tandem with her husband but she was by far the stronger character. One man whom she left for dead survived and would later testify that she marched him into the woods, taunted him verbally and shot him in the back. She also tortured a thirteen-year-old girl in a remote canyon before shooting her. In both instances Judith's husband was out of sight.

In almost all of the thirteen cases profiled in the book, the woman was keen to initiate the crime. The exception is Myra Hindley who was a caring childminder and well liked teenager until she met the handsome and persuasive – but disturbed – Ian Brady. She fell hopelessly in love. Myra was a prudish and religious virgin yet under his influence she was soon posing naked for his camera. But after he drugged and photographed her illicitly she became afraid of what he might do and gave a letter to a friend explaining that she feared for her own life and that of her relatives. Later, as Brady's influence over her deepened further and she became temporarily as callous as he was, she asked her friend to tear the letter up. Whilst researching the book I interviewed the Rev. Peter Timms, the former prison governor and Methodist minister to whom Myra Hindley ultimately confessed. The Rev. Timms explained that Myra was with Ian Brady constantly, so he had endless time to influence her with his humanity-hating beliefs. Myra and Ian

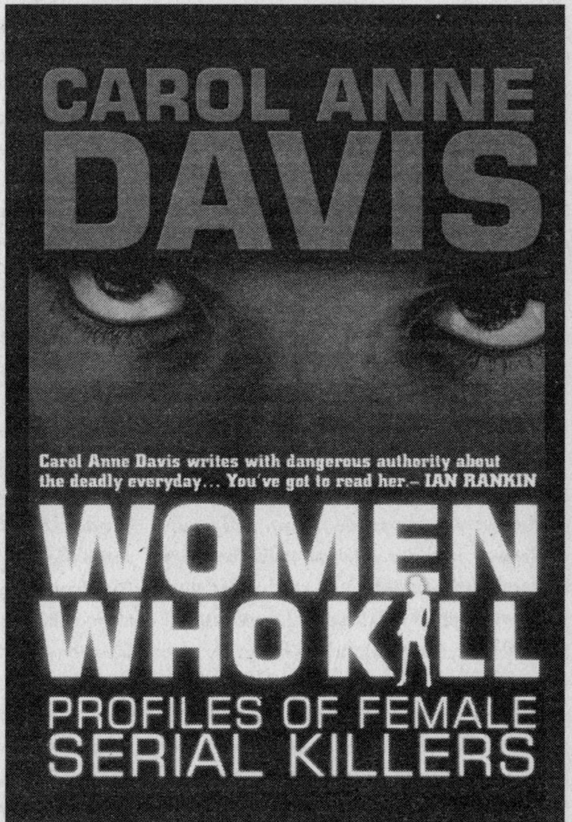

lived together, travelled to the office together, worked together and spent their evenings at home or on the moors together. They were hardly ever separate. Ian drew out her suppressed rage, a dark side formed through being rejected by her violent father. For a time she became as heartless as her lover, luring five innocent teenagers and children into her car knowing that he would strangle or in one case axe them to death.

Catherine Birnie's history was also a rejection-filled one. As such, she showed no compassion for the females that she and her common law husband David abducted. Catherine photographed him raping the girls and she participated in some of their prolonged sexual assaults. (An Australian policeman told this author that animals don't treat their prey as viciously as the Birnie's treated these girls.) Catherine eventually drove the still-living victims to the forest where she helped her husband dig their shallow graves. She obligingly held the torch so that he could focus on bludgeoning the dying girls more :ffectively.

Certain newspapers would like their r· aders to think that such serial killers are :imply born evil, a biological mutation. 3ut they aren't – they're very much man-made and woman-made. Again and again my research showed what these females had endured as children: being hit and verbally rubbished and sexually assaulted throughout their childhood, often by the very people who had created them. None of these girls had enjoyed the love and approval that helps children grow into caring and confident young adults. Instead, they had been battered down the long, hard road that turns a loving baby into a potential torturer and murderess.

Women Who Kill: Profiles of Female Serial Killers *by Carol Anne Davis is published in hardback by Allison & Busby, £16.99*

And Russell James looks at another book by Carol Anne Davis...

Noise Abatement (Do Not Press, £7.50)

Carol Anne Davis specialises in transforming the mundane to the macabre. Here, she trespasses further into Patricia Highsmith territory by subjecting her hero, Stephen Day, to a severe case of everyday irritation: the lads in the flat upstairs are driving him and his wife mad by their noise. Loud noise erupts at any time – the middle of the night, mid-afternoon, whether the lads are home or not. The horrors are those of a bad dream rather than a nightmare: the lads upstairs are not monsters from hell. They apologise, turn down the noise for a few minutes, then carry on as before. Police and Environmental Health are too busy to do anything.

Meanwhile, Stephen's work is suffering. His wife develops spastic colitis. Something must be done. But what? They can't sell the flat because every time someone calls, blasts of noise come from upstairs. They can't persuade the boys to stop. They can't force them. They have no way out. Many of us have fantasised about how we would deal with this situation – like Stephen, we'd like to kill the blighters. Unlike Stephen, we don't do it. *Noise Abatement* shows how easily – as if sleepwalking or staggering from loss of sleep – any one of us could cross into that world of living nightmare.

WHERE DO YOU HIDE THE BODY?

Doug Swanson *on* House of Corrections

House of Corrections *(No Exit Press) is something special – in the avalanche of new titles that besiege the offices of CT, this struck us a one-of-a-kind crime novel, with a highly individual authorial voice. We asked the affable Mr Swanson to talk to us about it…*

I'm sure there are lucky bastards somewhere whose book ideas spring fully formed and on schedule. Mine arrive inconveniently, vaguely and not to be ignored, something like the early onset of the flu.

A few years ago I used to swim every night in a backyard pool, doing laps, hoping for a swimmer's body that never quite materialized. It's a boring business, back and forth in a concrete pond. Your mind wanders to strange places: I had this vision one night of a young woman swimming as I was, while a fat man spied on her from a nearby tree and took photographs. Who? Why? I tried to work it out in a screenplay. Three months later I found myself lost and out of gas in the middle of the second act. I put the story aside and wrote something else.

Two years after that, I was trying to come up with a plot for the fifth novel in the Jack Flippo mystery series. Nothing was working until I remembered the woman swimming and the fat guy in the tree. I plugged my man Jack into the story, and it took off. Only one other problem remained to be solved: I needed a good, offbeat spot for my protagonist to discover the requisite dead body. I flew to Galveston, the Texas island on which the story is set, and walked around for a few days, searching vainly for a concrete bunker I dimly remembered from a beer-soaked beach trip twenty-five years back. The bunker was gone, replaced by a luxury hotel. But I eventually found my corpse-hiding spot in a weedy, forgotten park with land-locked, rusting Navy vessels from World War II.

Vision explained, corpse stashed – writing the rest of the novel was just a matter of following my map. So that's how *House Of Corrections* was done.

Now I'm working on a notion that came to me in California, that of a small man being electrocuted at night on a city street. Who is he? How did he get there? What happens next? Don't have the slightest. Ask me in a year or so. In the meantime, I'll be visiting San Francisco often, looking for a place to hide the body.

House of Corrections *is published by No Exit Press*

FASCISTS AND RECALCITRANT PUBLISHERS

Russell James

Russell James's new novel Painting in the Dark *is a controversial and exciting modern crime novel set against the 1997 General Election when Blair's New Labour swept to power. An unscrupulous and gargantuan art dealer, Gottfleisch, believes that eighty-five year old Sidonie Keene is hiding a small hoard of her notorious sister Naomi's valuable paintings. Naomi was a British Fascist in the 1930s, a friend of Goering and Hitler, and was denounced at the time as a traitor. She died a forgotten artist but after her death her intimate portraits of Hitler and his friends became collectors' items, commanding high prices. Gottfleisch and his evil sidekick, Little Ticky, set out to steal the paintings from the old lady, not realising that there is more to her than meets the eye.*

Russell spoke to Crime Time:

Painting in the Dark will surprise my regular readers. I'm a crime writer and I'm not known for having right wing views – so why have I placed at the heart of his new novel a sympathetic portrait of a British Fascist from the 1930s? *Painting in the Dark* is a crime novel, and like many crime novels it shines a bright light into murky corners (from teenage runaways to skulduggery in the art world). But it also investigates a mystery: how it was that throughout Europe so many of the intelligentsia and the ruling classes became drawn to extreme politics – communism and fascism. The book does this by placing you, the reader, in the shoes of a woman caught up in the spirit of her times.

Back in the 1930s – when the century still seemed quite young – people were fascinated by the new. Technology was a god (a radio in every home, bringing the voice of the world into your living room); telephones through which, with some difficulty, you could speak to someone on the other side of the world; aeroplanes by which, again with some difficulty, you could fly to the other side of the world. Cinemas which talked, new materials in the home, electricity in the home. Art reflected this youthful excitement – we had Cubist and Futurist paintings, extraordinary experiments on stage and screen. Indeed, if a cartoonist at the end of the twentieth century wanted to show a piece of 'modern' art he probably did a pastiche of a 1920s progressive painting. At that time, people were thrilled by 'the future': everything old should be swept away. Old politics should be swept away. What we wanted was a dynamic, charismatic *new* type of leader – a new way.

In Britain, Mosley was charismatic, and (though we refuse to admit it) Hitler – with Goering and Goebels even more so – were all charismatic. They promised to drag their countries out of the stifling clutches of old corrupt politics and replace it with something rather vaguely described but which sounded exciting and new. Hitler said he would transform his country in four years. And in those first four years it seemed, astonishingly, that that's just what he did.

Hitler led the National Socialist Party, though for him 'socialist' was a dirty word. When people elected him, what did they think they were electing? Did they vote for policy or charisma? My book raises these questions – but is a fundamentally a modern crime novel; it does not preach a message. *Painting in the Dark* is a crime novel, set against Tony Blair's triumphal election of 1997, but looking back to Hitler's rise and fall sixty years before.

This is a confession. Instead of telling you how wonderful my latest book is, I am going to tell you something a writer should never tell anyone – one of those secrets best kept in a bottom drawer. It is this: although five big UK publishers praised my book they hesitated to take it. "I like the characters, I like the plot, I like his writing...", said one British publisher. "Russell is an unusual and original writer – and therein lies the difficulty, I think. It's an impossible novel to categorise, and I'm afraid I just can't see a way for us to publish it successfully. So, I shall say no, with considerable regret because there is so much to admire here", said the second major British publisher. One publisher hated it: because of its historical theme, he said, he wouldn't have it in the house. "I found it quite compelling. You certainly have no idea at the beginning where the plot is going to take you, and it retains a couple of tricks up its sleeve right to the end," said another major British publisher – but he too didn't take it! So which books do you buy – only those that are safe? But sometimes an author has to be controversial. As The Times once said, "Russell James goes looking for trouble where more circumspect writers would back off".

The book is published now. I am proud of it. Every author praises his latest book but my feelings for *Painting in the Dark* go beyond that. I think it is the best book I have written. Perhaps it is the best book I shall ever write. With its background sweep, from the 1930s to Blair's triumphant election victory in the late 1990s, this is *my* twentieth century novel.

The chances are that you'll find few titles from small presses and mid-list authors in your local bookshop. You'll have to order mine. But please do so – either from Do Not Press themselves, or from your struggling local shop. They'll be delighted to get it for you.

Painting in the Dark *is published by Do Not Press (hbk £15 (1 899344 63 2), pbk £7.50 (1 899344 62 4))*

DANCING WITH THE VIRGINS

Stephen Booth

1 On the day the first woman died, Mark Roper had radio trouble. At the start of his shift, he had been patrolling in the valley, in the deep dead spot where the gritstone plateau blocked out the signal from the telephone interface point at Bradwell. The silence had been unnerving, even then. It had made him conscious of his isolation in the slowly dying landscape, and it had begun to undermine his confidence and stir up the old uncertainties. But Mark wasn't frightened then. It was only later he had been frightened.

Normally, this was his favourite time of year – these few weeks of hesitation before the start of winter. He liked to watch the hills changing colour day by day, and the Peak District villages emptying of visitors. But he could tell that today wasn't quite normal. There was a feeling about this particular Sunday that made him uncomfortable to be alone on Ringham Moor. There was something strained and uneasy in the way the trees stirred in the wind, in the way the dry bracken snapped underfoot and the birds fell silent in the middle of the afternoon.

As Mark climbed out of the dead spot, his horizon widened until he could see across to Hartington and the Staffordshire border. But even on his way back across the moor towards Partridge Cross, he could not raise his Area Ranger. Maybe the radio handset he had picked up from the briefing centre that morning was the one with the faulty battery connection. Little things like that could change your life forever.

'Peakland Partridge Three to Peakland Zulu. Owen?'

No matter how many times he tried, his call sign went unanswered.

Earlier in the year, they had been burning the heather on this part of Ringham Moor. An acrid charcoal smell still clung to the vegetation, and it mingled with the sweet, fruity scent of the living flowers as it rose from the ground under Mark's boots. In places, the stems had been left bare and white where the bark had been burned off completely. They showed up in the blackened carpet like tiny bones, like a thousand skeletal fingers poking from the earth.

Mark's father had helped the gamekeepers many times with the swaling, the annual burning of the heather to encourage the growth of fresh shoots for red grouse to feed on. Conditions for burning had to be just right – the heather dry, but the ground wet enough to prevent the fire spreading down into the peat. You could get so hot controlling the flames that you thought your skin would be burned to a cinder, and if you were standing in the wrong place when the wind blew, you could end up black from head to toe. Sometimes, Mark recalled, his father had smelled like Bonfire Night for days.

The scent of the burned heather brought the presence of his father back to him now. It was a sensation so powerful that the tall figure might have been striding alongside him, swinging his huge, reddened hands, talking of working dogs and trout flies, and promising that he would take Mark and his brother on a shoot one day. But he had never carried out his promise. And he hadn't walked with Mark again, not for a long time now.

The impression left as quickly as it had come, leaving Mark clutching desperately at a memory, reaching for an image that dissipated like a wisp of smoke in the wind.

Fumbling at the radio, he tried again. 'Peakland Zulu. Can you hear me, Owen? Owen?' But still there was nothing.

As he climbed to the plateau, the weight of Mark's rucksack gradually increased, chafing his skin through the fabric of his red fleece, pulling down his shoulders and pressing on the muscles in his back. Despite the chill, his neck was wet with sweat, and he shivered as he came over a rise and the wind grabbed at him. The shadows of clouds were moving across the landscape below him. Brief patches of sunlight revealed a field dotted with sheep, a narrow stretch of tarmac road, an oak spinney, or the roof of a distant farmhouse. Yet the sight of human habitation only heightened his sense of being alone.

It was the environment, not the welfare of people and property, that had led Mark to volunteer as a Peak Park Ranger in the first place. Once, he had wanted to save the entire world, but in the end he had settled for helping to protect one little bit of it. He had not imagined that he would be called on to tolerate the actions of people who destroyed and defiled the environment, people who had no respect for nature and the lives of animals. It was the most difficult thing he had to learn. Maybe even Owen Fox would never be able to teach him that.

One thing Owen had taught Mark was the importance of good communication; he had told him to stay in touch, always. But this early November day had been the wrong time for Mark to choose for his first solo patrol. Entirely the wrong day to be on his own.

'This is Peakland Partridge Three. Owen? Owen? Where *are* you?'

And, of course, it had been the wrong day for Jenny Weston, too.

Jenny had been riding a yellow six-gear Dawes Kokomo. It had one-inch tyres, and a wire basket bolted over the rear wheel. It was hired from the Peak Cycle centre at Partridge Cross on a three-hour ticket, and Jenny had already ridden nearly five miles to reach the plateau of Ringham Moor.

The moor was littered with prehistoric burial mounds, cairns and stone circles, some so small or so ruined and overgrown that they were barely visible in the heather and bracken. It was not as well used as the moors to the south and west, Stanton and Harthill, but its tracks were more accessible to a mountain bike, its open spaces more solitary, its face that bit closer to the sky.

Ringham had become one of Jenny's favourite places. There were many reasons that brought her back, needs and compulsions that had worn a track for her bike tyres right to the base of the Hammond Tower on Ringham Edge. She carried an impression in her mind of the view down into the valley from the tower – that steep plummet through the trees on to a litter of rocks at the bottom.

It had been a blustery day, with showers that blew across the hills in squalls, bludgeoning the birches and scattering dead leaves into the heather. There seemed to be little life on the moor. But at the bottom of the track, Jenny had passed a youth wearing a red woollen cap pulled low on his forehead, with large ears that stuck out like table-tennis bats. He had been walking very quickly towards the road, and had refused to raise his head to meet her eye as she passed. Jenny had pressed down harder on the pedals, seeking to gain distance from the youth, so that she over-exerted herself on the slope and had to stop further on, gasping from painful lungs as she looked back. The youth had gone, and there was no one else to be seen – only a fistful of jackdaws drifting against the face of one of the abandoned quarries, and a herd of cattle lying restlessly in a field on the slope below the Virgins.

Jenny had always believed she was safer on a bike. Two wheels and the extra speed gave her the confidence that she could get out of trouble, if she needed to. A woman on her own, in a place like Ringham Moor, ought to think about being careful.

To get to the top of the moor, Jenny had

to dismount and wheel the Kokomo up the steepest part of the path. She knew she was almost there when she reached the twisted Heart Stone, twelve feet high, with iron hand and foot holds driven into its sides.

At the top, the sandy track was cycleable, as long as you avoided the exposed rocks in the middle. It crossed a plateau of dark heather and whinberry, with patches of rhododendron on the southern slopes. There were old quarries on two sides, and sharp crags and edges on the east and south, where the plateau fell away into the valleys.

The crossing of the main paths was marked by a wooden sign scrawled with the name of the Nine Virgins and a yellow arrow. Around the sign was an area worn by many feet. Someone living in the valley had a peacock; its long drawn-out shriek drifted across the moor before dying away in the wind.

By the time she reached the Virgins, Jenny could feel the perspiration standing out on her forehead. Her Lycra cycling shorts were tighter on her hips and buttocks than they should have been, and the skin of her legs was pink and blotched from the exertion and the chafing of the wind.

She didn't mind the wind, or the cold, or even the exertion. Up here on the moor they helped to blow away the thoughts that would sit in the corners of her mind all the rest of the week, dark and evil-eyed. Nowhere else could she do that; certainly nowhere in Sheffield, where the crowded streets and the traffic only fed her anxieties.

In early November, the weather kept most people off the moor. But she could see that someone was sitting against the trunk of a tree near the stone circle, playing a few notes on a flute, toying with a tune that was vaguely familiar. She couldn't see the musician clearly, but she had an impression of long, fair hair and a multi-coloured sweater.

Jenny turned the handlebars of the bike away from the Nine Virgins and headed towards a path that ran down through deep bracken. The path turned into a stream bed later in the winter, and the ground was scoured to its sandy bottom. Tree roots ran close to the surface, bursting through to form ragged steps in the steepest parts. Beechnuts crunched underfoot and the bracken was head high. It pressed close around her, its brown, dead hands brushing against her legs and rattling on the spokes of her wheels.

Beyond the dip, the Hammond Tower stood at the top of the slope. It was prominent on the horizon, tall and built of grey stone, but serving no apparent purpose. A walled-up doorway faced a flight of roughly cut steps and a steep drop off Ringham Edge. Fallen leaves filled a wide hollow between the tower and the rock outcrops they called the Cat Stones.

Jenny sat for a while on a broken ledge at the base of the tower, staring at the view across the dale, waiting for her breathing to slow down, but feeling the chill begin to creep over her skin. She shouldn't stay long, or her muscles would stiffen.

Down in the valley, she could see the farm, with a field full of cows, a cluster of gritstone buildings and a bigger, newer shed with a dark green steel roof. A track ran past the farm, and she studied it carefully for figures walking by the gate and heading up towards the tower. But there was no one today.

As she stood up to retrieve her bike, she noticed a crevice in the stones of the tower which had been crammed with crumpled drinks cans and cigarette packets. Jenny shook her head in irritation, but did nothing about the litter. It was a job for the Rangers who patrolled the moor.

A few minutes later, she had reached the stone circle again. The Nine Virgins were only about four feet high, and they stood in a clearing of flattened and eroded grass between clumps of birch and oaks. Fifteen yards from the circle was a single stone on its own, an outlier – the stone that they called the Fiddler. According to the legend, nine village maidens had been caught dancing on the Sabbath and had been turned to stone for their sin. The fiddler who played for them had suffered the same fate. Now the single stone looked lonely and isolated, condemned for ever to stand outside the circle.

Jenny stopped the bike and wiped her palms on a tissue. The hills were already misting into grey over the banks of bracken, but the clouds broke and allowed a trickle of sun on to the moor. There was no sound but for the wind whispering across the heather. There was no one to be seen now; she was alone. And it was perfectly safe on a bike – as long as you didn't get a puncture.

'Oh, damn!'

She dismounted and struggled to turn her bike upside down to inspect the back tyre. Immediately she saw the glitter of a sliver of glass. It had slit a gaping wound in the rubber tread and gone straight through to puncture the inner tube. She pulled the glass free, flinching at the sharp edges, and listened to the last gasp of escaping air. The tyre looked peculiarly lifeless as it hung from the wheel, the soft grey skin of its collapsed tube protruding under the rim.

Jenny knew what a hassle it was to get the tyre off the back wheel, repair and replace it, and she was already reaching that state of tiredness where everything felt like a major task. But there was nothing else for it. Sighing, she flipped the quick-release lever and dropped the wheel on the ground. The forks of the bike pointed into the air in an undignified posture, like a dead animal on its back.

She was reminded of a photograph that had been taken at the height of the panic over mad cow disease. It had shown a slaughtered British Holstein cow, a huge animal with its stomach bloated, its vast udder shiny and leaking a dribble of milk, and its four stiff legs pointing ludicrously to the sky. The cow had been waiting its turn to be rolled into an incinerator. Its photograph had been on the front of leaflets that Jenny had helped to distribute, and she had seen it so many times that the details had stayed with her ever since, along with other images of things that had been done to animals.

Automatically, she patted the pouch she wore round her waist, to make sure it was still there. Soon, she would have to decide what to do with what it contained.

Jenny shivered. The weather had changed, and the evening would be cold. The feathery stems of cotton grass created patches of golden mist close to the ground. They hovered just above the heather, moving in the wind like live creatures stirring in their nests.

It was the noise of the wind in Jenny's ears that covered the soft sound of footsteps until the walker was only a few feet behind her.

In half an hour, Mark was due to go off duty. Owen had given him exact instructions for his first solo patrol – a pass across the face of Ringham and a descent into the valley on the far side, where the moor turned into farmland. There he was to take a look at the walls and stiles and signposts for recent damage, and have a scout around for the worst of the litter left by hikers.

On the way back, he should have a glance at the Nine Virgins to see that the ancient monument was no more scarred than usual; have a word, perhaps, with any campers foolhardy enough to have pitched their tents in the woods. Mark couldn't imagine why anybody would want to camp on the moor at any time of the year, let alone in November. But still they did it. And they were breaking the law when they did.

Near the top of the track he noticed a crumpled Coke can, dropped by some careless visitor. Muttering angrily, he picked it up and slipped it under the flap of his rucksack, where it joined a small pile of chocolate bar wrappers, aluminium ring-pulls and an empty Marlboro packet and some cigarette ends he had found near the Hammond Tower, to be disposed of later. Mark couldn't tolerate the attitude that made people think it was OK to scatter the environment with litter. They thought their own convenience was more important.

If he had his way, Mark would ban these people completely from the national park. He would put tollgates on all the entrance roads and issue passes for admission. It might come to it one day, too. The park couldn't cope with the constantly rising numbers.

There were tyre tracks in the sandy soil here. That meant there had been a mountain biker this way recently. Mark knew his by-laws; he had read the regulations carefully, and he knew what was allowed and what wasn't. The Peak District National Park Authority had prosecuted mountain bikers before.

He smiled in satisfaction, then immediately felt guilty. Owen said the main skills you needed as a Ranger were tact and diplomacy. Why get into an argument when you could achieve more with a friendly word of advice? Mark knew he had a lot to learn. Sometimes he couldn't find the right things to say to people who appalled him with their stupidity and their disregard for their own safety, the property of others – and, above all, for the environment and its wildlife. That was their greatest crime, these people who desecrated the moors. The last thing they deserved was diplomacy.

Though it was only two o'clock, it would be starting to go dark in a couple of hours' time. For a few days now, Mark had noticed that peculiar half-light, like full moonlight, that came at five o'clock in the afternoon, when all the colours seemed to change and glow for a few minutes before fading into the darkness. The turning back of the clocks at the end of British Summer Time always worried the Peak Park

Rangers. Walkers were liable to miscalculate and still be on the hills when it went dark.

The afternoon was turning cold, but Mark didn't feel the chill. The red fleece jacket he wore proudly, with its silver Peak Park insignia, kept him warm. It was also a reassuring sight for the visitors a Ranger came across – those who were lost and bewildered, exhausted or injured, or simply inadequately dressed and too poorly equipped for walking the moors. The sight of the red jacket was like a friendly beacon. It meant a Ranger approaching.

Jenny Weston had been in the act of smiling when she died. Her smile had stiffened and shattered, twisting into a grin of fear as the knife slipped under her ribs.

The blade was sharp, tungsten coated, and with a lethal tip. It slit the cotton of her T-shirt and sliced easily through her skin and a layer of subcutaneous fat as it thrust towards her heart. A small patch on the front of her T-shirt turned red and a single spurt of blood splashed on to the handlebars of the Kokomo.

As soon as the knife was withdrawn, the wound closed and ceased to bleed on the outside. Jenny looked down, astonished, and pressed her hand to the red patch. Inside her ribcage, her heart sac was already filling with leaking blood; the pressure of it squeezed her heart and constricted its movement. Then her left lung deflated and a gush of fluids filled the cavity. She began to feel light-headed; her hands and feet turned numb, and her legs lost the strength to hold her body upright.

She made no resistance as she was grasped under the armpits and dragged across the clearing, with her heels leaving trails in the sandy soil. As fresh blood failed to reach her brain and extremities, her skin turned a dirty white; her legs and belly looked like lumps of boiled fish as they were deliberately exposed to the light.

The blade of the knife left a red smear where it was wiped on the grass. From the handlebars of the bike, a small trickle of blood had run down on to the front wheel. It dripped slowly from spoke to spoke, already darkening and thickening in the air, until it was absorbed into the ground.

By the time her attacker had finished, or not long after, Jenny Weston was dead.

Mark knew it happened sometimes, but it was such a pointless thing to do. Mindless and irresponsible. Now and then the Ranger briefings mentioned a bike that had not been returned to the hire centre. Hirers had to give proof of their identity and leave a name and address, as well as a £50 deposit, so it was hardly worth trying to get away with a mountain bike, considering how easily you would get caught. But sometimes there was one who took the bike away with them. Occasionally, they simply abandoned it on one of the tracks, in a car park, or up here on the moor, like this one. None of it ever made sense to Mark.

The sight of the Kokomo under the gorse bush angered him unreasonably. Its presence was like a violation – the evidence of selfish humanity intruding into his world, like children pawing his most precious possessions with grubby fingers. The bike had been treated as just so much rubbish.

Then Mark looked more closely. A streak of red had stained the canary yellow paintwork of the front stem and left rust-like spots on the spokes. He shivered with misgiving and fingered the radio in his pocket. Suddenly he wished he hadn't come out alone, after all. There was no reassuring presence alongside him, no Owen there to know exactly what to do.

With a shaking hand, Mark made a note of the colour, model and number of the bike, crumpling the pages of his notebook in his haste to get it out of his pocket. The act of writing made him feel better, more in control, as if the ink marks on the page had magically brought a familiar voice from the air: 'Observe, keep a note, report back.'

'Yes, Owen,' whispered Mark.

Feeling the sweat drying on his forehead and the back of his neck, he forced himself to walk past the bike to where the stones were clustered among the spindly birches. Somebody had lit a fire here recently, leaving scorched earth and a pile of white ash. People were always lighting fires near the Virgins, as if they thought the flames might melt their stony hearts. At the midsummer solstice, there were hundreds of folk up here at night, and they did a lot more than light fires.

Mark stopped abruptly as he looked into the circle. The sensations that came reminded him of the terrors of his puberty, the physical sickness and the guilt. He tried to concentrate on studying the ground, to look for evidence of bike tracks or footprints. He tried to think about casting around for telltale objects that might have been dropped by someone who had been in the area. I'm observing, he told himself. I must observe. Be professional and calm, and don't rush into anything.

But he couldn't keep up the pretence for long. His eyes just wouldn't focus on anything else. With shameful fascination, Mark found his attention drawn to the centre of the stone circle, where the white shape lay in such startling, rousing incongruity.

'Oh, Jesus.'

The body of the woman sprawled obscenely among the stones. Her half-naked torso had been flung on the rough grass, her arms and legs twisted in provocative gestures. Her right knee was lifted high, to the level of her waist, and her left leg was stretched taut, as if she might be about to spring into the air.

Mark could see every detail of the muscles in her legs, the tendons rigid under the skin at the top of her thigh, the faint crinkling of cellulite on her hips. Her pose was a caricature of life, a cruel parody of flamboyance and movement. Her hands were tilted at the wrist, her toes pointed downwards, and her head nodded to silent music. She was spread against the ground in a final arabesque, in a fatal pirouette, or the last fling of an abandoned tango.

Mark wondered whether to write it down. But it sounded too strange, and his hand wouldn't write any more, anyway. Instead, he repeated it to himself, over and over, in his head. A dead woman dancing. She looked like a dead woman, dancing.

2

Fifteen miles to the north, in the town of Edendale, the battle had been going on for an hour and a half already. The police officers in the front line were battered and breathing hard, their faces swollen with exertion, and their hair stuck to their foreheads with sweat. One or two had their shirts ripped. Another had blood trickling from a cut on his eye.

Detective Constable Ben Cooper could see his colleague, Todd Weenink, deep in the thick of it. Weenink had two PCs from the Tactical Support Unit close on either side of him, and there were more men coming in from behind to assist them. They looked exhausted, their expressions grim, but determined. They were struggling against the odds, fighting a battle of containment that they were constantly in danger of losing.

The students were charging forward in a solid mass, forcing the police to give ground under the onslaught. In the melee, close up, anything could be happening – a poke in the eye, a boot in the crutch, teeth sinking into an ear. The police had not been issued with riot shields or helmets today; there was no body armour, no snarling Alsatians or horses to keep the students at bay. There had been no authority given for the use of special weapons, no tear gas canisters held nervously in reserve.

In addition, the police had to face a ceaseless barrage of noise – chanted slogans, shouts of abuse and a constant stream of profanities from a hostile crowd.

Cooper pulled his hands out of his jeans pockets and turned his coat collar up to try to shut out the cacophony. If he could, he would have closed his eyes, too, to avoid seeing the slaughter, to stop himself from imagining the consequences if the police line collapsed. In another moment, the day could end in total humiliation for Derbyshire Constabulary E Division. And not a single arrest made so far.

'What are we going to do, Sarge?' he said.

Detective Sergeant Rennie was an old hand. He had seen it all before. He rubbed his jowls, pulled his anorak closer around his shoulders, and winced as a PC went down and was trampled underfoot.

'Conduct a survey,' he said. 'We'll send out a questionnaire.'

Cooper nodded. 'I suppose so. But it's a bit pathetic, isn't it?'

'We'll make sure there are lots of tick boxes to fill in.'

'Even so ...'

Rennie shrugged and sighed. 'It's all we can do, Ben. Otherwise, we just have to sit back and let it happen.'

The police formed a wall and turned to face their attackers again. Beyond the opposing lines, Cooper could see the main buildings of the High Peak College campus, set on the lower slopes of the hill. They looked down on Edendale like benign giants, the educational heights of the Eden Valley.

He began to search his pockets for a packet of mints to take the taste of nausea from his mouth. He had a lot of pockets – in his jeans, in his checked shirt, on the inside and the outside of his waxed jacket. But all he found was a scatter of cashpoint receipts, two empty shotgun cartridge cases and half a packet of dog biscuits.

Cooper knew there was more than just education that went on in those college buildings on the hill. He had been there himself, for long enough to collect the A-levels he needed to get into the police service. His fellow students had accused him of being single-minded, as if his determination made them guilty about their own pursuit of parties and casual sex. But there had been a demon driving Ben Cooper that his contemporaries would never have understood – a jealous God who would not have tolerated parties.

Dave Rennie sat back comfortably in his seat and unscrewed the top of a vacuum flask. He offered Cooper a plastic cup, which he refused as soon as he got a whiff of the metallic tang of the coffee. The sergeant's expression was serious, his forehead creased with anxiety, like a man with a great responsibility on his mind.

'You see, if they get rid of the kitchen and sack the canteen staff, that means they'll put vending machines in instead,' he said. 'And then what would happen? I mean, would anybody use them? There's no point in spending money on vending machines if they don't get used. It would look bad in the budgets, wasting money at a time like this.'

Cooper watched Todd Weenink duck his head and drive his shoulders forward to meet a wiry-haired youth who'd been tormenting him all afternoon. There was a thud as their skulls connected and a scuffing as their feet lashed out.

The crowd behind Cooper began yelling. Then the police back-pedalled. Officers fell and were trampled as they lay on the ground. But Weenink broke away and looked around, bemused. His eyes were dazed, as if he might have taken a knock on the head. Then he looked up and caught sight of a student running past him, and made an instinctive grab. The student's legs folded beneath him under the impact of Weenink's sixteen stone, and they both sprawled in the mud, exhausted and gasping.

Cooper smiled. Quite by chance, it had been the right student Weenink had flattened. The High Peak College wing-three-quarter happened to be in possession of the ball, and had been racing for the touchline, within seconds of scoring the winning try of the match. Even while the two opposing players were struggling to get up again from the tackle, the referee blew the final whistle. The match had been saved: 12–10 to Edendale Police.

'Thank God for that,' said Cooper.

'Honour preserved, I suppose,' said Rennie, putting away his flask.

'I don't know about that, Sarge. But our lot always trash the bar if they lose.'

Cooper left the touchline and headed for the clubhouse. In his early days in E Division, they had tried to recruit him to the rugby team. They had thought he looked tall and fit enough to be an asset, but had accused him of lacking ruthlessness in the ruck. Now his job was to order the jugs of beer for the changing-room celebrations. Loyalty to your colleagues meant doing such things on a Sunday afternoon, even when you would rather be at home watching videos with your nieces.

After ten years, Cooper was able to look back on his days at High Peak College with some nostalgia. His life had possessed a definite purpose then. Succeeding in his exams had been his role in life, and joining the police his destiny. The feeling had stayed with him through his time as a uniformed constable on the beat; it had followed him as he moved into CID and began to learn a different way of policing. His progress had been watched every inch of the way, and mostly approved of. Mostly. The times when he had made mistakes or expressed doubts were still imprinted in his memory.

Then, two years ago, everything had changed. With the violent death of his father, Police Sergeant Joe Cooper, a prop had been knocked from under him, and a great weight had been lifted from his back. His guiding hand had been taken away, and his life had been given back to him. But it had already been too late for Ben Cooper. He had become what his father made him.

'So that's why we have to do this Vending Machine Usage Survey,' said Rennie, pronouncing the capital letters carefully as he walked at Cooper's shoulder. 'To get an idea of the possible take-up on the proposed new refreshment facilities. It's so that somebody in Admin at HQ can make an informed decision. A decision supported by constructive feedback from the customer base.'

Cooper could practically see the internal memo that Rennie was quoting from. The sergeant had coffee soaking into his moustache. He was wearing knitted woollen gloves, for Heaven's sake. He looked like somebody's granddad on an off-season outing to Blackpool.

Cooper was conscious that his own thirtieth birthday was approaching next year. It loomed in the distance like a summer storm cloud, making him feel his youth was nearly over before he had got used to being in his twenties. One day, he could be another Dave Rennie.

'I think Todd might have got a bit of concussion, Sarge.'

'He always looks like that,' said Rennie. 'He got a knock on the head.'

'Don't worry – Weenink doesn't let anybody mess with him. He always gets his revenge.'

Todd Weenink was different, of course. During the last couple of months Cooper had found himself thrown together with Weenink in the latest round of restructuring in the division. In these circumstances, the relationship became almost like a marriage. The issue of 'them and us' became focused on a single individual. But there were times when you needed another officer at your side.

Without the man or woman at your side, you could find yourself looking the wrong way at the wrong time. You had to have a person you could put your trust in. They supported you; and you supported them. Cooper knew it was a law written in invisible ink on the back of the warrant card they gave you when you were sworn in as a constable. It was sewn into your first uniform like an extra seam; it was the page that they always forgot to print in the Police Training Manual.

Only a couple of weeks earlier, Weenink had been the man at his side when they had raided a small-scale drugs factory in a converted warehouse on the outskirts of Edendale. One of the occupants had produced a pickaxe, but he had been too slow, and they had executed a takedown between them, with no one injured.

Cooper reassured himself by thinking of his date with Helen Milner later on. Within an hour, he would be out of the rugby club and away. He and Helen hadn't decided where they would go yet. Probably it would be a walk to get the noise out of his head, then a drink or two at the

Light House before a meal somewhere. The Light House was where they had gone the very first time they had gone out together. It was hardly more than two months ago that they had met again at Helen's grandparents' house in the village of Moorhay and resumed a relationship that had started when they were school-friends. But their new beginning had not been without difficulties. Nothing ever was.

The clubhouse corridor smelled of sweat and mud and disinfectant, with a permanent underlying essence of embrocation. Dave Rennie helped Cooper carry the jugs of beer to the players in the visitors' changing room. Then the sergeant's pager began to bleep.

'Oh, God damn it. What now?'

Cooper watched Rennie go to the phone in the corridor. He looked back over his shoulder at the changing-room door, which swung open with the constant passing to and fro of players and supporters. Todd Weenink was out of the shower, towelling himself in the middle of a raucous mob, his naked bulk perfectly at home in a melee of pink male flesh and echoing laughter.

Weenink already had a beer in front of him. It was amazing that he could keep up the pace. He had arrived for the match only at the very last minute, when everyone else was changed and ready to go out on the pitch, thinking they were going to have to play a man short, and cursing him for letting them down. No doubt Weenink had been out on the booze the night before and had woken up in someone else's bed many miles away, with rugby the last thing on his mind.

Cooper shook his head at the intrusive thoughts that came to him – the contrast between Weenink's muscular, hairy nakedness and the picture he carried in his mind of the last colleague he had worked so closely with. Todd's open, up-front, relaxed maleness was a world away from Detective Constable Diane Fry. Former Detective Constable, he should say. Now Acting Detective Sergeant.

It was a subject Cooper didn't really want to think about. It brought with it painful memories, some of which he still didn't understand but suspected might be his own fault.

After a few minutes, he realized Dave Rennie hadn't come back into the bar. In the steamy atmosphere of the changing room, he couldn't see Todd either. He had to shout to make himself heard, even when close enough to tap one of the players on the shoulder.

'Have you seen Todd Weenink?'

'He's gone,' said the player. 'Control bleeped Dave Rennie, and Todd went off with him. They went off in a hurry, too. Todd hadn't even managed to put his trousers on.'

'You're joking.'

'No, mate. I saw him myself, with his arse hanging out. Should you be with them?'

Cooper stared bleakly at the player. 'I'm not on call. Control wouldn't have asked for me.'

'Right. You're the lucky one, then. You can have a few beers.'

'A few beers, yeah. What more could I ask for?'

Suddenly, Cooper's mood plummeted.

He felt as if he had just been jilted by a lover. If there was a job on, he wanted to be there. He wanted to be part of the team. He wondered why loyalty had to be so painful. And when would he learn to give his loyalty in the right direction? He ought to have learned that lesson from Diane Fry – their brief relationship had certainly been difficult enough to drive it home. Cooper shuddered at a premonition. He thought it likely that she could inflict more pain on him yet, given the chance.

The police vehicles cluttering up the roadsides at the bottom of the main track on to Ringham Moor made Diane Fry frown in exasperation. The scene looked chaotic, as cars with beacons flashing arrived one after another in the gathering dusk and slewed across the narrow verge. A minibus carrying the Tactical Support Unit was unable to squeeze through the gap left by the parked cars until a uniformed sergeant yelled at someone to move. Figures in reflective yellow jackets were caught briefly in the headlights as they passed aimlessly backwards and forwards.

Fry itched to take control of the situation, to bring order and a bit of sense to officers so charged with excitement and adrenalin that they were causing more trouble than they were worth. But, in fact, she shouldn't even be here at all. She had thought she had got away from E Division, that her few weeks in Edendale had been a bad dream she could soon put behind her. But here she still was, answering the call. And before she knew what was happening, she had found herself out in the Peak District countryside again, where civilization seemed like a dim memory and the 21st century was reduced to the fantasy of a Victorian novelist.

She stood with Detective Inspector Paul Hitchens on the rocks overlooking the road. A fine drizzle was settling on their clothes and in their hair, and turning the gritstone slab under their feet a shade darker. With Hitchens at her side, Fry felt as though she had taken another step closer in her ambitions. She was already 'acting up' as a detective sergeant, with a transfer to a permanent DS's job in the offing when the imminent re-shuffle took place.

A move couldn't come too soon for Fry. At all costs, she must avoid the crazy distractions and misjudgements that had plagued he in a spell shortly after her arrival in E Division from West Midlands. The name of her biggest misjudgement was Ben Cooper.

The thought of him immediately sparked the surge of anger that always bubbled somewhere deep in her stomach, churning thick and corrosive like an acid that flowed in her small intestines. It happened every time; it only took the mention of Cooper's name, or even a burst of the wrong music. There were cassettes that she used to play often in her car which she had been forced to throw away – not just casually chucked on the back seat, but hurled into the nearest wheelie bin, with their spools of magnetic tape ripped out and shredded like the innards of a rat she had once seen killed and torn apart by a police Alsatian in a derelict warehouse back in Birmingham. If there had been an open fire in her flat, she would have burned the tapes; she would have happily watched their plastic cases crack and twist and bubble, as they melted into a greasy smear.

Fry wiped a sheen of drizzle from her face, where it was starting to make her cheeks feel damp and uncomfortable. No, she hadn't quite managed to erase Ben Cooper from her memory yet. But she was working on it.

'We've arranged for you to see Maggie Crew at six o'clock,' said DI Hitchens. 'You'd better get going, as soon as this lot are out of our way.'

'Was she willing to see me?'

'Willing isn't a word I'd use. She's bloody hard work.'

'She's uncooperative? But why?'

'You'll see. Form your own impressions of her, Diane, that's the best way. We want you to get to know her. Get under her skin. Be an irritant, if you like.'

Fry knew she was being presented with a chance to do something different, to escape the routine chores that the Ben Coopers of the world would be allocated during this enquiry.

'I'm looking forward to it,' she said.

Hitchens nodded in approval. 'When *are* they going to stop messing about down there?' he said.

DI Hitchens was dressed casually, in denims and trainers, and he looked like a man who should have been doing something else. His cheeks were dark and unshaven, and there were specks of white paint in his hair.

'We've got to keep the road open,' said the sergeant importantly as he passed below them.

'Yeah. You're doing a great job. We can see that.'

'Control reckons the cavalry's on the way, Inspector. They tracked down a couple of your lot at the rugby match.'

Fry knew exactly what that meant. The rugby match was where Ben Cooper would have been with his friend, Todd Weenink, and no doubt DS Dave Rennie, too. Cooper wasn't a rugby-playing man himself. From her own experience, Fry reckoned he was more likely to be taking out the half-time oranges and cleaning the players' boots, generally getting in the way and making helpful suggestions. But he would have been at the match to support his colleagues. Oh yes, Ben Cooper was a great one for supporting his friends.

'Oh, and you'll be pleased to know our lads won too!' called the sergeant.

Fry blew through her teeth and jammed her hands into the pockets of her coat, squaring her shoulders like someone bracing herself for a fight. Rennie, Cooper, and Weenink. The dream team. Just what E Division needed to stamp on a spate of attacks on women.

At last it looked as though someone had located another place to park. Radios crackled, the sergeant shouted, and cars began to move off, flashing their headlights and spinning their wheels dramatically on the grass as they went. But as the patrols and vans made space, another car arrived. It was an unmarked Mondeo – a private car, not a police vehicle. The doors popped open and a warm fug seemed to ooze out into the evening chill. A voice was raised in complaint from the back seat.

'I can't *believe* we left those uniformed bastards with all the beer,' it said.

Fry recognized DC Weenink immediately. He was damp-haired and pink-faced, and his voice sounded petulant, like an overgrown child. She watched in disgust as he poked bare, muscular legs out of the car door and struggled to pull his trousers on over his jockey shorts. Parts of his anatomy bulged dangerously from his underclothes, and the buttons of his shirt were unfastened over his hairy chest. Even from several yards away, Fry knew that his breath smelled of alcohol.

She watched DS Rennie get out of the driver's seat. But no Ben Cooper. Suddenly, Fry felt more cheerful. Her shoulders relaxed, her lips formed a contemptuous smile.

'Well, if that's the cavalry,' she said, 'my money's on the Indians.'

DI Hitchens laughed. Weenink heard the laugh, and he looked around for its source. He grinned up at Fry, with his zip still open, his hands pressed round his crotch, the position of them emphasizing rather than concealing the bulge in his shorts.

'Excuse me, Sergeant,' he said. 'Can you use me at all?'

Fry stared at him, but Weenink's grin only grew broader, until it became a smirk. She turned to stride away from the road. She had no time to waste on petty irritations – not when a woman's entire life had already been wasted up there on the moor. She had seen enough wasted lives, and her own had almost been one of them. But not any more.

Ben Cooper took a swig from his bottle, conserving the beer carefully, anxious about drinking too much. He didn't want to become a solitary drinker, though the temptation was strong.

A few minutes ago, he had rung Control to find out what was happening. They said the body of a woman had been found on Ringham Moor, fifteen miles south of Edendale. A suspected murder. The control room operator didn't need to mention the other attack that had taken place not a mile away from the same spot six weeks before. In that case, the victim had survived – just about.

Now Cooper's mind was no longer with him as he sat in the sweaty rugby club bar. It was elsewhere, drifting across the moors towards a flutter of tape and the flashing lights, the sound of urgent voices, and the scents and the electric crackle in the air that never failed to give him a buzz of excitement. That sense of satisfaction from taking his place in the team was a thing that couldn't be explained to someone who had never experienced it.

Yet tomorrow morning, he knew he would be sitting in the monthly Crime Strategy Meeting for Edendale Section. He would be discussing the section's annual local objectives, the implementation of liaison policies and the measurement of performance. Occasionally, in these meetings, they talked about crime. But they hardly ever talked about the victims.

Cooper watched the rugby players reach the traditional highlight of the evening, when they began to pour pints of beer over each other's heads. The bare wooden floor of the bar was already awash and turning sticky underfoot. Some of the students looked irritated at the way their clubhouse was being taken over by the more boisterous and more aggressive celebratory style of the police. Soon it would reach the point when it might be better not to have to witness a colleague committing a breach of the peace.

It was time for Ben Cooper to leave. He needed to be awake and alert for the meeting in the morning, and he had a stack of burglaries to work on, as well as a serious assault on a bouncer at one of Edendale's night clubs. With officers seconded to the murder enquiry, no doubt there would be someone else's workload to take over as well. Besides, if he stayed any longer, he would drink too much. It was definitely time to go home.

But home was Bank End Farm, in the shadow of Camphill. Though he was close to his brother Matt, Matt's young family were gradually making the house their own, until their video games and guinea pig cages left little room for Ben. So for a while he sat on in the bar, like an old man in the corner watching the youngsters enjoy themselves, and he thought about the body on Ringham Moor.

With a bit of luck, the police team would find some obvious leads and get an early closure. There would be initial witness statements that pointed with clunking obviousness to a boyfriend or a spurned lover. Sometimes it was as if the perpetrator carried a giant, fluorescent arrow round with him and the word 'guilty' in bright red letters that were visible five miles away in poor light. All the team would need to do then was make sure they collected the forensic evidence at the scene without either contaminating it, losing it or sticking the wrong label on it so that no one could say afterwards where it had been found. It was amazing what could happen to evidence between the first report of a crime and the day a case came to court.

Cooper fought his way to the bar, shouting to the barman to make himself heard above the din. It seemed as though no one else in here wanted to sit down – they were all up on their feet, shouting at each other. The police were singing triumphal songs, having a great time. The students were starting to look hostile.

The American beer Cooper was drinking came in a brown bottle, with a black label and a faint wisp of vapour from its open neck. It was cold, and he closed both his hands round it, drawing a strange comfort from its chill for a moment before he turned and carried it away from the bar. Instead of returning to his corner, he slipped out of the door into the cooler air outside.

For a while, he leaned against a rail near the changing rooms, gazing at the empty pitch, watching the starlings that had arrived in the dusk to pick over the divots in the turf, searching for worms exposed by the players' studs. He became distantly aware of a more aggressive note to the shouting in the bar behind him, but decided it wasn't his concern.

Cooper continued to believe it was nothing to do with him right up until the moment that a six-foot six-inch student lock forward put a hand like a meat plate on his arm.

3

Diane Fry had never seen Detective Chief Inspector Stewart Tailby quite so agitated. The DCI loomed over his group of officers like a head teacher with a class full of pupils in detention, and he was shouting at the Senior SOCO from the Scientific Support Unit. Tailby's strangely two-tone hair was trembling in the wind as he turned and paced around the crime scene.

'We've got to hit this area fast,' he said. 'We can't possibly seal it off – we'd need every man in E Division. We need to get what we can before the public get up here and trample over everything.'

'Well, we *could* do it in a rush, but it won't be very selective,' said the SOCO.

'Sod being selective,' said Tailby. 'Take everything. We'll worry about being selective later.'

A few yards away, DI Hitchens manoeuvred to keep his senior officer within distance. Other officers ebbed and flowed awkwardly around them, like extras in a badly staged Gilbert and Sullivan opera, who had just realized that nobody had told them what to do with their hands.

'The light's failing fast,' said Hitchens, gazing at the sky.

'Well, thanks for that,' snapped Tailby. 'I thought I was going blind.'

The DCI strode over to the side of the stone circle and looked down into the disused quarry beyond it. There was a barbed wire fence, but it was too low to keep anybody out. On the other side could be seen the last few yards of an access road, which ended on the lip of the quarry. Diane Fry stretched her neck to see what Tailby was looking at. Someone had been fly-tipping from the roadway. She could just make out tyre marks, and a heap of bulging black bin liners, some yellow plastic sheeting and a roll of carpet that had been heaved off the edge. The rubbish lay scattered on the slope like the debris of a plane crash.

'Find out where the entrance to that quarry is,' said Tailby. 'And somebody will have to go down there. We need to find the rest of the clothes. Top priority.'

Hitchens had to dodge as Tailby wheeled suddenly and strode back towards the stones, avoiding the lengths of blue tape twisted together between birch trees and metal stakes. In the centre of the circle, the pathologist, Mrs Van Doon, still crouched over the victim under makeshift lighting. Tailby's face contorted. He seemed to find something outrageous and obscene in the posture of the body.

'Where's that tent?' he called. 'Get the tent over her before we have an audience.'

He turned his back and walked on a few yards from the circle, where a single stone stood on its own. DI Hitchens trailed after him at a safe distance.

'There's an inscription carved on this stone,' announced Tailby, with the air of Moses coming down from the mountain.

'Yes. It looks like a name, sir.'

'We'll need a photographer over here. I want that name deciphering.'

'It's well away from the path,' said Hitchens. 'We think the assailant probably brought his victim from the other direction.'

'So?'

'The inscription has probably been there for years.'

'Do you *know* that? Are you familiar with these stones?'

'No, sir.'

'Ever seen them before in your life?'

'No, sir.'

Tailby turned. 'No point asking you, Fry, is there?'

Fry shrugged, but the DCI wasn't waiting for an answer. He looked around to see who else he could find. 'You lot, there! Anyone seen these stones before? They're a famous landmark, they tell me. A significant part of our ancient heritage. They're an attraction. Visitors flock to see them. What about you?'

The officers shook their heads. They were the sort of men who spent their free time in the pub or in front of the telly, doing a bit of DIY or visiting the garden centre. The ones with kids went to Alton Towers and Gulliver's Kingdom. But this thing in front of them wasn't a theme park. There were no white-knuckle rides or ice-cream vans. Tailby turned back to Hitchens.

'OK, see? We know nothing about it. We're all as ignorant as a lot of monkeys. This stone circle might as well be a Tibetan yak compound, for all we know about the place.'

'Yes, but –'

'Just see that it's done,' snarled Tailby.

Then the DCI looked back to where Mrs Van Doon was working. Fry could see that more inscriptions had been scratched into the dirt in the centre of the circle, close to the body. The letters were big and bold, and they spelled out 'STRIDE'. Whoever had made these was less interested in leaving a long-term record of his presence, though. The drizzle was hardly touching the marks, but a couple of heavy showers would wash them clean away.

'What about those, then?' said Tailby. 'You're not going to tell me those have been there for years?'

'No,' admitted Hitchens. 'They've got to be more recent.'

'When did it rain in this area last? Properly, I mean?'

Tailby stared around him. The officers gathered nearby looked at each other, then up at the sky. Fry sympathized. They were detectives – they spent all their time buried in paperwork or making phone calls in windowless offices; occasionally they drove around in a car, shuttling from pub to crown court and back again. How were they supposed to know when it had rained?

It was well known that DI Hitchens had just bought a new house in Chesterfield. Tailby himself had a ranch-style bungalow in a desirable part of Dronfield. Most of the other officers lived miles away, down in the lower valleys and the dormitory villages. Some of them were from the suburbs of Derby. It could be blowing a blizzard up here on the moor, piling up six-foot drifts of virgin snow, and all these men would see was a faint bit of sleet in the condensation on their kitchen windows.

'Does it matter?' said Hitchens.

Tailby smiled like a fox with a rabbit. 'It matters, Inspector, because we can't say whether the inscriptions were written in the last twenty-four hours or the last two weeks.'

'I suppose so, sir.'

Teeth bared, Tailby glared round for another victim. There was a shuffling and looking away, a lot of thoughtful glances at the grey blanket of cloud.

'You useless set of pillocks! Doesn't *anyone* know? Then find me someone who does!'

Mark Roper finally opened his eyes as Owen Fox parked the Land Rover behind the Partridge Cross briefing centre. The cycle hire staff had closed up for the night, but there were still a few visitors' cars left outside. A couple were securing their bikes to a rack. It occurred to Mark Roper that one of the cars that still stood dark and unattended probably belonged to the woman whose body lay on the moor.

'Come on, Mark. Let's get you inside,' said Owen.

For a moment, Mark didn't move. Then, slowly, he unfolded his legs and got out. He felt stiff, like an old man with arthritis. His jacket was crumpled, there were grass stains on his knees and black marks on his hands. He couldn't think where the marks had come from, but his hands felt unpleasant and greasy, as if there was something on his skin that would take a long time to remove.

He swayed and supported himself on the side of the Land Rover. Owen moved nearer, not touching him but hovering anxiously.

'We have to wait while the police come to speak to you, Mark,' he said.

'I know.'

'Are you up to it?'

'I'm all right.'

Owen Fox was a large man, a little ungainly from carrying too much weight around his upper body. His curly hair and wiry beard were going grey, and his face was worn and creased, the sign of a man who spent his life outdoors, regardless of the weather. Mark wanted to draw reassurance from his presence, to lean on his comforting bulk, but an uncertainty held him back.

Owen finally took Mark by the arm. But the reassurance failed to come. The contact was safe and impersonal, Owen's fingers meeting only the fabric of the young Ranger's red fleece jacket. Mark shivered violently, as if his only source of warmth had suddenly been withdrawn.

'Let's get inside,' said Owen. 'It's cold out here. You look to me as though you need a hot drink. A cup of my tea will bring some colour back to your cheeks, won't it? Green, maybe – but at least it'll be colour.'

Mark smiled weakly. 'I'm fine.'

'You're probably suffering from shock. We ought to get a doctor to look at you.'

'No. I'll be all right, Owen.'

The briefing centre was empty, but warm. The blackboard on the far wall contained white chalk scrawl that gleamed in the sudden light. The words meant nothing to Mark now. In the corner, the assistant's desk was scattered with papers – reports and forms, the encroaching paperwork of the modern Peak Park Ranger. Soon, a computer would arrive, even here.

Mark needed no encouragement to collapse into a chair near the electric heater. Owen watched him, his face creased with concern, then turned to switch on the kettle.

'Plenty of sugar in your tea, for the shock.'

Sugar, and a reassuring voice, thought Mark. The things that people needed were simple, really – such as stability and their own part to play in life. But it was Owen he had learned to looked to for stability. Now he had an inexplicable fear that it would be snatched from his life again.

'The things people leave on the moor,' said Owen. 'Litter and rubbish. You'd think they'd at least take their dead bodies home with them.'

This time Mark couldn't smile.

Owen looked at him. 'I did tell you to keep in touch, Mark,' he said.

'I tried, Owen. But I couldn't get an answer.'

Owen grimaced. 'Those radios.'

I mustn't make him feel guilty, thought Mark. Don't make him take this burden on himself as well as everything else. Mark was aware that there were things he didn't know about Owen, that in their relationship he only saw the surface of the older man. But there was one thing he did know. Owen needed no more burdens.

Ben Cooper jumped at the hand on his shoulder and tensed his body for trouble. He cursed himself for having allowed someone to find him on his own in a vulnerable position.

The hand felt like a great weight. The tall student was massively built, with a red, sweaty face and a squashed nose. He leaned down and spoke into Cooper's ear with a voice that growled like a boulder in a landslide. At first, Cooper had no idea what he was saying. He thought the noise in the bar must have damaged his hearing permanently. He shook his head. The student leaned closer, breathing beer fumes on his neck.

'You *are* Constable Cooper, aren't you?'

'Yes.'

'I said there's someone on the phone for you. Some daft bastard who wants to know when it rained last.'

Ten minutes later, Cooper slid into the passenger seat of a Ford Mondeo as it scattered gravel on the sports ground car park.

'It's a what, Todd?'

'A cyclist from Sheffield,' said Weenink. 'She was found in the middle of the stones on Ringham Moor.'

'You mean the Nine Virgins?'

'That's the place. You got it in one. I can see why the DCI loves you.'

'Everybody knows the Nine Virgins,' said Cooper.

'I wish you'd introduce me, then. I can't find even one virgin where I live.'

Cooper could detect the sweet smell of beer in the car. He wondered if Weenink was fit to drive. It would be ironic if they got stopped by a Traffic patrol. Todd could lose his job, if he was breathalysed.

'Is Mr Tailby in charge up there?'

'He's SIO until they manage to pull a superintendent in from somewhere,' said Weenink. 'He's not a happy man. He's got a wide-open scene, public access, SOCOs scattered over a space as big as four football pitches. Also, he has a temper on him as foul as my breath on a Saturday night. But we have to report to DI Hitchens. And let me tell you, we're bloody lucky Hitchens arrived.'

'Yeah?'

'Earlier on, it was DI Armstrong at the scene. The Wicked Witch of West Street.'

'Don't say that.'

'The Bitch of Buxton, then.'

'Shut up, Todd.'

Weenink stopped at the junction of the A6, and seemed to spend a long time waiting for distant traffic to pass on the main road. Finally, he pulled out behind a tanker carrying milk for Hartington Stilton.

'You don't understand, Ben,' he said. 'That Kim Armstrong, she's so scary. I'm frightened she'll put a spell on me and turn me into a eunuch.'

'Will you cut it out?'

'No, seriously, Ben. They reckon she cursed Ossie Clarke in Traffic one day, and his balls shrivelled up like cashew nuts. The doctors are baffled. He's been off sick for weeks.'

'Todd –'

'Well, he has, hasn't he? Eh?'

'Ossie Clarke is one of the bad-back brigade. He has a slipped disc.'

'That's the official line. Don't let it lull you into a false sense of security. Anyway, we're in luck. They couldn't spare Armstrong from this paedophile enquiry. Apparently it's warming up for some arrests. There was the little girl that was killed –'

'Yes, I know.'

'So Hitchens has had to come in off leave. And you know he's just moved into a new house with that red-headed nurse? So *he's* not happy, either. It's a barrel of laughs up there, all right. Couldn't wait to get away for a bit, myself.'

Weenink was taking the back road past the fluorspar works to avoid the bottleneck in Bakewell. He took the bends gently, as if he was just one more pensioner on a Sunday afternoon outing.

'Todd? Can't we go a bit faster?'

'Mmm, the roads are a bit slippery with all these leaves,' said Weenink. 'Can't be too careful.'

The atmosphere on the moor was gloomy. It made Ben Cooper feel almost guilty about the buzz of anticipation that had stayed with him even in the car with Todd Weenink. The entire stone circle had been taped off, and lights were being set up to illuminate a small tent in the centre. More tape created a pathway as far as a gorse bush a few yards away. The tape twisted and rattled in the wind with a noise like a crowd of football supporters half-heartedly encouraging their team.

'There was an inch or two of rain during Thursday night, but it had dried up by morning,' said Cooper.

Several faces turned to stare at him. Hitchens raised an eyebrow, but Tailby nodded.

'Well, the ground was fine for lifting the sugar beet that morning,' explained Cooper. He drew a finger through a hollow on the top of one of the stones. 'On the other hand, there hasn't been enough sun since then to dry the moisture out where it's sheltered from the wind.'

He became suddenly aware of the nature of the looks he was being given. 'It's what you asked me,' he said.

Hitchens shrugged. He was wearing an old rugby jersey over his jeans, and might once have played for the divisional XV until he became senior enough to be more at risk of injury from his own side than from the opposition.

'Could Stride be a name?' he asked.

'What kind of man would leave his name written in the dirt when he had committed a murder, anyway?' said Tailby. 'And these stones ...'

'The Nine Virgins,' said Cooper.

'What are they all about?'

'They're the remains of a Bronze Age burial chamber. But local people call them the Virgins because of the legends ...'

'How old?'

'Three and a half thousand years, give or take.'

'The last virgins in Derbyshire, then,' said Hitchens.

Cooper kept his mouth shut. He watched a SOCO scoop up a tiny patch of bloodstained earth where the body had lain, while he listened to the faint laughter drop hollowly into the wind and disappear with a scatter of dead leaves.

In a short while, no doubt, a detective superintendent would arrive from another division to take over as senior investigating officer. He would be grumbling about the continuing vacancy in E Division that meant he had to be dragged away from his own patch, where there would be several other major incidents to be dealt with as well.

But this was the second attack on a woman in a small area, and this victim was dead. Panic would be setting in at higher levels, and those being kicked by the chiefs would soon be kicking the dog.

Though he knew Ringham Moor well, Ben Cooper found the area around the Nine Virgins disturbed him in a way it had never done before. The atmosphere was all wrong. There was nothing dark and claustrophobic about this murder scene, unlike so many others he had come across. Very often a killing occurred within a close relationship, usually within the confines of a family, where emotions ran high and someone was finally driven to extremes. Here, though, the feeling he got was of space and timelessness, a place where everything ran to its natural sequence, just as it had done for thousands of years. Here, the slow dance of the seasons repeated itself endlessly on an almost empty stage as nature rolled from life to death and back to life again.

Cooper had learned to keep quiet about his thoughts at times. Most senior officers, like DCI Tailby, prided themselves on being practical, logical men. Tailby was from Nottingham, raised in suburban streets and comprehensive schools. He preferred to leave it to people like Ben Cooper to be imaginative – he seemed to regard it as some kind of local idiosyncrasy, a queer characteristic inherited from the distant Celtic ancestors of the Derbyshire hill folk.

Cooper watched his fellow officers. Some of them certainly looked as though they felt disorientated and isolated from the realities of the twenty-first century up here. As if to emphasize the point, the sound of a steam train starting up seemed to reach them from the valley below.

'There's the train,' said Cooper.

'What?' said Tailby.

'It's the Peak Rail line. They run restored steam engines on it. For the tourists, you know.'

A white plume hung across the lights in the bottom of the valley, drifting with the breeze back towards Matlock and vanishing into the darkness as the chug of the engine receded.

Tailby spun on his heel. 'Time to talk to the Rangers,' he said.

'We'll need to get proper lights set up here, you know,' said the Senior SOCO, 'if you really want photos of that inscription.'

'Believe me,' said Tailby, 'I want *everything*.'

Stephen Booth's *Dancing With The Virgins* is published by HarperCollins

CAUSE FOR CELEBRATION: HOUSE OF STRATUS

Judith Gray

We all have our favourite crime and thriller writers whose works have fallen out of print. Such are the vagaries of fashion, that it's difficult these days to find the first-rate thrillers of James Leasor, Adam Hall and (until Pan Macmillan began its welcome series of reissues) Eric Ambler. One of the saddest omissions from the lists has been the excellent thriller writer Desmond Bagley, once a literary high-flier but now only to be found in church jumble sales. Not any more. The appearance of House of Stratus, a new publishing house specialising in reissues of classic crime and thrillers (along with other non-genre material), is something that every reader of this magazine must give three cheers for. And this is no soft launch, just dipping its toe into the market. The first batch includes four books apiece by writers who have fallen from favour, and are here restored to print in beautifully produced new editions, each with a separate identity. This first batch includes Desmond Bagley, Erle Stanley Gardner, Freeman Wills Crofts, James Leasor's non-fiction and (more controversially) James Hadley Chase, and one can only wish the group the greatest success in this brave reissue programme.

Desmond Bagley was a British thriller writer born in South Africa, and specialised in creating tension by placing ordinary pro-

tagonists in very difficult situations. His use of exotic settings was his speciality, and his research in these territories made for a powerful sense of authenticity. In this regard, many would count *Running Blind* as his masterpiece; with its superb thriller plot set against a vivid Icelandic background. This is in this first House of Stratus batch, as is his *Bahama Crisis, Wyatt's Hurricane*, and the much-acclaimed *High Citadel* (Crime Time will be covering the considerable number of Bagley titles in the House of Stratus programme at a later date).

Crofts is a British detective story writer that many will be glad to see back in print. Crofts' speciality was the cracking of alibis, set in beautifully constructed tales with an outrageous but plausible logic. The other pleasure of his books comes from the careful recreation of life in 1930s Britain. Crofts is represented in this batch by *The Box Office Murders, Found Floating* and *The Groote Parker Murder*. But many will find *Death of the Train* the most beguiling book by him here.

About the Erle Stanley Gardner Perry Mason books, little needs to be said (at least one would have thought not, for readers of this magazine) and *The Case of the Phantom Fortune* is probably the most accomplished title in this batch.

Is it time for a reappraisal of James Hadley Chase? His reputation is, to say the least, in flux: at least the House of Stratus reissues of *An Ace Up My Sleeve* and *Hit and Run* will open up the debate. Hopefully, the company will reissue the 'director's cut' version of Chase's notorious *No Orchids for Miss Blandish*. It is always salutary to read the bland, toned-down version that has been available for so many years

after reading George Orwell's famous attack in *Raffles and Miss Blandish* – the book Orwell is excoriating is not the one most readers encounter, and the uncensored version sounds like far more fun. Knife murders in this version are NOT accompanied by orgasms – the touch that so upset Orwell.

Finally, though, one has to wish this company every success, and readers everywhere will be compiling their own lists of favourites on which the axe has fallen – and which House of Stratus might introduce again. If one's only caveat is the ultra-thin card on the covers that curls almost immediately, that's a minor one.

James Hadley Chase

James Hadley Chase was born in London and initially worked as a book wholesaler. He was heavily influenced by American crime and gangster writers and his own books fall within that genre, with many of them based in the US. Chase developed a number of series characters, with several books dedicated to each, and all are fast moving tales of murder, intrigue, blackmail and espionage. Characters include ex-commando Brick-Top Corrigan, Californian private eye Vic Malloy, former CIA agent Mark Girland, and millionaire Don Miclem. Hailed as 'the thriller maestro of the generation', Chase died in 1985.

A major influence on modern day writers such as James Elroy and Carl Hiaassen, the intricate plots with deceptive twists make these novels an essential part of any crime and thriller library.

Bibliography

Titles Available from House of Stratus:

An Ace Up My Sleeve

An Ear to the Ground

The Fast Buck

Goldfish Have No Hiding Place

The Guilty Are Afraid
Hand Me a Fig Leaf
Have a Change of Scene
Have this One on Me
Hit and Run
Hit Them Where It Hurts
Just a Matter of Time
Knock Knock Who's There?
Like a Hole in the Head
Make the Corpse Walk
More Deadly than the Male
My Laugh Comes Last
Not My Thing
So What Happens to Me?
Tell it to the Birds
The Whiff of Money
You Have Yourself a Deal
You're Dead Without Money

An Ace Up My Sleeve (ISBN 1 84232 100 5)
When three very different people come together, all out for the same thing and prepared to go to any lengths to get it, the stakes are likely to be high. But, for a wealthy middle-aged woman, an international lawyer and a young American, games of bluff and counter-bluff quickly develop into a dangerous and deadly battle. As the action hots up, Chase weaves a fast-moving story of blackmail, intrigue and extortion with a hair-raising climax.

An Ear to the Ground (ISBN 1 84232 101 3)
When a necklace is as beautiful as the Esmaldi necklace with its hundred sparkling diamonds, it is not surprising that it causes powerful emotions. It is an object that people will do anything to obtain – even murder. For Al Barney, general idler and layabout, this comes as no surprise for he knows the peculiar history that the necklace holds – an ancient story of passion, jealousy and hatred. Yet as events unfold, it becomes clear that this violent story is far from over…

"Jewel-snatch gang stuff, set in Miami. Quite the best thing Chase has done for years" *Sun*

The Fast Buck (ISBN 1 84232 102 1)
International jewel thief, Paul Hater, knows a secret that everyone wants to know – and will go to any lengths to uncover. How long can he remain silent? When Hater is arrested in possession of a stolen necklace, the police use every possible means to persuade him to reveal the location of the rest of the collection. He remains silent and so begins his twenty-year prison sentence. Having exhausted all their leads, the International Detective Agency, acting on behalf of the insurers, must patiently await Hater's release before they can hope to find out more. But just as his day of release approaches, Hater is kidnapped by a ruthless international gang determined to force the secret from him and prepared to go to any lengths to do so…

Goldfish Have No Hiding Place (ISBN 1 84232 103 X)
Eastlake is the kind of place where 'nice' people live – nice, well-off, civilised people. People who know all about each other and where everyone knows everyone else's business – rather like living in a goldfish bowl. So when scanners are set up in the self-service shop in an attempt to catch petty shoplifters, it comes as rather a surprise when some dark secrets begin to emerge. A perfect opportunity for blackmailers…

The Guilty are Afraid (ISBN 1 84232 104 8)
When Jack Sheppey ends up dead in a beach hut in a wealthy town on the coast of the Pacific, his former partner in their detective agency starts a desperate quest to find his killer. But as private investigator Lew Brandon soon learns, this becomes a non-stop, terrifying and deadly hunt that will take him right to the heart of gangster territory.

Hand Me a Fig Leaf (ISBN 1 84232 105 6)
When Johnny Jackson unaccountably disappears, his grandfather contacts the police for help. As they prove to be uninterested, he turns instead to Colonel Parnell of the Parnell Detective Agency. It seems at first to be a simple case of a missing person but they soon find themselves in the middle of a complicated web of deceit, intrigue and murder.

Have a Change of Scene (ISBN 1 84232 106 4)
Larry Carr is a diamond expert in need of a break. So when his psychiatrist suggests he has a change of scene, he jumps at the opportunity to move to Luceville, a struggling industrial town, and become a social worker. This, he thinks, will give him all the rest he needs… until he runs into Rhea Morgan, a ruthless, vicious thief who also happens to be extremely attractive. He falls headlong into the criminal world and embarks upon a thrilling, rapid and dastardly adventure in true Hadley Chase style.

Have This One on Me (ISBN 1 84232 107 2)
Mark Girland, good-for-nothing secret agent with a distinct weakness for money and women, finds himself in Prague for his latest adventure. Events in the Communist country prove all too much for Girland as he comes face to face with a sinister world of deception, fraud and corruption. The result is another gripping thriller from the James Hadley Chase Library.

Hit and Run (ISBN 1 84232 108 0)
Lucille Aitkin was the kind of woman who encouraged men to run around after her and most men were more than happy to do so – so why did she suddenly want to learn to drive rather than being chauffeur-driven in style? And why was Chester Scott's Cadillac covered with bloodstains on the *wrong* side? And at the same time, why was patrol officer O'Brien run over on a deserted beach road when he should have been on duty on the highway? It seems that somebody knows how these events are connected, and whoever it is seems intent on blackmail.

Hit Them Where it Hurts (ISBN 1 84232 109 9)
Somebody is blackmailing Mrs Thorsen's daughter and Mrs Thorsen wants it to stop. She approaches the Acme Detective Agency and enlists the help of Dirk Wallace. But Wallace soon learns that he is way out of his depth and must go it alone if he has any change to succeed – after all, he is taking on the Mafia…

Just a Matter of Time (ISBN 1 84232 110 2)
An old lady's will seems to be causing quite a stir. Suddenly everyone wants to get in on the action, everyone that is, including a master forger, a hospital nurse, a young delinquent, a bank executive and, to make matters worse, a professional killer. With such ingredients, a showdown seems inevitable and James Hadley Chase adds enough suspense to keep you guessing right up to the very last page.

Knock Knock Who's There? (ISBN 1 84232 111 0)

Johnny Bianda is a man with a dream. He wants to own a boat off the coast of Florida and he only needs $186,000 to buy it. He steals the money from his firm, knowing that one day they'll notice and one day they'll kill him for it – after all, it is the Mafia. But for Johnny Bianda, the risk is worth taking and he knows it will be at least a year before they catch up with him... Unfortunately for Bianda, the knock on his door comes sooner than he thinks.

Like a Hole in the Head (ISBN 1 84232 112 9)

Ex-army musketry trainer, Jay Benson and his wife Lucy's dream of running a shooting school turns sour as the school heads towards certain closure. They need money – quickly, and a lot of it. At the eleventh hour Augusto Savanto, head of a vast corporation in Venezuela, walks into their lives with a proposition they can scarcely refuse – he will pay them $50,000 to turn his son into an expert marksman in nine days. Desperate for money they accept the challenge but find themselves in a deadly game of ruthless vendettas and vengeful murder.

"genuinely tense" *Observer*

Make the Corpse Walk (ISBN 1 84232 113 7)

Crazed millionaire Kester Weidmann believes money can buy everything – even life and death. So when his brother dies, Weidmann seeks the services of a voodoo expert to bring him back to life. He finds Rollo, a crooked nightclub owner who seizes the opportunity for the biggest con of the century. But Rollo had not reckoned for the involvement of Celie, his exotic mistress, and Butch, the nightclub's bouncer. And he had certainly not reckoned they would decide the Weidmann fortune was more important than his own neck...

More Deadly than the Male (ISBN 1 84232 114 5)

George Fraser is a lonely man, and a bored man. But he has exciting dreams. In his dreams, he lives in a thrilling world of gangsters, guns, fast cars and beautiful women. And of course, in his dreams, he is the toughest gangster of them all. George Fraser prefers his dream world to his real, ordinary life so he begins to boast about it, pretending that he is, in fact, a hardened and ruthless gangster. But George Fraser boasts to the wrong people and suddenly his dream world becomes all too real.

"an intelligent and harshly revealing piece of work with not a little serious penetration and power" *The Times*

My Laugh Comes Last (ISBN 1 84232 115 2)

Farrell Brannigan, President of the National Californian Bank, is an extremely successful man. So when he builds another bank in an up-and-coming town on the Pacific coast, he is given worldwide publicity, and this new bank is hailed as 'the safest bank in the world'. But Brannigan's success came at a price and he made many enemies on his way up the ladder. It seems that one of them is now set on revenge and determined to destroy both the bank and Brannigan himself.

Not My Thing (ISBN 1 84232 115 3)

Sherman Jamison is rich, very rich. He has amassed millions and now wants someone to pass them on to, the next in the family line. But he has no heir as his wife has been unable to have children. Refusing to let this stand in his way, Jamison pleads for a divorce but his wife, a devout Catholic, refuses to give into his demands. If she will not agree, she will have to be removed. Jamison hires a professional killer to do the deed but this is only the beginning of a thrilling and electrifying story of revenge, betrayal and murder.

So What Happens to Me? (ISBN 1 84232 116 1)
Hijacking aircraft seems to have become the latest fashion. Everyone is at it. Colonel Bernie Olson, ex-bomber pilot, decides to cash in on this latest trend and enlists the support of his ex-flight mechanic, Jack Crane, to lend a hand. Planning a simple hijack shouldn't be that difficult, but they soon discover that they didn't account for every eventuality. This is no ordinary hijack and the plot twists and turns in true Hadley Chase style until it reaches a thrilling, nail-biting conclusion.

Tell it to the Birds (ISBN 1 84232 117 X)
When a small-time clerk insures his life for $50,000 and then suddenly dies ten days later, it doesn't take a genius to work out something suspicious is going on. So when Maddox, the top man in the insurance business, finds out, he is determined to get to the bottom of it. And this means trouble for someone. In fact it means trouble for the beautiful, auburn-haired Meg Barlowe, a woman with a serious past.

The Whiff of Money (ISBN 1 84232 118 8)
Secret Agent Mark Kirkland has been given the task of locating and retrieving three pornographic films. His mission must remain top secret as the films, rather embarrassingly, feature the daughter of the future president of the United States. His quest leads him to the depths of Bavaria where he finds Soviet agent, Malik, and sidekick Lu Silk also rather interested in the whereabouts of the films. Who will find them first? And once found, who's to say they won't immediately disappear again?

You Have Yourself a Deal (ISBN 1 84232 119 6)
On a dark, sinister night, a woman is found wandering around Paris' fourth *arrondissement* suffering from amnesia. This appears at first to be a simple case of a missing person turned up – until the initials of the leading Chinese atomic scientist are found tattooed on her buttock. This is the beginning of a dramatic adventure into the world of international espionage and intrigue with a thrilling and breathtaking conclusion.

You're Dead Without Money
(ISBN 1 84232 120 X)
Joey Luck and his daughter Cindy were small-time criminals going nowhere fast… until they joined forces with Vin Pinna, a hardened criminal on the run from Miami. They begin to set their sights higher and turn their hands to kidnapping. But their hostage, ex-movie star Don Elliot, seems to have different ideas. He wants in, so they form a 'quartet in crime' and this time the stakes are higher still – eight Russian stamps worth a million dollars.

"realistic and suspenseful far above his average" *Observer*

Good books should never go out of print.
FREEMAN WILLS CROFTS
THE GROOTE PARK MURDER
The Groote Park Murder
£6.99 ISBN 1-84232-395-4
DORNFORD YATES
NE'ER DO WELL
Ne'er Do Well
£6.99 ISBN 1-84232-977-4
FREEMAN WILLS CROFTS
DEATH OF A TRAIN
Death of a Train
£6.99 ISBN 1-84232-386-5
C P SNOW
Death Under Sail
£6.99 ISBN 1-84232-420-9
HOUSE OF STRATUS
www.houseofstratus.com

ROBERT WILSON'S INSTRUMENTS OF DARKNESS

Barry Forshaw

Many people discovered the superb novels of Robert Wilson with CWA Gold Dagger Award winner *A Small Death in Lisbon,* and more than a few readers were sent to the bookshops to explore the back catalogue of this remarkable writer. Who was Robert Wilson? Actually, those who had been reading such novels as *Instruments of Darkness, Blood is Dirt, A Darkening Stain* and *The Big Killing* were fully aware that this was a writer of rich imagination and stunning narrative ability. Such commodities are relatively common these days, but Wilson has another element that distinguished him from most of his contemporaries: his Bruce Medway novels have the queasy moral sense and impeccable scene-setting of such notable predecessors as Graham Greene and Eric Ambler. HarperCollins' packaging of his earlier books gave little hint of the crime or thriller aspects of his work: in fact, festooned with quotes from The Literary Review, this first quartet appeared to be aimed fairly and squarely at the more literary end of the market. Fair enough: Wilson undoubtedly belongs there, and is more than the equal of most serious talents. But with the phenomenal success of *A Small Death in Lisbon* HarperCollins acknowledged that perhaps another approach would be apropos, and on the latter book there's no literary quote. Also it has been packaged in the smaller

format associated with crime thrillers, and bears the CWA Dagger Winner legend. With the appearance of *The Company of Strangers*, Wilson continues to confound expectations, and strenuously resists categorisation in any easy fashion. This is his most ambitious book yet, set in Lisbon in 1944 and dealing with the lethal consequences of espionage, set against an epic backdrop of Europe in the dark days of World War II.

Wilson (who now lives in Portugal) worked as a shipbroker and an advertising video producer, among other things. But it is his full-time writing, inaugurated in 1992, that has provided so much pleasure for his growing band of readers. Those coming fresh to his work are probably best advised to start with *A Small Death in Lisbon*, in which the violent death of a girl in modern Portugal brings to light the malign activities of an SS officer in wartime Lisbon. It's like all his work; a fascinating picture of a society conjured up along with the imperatives of a thriller narrative. The best advice to someone new to Wilson's work is simple: buy them all – you won't regret it.

(The new audiobook recording of A Small Death in Lisbon *is reviewed in the Audiocrime section)*

Robert Wilson on
The Company of Strangers

The Company of Strangers is a spy thriller / love story which is set primarily in Lisbon in the July of 1944, has its continuation in East Berlin of early 1971 and a denouement in England in the early 1990s. The book is dedicated to my father who died twenty years ago at the age of fifty-seven when I wasn't quite twenty-three. I'd just started to get to know him as an adult. This book is very much his book, not that his story actually appears here but he was an inspiration for the kind of story I've told.

The first time I really thought about what my father did in the war was as I was travelling with three student friends in a van on a rough road through the foothills of the Himalayas in 1978. It was dangerous terrain and we were all feeling adventurous, especially when there was a rock fall in front of us which we had to clear to be able to continue. Feeling that our mettle was being tested, it suddenly occurred to me what my father had been doing when he was twenty-one. It would have been 1943 and he would have just finished his second year as a bomber pilot. He survived the war having flown three and a half years of bombing missions over Germany and northern Italy, which, given the survival rate of bomber crews in WW2, was close to a miracle. He'd never spoken about the war until one day in the pub I asked him my first direct question about it. He told me very quickly that the main part of his job was to drop flares and a bomb load before flying around the target for some time whilst directing the other crews in. He described it as a shit job and that was the end of it. How many friends and colleagues he lost, blown out of the sky by the endless flak, didn't bear thinking about.

So this is a story that, in part, attempts to honour what his generation sacrificed for a safer world. However, there was another side to my father's life, one that was also completely unknown to me and my sister, which made him an even more extraordinary man and added another, quite different dimension, to the book. We knew that he'd been married before but it wasn't until we were much older that an aunt told us that his first wife had died in childbirth and that the infant had not survived. It's difficult to imagine what it must have been like to reach a moment in your life, which you believe will be the start of true happiness – your wife having your first child – and then to lose it all in a matter of hours. It must have burdened him terribly but it never embittered him, but rather made him very sympathetic to his fellow human beings.

So, *The Company of Strangers* grew from that primary source – what we hide from others that makes us truly human. I had also done a lot of research on Lisbon for my previous book and knew that in WW2 it was pretty well the only place in Europe where all sides could meet on neutral ground. It therefore became a city of spies. The idea of the spy culture was particularly interesting because we are all spies. We all have our secrets and we are all fascinated by the secrets of others. I also learnt from reading about the radio games played out in Resistance France in the earlier part of WW2 how fantastically illusory the secret world can be. It was a short step to put two spies from opposite sides into the cauldron of paranoia that was 1944 Lisbon and see if they could fall in love.

As I described in *A Small Death in Lisbon*, Portugal was an important economic battleground, especially for the mineral wolfram. By July 1944 the Allies had landed in Normandy and all the wolfram mines were closed. All that was left was the vital trade in industrial diamonds, used to produce the machine tools indispensable in the production of the German V1 and V2 rockets that were falling on London. There was also a great deal of talk about Hitler's secret weapon and, given the quality of the physics coming out of Germany at the time from scientists such as Heisenberg, Weizsäcker, and Hahn, it was feared that these rockets might end up carrying atomic warheads. This was the intelligence game I set rolling in *The Company of Strangers*.

Our heroine, the twenty year old Oxford University mathematician, Andrea Aspinall, is thrown in at what her spymasters assume is the shallow end but, within a matter of hours, proves to be deep and very hot water. She is left, after a savage denouement, holding a personal secret which she cannot reveal to anyone and, ironically, only then begins to understand the true nature of the spy. The first part of the book shows her entering the complicated world of adults, seeing at first hand the destructive nature of the secret world but within it finding the one truth to sus-

tain her, which is destroyed by an act of betrayal. The second part shows the resolution as gradually all, or almost all, personal secrets are revealed and confronted. The third part provides a denouement to the fundamental betrayal in book one and a coda which is designed to show that, although we glorify the importance of work and our value within its structure, it is our connectivity with our fellow humans that matters most.

And Eve Tan Gee looks at the new book...

A dedicated (but not massive) band of readers has acquired a taste for the remarkable novels of Robert Wilson, with such books as *A Darkening Stain* and *Blood is Dirt* marking him out as the heir apparent of such writers as Graham Greene. His tales of danger and betrayal in brilliantly realised foreign settings echo Greene, but add an individual strain that is entirely Wilson's own. When he won the CWA Gold Dagger Award for *A Small Death in Lisbon*, the secret was out, and he quickly acquired the literary gravitas that goes with this kind of celebrity. Following up this novel must have been a daunting prospect, but in *The Company of Strangers*, he has succeeded triumphantly. This tale of divided loyalties and a bitter war fought behind polite façades is his most ambitious and sprawling novel yet, set in the stupefying heat of Lisbon in 1944. We are vividly shown a city that echoes Bogart's Casablanca, where spies and informers make every conversation a minefield. The Germans have developed rocket technology, and are on the brink of atomic breakthrough. The allies are keen to stop the German secret weapon, and their operative is Andrea Aspinall, a young mathematician struggling to come to terms with the sophisticated world she finds herself in, living at the house of a rich Irishman who may well be a German sympathiser. Andrea (now called Anne) meets Karl Voss, a military attaché to the German legation, who is embittered and compromised by his part in the death the Reichsminister, and traumatised by the death of his beloved brother in Stalingrad. This ill-assorted couple attempts to forge a relationship in a world of treachery and death. After a terrifying climax, the novel moves to the paranoid world of Cold War Germany, and Andrea finds that she must make grim choices in a snowbound East Berlin.

Wilson tackles his epic canvas with the kind of assurance that is no surprise to his admirers, and at nearly 500 pages, this is truly a book of ambitious reach. But Wilson's speciality is, of course, characterisation, and both Andrea and Voss are painted with the utmost subtlety and intelligence. Andrea's development from naive young girl to the woman that war makes of her is very sharply handled. It must be said, though, that this may not be the best novel for those new to Wilson: after a mesmerising opening scene with Voss watching Hitler's madness infect those around him, the author undoubtedly takes his time to create his minutely detailed world, and the tautness of the early books is replaced by a more leisurely inclusiveness reminiscent of late le Carré. But those who allow themselves to fall under the author's Ancient Mariner-like spell will find this among his most rewarding and complex novels.

HOW I WROTE:

top Pros tell us how...

How I wrote *Blind Fear*

Hilary Norman

Without giving away the plot of my new novel, the idea for the particular – and peculiar – evil at the heart of *Blind Fear* came to me several years ago, during a weekend trip to Scotland. Mere weeks later, however, I picked up a newspaper and discovered that yet again life had imitated art, in that a gruesome crime, with slight, but nonetheless alarming similarities to my fictitious idea, had not only been committed, but its perpetrator had been arrested and was facing trial. For one thing, it seemed clear that people reading my story might now wrongly assume I'd 'lifted' it from this real-life case; for another, it seemed suddenly rendered too distasteful to write.

Time passed, the real case blurred into

comparative insignificance, sensibilities fell by the wayside and, the idea being a compelling one, I returned to it, built upon it, and as so often happens, the first idea became mere underpinning for something vastly different from the original – and from that real-life crime. In effect, that piece of wrongdoing was child's play compared to what goes on in *Blind Fear*. More proof, if any were needed, of my perverse imagination.

Since I seldom write about what I know, I have to research a good deal. In *Blind Fear*, one of the central characters, Jack Donovan, is a blind American sculptor (surrounded by adoring, over-protective friends and colleagues) who needs a very special new guide dog to fit into his unusual lifestyle; the other, Joanna Guthrie, is a British guide dog trainer who ventures into Donovan's world to help him out, and stumbles into sheer horror. Plot and background indicated an unusual blend on the research front: meetings with a brilliant, generous-hearted sculptor, and with the amazing humans and animals at one of Guide Dogs for the Blind's training centres. Throw into the pot a sprinkle of Taoist mythology, a dollop of basic anatomy, a touch of shamanism and photography, lashings of bizarre imagination and, above all, as always, huge quantities of hard slog, and – to continue in the cookery vernacular (or is it Blue Peter?) – here's one I made earlier.

Blind Fear is my twelfth novel, and fourth thriller. For the time being, my killers seem to be growing ever more psychotic, but full-blown thriller writing does have a liberating aspect to it. As I work on number thirteen, though, and plant the seeds of the fourteenth, I sense a shift within me, perhaps the start of a return to *slightly* gentler tales. Still suspense, of course, but more of the psychological, and a little less of the psycho, maybe... Or maybe not. These things are not to be contrived too far ahead of time. They come as they will.

Blind Fear *is published in paperback by Piatkus*

Writing *Deadline*

Campbell Armstrong

Deadline came out of a desire I had to write a novel compressed into a specific number of hours and the amount of pressure that could be borne by a central character obliged to act decisively within that period. I also wanted to write in the first person, which – in spite of its limitations – would give the narrative even more urgency. The kidnap scenario lent itself well to the terse idea I had in mind. But that had been done many times before, so I realised I needed a twist on the old ransom plot line. In fact, I needed a series of twists and surprises if I was going to inject puzzlement and mystery into the proceedings. I also wanted *Deadline* to be outside the currently fashionable category of the serial killer variety: forensic fiction, which invariably involves a cop with heavy baggage – a failed marriage, alcoholism, disrepute inside the department, whatever – and a murderer who leaves increasingly cryptic clues as to his motives. I made my central character a psychiatrist, because he's privy to dark secrets, and because he obeys a stressful code of confidentiality almost as strict as that of a priest. He's a man who carries the problems of other people around twenty-four hours a day. So how does he react when he has a seriously difficult problem of his own, one that is a matter of life and death? How does he cope when he's cut off from the props of all his book learning and his experience of therapy, and has nobody to help him? How does he survive in this kind of solitude, when his wife is in the hands of a kidnapper, and the clock is running?

Most novels of suspense are acts of fictional sleight-of-hand. You show the reader a certain situation and then you suddenly turn it around, you show them it wasn't a dove in the hat but a rabbit, you play with their expectations – and the more successfully you can do this, the more intriguing and compelling the book will be. It's a tough act, and the tricks are difficult to pull off, because most readers of suspense fiction are hardened to the hairpin turns of story lines. They're a sceptical bunch, by and large, and it's not easy to surprise them. I hope *Deadline* has a couple of unexpected turns in store.

Judith Cook

One of the panels at this year's Dead on Deansgate jamboree asked if it was ever right to put real historical characters into crime fiction, even if they only play small roles. Obviously there are differing views on this, but I'm in the position of putting a little-known sixteenth century doctor into a crime series as a sleuth, then becoming sufficiently interested in him to research and write his real biography. After spending an awful lot of time in the Bodleian (which has his case notes, jottings and diary) and King's College Library, Cambridge (for his medical books and more notes), I discovered a character who is both like and unlike his fictional counterpart.

The real Simon Forman was something of a maverick and did have countless fights with the College of Physicians over his methods of practise. He, and his friend Richard Napier, also left behind the most meticulous case notes so that we know who he treated and how. My fictional Forman accepted sex when it was offered and had a long-term mistress, but his activities pale into insignificance beside the real thing: Forman slept with his maids, his patients, his friends' wives, Bankside whores ('Julia in Seething Lane') and with a possible contender for Shakespeare's Dark Lady. Sometimes he slept with three or four in a day, and, since he wasn't writing with posterity in mind, possibly he was telling the truth. Finally, at the age of forty-seven he married a child bride of seventeen.

Sometimes real life eerily copied fiction. I started one book, *Blood on the Borders,* with two young cousins from the Borders being chased through London, one ending up dead on Forman's doorstep, only to discover that the real Forman was called out to deal with the aftermath of just such an incident, though the victims came from this side of the Borders and not from Scotland. I gave the fictional Forman a link with Cecil's secret service and found that when the College of Physicians put him in prison, it was Cecil who go him out. I made him something of a philanthropist, treating the poor whether they could pay or not. In 1592 and 1593 Forman stayed behind to treat Plague victims free when virtually all other doctors had fled for safety outside London. And the real Simon Forman was involved in a spectacular poisoning case. Has the truth made any difference? In some ways it was bound to, I suppose. Though whether or not the series continues – at least with Headline – remains to be seen. But I hope those who like the fictional Forman might also be attracted to his colourful, maddening, real-life counterpart.

Dr Simon Forman – A Most Notorious Physician *is published by Chatto and Windus*

Notes on Harvesting Ice in the More or Less Contemporary Midwest

Scott Phillips

One afternoon in the late 1980s I was killing time waiting to get my hair cut, and I stepped into a bar a few blocks from the barbershop. A young man, drunk almost to the point of losing consciousness, sat at the bar with a burning cigarette in his hand, and the barmaid was talking on the phone and pretending not to notice me. When the young man caught his hair on fire the barmaid took his smokes away but she gave him another drink. She finally acknowledged my presence, and as I stood there savouring my watery, tasteless and nearly alcohol free Miller High Life I remember thinking 'someday I can use this'. It took more than ten years, but I was finally able to use the incident as the jumping-off point for a novel I was ill-advisedly going to call *The Guano Harvest.*

I had just finished a collaborative writing-for-hire job which, since my partner and I had little or no control over our material, had proved frustrating in the extreme. Out of disgust at this process and disappointment in the final product (a low-budget movie I won't name here), I decided to write something to please myself, with no regard whatsoever for anyone else's opinion. I'd been reading lots of noir novels, ranging from James Crumley (who was and is a friend) and the great Charles Willeford, to the terrific pulps Barry Gifford had reissued at Black Lizard: Peter Rabe, Harry Whittington, Dan J. Marlowe and of course Jim Thompson, among others, and it seemed natural at that point to try my hand at writing one myself. I started with a lawyer in that bar with the pompadour-burning drunk, and I made it Christmas Eve in 1979, and before I knew it I had Charlie Arglist at the wheel of a 1980 Lincoln Continental on his way to a strip joint, drinking and driving and eventually committing a variety of other sins, venial and mortal. My original plan was to alternate chapters between Charlie's point of view and that of Roy Gelles, a hit man who's come to Wichita from Kansas City to kill Charlie and his partner, Vic. They were only to actually meet at the end of the novel, and then and only then would I decide which of the two would survive the encounter. I wrote some great stuff (I thought) for Roy, but before I was halfway through the first part of the book I realised that Roy's chapters were getting shorter and shorter as Charlie's were getting longer and longer. I found myself a lot more interested in Charlie, in who he was and how he'd got that way, than I was in Roy, and so regretfully I tossed Roy's chapters, demoting him from the book's second most important character to (without giving away too much) a mere voice coming from inside a footlocker that Charlie and Vic are threatening to drop into a lake.

In addition to having the liberty to make such radical structural changes without asking anyone's permission, I was free to make it as dark and dirty as I wanted; there was no one reading over my shoulder saying I had to take out the funny parts, or the sad ones, no one telling me I had to make Charlie likeable, no one to tell me whether he should live or die or go to El Paso, to paraphrase Chandler. And as I got further along, and the story got progressively grimmer yet somehow funnier, I found to my great surprise that I was having the best time writing I'd had in years. Charlie's evening was deteriorating with each passing chapter, but I was having a great time. When it was finished and I discovered that people liked it far more than the things I'd been writing with a keen eye on the commercial marketplace, I was amazed. I still am.

The Ice Harvest *is published by Picador*

To write or not to write?

Judith Cutler

Thus conscience doth make cowards of us all...

At three in the morning, one of the questions that keep me awake is one concerning the morality of some of the things we do as writers. I'm not concerned here with the depiction of sex and violence, and whether writing about violent crime encourages sick readers to go out and emulate crimes we've written about (though I'm sure all crime writers worry about those issues a great deal of the time). I'm concerned with the way we may implement the advice we all give to aspiring writers: *write what you know.* Are we at liberty to pillage our lives for ideas? The sad truth is, that whether I am or not, I do it.

There are certain things I'm positive I'm free to draw on: my experience of real life crime, for instance. The early Sophie novels were set in my own background as a teacher in further education. This was once an innocent if tatty grove of academe, but, under the Thatcher government, it became a seething mass of management corruption and bullying. I'm assured that things have now improved, though the efforts of a leading London college to evade their responsibilities under European employment law recently made The Times legal correspondent raise his hands in horror. *Dying by Degrees* (Headline) took me back into education, but at university level. I leave you to work out how much the plot draws on a real-life scam defrauding real-life students. As for the subplot, a glance at your newspapers will remind you that it is not unknown for people to con their illegitimate way into senior and lucrative positions – unqualified successes, you might call them. I regret that I never formally whistle-blew when I was a college lecturer – there was too much at stake, the penalties too high – but I'm glad I've had a chance to tell a wider audience that there are things in the real world against which someone should take action.

Anyone who has been burgled, robbed or assaulted is surely entitled to convey in their writing their sense of violation. I'd go further: experiencing, as I do, the long-term effects of being beaten up, I'm very careful to show that bruises and tissue damage hurt – and not just for ten minutes afterwards. How police officers manage to pick themselves up and go back into situations likely to cause them similar or worse injuries, goodness only knows. Since I've discovered just how vulnerable I am, I find I'm a coward. Those of you wishing to write to the Crime Writers' Association (I'm the Secretary) will find we have a Post Office number. This is because one morning, when my home address was in the public domain, I found on my front doormat a hand-delivered letter from a self-confessed killer asking for advice. Of course, I'm happy to help anyone, including, indeed especially ex-lifers, but it's got to be on my terms – which do not include their unheralded arrival on my territory. On a more mundane level, I avoid lonely walks, dark alleys and ill-lit car parks. After all, my assailant was a girl – what if it had been a hefty man? And, dear reader, having had my previous house done over three times (who on earth would want to nick CDs by both the Bee Gees and Yuri Bashmet?) I always set my burglar alarm. The problem is, how much fear should my protagonists feel? Sophie, as a civilian, is, I suspect, entitled to have weaknesses Kate should strive to overcome – and police services are now actively implementing treatment to prevent post-traumatic stress disorder. Furthermore, Sophie has acquired a nearest and dearest: knowing that there's someone at home worrying about her, and that truly she's poking her nose into business that is someone else's entirely, will she have the sense to leave fighting crime to Chris Groom and his colleagues? Or will she still put her life at risk?

Perhaps it was intimations of my own mortality that sent me off to make a will. My solicitor is a kind old friend, who noticed the trembling of my hand as I signed it. He sought to cheer me up by telling me the consequences of failure to consult experts. Every writer knows those embarrassing moments when a tedious interlocutor pins you against the wall with the ominous words, "I'm sure you'll want to put this in one of your novels", and you know you're going to have your socks bored off. My solicitor's narrative was the opposite: completely riveting. But to see the effect it had on me, you'll have to wait till next year…

Writing *Six Days*

Brendan DuBois

One of the most popular questions authors get is, "Where do you get your ideas?" Most authors I know are like myself, information vacuum cleaners, sucking in stories, newspaper clippings, magazine articles and other bits of information, working and reworking them as part of an odd construct, trying to make something come out that would work as a story idea. Sometimes, though, ideas come through loud and clear, which was the case of *Six Days*. A few years ago, I came across an article in the New York Times, which revealed the existence of a secret US Government agency called the National Program Office.

Simply put, the job of the National Program Office is to ensure that there is always a President of the United States. Under the US Constitution, there is a clear line of succession from the President to the Vice-President, in case the President is incapacitated or killed. In 1963, Vice-President Lyndon B. Johnson quickly took the oath of office after the assassination of President John F. Kennedy. In 1974, Vice-President Gerald Ford was sworn in following the resignation of President Richard Nixon. There are also provisions in case the President and Vice President are both killed or removed from office. The line of succession then goes from the Vice President to the Speaker of the House of Representatives, to the President Pro Tempore of the Senate, and from there to the Secretary of State through to the rest of the Cabinet.

But in the 1980's, the National Program Office took this to another step. Suppose some disaster – a nuclear or terrorist attack upon Washington, DC – removed everyone in the line of succession, from the President of the United States through to the Secretary of Veterans Affairs? There would then be no-one to assume the office of President. Based on the way the American government and military force is set up, there must always be a President, a commander-in-chief, to issue the necessary orders. Without this national command authority, nothing could legally occur from any part of the military. The National Program Office found this situation intolerable. Then, what was to be done?

Operating outside of the Constitution, the National Program Office established a top secret program to identify former government officials – such as former Secretary of Defence Harold Brown, former White House Chief of Staff Howard Baker, and former Secretary of State James Baker – to step in and serve as Acting President in case a disaster removed the entire, legitimate line of succession. In the New York Times article I mentioned earlier, what little was known about the National Program Office was written about, outlining those government officials who agreed to serve as Acting President, and also making note of top secret retreat bunkers and transportation systems to assist the Acting President in case of natural or manmade disaster. One troubling aspect of the story was that this secretive office – staffed by unelected officials – apparently operated without congressional oversight. And that's when the writer's imagination kicked in, with those two special words: what if?

What if the United States was facing an economic crisis at home, and a political crisis abroad? What if the President and Congress were seen as ineffective, tied up in scandals and partisanship? What if the people running the National Program Office didn't like the people governing the country, and the decisions they were making? And most importantly, what if the people running the National Program Office decided it was their God-given duty to take back the country, by installing an Acting President chosen only by them. One stolen Russian tactical nuclear weapon later, their plans begin to take fruition, until there were only six days left to stop the conspiracy.

Outlandish? Perhaps. But one of the least known stories about the United States during the Depression was a conspiracy by certain wealthy industrialists and veterans to overthrow President Franklin D. Roosevelt. And as I write this article, it has been more than two weeks since the November 7 presidential election in the United States, and the people of the world still don't know who the forty-third President of the United States will be. We in the United States pride ourselves on the integrity and longevity of our political institutions. But as shown by this election, by the impeachment efforts against President Clinton, and previous scandals all the way back to Watergate, sometimes the binds that keep us together in this country began to fray. Fray until there just might be a time when there really are, just *Six Days* left.

Six Days *is published by Orion*

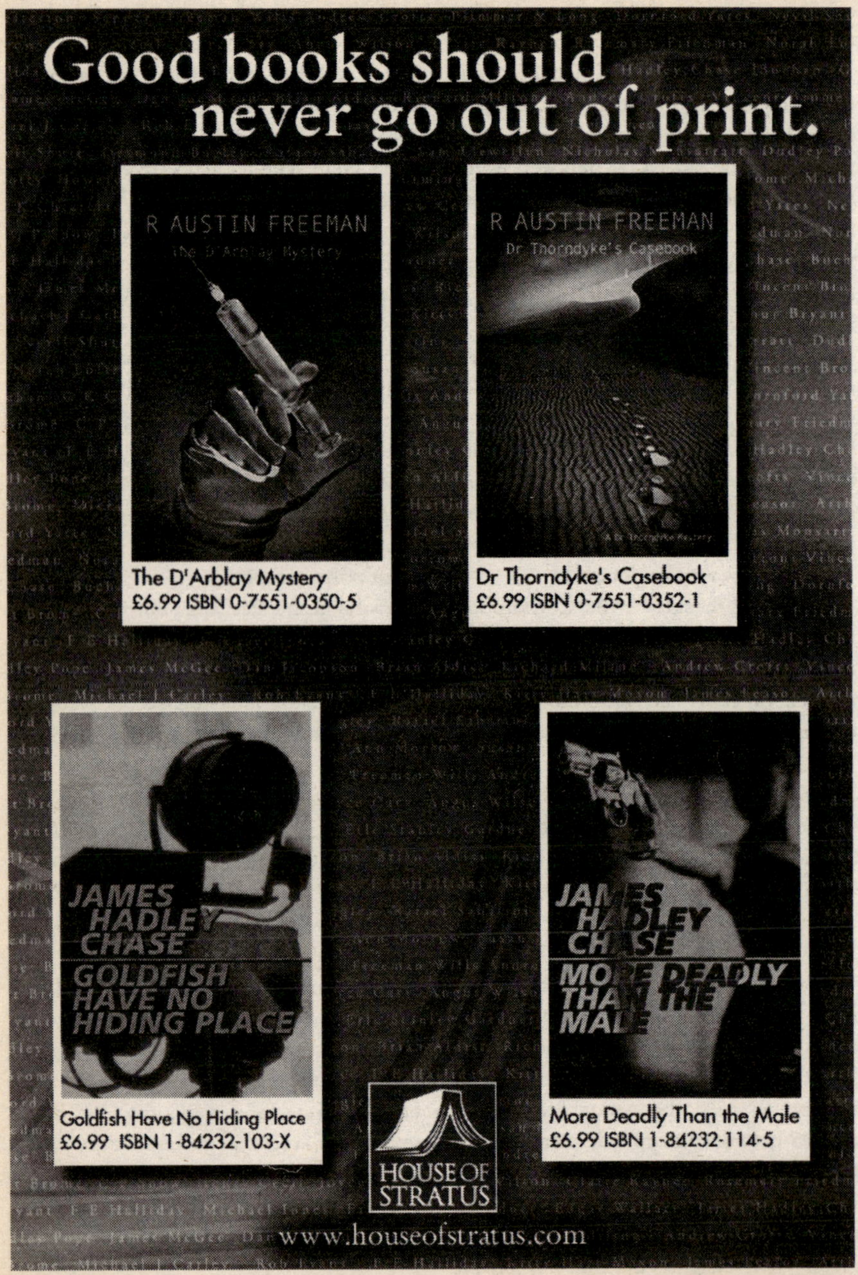
Good books should never go out of print.
R AUSTIN FREEMAN
The D'Arblay Mystery
The D'Arblay Mystery
£6.99 ISBN 0-7551-0350-5
R AUSTIN FREEMAN
Dr Thorndyke's Casebook
Dr Thorndyke's Casebook
£6.99 ISBN 0-7551-0352-1
JAMES HADLEY CHASE
GOLDFISH HAVE NO HIDING PLACE
Goldfish Have No Hiding Place
£6.99 ISBN 1-84232-103-X
JAMES HADLEY CHASE
MORE DEADLY THAN THE MALE
More Deadly Than the Male
£6.99 ISBN 1-84232-114-5
HOUSE OF STRATUS
www.houseofstratus.com

EVOCATION OF AN ERA: ED GORMAN'S SAM McCAIN TRILOGY

Barry Forshaw

Long a reciprocal favourite of CT (Gorman edits our US sister mag, Mystery Scene), we're always pleased to lay our hands on his Sam McCain mysteries – a world away from some of his grimmer material. With the appearance (from Carroll & Graf) of Wake Up Little Susie, The Day the Music Died *and* Will You Still Love Me Tomorrow, *we have some of the richest and most allusive writing in the PI genre. The careful evocation of an era (the late Fifties – check out the music-related titles) is as important as the strongly-wrought mystery elements, and the books have an effortless grip on the reader – even the reader without a special affection for the era. All three are Gorman at his caustic best, but* Wake Up Little Susie *is probably the best entrée for the Gorman tyro.*

We asked Ed why he wrote the new trilogy...

As much as I liked the Beats of the late Fifties and early Sixties – Kerouac, Ginsberg, Corso, all that 'spontaneous bop prosody' – I never felt any kinship with them or their writing. Too narcissistic. Too self-consciously hip. Too unaware of the world at large. Strange as it seemed for a teenager living in Iowa, my favourite contemporary writers of that period were the Brits known as The Angry Young Men – John Osborne, Colin Wilson, Alan Sillitoe, Kingsley Amis, John Wain, etc. – the working class writers of Britain. They were not only far better writers than their American counterparts, they had something to share with the rest of the world. My favourite novel of that period was – and remains – *Room at the Top* by John Braine. It's very Raymond Chandleresque in its prose, its structure and its attitudes about class.

I reread *Room* before I wrote my first Sam McCain, of which there are now three. My idea was to set a novel in small-town Iowa in the Fifties. In such a microcosm I'd be able to show what the era was really like – too many people, even people who lived through that time, seem to think it was like *Happy Days* – good and bad alike. I wanted a Mark Twainian semi-naif as my lead, a young lawyer who was able to love his little town despite its many

flaws – racism, sexism, and a very strong class system – a man who could be fooled sometimes but who was rarely foolish. A good-hearted man but one who could recognise evil when he saw it. I wanted a lot of comedy, a lot of social observation, and a good deal of melancholy – all of which I found every time I returned to *Room*.

The idea was to write Sam McCain's life story over a number of books. As the Fifties fade in the fourth novel, the Sixties come creeping along – not much different from the Fifties at first. But then suddenly the Free Speech movement at Berkeley, the Vietnam war, hippies, drugs, draft riots, race riots, etc.

Each book would have a broad theme – the first about the death of Buddy Holly in a plane, my having lived forty miles from the crash site when that occurred; the second about the day the Edsel car went on sale and was an utter disaster, symbolising that one period of wretched excess was drawing to a close; and the third about the effects of the Joe McCarthy hearings on small-town America, the effects being quite vicious.

The first three novels have proved to be my most successful over here. I hope they'll someday be available to my friends in the UK.

Ed Gorman Bibliography

The Sam McCain Series:

The Day the Music Died (1999)

Wake Up Little Susie (2000)

Will You Still Love Me Tomorrow? (2001)

The Jack Dwyer Series:

New, Improved Murder (1985)

Murder Straight Up (1986)

Murder in the Wings (1986)

The Autumn Dead (1987)

A Cry of Shadows (1990)

The Tobin Series:

Murder on the Aisle (1987)

Several Deaths Later (1988)

The Robert Payne Series:

Blood Moon (1994)

Hawk Moon (1995)

Harlot's Moon (1997)

Voodoo Moon (2000)

Suspense Novels:

Night Kills (1990)

The Night Remembers (1991)

Black River Falls (1996)

Thrillers:

The Marilyn Tapes (1995)

The First Lady (1995)

Runner in the Dark (1996)

Senatorial Privilege (1997)

Short Story Collections:

Prisoners (1992)

Moonchasers (1994)

Cages (1995)

Dark Whispers (1996)

Famous Blue Raincoat (1999)

The Dark Fantastic (2001)

Such a Good Girl (2001)

FIGHTING CHEEK: ELIOT PATTISON

Barry Forshaw

The acclaim for American writer Eliot Pattison's first novel, The Skull Mantra *(published by Arrow) has been loud and long, with a new voice in crime fiction being comprehensively recognised. Set against the vividly drawn landscape of a beleaguered Tibet (with the struggle of its people against Chinese oppression), the novel features veteran investigator Shan Tao Yen, released from a hard labour prison gang to investigate the mystery behind a decapitated body. Crime Time was highly impressed by the book, and caught up with the author on a recent trip to London.*

Did you have a quiet confidence that *The Skull Mantra* would glean the applause it has?

No – I was devoutly hoping it would receive some attention, but obviously it's flattering that it's been so well received.

Winning the Edgar must have been exhilarating...

Yes, although collecting that was an intimidating experience. But it was a breakthrough for me, certainly.

Did that quickly transfer itself into actual sales?

Undoubtedly. You can't ignore that as a factor when you receive awards like this.

The Tibetan setting is brilliantly realised, and you always avoid proselytising with the book, although it makes its points sharply.

Well, many people know what China has done to Tibet, and I felt that those points could be made within the context of the narrative. After all, the story is all, and I wanted to avoid any lecturing.

Presumably you also wanted to avoid accusations of adopting Tibetan chic, à la Richard Gere.

Richard Gere has some strongly held views, but there's no doubt that some people perceive his convictions as a fashion thing.

Are we right to detect a certain influence of Martin Cruz Smith: foreign cop in a strongly drawn foreign setting; oppressive government, etc.?

I make no bones about the fact that Martin Cruz Smith is a great influence on me, and *Gorky Park* was a remarkable book. If I manage to achieve anything even half as good as that, I'm happy.

One of the tricks that Umberto Eco pulled off so successfully in *The Name of the Rose* was ensuring that his medieval monk hero never appeared to have a modern sensibility. You seem to work hard to give your hero the correct mindset.

I've been to these countries many times, and I'm very familiar with the people. I knew that it was important to make this authentic – almost in fact the most important thing in the book. And I think it comes off.

Did you consider *The Skull Mantra* a thriller or a literary novel with thriller overtones?

A guarded answer, but the latter. But I'm not putting down the thriller genre!

Shan is too good a hero to use in only one book: Do you have another outing lined up for him?

Yes, the second Shan book is underway.

At the beginning of *The Skull Mantra*, he is under a sentence of hard labour. You must have another handicap lined up for him?

At the end of *The Skull Mantra*, he is a renegade, so his life isn't going to be any easier in the new book...

DEAD ON DEANSGATE

Barry Forshaw

Crime writers are a hardy breed. If the indifference of literary editors to their best efforts doesn't give them pause, the extremes of British weather and Railtrack chaos that fell on the weekend of Dead on Deansgate 2000 was received by the delegates with nary a complaint. Manchester's annual crime writing festival (organised by Waterstone's) is now a red-letter event in the crime calendar, and an impressive list of luminaries at the third festival ensured some lively moments. The cream of Britain's crime writers (along with token Americans such as the dryly self-deprecating Janet Evanovich) made sure that the various panels and (particularly) the bars at such hotels as the Renaissance were hotbeds of gossip and criminous conversation. International guest of honour was Ruth Rendell, and last year's Cartier Diamond Dagger winner Peter Lovesey was much in evidence, along with the legendary Harry Keating (beard more awe-inspiring than ever), the always unmissable Paul Johnston – and Lindsey Davis (whose Falco series set in ancient Rome was a favourite of both the writers and enthusiasts who attended). Joolz Denby (who famously fell out with fellow delegates in a discussion about class last year) lost out to American Boston Terran, who won (in absentia) the prestigious John Creasey award for his much-acclaimed *God is a Bullet* – his British editor collected the award.

Crime Writers' Association chairman Natasha Cooper demonstrated her usual skill at whipping recalcitrant authors into shape, and the various panels were lively affairs (although only thirteen delegates turned up at what was generally considered to be the best: Paul Johnston's brilliant analysis of a single Sherlock Holmes short story, *The Dancing Men*).

At the final gala dinner, guests cheerfully ignored the indifferent catering and enjoyed the wry and cutting comments from MC Robert Barnard and British guest of honour Reginald Hill. But when Hill observed that while crime scribes may rarely attain the financial clout of such writers as Lord Archer, at least they didn't have to mix with him, fellow habitué of the House of Lords Ruth Rendell looked distinctly frosty – peer of the realm solidarity, perhaps. Waterstone's David Kneale, when thanking the splendid organisation of the Deansgate staffers such as Jude Davies, avoided any reference to Robert Topping as *corpus delecti*.

Fringe events (such as the Headline party) kept delegates entertained while the elements pounded the Renaissance hotel, and Headline's Lucy Ramsey ensured that the glasses of such star scribes as Martina Cole and the always-approachable John Connolly were well filled. Cole, as ever, dispensed cool Cockney wit, while Connolly reminded delegates how he remains the least likely dispenser of extremely grisly serial killer tomes. On the final day, the various delegates faced their daunting journeys home with considerable equanimity after a diverting weekend. Little blood was spilt.

ROBBERS OF VIRTUE

Christopher Cook

•

CT's latest rave is Cook's Robbers *(No Exit Press); we spoke to him about it ...*

A famous songwriter (whose name I don't recall) once said that to live an honest life a fellow's got to break the law. A lot of books have been made off that idea. And, it occurs to me, so has many a crime. Maybe that's why I write literary noir. It goes to the heart of motive. I've always thought it odd that when a person commits a generous deed, he's assumed to have acted from virtue, whereas the criminal is presumed to have been driven by immorality, or at best amorality. That such presumptions hold strong in Judeo-Christian cultures especially interests me. After all, the rabbi who passes an unconscious, beaten man in the road justifies his behaviour by citing a moral precept, while the Samaritan proves the better man precisely by breaking the rule. So much for the law.

What we are left with is motive. A generous man in fact may be acting out of self-interest. Indeed, free-market economists base an entire social ethic on that premise: charity holds down taxes. Meanwhile, a man who steals a loaf of bread because an

entire social system is out of whack is labelled a criminal, as Victor Hugo so ably described. Given such confusion, where do we draw the line between the law and the criminal act, between the lawman and the lawbreaker? It's an honest question, and the answer is not so clear as the idolaters of law (or crime, either) would have us believe. But the lack of clarity does offer rich soil for the tilling of a good story. So why not get right to it? In my novel *Robbers*, the question of motive is established in the first two lines: Eddie didn't intend to shoot the guy, and didn't intend to rob him either. But he did. He got into an argument over a penny and committed the crime, and all that's left to see is how he pays for it. Or doesn't.

I've heard many a writer say that his or her novel began with a situation as simple as that. Mine certainly did. Unemployed, I was living in a small town in the mountains of central Mexico, paying my meagre way by shuffling money back and forth between half a dozen credit cards – a possibly criminal act in itself – when I thought of Eddie and his running buddy Ray Bob, both living on the drift, getting into a jam because they lacked the necessary funds for a packet of cigarettes. Next thing I knew, they were on the lam in a boosted Cadillac convertible. Naturally, I wanted to see where they were going. They weren't certain, nor was I. So we went together. Several months later, when I finished writing the book, we all knew. But I still wasn't sure who were the bad guys and who were the good guys. After all, life ain't simple. Neither is ethics. Maybe the most honest character in the book – and the smartest – turns out to have acted the basest. And maybe the least honest acted no better. Such circumstances drive those who categorise books nuts. Is this a mystery or a suspense novel? Is it a crime story or a police procedural? Or is it another animal altogether? Dostoevski gone off the rails, perhaps. This state of affairs, to my thinking, is why God created the handy genre called 'literary noir'.

The French first broached a philosophy we refer to as 'existential', in which any moral standards left standing after Nietzsche (however uneasily) were guillotined and neatly separated from theological authority. Any tenuous standards that are left emerge from our own frail humanity. It has been a great disappointment to many, this moral ambiguity, but not so disappointing as our inability to forge another moral authority from our own entrails. No-one could dissect this quandary as readily as Bertrand Russell, nor dismantle pretenders of a solution as quickly. But who reads philosophy nowadays, besides theologians? What is left for the average man or woman who pretends that existential questions apply only to others – who are muddled in their thinking and lack basic common sense, the only moral compass we seem to have found as of yet – is that red-headed offspring of the naughty French: literary noir. Having written *Robbers*, I was gratified to learn there was a category ready-made for it. I salute the one-eyed cyclops, Sartre, who made it possible for a character to shoot an innocent man and still seem charming. It was an honest act, and a crime.

So impressed was CT by* Robbers, *that we've trawled the US reviews...

The following pre-release review was pub-

lished in the fiction section of Publishers Weekly on October 9, 2000:

The harsh, foreboding essence of rural Texas dominates Cook's bloody, bittersweet debut novel, charting the adventures of two criminal drifters and their pursuers. The boys' aimless adventure eventually includes Della, a woman who patterns her life on women's magazines and desperately aspires to middle-class respectability. Crafty Texas Ranger, Rule Hooks, picks up their scent. Hooks, a tracker by training and instinct, relies on modern police methods as well as his gut instincts to sniff out his prey. Cook's plot tumbles from scene to scene with jarring brilliance, the pathos of his characters lending his otherwise brutal world a certain beauty. His imagery is striking, almost lyrical. This gritty crime drama is not for the faint of heart, but Cook's prose sets it a notch above many like novels. The publisher compares the book to the work of James Lee Burke; if booksellers push this comparison, or if they aim the title at a hip, youthful readership, it could make out like a bandit.

The following starred and boxed pre-release review by Bill Ott was published in Booklist on October 15, 2000:

Eddie and Ray Bob are runnin' buddies, and they run for all they're worth, through Texas and Louisiana, in this high-octane first novel. Eddie starts shooting first, but it's really sociopath Ray Bob we have to worry about. Then there's Della, a hairdresser who hitches a ride in the runnin' buddies' ragtop caddy, and naturally three's a crowd. This may sound like a cross between *Natural Born Killers* and *Will and Grace*, but, in fact, it's something very different. Cook takes the noir chase novel (there's a persistent Texas Ranger on the boys' trail) on some remarkable detours. Yes, we feel the pathos of white-trash lives gone wrong, but soon enough, we've forgotten the big picture; we're runnin', too.

The following pre-release review was published in Kirkus Reviews in its November 15, 2000 issue:

First-timer Cook, a former journalist and human-rights activist, serves up 'running buddies' Ray Bob and Eddie, who follow up their prison stint with a killing spree motivated by a need for cold beer, pocket money and an amorality so deep it must have been implanted prenatally. Their demonic swathe through most of Texas leads them to Della. Meantime, Texas Ranger Rule Hooks and his tracking dog Lucky are closing in, as is another old-time lawman, out to avenge a relative who became one of the buddies' victims. Della, whose mentors are drawn from soap operas and the sleazier talk-show hosts, is appallingly funny, while Ray Bob's behaviour makes a powerful case for capital punishment without trial. Despite some schmaltz towards the end, an impressive first effort.

The following review by Reed Holland appears in the December issue of TCP magazine:

Robbers falls within the genre of darkly comic, smart-talk thrillers of Elmore Leonard, James Ellroy and James Lee Burke. Cook, whose novel will soon be published in England, France and Japan, writes with evangelical rhythms and a sheer joy for words that can make his prose read like Faulkner's or Cormac McCarthy's: "Vast stretches of land to a horizon unbroken save for lonely trailer homes perched queerly in the stepped green-brown expanse, as if dropped from the sky as an alien afterthought." Cook, who lives in Austin, aspires to the literary noire. He finds it in the wasteland along the Houston Ship Channel that once was a leper colony, a highway on the Bolivar Peninsula broken away by the Gulf of Mexico, and a hardwood overstory so thick in Jasper County that a deluge of rain roars on the canopy, slowly dripping through, as the action takes a hair-raising turn. Make what you will of Cook's antiheroes, violence and frank carnality, but here's a Texas writer whose eye is keen, and whose voice is sure and strong.

Some more excerpted reviews for Robbers:

Texas Monthly magazine, December 2000:

Vice Grip: Cook's Recipe For Crime

In one sense this earthy first novel by Christopher Cook is a feel-good book: compared with the title character, you can't help but feel good about your own relatively decent self. In *Robbers*, two aimless outlaws, Ray Bob and Eddie, hook up and, in a sort of quien-es-mas-macho contest, set out on a killing adventure that is far too casual to be called a spree. A surly Texas Ranger lopes after them in determined pursuit, a chance encounter with a wayward beautician causes even more tension for the gunning buddies. The characters are hardly sympathetic, but Cook clearly has the suspense-building gene; his writing, fluid yet visceral, compels the reader to hang in there while the nerve-jangling plot tick-tick-ticks toward its explosive end. The author especially excels in the laconic, cuss word-laced dialogue of Western menfolk (cuss word-laced? Hell, it's filthy!) and in clever coinages all his own: For example, he dubs the West Coasters moving to Austin 'cyberokies' and the brutish, red-headed Ray Bob is a 'coppernob'. For such a writer, crime (fiction) can't help but pay.

The New York Times Book Review, December 24, 2000 (from Crime by Marilyn Stasio):

Bad boys like Ray Bob and Eddie need no introduction; they are just what they are, 'outsiders from the rural frontier: young and unemployed and broke, trawling boredom after a late greasy lunch.' Christopher Cook puts the match to these combustible 'running buddies' in *Robbers*, a debut novel with classic noir bones, when he sets them down in Austin, Texas, in a stolen Eldorado and points them to the highway. Cook covers it with fearless originality, in a lyric voice that sings itself raw.

And life imitates art...

A massive hunt for a gang of dangerous escaped convicts is intensifying in Texas four weeks after the men escaped from prison. All the law enforcement agencies, from state police to the US Marshals, are now on the trail of the fugitives. It is the biggest manhunt in Texas history and the state, which once hunted down Bonnie and Clyde, is in pursuit of even more dangerous fugitives. Several times they thought they had them cornered but each time the Texas Seven managed to slip away. The gang includes two murderers, two rapists, a kidnapper, a child abuser and a robber.

The seven men tricked their way out of a maximum security prison in southern Texas and with help from the outside they quickly disappeared. Finding them was never going to be easy and on Christmas Eve it became even more difficult when they walked into a sporting goods store in the suburb of Dallas dressed as security guards. By the time they left through the rear exit they had got away with $70,000 dollars in cash, clothing and supplies for the winter, radios capable of picking up police frequencies and yet more guns and ammunition. As they left they were intercepted by a single police officer, who died in a hail of bullets...

MORE THAN NIGHT

Michael Connelly *talks about* A Darkness More Than Night

A Darkness More Than Night (Orion) gets its title from Raymond Chandler. Once, while writing about what made his early hardboiled stories popular, he stated that it was because in these stories the "streets were alive with a darkness that was more than night." I read that a long time ago and it always stuck with me. In this book, my tenth, my plan was to make it an exploration of Harry Bosch and the costs of going into the darkness. The philosopher Friedrich Nietzsche once wrote that when you look into the abyss that the abyss looks into you. Probably no other line or thought more informs my work. By virtue of his job, Harry Bosch has spent most of his life looking into the abyss, into the darkness of the human soul. What has been the cost of that? What

did going into the darkness do to him? These questions became the basis of this book. To me this book is a study of the costs of going into the darkness. At one point a character in the book likens it to physics, saying that you can't go into the darkness without changing it and yourself. For every action there is an equal and opposite reaction.

Because all of the prior books about Harry Bosch have been constructed so that the world is seen through his eyes, my goal with this book was to change that a bit. There are many sections of the book where this is still the case. But the majority of the book is seen through another character's eyes – Terry McCaleb, who I brought back from *Blood Work*. In *Darkness* we get a view of Bosch through McCaleb's eyes. It allowed me to reveal things about him that would have been awkward in the prior Bosch books. I think it allows the reader a different view of Harry.

The other key part of the book, for me at least, was the use of the paintings of Hieronymus Bosch. Harry's real name is Hieronymus Bosch. He is named for the fifteenth century painter whose work is replete with depictions of the wages of sin. When I first created Harry Bosch and gave him the painter's name, I did it with the idea that the name was a metaphor. Bosch the painter created strange landscapes where good and bad actions are played out in chaotic scenes. Five centuries later Bosch the detective moves across a chaotic city where good and bad actions are played out before his – and therefore, the readers' – eyes. I wanted with this book to really explore this and therefore I made the paintings a pivotal part of the story.

I think that what is also explored in the book is the difference in styles between Bosch and McCaleb. Both are very good investigators. But they operate on different levels of motivation. Bosch has deep emotional conflicts from which he draws his fire. In a way, he is making up for wrongs done to him when he rights wrongs as a homicide detective. In a way, he is an avenging angel, as McCaleb himself notes in the book. But McCaleb is different. He is less instinctual and more intellectual about putting the puzzles of crimes together. He is not an avenger. I think he is someone who is motivated by common decency and a desire to see that no bad deed goes unpunished. I think putting these two different men and different views of the world and different styles together makes for interesting conflict and story.

Michael Connelly

WINNERS OF THE MACALLAN DAGGERS 2000

The Macallan Gold Dagger for Fiction
Jonathan Lethem for *Motherless Brooklyn* (Faber & Faber, £9.99)
This New York thriller is idiosyncratically narrated by Lionel Essrog, aka The Human Freakshow, a victim of Tourette's syndrome, as he doggedly unravels the reasons behind the death of his gangland protector.

The Macallan Silver Dagger for Fiction
Donna Leon for *Friends in High Places* (William Heinemann, £15.99)
The latest elegant thriller about the Venetian policeman Guido Brunetti and his attempts to negotiate the narrow path between personal intrigue and political corruption in modern day Italy.

The Macallan Gold Dagger for Non Fiction
Edward Bunker for *Mr Blue* (No Exit Press, £16.99)
A relentlessly honest life story from the ex-San Quentin inmate, written in lean, sinewy prose by the reformed con who played Mr Blue in *Reservoir Dogs*.

The Macallan Short Story Dagger
Denise Mina for *Helena and the Babies* (from *Fresh Blood* 3 edited by Mike Ripley and Maxim Jakubowski, The Do Not Press, £8)
Set in the babies room for confused and incontinents in Roseybank Nursing Home, this new slant on the country house mystery is dark but tremendously humane. Denise Mina sets the scene economically and very successfully.

The Macallan Daggers are sponsored by the Macallan, distillers of the finest single Highland malt whisky, in association with the Crime Writers' Association. The Macallan Daggers were founded by the Crime Writers' Association in 1956 and the CWA continues to manage the awards today.

Good books should never go out of print.
Erle Stanley GARDNER
The Adventures of Paul Pry
The Adventures of Paul Pry
£6.99 ISBN 1-84232-081-5
Erle Stanley GARDNER
A PERRY MASON MYSTERY
The Case of the Restless Redhead
£6.99 ISBN 1-84232-090-4
MICHAEL INNES
Appleby's Answer
£6.99 ISBN 1-84232-714-3
MICHAEL INNES
An Inspector Appleby Mystery
LAMENT FOR A MAKER
Lament for a Maker
£6.99 ISBN 1-84232-741-0
HOUSE OF STRATUS
www.houseofstratus.com

DOUGLAS E. WINTER: RATCHETTING UP THE PROSE

Mark Campbell

Douglas Winter was born in 1950 and grew up in the steel town of Granite City, Illinois. His mother encouraged him to read and write, even if it meant buying him subscriptions to Famous Monsters of Filmland. *He attended Harvard Law School, from where he graduated in 1975. His first job was with Judge William H. Webster, later director of the FBI and CIA. By the 1980s, Winter was a partner in one of the nation's leading law firms, where he specialised in air disaster cases.*

His criticism, reviews and interviews have appeared in countless US magazines and newspapers. Among his published books are the definitive biography of Stephen King, The Art of Darkness, *and the anthologies* Prime Evil *and* Revelations. *His short stories have been published with increasing regularity and have won several awards.*

Winter lives in Oakton, Virginia, a suburb of Washington DC, with his wife, Lynne, and

their three dogs. Although he's now retired as a partner of the law firm, he continues to work on a limited basis. On his days off he can be found at home hunched over a computer, writing to the accompaniment of eclectic rock music and his ever-growing collection of obscure film soundtracks.

Run feels like it was written in one go – exactly how long did it take you to write?

I wish it had been that easy! *Run* was written over several years, in the aftermath of an air disaster case that consumed my life for almost a decade. I honestly don't know how much time I spent on the book – sometimes months would pass when I couldn't write a word. And the style is deceptive. Because the story is narrated conversationally, it was difficult at times to sustain an authentic voice, straight off the street; to lure readers into the criminal mindset, urge them along on the doomed 'run' that is the focus of the novel's first half. Certainly it was a book where less words meant more work.

How did you get back into character each time?

Because I didn't have the luxury of being able to write every day, it was often difficult. But it was important to honour the first person narration, to filter every element of the novel through Burdon Lane's perspective. So I guess part of the process was learning to look at the world through his narrowed and jaundiced eyes. What helped the most was to learn the rhythm of his voice, and his idiosyncrasies of speech – for example, the way he uses proper names as adjectives, like 'this Dickie Mullen guy'. Another great help was to write in a run-on style, which produced lengthy rants that I would later edit dramatically – but which carried me over into his voice.

The subject matter is harrowing – did you find yourself drawn too deep into it?

I wrote *Run* in an effort to make sense of tragic violence – things like school shootings – which the media prefer to describe as 'senseless'. That's one reason for the novel's intimate style. I didn't want to distance readers. I wanted to put them right inside the story. Originally, the ending was darker and more violent; but when I finished the book, it was obvious that, in your words, I was 'in too deep', and that the novel worked more convincingly than I had hoped. Which meant, in turn, that my original vision of the ending was moot, and the finale became even better than the one I'd intended.

How important is it to you to put forward a viewpoint that may be morally repugnant?

It was essential. I wanted to tell the story from the inside out – to take readers into the criminal underworld, and into the culture of bigotry and violence that haunts America. You can't do that honestly or convincingly without offering attitudes and words that are impolite and, indeed, repugnant. And we've seen far too many novels and films that gloss over the demons, that wrestle with symbols – swastikas, for example – without ever getting to the pathology that gives the symbols their power. My narrator, Burdon

Lane, tells you from the outset that he's not the good guy; but readers soon realise that Burdon's world is one of bad guys and worse guys; that an either/or mentality – good or bad, black or white, criminal or cop – is not only superficial but dangerous. And that there is no redemption without damnation.

Was it difficult getting it published?

No. While I knew that publishers who liked bland, safe, so-called 'commercial' prose might balk at the style and the subject, other publishers wanted *Run*, and intensely so, because it took risks and tried to be different. The response was very gratifying. I knew the risks when I started the book, but I wanted to write a novel that was mine, a novel sufficiently unique that, whether you closed it after page one or the final page, you knew it was written by Douglas Winter. At the same time, I knew I was working within a great tradition, and I hoped that publishers would see *Run* as an extension of that tradition. I wanted, among other things, to take noir sensibilities and wrench them out of the forties and fifties and into the next century, and, at the same time, to ratchet up the prose, to make this book true to its title – something that moved with a speed that would leave readers breathless.

You cite cinema as an influence on some of the shoot-outs, but doesn't this glamorise the violence?

Cinema does glamorise violence; but glamour is the essence of cinema, at least in Hollywood, which has managed to glamorise everything from the Holocaust to HIV. The cinematic influence on *Run* was contrary: I wanted to depict the gunplay and its aftermath in a realistic and decidedly non-glamorous style, although I admit there are moments where I try to evoke the strange, seductive beauty of guns. But otherwise, especially in the two major shoot-outs, the gunplay is dense and chaotic, with the fog and confusion of combat – an inversion of the choreographed and romanticised 'bullet ballet' seen in the films of Sam Peckinpah and John Woo.

Was it a 'healthy' diversion from the incisiveness and logic of your law job?

Yes, it was a wonderful diversion from legal writing, which requires orderly, grammatical structures and polite lan-

guage, even at the worst of moments. One of my favourite reviews told readers not to fret because I was a lawyer: that *Run* wasn't a 'lawyer novel' but read like it had been written inside a prison cell!

What other sort of feedback have you had?

Well, when I finished *Run*, my wife and I agreed that we would only care about whether the book was published. Anything else – whether it sold for $5,000 or $5 million, whether it was panned or praised – would be meaningless, because the point was to see my first novel, written on my own terms, in print. But the response has been terrific. From publishers in New York, and then around the world, to reviewers and readers. Being published by Knopf is the dream of any writer in the States, and being published by Canongate in the UK is another delight, since I'm a great fan of their Payback series and now their new crime series.

Tell me a bit about your *Prime Evil* anthology.

Prime Evil was meant to offer readers a collection of original stories by the best (and bestselling) writers of horror and suspense fiction at the close of the 1980s, and to champion my argument that horror is not a genre but an emotion. The anthology was based on good writing, and featured writers whose voices are genuine and idiosyncratic. It included fine work from 'name' writers like Stephen King, Peter Straub and Clive Barker, but it also helped bring lesser-known talents like Thomas Ligotti and Jack Cady to the public eye. And it's stayed in print for more than twelve years now, which is very gratifying.

Influences – who are your literary heroes?

It's difficult to offer anything approaching a definitive answer. Joseph Conrad, and particularly *Heart of Darkness*, is immensely important – it is, for me, the finest horror novel ever written. In the realm of crime fiction, I have a definite fondness for Raymond Chandler and the more desolate writers of noir: David Goodis and Jim Thompson, certainly; the early novels of George V. Higgins; the darker works of Elmore Leonard. Among more contemporary crime and thriller writers, Michael Connelly and George P. Pellecanos and, of course, Thomas Harris; I think *Red Dragon* is a masterpiece. Peter Straub and Stephen King. Clive Barker (for his ambition), Robert F. Stone, if only for *Dog Soldiers*. James Herbert and David Morrell, whose early novels, in particular, taught me so much about momentum. And then – to underscore my eclecticism – some less obvious names: Alain Robbe-Grillet, J. G. Ballard, the fantasist E. R. Eddison, and the bitter black comedies of Harry Crews and Thomas McGuane.

What's your ultimate goal in *Run* – to entertain, or to challenge?

To me, these goals aren't mutually exclusive. I write to entertain, but I don't like 'mindless' entertainment. I want to challenge readers, to give them something that works on multiple levels – to have, in a sense, stories inside of stories. To entertain and, hopefully, edify. Films and television seem increasingly superficial – for the most part, what you see is what you get. But in fiction you can work so effectively on multiple levels, giving readers things to thrill them, like murder and mayhem, at the same time that you're giving them things to think about. Myth and meaning.

Do you enjoy publicity work?

Well, I guess in a perfect world, *Run* would speak for itself. But with competition from everything from video games to the internet, you really need to distinguish your work and find ways to communicate your ideas to an audience. And a first novel presents a unique difficulty in the marketplace, since no one – bookstores, reviewers or readers – knows who you are, or why your book ought to be read rather than one by, say, the tried and true folks who have published ten novels. So publicity work seems inevitable; it can be stressful, but it's also a lot of fun. Writers work for a long time in the shadows, then emerge every year or two, or ten, with a new book. The isolation is nice, but I like interacting with others, particularly on subjects that are dear to me. That is an added benefit of doing interviews or speaking about the book.

Your role on the Book Critics Circle must mean you see an awful lot of books – what's the state of fiction in the US like at the moment?

I think it's very good. The nineties were a difficult time for publishing in America, with so many houses consolidated or dissolved through mergers and the advent of competition from electronic media and the Internet. There was something of a shake out, and a healthy benefit was that books published more for their type than for their merit lost favour. In the aftermath, there seems to be renewed interest in original voices, and the way in which books are written. There is still too much emphasis on publishing 'safe' books – novels that seem to replicate other successful books – but there is also great interest in evolution, in championing books that push at, or indeed reject, the expected.

Novels offer an experience unlike that produced by any other media – that delightful long-term collaboration between the author and the individual reader's imagination. We may witness changes in the format of that collaboration – from paper to electronic screen, for example – but I have no doubt that fiction is thriving, and will outlive us all.

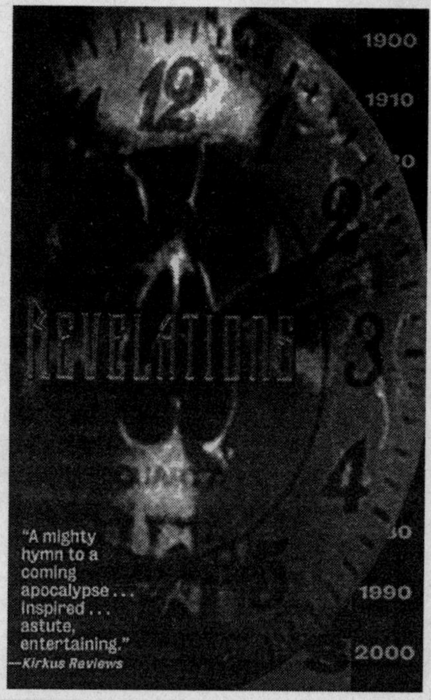

COLIN DEXTER

interviewed by **Brian Ritterspak**

The world of books had seen nothing like it before. When the closely guarded secret broke that The Remorseful Day *was to be the last novel to feature Colin Dexter's morose opera-loving detective Morse, the media went into overdrive. Such was the fame of the character (both through Dexter's brilliant and playful books and the phenomenal popularity of the John Thaw TV adaptations) that the TV cameras were beating a path to the bemused author's door. So, after delighting aficionados with such books as* The Jewel That Was Ours, The Dead of Jericho *and* Death Is Now My Neighbour, *why did Dexter put such a decisive end to the Morse saga? Crime Time set out for the dreaming spires of Oxford (Morse and Dexter's beat) to find out why.*

Were you expecting all the furore that happened when the news broke that

the *The Remorseful Day* was to be the last Morse novel?

Yes and no. When I had revealed that Morse's first name was Endeavour in the previous book, this had been treated as a serious news item in most of the media. So I certainly had an inkling that what I was going to do in the next book would create something of a fuss. But I must admit that I'd never seen so many cameras in my life – the response was phenomenal.

There was tremendous secrecy around the fate of Morse in this novel.

Well, we did try to keep it quiet. And everybody played along – we almost got away with it. Except, of course, for the *Daily Telegraph*, which I thought was very discourteous of them. I'm not a great fan of the paper anyway, but I thought it was naughty of them.

Did your publisher – or anyone else – put pressure on you to avoid this being the final book?

A little, yes. But I felt that it was a decision that had to be taken. I've never been a full-time writer anyway – I've spent most of my life in education. But I had written enough about Oxford and Morse. Look at the TV series alone: sixty-six hours about the character. My greatest fear was always that I would lose the freshness, and I thought it was time to end things before I started to repeat myself. And, anyway, I don't think many people get better as they get older, do you?

***The Remorseful Day*, surely, is one of the best Morse novels, with deeper and richer characterisation than in any previous book.**

Even so. And there's another factor: the body count among the academic population of Oxford was becoming so high...

Yes, you've made wry references before to the bloody swathe you've cut through this city.

Well, I thought it was time to make Oxford a slightly safer place, having had to provide so many corpses for Morse. I'd made the city the literary murder capital of Europe.

Your readers have always loved the relationship between the abrasive Morse and the long-suffering Lewis.

There again, I felt it was time to call a halt before it became a cliché. For example, the thing about money: Morse is so mean, and will do anything to avoid buying a round. There's Lewis on about a third of his salary having to buy nine tenths of the booze... But there are only so many times you can utilise these characteristics. And in every book, apart from mentioning Housman and The Archers – well, you have to come up with new 'tics' for the characters.

Conan Doyle certainly reused familiar ideas in the relationship between Holmes and Watson.

Yes, but they are mostly short stories. And as for moving the character on: they tell me that everybody has to die... it's not sad from Morse's point of view, is it? It's sad from the point of view of Lewis' perception. As usual, throughout the book Lewis is about six furlongs behind – and he's still behind two or three pages from the end. But he finally realises that there are things he, Lewis, cannot put right – things involving Morse. And this is sad, denying him a sense of closure.

You seem to have a healthy sense of the unlikely in your books – do you think that readers are not prepared to suspend disbelief about, for instance, the number of capital crimes that take place in Oxford?

I suppose they are, but it was beginning to worry me, and that sense of verisimilitude is crucially important, surely.

Chandler famously remarked that Philip Marlowe was essentially an impossible figure: if he'd trodden on as many toes as he did throughout the books, he would certainly have been summarily killed. But don't readers ignore such inconvenient realities?

Well, I'm a great Chandler fan, and I similarly am concerned with such things. And although I admire Chandler more than any other crime writer, I did think he made a great mistake in marrying Marlowe off. What book was it in?

***Playback* or *Poodle Springs* – the unfinished one.**

Yes, *Playback*. You lose the dynamic that comes from all the familiar characteristics: Marlowe alone in his office taking a slug from the bottle in the filing cabinet, all that sort of thing. There is only so much you can do with a character before you retire him – or, at least it would be advisable to retire him. Hence Morse...

To get back to the relationship between Lewis and Morse: you've admitted that you allowed the character of Lewis to change from a Welshman to that of a Geordie, reflecting Kevin Whately's TV portrayal...

Yes, I did do that. But Whately is a remarkable actor. He's reading the audio book version of *The Remorseful Day*, did you know that?

Have you heard that yet? Do you listen to the audiotape versions of your books?
I must admit that I haven't had a chance to hear it yet, but I know that Kevin will do an exemplary job – although it's a little strange having an actor so completely identified with a particular character assuming the authorial voice. I know that more and more people are listening to audio books in their cars these days – it's definitely a growth industry.

How do you feel about British writers such as Dorothy L. Sayers? You share with her a love of language and word play...
My feelings about Sayers are this side of idolatry, but I admire her principally as a scholar. Books such as *The Nine Tailors* are wonderfully inventive (although it's highly improbable – the solution to the murder simply didn't hold water), but I do have problems with Wimsey these days.

P. D. James is sometimes criticised for making Adam Dalgleish such a lover of poetry – people point out that it's a highly unusual police inspector who has such rarefied tastes. But nobody seems to be worried about Morse and his love of Wagner and Schubert...
Perhaps it's because I also stress Morse's love of beer – now that's plausible in a copper, isn't it? And Morse is a very different character from Dalgleish.

When you talk about Morse and your books in public, you're often noticeably wry – which often seems to take audiences aback a little. Have you noticed that your readers take your books more seriously than you do?
To some degree – although that's not to say I don't take them seriously. But I am creating this character and this universe (or, more precisely, recreating Oxford and trying to do justice to a beautiful city), and readers sometimes have a tendency to start to believe the truth of what they're reading. As the author, you know it's all a fabrication.

Is there a separate audience for the literary Morse and the TV Morse, or have you found that they are usually the same?
From the letters I receive, I know that most people read the books, but I have had letters from people who admit to being familiar only with John Thaw's TV incarnation. It's a good thing, I suppose, that he's so good at it.

Now that you've written the last Morse novel, is it possible to have a perspective on the series? Do you have a favourite?
Do you mean a favourite, or what I consider to be the best book?

Both.
Actually, I know what my most underrated book is: it's *The Secret of Annexe 3*, which, in all modesty, has some of my best plotting. And then, of course, *The Jewel That Was Ours*.

I know a lot of Dexter aficionados are very fond of *The Dead of Jericho*...
Are they? Well, I'm always happy when Dexter aficionados are happy.

WRITING FOR THE MAVERICK READER: ALAN FURST

Woody Haut

Alan Furst's novels, of which Kingdom of Shadows *is his sixth (his other novels, all published by Orion, include* Night Soldiers, Dark Star, The Polish Officer, The World At Night *and* Red Gold*), are a literary version of black and white spy films from the 1940s. Filled with intrigue and shadows, they take place on trains and in various cafes of Europe- particularly Eastern Europe and Paris- and cover the period between 1933 and 1944. Born and raised in Manhattan, and of Jewish descent, Furst has lived for long periods in Paris, but now lives in Long Island, New York.*

You must do a lot of research for these books?

Quite a bit. Which is, of course, the most addictive thing in the world. You would love to do nothing but research. Why? Because you're reading extraordinary and fascinating accounts by people who were in an important place at an important moment, they think. Frankly, my period, 1933-1944 is endless. No one will ever tell all the stories, or even know all the stories from that period, because it was such an immense kind of thing.

Have you travelled a lot to Eastern Europe? Because your descriptions are extraordinarily vivid.

Just Russia. Then I was in pretty much all, or a lot, of the Balkans on a Russian river cruiser on behalf of *Esquire* when I was writing journalism. But even though I haven't travelled extensively, I know what those places look like. If you're going to ask me how I know, I'm not really going to be able to answer you. I have some kind of understanding of things that isn't necessarily empirical. But if it isn't that, I don't know what it is – I'm a very secular person. I don't say that it's received wisdom or anything like that. On the other hand, I know what European rivers look like. I know what European villages look like. I know what they look like in the Balkans as opposed to what they look like in Austria.

Your books are very cinematic. I was wondering if you were influenced by various 1940s black and white spy films?

Influenced by that. Influenced by the music. Influenced by the cultural sense of the moment that existed in that period. And that I understand very well indeed. I really can project myself into thinking like a Frenchman in 1940, hoping the axe wasn't going to fall. Then, after it did, hoping it wasn't going to be too bad. I also like black and white photographs from the period. I have a small archive. Being a historical novelist, I'm writing about near history. There are plenty of people around who fought in that war. So it's with us still, but just barely.

After I finished *Kingdom of Shadows*, I read Joseph Roth's *The Hotel Savoy*, which figures heavily in the book.

I'm very influenced by Roth. He's a wonderful novelist. That's why I did the funeral scene in *Kingdom of Shadows.* It's dedicated to him. His story is so strange. He started out in a ghetto in Galicia, and in the middle of his life decided to become a Catholic, a monarchist and a partisan of the Hapsburgs. This is a man who went from one end of the spectrum to the other, who fought on the Eastern Front as part of the Austrian army, along with Oscar Kokoschka and Ludwig Wittgenstein.

What about spy novelists like Le Carré and Graham Greene?

Absolutely. But as I tell everyone, those aren't the only ones. There are also people like Derek Marlowe, who wrote a wonderful book called *The Dandy In Aspic.* That's a terrific book. I don't think he wrote any other spy novels. I don't read that much contemporary fiction. I'm basically reading and doing research in the thirties and forties. That doesn't leave me time to work on the bestseller list.

I read Eric Ambler for the first time in a number of years not so long ago. People don't write like that any more.

In fact, the first paragraph of *Kingdom of Shadows* is a direct citation of Eric Ambler. It's nothing but that. It is Eric Ambler. I wrote an Eric Ambler paragraph to begin that book. And I meant for people, if they knew who Eric Ambler was, to look at it and read it in exactly that way.

Your books aren't really leftwing, though they've obviously been influenced by leftwing writing.

I'm a humanist. I think in a way that's what most writers are. But in those days one could be a communist writer. Like Malraux. Or Victor Serge, who certainly writes Trotskyist novels. Wonderful books. And Koestler, who is an anti-communist writer, but a former communist. Communism is a crucial element, because it was the idealism of the 1930s. If you wonder about that, take a look at photographs of the aristocracy of that period, and you see some very obnoxious people. In doing the research for *Kingdom of Shadows*, I came on a prescription for slapping peasants, and exactly how you were supposed to do that. The writer said you should slap them on the neck. I don't even remember why. It was bizarre that one human would slap another human, or would have the right to do so. He went on to say that the hard part is when it's an old man, because they start crying before you hit them. But they're crying from humiliation, not from pain. You read that stuff, and you go, well, I really wonder why people join the communist party.

One thing I like about *Kingdom of Shadows* is that you don't know exactly what's going on until quite a bit into the book.

You're not really supposed to know. I want you in the dark. Just like the character's in the dark. He doesn't know what's going on. He wonders what's going on. He also decides that he won't think about it too much. Because this is what his uncle tells him. He says, "Myself, I choose not to think about it." People are saying that, as we're sitting here, about a variety of things in the world. That's their privilege, though they may regret it later.

How much are your characters based on real people?

None of my characters are meant to be representations of real people. But the fact of the matter is, in *Dark Star* the lead character is a Russified Polish Jew who is a foreign correspondent for *Pravda*. So are we talking about Ilya Ahrenberg? Not really. But he's *like* that. Obviously there were Hungarians like Count Polanyi and Nicholas Morath. I don't know their names, but I'm sure they existed. And though you never see Stalin or Churchill in my novels, they're there, in the newsreels and newspapers.

What are you writing now?

I'm working on a book about Odessa. And thinking about Issac Babel, who is a writer that I really like. He had a very interesting life, though it didn't last all that long. Odessa was a place of Palladian balustrades and chicken markets. Home of Jewish gangsters, and substantial Greek, Italian and Polish populations. A city of intrigue, which it still is today. Babel was arrested and taken away in 1938 and apparently killed in 1939. Though my Babel-like character won't be executed. He might even know Babel. He will maybe think he could write as well as Babel does, given certain circumstances. But I want to write about fictional characters. I don't like being constrained by the lives of non-fictional characters. I think it'll be interesting. But, you know, when you start out, you start out going here and you think you're going there, and, in fact, you end up going some place completely different.

And Another View...

ALAN FURST

interviewed by ***Brian Ritterspak***

With Kingdom of Shadows, *the American writer Alan Furst has finally achieved the kind of recognition he has so long deserved as one of the most gifted and intelligent writers practising today. Furst, who has enjoyed favourable comparisons with Robert Harris, Graham Greene and John Le Carré, writes immensely rich and detailed novels that function as both serious literary pieces and (reluctant though the author is to admit it) utterly compelling thrillers. Books such as* The World at Night *and* Red Gold *had already created considerable word-of-mouth acclaim, but his move to a new publisher, Orion, has produced a book that he considers his very best work – and it's hard to disagree with him.* Crime Time *caught up with him on the fifteenth floor of his hotel near the BBC and talked to the confident but unassuming Furst as he gazed out at a breathtaking panorama of London.*

Looking out at London like this, do you still feel more European than American, as you've described yourself in the past?

Oh, I'm a European. My family's time in America has been brief compared to their European legacy.

And many of the writers who inspired you – Greene, Conrad, Eric Ambler – were European.

One of the reasons I started writing was to produce the kind of books that these writers were famous for: Greene's *This Gun for Hire* (which I believe is *A Gun for Sale* in the UK), Ambler's *The Mask of Demetrios*. These were beautifully written, stunningly plotted – and I knew many people like me still wanted to read this kind of fiction. But so much indifferent writing was clogging the bestseller lists, and I wasn't sure that there were enough people around who wanted something better. But I hoped that I'd be able to produce something approaching that kind of quality – and that readers might be hungry for it.

You have certainly acquired a reputation as a writer who principally appeals to readers who want something a touch more challenging.

Well, fiction that entertains can be challenging: have you tried reading Dorothy Sayer's *The Nine Tailors* recently? That's a tough book! But she knew that her readers would want this – there was no Danielle Steel crowd then. And I'm glad that the appetite for something more substantial seems to be out there.

Yes, writers like Greene and Ambler

were able to make telling political points within the context of the thriller.

Absolutely. But there are so many writers who could invest the form with much more than conventional excitement: Derek Malcolm's *A Dandy in Aspic* is another favourite of mine. Speaking to my publishers, we all loved these books…

But you move in a bookish circle, and such people are more likely to want to read more substantial work, surely?

No, there are far more people out there making these demands. There is always a counter-current: readers who regard themselves as maverick. Although we might look in despair at many of the books that people buy these days, there is always an appetite for something better. And I don't just mean older readers: I've had young people tell me how much more they enjoyed *Kingdom of Shadows* than the more formulaic thrillers they'd read.

Well, that book has every sign of enjoying even more success than your earlier books. But did you always have a strategy of slowing accruing a reputation, and avoiding easy crowd-pleasing tactics in favour of something far more powerful?

I always tell people that the only way you can achieve something is to work at the absolute top of your ability. That's what people like Sidney Sheldon and Jacqueline Suzanne did in their fields – really! – and it's true for me too.

So you're writing at the very limits of your ability now?

I'm hanging by my fingertips, and desperately trying not to fall off. It's the only way I can work. So there was no strategy in the way the books were written or published. Although I suppose that the reason I feel that the new book is my best is because it took me five books to perfect exactly what I was trying to do. This was the book I always wanted to write.

Rather lucky for your new publishers, Orion, that you made the move with this book!

Well, Malcolm Edwards at Orion was closely involved this. And, of course, there was a definite impetus with a new publisher to launch yourself with something really special.

So when you were writing *Kingdom of Shadows* were you saying to yourself "Something is happening here that hasn't happened before"?

Yes. I determined to change certain things, and cast off certain constraints.

Such as?
It's commonplace in a novel to have eight characters, and at the end of the book, you know what happened to all of them. I made sure that this slightly artificial convention didn't apply to *Kingdom of Shadows*. Plus, I tried to initiate something that felt very weird to me: why couldn't I write a book in which the hero is in ignorance about certain issues, and remains in ignorance even at the end. Just like the rest of us! In life, things are not packaged that neatly.

But that's taking away one of the comforting pleasures of books: the sense of order being wrought from chaos...
Well, the important things are sorted out in the book – I couldn't ignore that imperative. But I also thought that if you were a man like my protagonist Polanyi who operates in a shadowy world, why would you tell your nephew anything? Polanyi's nephew Nicholas Morath, who undertakes this dangerous work for him, is never in full possession of the facts.

The reader always senses that change of gears in bad writing, when the paragraph of explanation kicks in.
That's right.

In books like this one, and *The Polish Officer*, your characters inhabit a world of queasy values in which there are no moral certainties. They are always caught in a kind of shifting morass...
I think I feel that is the way life is. You view things from a certain angle, and then you discover that viewpoint simply isn't valid any more. The paradigm for United States history used to go: Abraham Lincoln fought the Civil War to free the slaves. Then, it was: Abraham Lincoln fought the Civil War so that the North, which was industrial, would be triumphal over the agrarian South. Then, no: on the third level, he fought the war to free the slaves. That paradigm works for fiction, and it works for everything else.

Although you don't principally identify yourself as a thriller writer, you've just encapsulated the tension that underlines all your books: the reader is cast adrift in this uncertain universe.
But closure is possible, both in fiction and the real world. When the right thing is finally done (as witness Albania, as witness Bosnia) we all breathe a collective sigh.

But even there, in many such cases, the rug is pulled from under our feet again very quickly. The Middle East, Northern Ireland...
That's exactly right. But all I'm doing is trying to suggest that the world is redefined on a daily basis. And it always was, even in the periods I cover: Hungary in the Second World War in the new book for instance.

In your earlier books, was there ever any pressure to streamline you, to make you a more conventional writer following all the standard bestseller shibboleths?
No. I've been really lucky in that regard: my editors have always seen what I've been trying to do and have supported me. And as long as I can deliver the goods, I hope that will continue to be the case.

THE CRIME TIME ONLINE COMPETITION

Why not test your wits against fellow Crime Time *readers and add to your crime fiction library? All you have to do is e-mail your answer (along with your address) to editor@crimetime.co.uk – and if you're one of our twelve lucky winners, we'll arrange for you to be sent the goodies below.*
This is an e-mail competition – but if you're one of our readers who aren't yet online, you must know somebody who is – so don't let that stop you!

TWO BY NADEL

Barbara Nadel (according to her publisher) is either the "Donna Leon or the Michael Dibdin of Istanbul" – but we feel that she doesn't need to be "belied with false compare" – Nadel is quite one of the freshest talents around.

To win her first two books (*Belshazzar's Feast* and *A Chemical Prison),* simply answer the following questions:

Which novel is Barbara Nadel's debut thriller?

Now's your chance to meet the canny Inspector Ikmen…

APPLEBY AT ALLINGTON

Michael Innes

However it may have been with Owain Allington, Appleby had seen too many dead men in unexpected places and mysterious circumstances to be particularly staggered upon the present occasion. He even detected himself as reflecting that, had he been sufficiently strong-minded to decline this poking around the scene of the son et lumière, he would not have got himself thus tiresomely involved with whatever unfortunate thing had happened.

He also found time to be thankful – and rather brutally to tell Allington that he should be similarly thankful – that he wasn't dead himself. For what had taken place was presently fairly clear. This ridiculous elevated box, with its mass of electrical equipment, had been casually left by the persons responsible for it in a highly dangerous state. Or – for it would be necessary to be very fair in the matter – in a state that was decidedly far from fool-proof. And this chap had climbed in and got himself electrocuted.

It could hardly be anybody's excuse that he was trespassing, and that nothing of the kind was to have been expected. The son et lumière at Allington Park must have been the talk of a dozen surrounding villages, and curiosity about this structure was as natural as if it had been a tripod arrived from Mars. Appleby's brow darkened as he reflected that half a dozen venturesome children might have gone scrambling up that ladder in the dark.

Allington had found a master-switch, and the place was now safe enough. But, for the moment, this seemed to represent the limit of his nervous resources. He was badly shaken – which wasn't, Appleby reflected, surprising in the least. Here were the two of them, in darkness except for an unimpressive electric torch, perched at the top of a ladder with a totally unexplained and unexpected corpse.

'A tramp,' Allington said. 'He must have decided to find shelter here for the night.'

'Perhaps so.' Appleby made a further, and necessarily imperfect, examination of the dead man. He looked about twenty-five, and he had ginger hair. He certainly bore no appearance of belonging to the higher classes of society. 'It's a pity that even the lights on your terrace are out. I suppose they're the only part of the electrical equipment over there still to be tied up with all this?'

'Oh, certainly. I had most of that part of the damned nonsense cleared up this morning.' Allington no longer seemed particularly proud of his son et lumière.

'It can't be helped. You'd better get back to the house, and leave me here. Take your torch. Call the police. And call your own doctor, as well. He won't thank you, but he'll no doubt turn out promptly for the squire. When this sort of thing happens, it's sometimes useful to have an additional observer around. And it might be useful with the insurance people.'

'The insurance people?'

'Certainly. You were talking about them. Whoever this chap is, and however unauthorized his entry here, anybody who depended upon him would have a bit of a case against someone.' Appleby spoke dryly. 'It may sound callous, but one has to have a thought to these small practical matters. And rouse your servants, and have them bring over rugs and hot-water bottles as quick as they can.'

'But surely – '

'The man's dead, all right, but we're not doctors. It's prudent to take every practical measure. You'll sound less of a fool at the inquest.' Appleby checked this note of irritation, since it was something not very decent to express. 'I'm afraid you're a bit shaken, Allington, and I'm sorry to sound brusque. But the sooner we have the proper measures under way – well, the sooner we can relax a little.'

'I'll go at once.' But Allington was still irresolute. 'I wish Martin really had turned up this evening. I rather expected him, as I think I told you. He'd be a support.'

'You're going to have plenty of support tomorrow – and a church fête as well. Meanwhile, I'll do what I can myself.'

'My dear chap, you're very kind. And I'm sorry that the place has produced so shocking an end to your dining with me. I feel it almost as a breach of hospitality.'

Judging this proposition to be decidedly overstrained, Appleby made no reply to it. He watched Owain Allington climb down the ladder and begin to cross the strip of park in front of the invisible house. Then he turned back to keep his vigil by the dead man. The son et lumière at Allington had certainly had an unfortunate close. But in about half an hour, he told himself, it would cease to be his affair. No doubt he would be required to give evidence before the coroner. But that, after all, was something he had done before.

Meanwhile, inactivity was his role. He had satisfied himself that the man in the corner was dead, and further than that he had better not go. There must be an investigation, no doubt, although there didn't really seem to be all that to investigate. But it wasn't for a retired Police Commissioner to start poking around. If he did so, the local people would be entirely respectful. They would feel mildly outraged, all the same.

But inactivity wasn't natural to him. He moved over to one of the glass panels shutting him off from the night, and found that it was designed to slide back in a groove. There would be no harm in letting in a little more air. He did so, and was presently leaning out into the darkness. Being thus less immediately in the presence of death, he decided it wouldn't be too strikingly improper to light a cigarette. For a moment the brief flare of the match blinded him. Then he realized that the summer night into which he was gazing was no longer all but impenetrably dark. For a moment he thought that the dawn was breaking, and then he saw that he was witnessing one of those odd meteorological occasions, disconcerting to nocturnally-behaving persons, in which the moon heaves itself into the sky not all that far ahead of the sun. It was a very faint moonlight that was seeping with a slow stealth into the park.

It was with a sense that time had been behaving in some obscurely curious fashion that night that he now glanced at the illuminated dial of his watch. There would certainly be little of the night left by the time he got to bed. Meanwhile, there was this mild lunar manifestation. It would be soothing, even perhaps poetic in suggestion to anyone less gruesomely circumstanced than he himself happened to be. Even so, he watched with satisfaction great trees beginning to define themselves – beginning even, or so he fancied, to cast a ghost of shadow on the grass. He remembered the story about King Charles' treasure being buried under one of them. He was very far from believing in it, and it was his impression that Owain Allington was very far from believing in it too. But there had apparently been people taking it seriously – even to the point of doing a little quiet trespassing and prospecting at an hour very much like this. It suddenly occurred to Appleby that the dead man might have been one of them.

He turned back irresolutely towards the body, almost as if prompted to seek verification of this suspicion in some way. But that was nonsense, like a notion out of a boys' adventure story – in which the dead man would prove to have an ancient map in his pocket, with the hiding-place marked with a cross in rusty red.

Appleby returned to the window. He could now see the glimmer of the lake, and even the white line of the long drive that skirted it. Low on a near horizon, a beam of light appeared, circled, vanished. That was a car or lorry on the high road. Presently the arrival of the county constabulary would be signalised in that way. And he himself would drive home in the first dawn – drive home without having interfered.

Of course, one can't help one's thoughts. Appleby found himself at least thinking about the dead man. How long had he been dead? He remembered the first feel of the body under his hand. He and Allington – he had told Allington – were not doctors. But there are some things one develops an instinct for if one has become Police Commissioner by the long, hard road of half a lifetime of criminal investigation.

No time at all, Appleby had to tell himself. The fellow had been dead no time at all.

'It sounds very odd to me,' Judith Appleby said.

'It was no business of mine,' her husband replied. 'I must get that bird out.' A thrush had got under the net guarding the raspberries, and for a couple of minutes he devoted himself to ejecting it. 'I'm not a policeman,' he then said. 'Or not any longer.'

'John, dear, whenever you meet anybody you judge to be a socially pretentious person, the first thing you announce is that you are a policeman. It's like some City gent in a Victorian novel, bellowing that he's a plain British merchant.'

'All right, all right. But stick to the point.

This rum death at Allington is not my concern. And there's another of those confounded birds. These nets are no good. They're a notion out of Noah's Ark. This winter we'll have Hoobin and his boy build cages. We'll put all the soft fruit inside cages. It's the only way. I've been thinking about it for some time.'

'Cages, by all means.' Judith clapped her hands expertly behind the second thrush. She had come home by the mid-morning train, and they were making a round of the garden. 'And perhaps you should keep bees. There's said to be a lot of intellectual interest in them. You could embody your observations and researches in what used to be called a monograph.' She lowered the net into place again. 'Of course, I can see that this affair is very old-hat.'

'What do you mean – old-hat?'

'Death at Allington Park. It sounds like the most antique sort of detective story. But, in fact, it's something that has happened to one of our neighbours. And it's unexplained.'

'It doesn't seem to be a neighbour who got himself killed. The body conveyed nothing to Owain Allington. As for its being unexplained – it's early days to say that. No doubt the police and the medical people will work it out.'

'I suppose, John, you'll have to answer questions yourself?'

'No doubt.'

'Do you know, I doubt whether you're going to strike your local colleagues as a man of much observation. How large is this gazebo-thing the show was run from?'

'Surprisingly large to be perched up on stilts like that. Perhaps twelve feet square – if my observation is any good, that is.' Appleby looked dubiously at Judith. What she was going to say wasn't exactly obscure to him.

'And you were shut up in it for quite some time, fooling around with that lumière, and quite unconscious that you were cheek by jowl with a corpse?'

'There was only a very low light. And no question of being cheek by jowl with the thing. It was crumpled in a corner, and more or less under a bench.'

'That's one of the things which don't make sense. The electrocuting was of the instantaneous sort, and not the nasty hang-on-until-charred business?'

'It was nasty enough. But you're quite right.'

'Otherwise, there would have been a kind of cook-house smell.' Judith made this revolting point dispassionately. 'So I don't see how – '

'No more do I. It was curious that the chap tumbled himself so unobtrusively into a corner.'

'It was Owain Allington who went up the ladder first?'

'Yes.'

'Into the dark?'

'Yes.' Appleby smiled at his wife. 'We're quite getting somewhere, are we not?'

'The first thing Allington did was to shove the corpse out of the way. Then he switched on this low light as Sir John Appleby – a dignified figure who is not to be hurried – lumbered majestically up the ladder.'

'Laughter in court,' Appleby said. 'The witness appeared discomfited.'

'But it still doesn't make sense. For why should he do anything of the sort?'

'Why, indeed?' Appleby looked worried – but this was because he had failed to count accurately the peaches on the old brick wall which they were now facing. 'Perhaps I haven't made it clear that my lack of observation continued to the end. I'd have left the blessed gazebo as ignorant of the corpse as I'd entered it, if Allington himself hadn't absolutely invited me to find it.'

'You mean that he said, "Look, Appleby, there's a dead body"?'

'Not precisely that. He said, "What's that bundle of stuff in the corner?" And I went over and found what I found. If he knew the body was there – and it's a perfectly fantastic notion, anyway – and wanted me to find it, he might as well have let me find it at the start, and not made a dive for it when he first entered the place, in order to shove it out of sight for a time. Isn't that obvious?'

'Not in the least. He may have felt that an extra ten or fifteen minutes would make it more certain that the chap really was dead.'

'You have the most macabre imagination of any woman I have ever known. Here is some wretched accident with a live electric cable, and you start fumbling round to find something suspicious in the behaviour of a highly respectable landed proprietor.'

'You oughtn't to expect me to do any more than fumble. I'm just an amateur. But you're a professional, and ought to be able to get straight at the truth.' Judith produced this argument with a great air of lucidity. 'It would be dreadful if poor Mr Allington did come under any sort of suspicion. So I think you owe it to – '

'Considering that you've just been cooking up a sheer rigmarole against the fellow – ' Words failed Appleby. 'I think I'll spray this one,' he said. 'I don't like the look of the leaves. I'll do it this afternoon.'

'But, John, we'll be at the fête.'

'Fête! What fête?' Appleby looked at his wife in alarm. 'I detest fêtes.'

'The fête at Allington, of course.' Judith seemed entirely surprised.

'There can't be a fête at Allington. A death yesterday, and a fête worse than death today: it just wouldn't do.' Appleby paused, but this fatigued joke raised no mirth in Judith. 'They're bound to put it off.'

'I don't think so.' Judith shook her head decisively. 'Not just for an unfortunate accident.'

'You've just been maintaining – '

'It will give you another chance to look around.'

THE AFFAIR AT LITTLE WOKEHAM

Freeman Wills Croft

Bellissa Plant had been correct when she told Christina that her husband was in some kind of trouble and that she imagined it was financial. The truth was that he did not know where to turn for money.

One evening a few weeks after the sisters' conversation and over a year after the Winningtons had moved to Hurst Lodge, Plant was seated in the deepest armchair in the study of his house on the outskirts of Weybridge, painfully taking stock of his position. Having ascertained just where he stood, his eyes were now staring before him into vacancy and his fingers trifled with the pad on which he had jotted down his figures, while he tried desperately to find some way out of the difficulties which beset him.

Guy Plant had not been intended for a business career. His father was a doctor in general practice in the country near Liverpool, and the old man's idea had been that his son should follow in his steps. He had taught the boy a good deal about medicine, particularly the routine of a country practitioner's life. But while Guy readily absorbed his teaching – as he did any information which came to him – his special aptitude for figures was not to be denied, and when the time came to make a definite choice, he decided for finance rather than medicine. Having qualified as a chartered accountant, he entered the accountant's department in the Liverpool office of the Yellow Star Line. His superiors, impressed by the young man's ability and grit, transferred him first for three years to their Marseilles office, and then to a good position at their headquarters in London. In this latter job he did excellent work for several years. As a result of the successful reorganisation of an unsatisfactory subsidiary business, he was promoted to second in command, and when his chief retired upon age-limit five years later, he succeeded him.

For a time his energies were devoted to improving the efficiency of his department, but when this had been brought to as near perfection as seemed possible and his work became largely routine, he grew tired of it and looked about for some other interest.

He found it through the conversation of a stockbroker friend with whom one day he was lunching. This man described how from following political trends he had been able to forecast first the fall and then the rise of a certain foreign government's stocks. The expected fall having taken place, he had bought to the limit of his ability. Presently the rise had followed and he had sold with a four-figure profit. If his friend had told the story in the hope of a commission he was disappointed. Plant wanted to repeat the trick himself. He was not particularly anxious to make more money; his tastes were simple and his salary ample for all his requirements. But the idea of pitting his brain against the market thrilled him. He began an intensive study of international finance.

For several weeks no trends such as his friend had observed suggested themselves; then he thought that a rise in oils and petrols was likely. He estimated the amount, sat back, and waited to see what would happen. Within the period he had forecast oils rose by very nearly the percentage he had guessed.

This disaster, for to him it was nothing less, confirmed his faith in his own ability. Now he felt satisfied that his superior intellect would enable him to foresee coming events more clearly than other men. For many more weeks he watched and studied; then he thought that a change of government in one of the South American republics, which he believed imminent, would raise the value of its stocks. He bought with every penny he could raise. The government fell, a more stable one took its place, the stocks appreciated, and Plant cleared a substantial sum. A few weeks later he tried again and scored a further success. The second and third of his disasters!

It was at this time that, already a little bored with his new hobby, Plant first began to notice his secretary, Bellissa Winnington. Up till then women had played but a small part in his life, but now, perhaps for this very reason, he fell devastatingly in love. His cautious nature would have liked to avoid matrimony, but he soon found that no progress with Bellissa was to be hoped for on other lines and presently he proposed. He was astounded and his desire was whetted when she did not immediately accept, but asked for a week to think it over.

His delight when eventually she consented was intense, and for a time he lived in a heaven such as he had not believed existed. Together they searched for a house, fixing at last on Ivy Cottage, in the southern suburbs of Weybridge. The painting and papering, the furnishing and the various other preparations, passed as an entrancing dream. Then came the wedding and the honeymoon in Italy.

It was during the honeymoon that the first pangs of doubt arose in Guy Plant's mind. Somehow being with Bellissa did not prove the joy he had expected. She was kind and pleasant, but he soon saw that this was due to her easy-going nature rather than to any particular liking for himself. Gradually he realised that he bored her, and then at long last that his presence was actually irksome to her. No longer could he hide the fact that the foundations of his happiness were laid upon sand.

While this was true, Bellissa's intentions had been of the best. She was out to make him a good wife, and had he accepted what she could give him and treated her with affection, their married life might have been successful enough. That he did not do so was his misfortune, if perhaps not altogether his fault. He found his discovery, with its revulsion of feeling, too bitter to hide. He felt cheated and grew harder and more self-centred, more sardonic, less pleasant to his subordinates and to her. He drew away from her in their home life, retiring in the evenings to his study and taking little interest in her affairs. While outwardly they remained on good terms, the possibility of real sympathy and understanding between them slowly died.

Under these circumstances it was perhaps inevitable that when the sharp edge of his disappointment had worn off he should have recourse again to his Stock Exchange operations. The excitement took his thoughts off domestic affairs. He was now less careful before he plunged, and he began to back fancies instead of considered opinions. The inevitable, of course, happened. He began to lose. His natural caution warned him to take no more risks, and for a time he did draw in his horns.

Then occurred the return of Clarence Winnington to England, the setting up of the Hurst Lodge establishment, and more important to Guy Plant, the disclosure of the fact that on Clarence's death Bellissa would, unless her uncle changed his mind, inherit the sum of twenty thousand pounds. This profoundly altered his outlook. He knew that, owing to Bellissa's easy-going character, twenty thousand left to her was twenty thousand left to him.

Somehow, with this sum in the background his Stock Exchange losses shrank in importance. Again he began to indulge in what was practically gambling, sometimes making a few pounds, but usually losing. Then in a moment of recklessness he plunged, buying a large block of Mexican shares which he could not cover, in the expectation that they would rise and that he could sell at a profit. Under normal conditions his action would probably have been justified, but unhappily a tornado wiped out the expected profits and he was faced with a ruinous loss. To meet it he had to borrow, and now he could not repay the loan. This was the disastrous fact that he was considering as on this evening, over a year after the Winningtons had moved to Hurst Lodge, he sat in his study taking stock of his position.

What an incredible fool he had been! He had meant to amuse himself, to relieve his boredom, to have a little excitement, and then to stop before he became in any way involved. Why had he not stopped? He did not know, except that the thing was more insidious than he had realised.

Irritably he pulled himself up. This kind of thinking would get him nowhere. Regrets were useless. He must have money or he would go under.

Money! The more Plant thought of it, the more the idea of his wife's legacy forced itself into his consciousness. Twenty thousand! If he had a twentieth of it his difficulties would be over.

All the same, there was no help here. Even if Clarence Winnington did not alter his will, which he might easily do, he was a hale and hearty man showing no symptom of an early decease. The fact that he was seventy-two counted for nothing: he might live another twenty years and more. But twenty thousand pounds in twenty years' time would be no use to Plant. He must have the money now. By mortgaging his house and insurance policy he could postpone the crisis for a few weeks. But it would only be a postponement. Without additional cash he was lost.

For the first time Guy Plant forced himself to consider what his failure to raise the money would mean. There was only one word for it: ruin, ruin utter and complete. It would mean personal misery and wretchedness. It would mean bankruptcy, leaving his home, giving up his possessions, losing his job and his salary. It would mean having to start life again at the age of thirty-nine, penniless and handicapped by a wife and son, and debarred from getting the sort of work he could do. He thought of himself more than of Bellissa – not, to do him justice, through mere selfishness, but because he felt Bellissa would find a home with her uncle. For himself death would be preferable: if only he had the courage to commit suicide. But had he? As shrinkingly he looked forward to the possibility, he doubted it.

No, a failure to get the thousand-odd he was in need of would be the end. He simply could not face it. No matter at what cost, be must raise the money.

It was then for the first time that a very horrible idea shot into his mind. Bellissa's legacy! Was there no way in which the existing conditions might be altered, so that he could get it at once?

When he realised what he had really thought, he felt a shock of horror. He, Guy Plant, a – Even in his mind he boggled over the word. A murderer! Never! It had been an idea only.

He tried to banish it, but it returned. If Clarence Winnington should die without altering his will, Bellissa would get twenty thousand pounds. Directly the death occurred she could, if she asked for it, get an advance on her legacy. And just such an advance would save him, would save her, would save their home and their name and their happiness. A solution of all their troubles: if Clarence Winnington were to die.

The sweat formed on Plant's brow. He must not think of such a thing. It was madness; he must retain his sanity. All the same, he would be saved: if Clarence Winnington were to die!

Relief surged back into his mind as he suddenly saw that his dreadful remedy was out of the question. Even if he wished to, he could not murder Clarence. He would be found out, inevitably and without hope of escape. There was no way in which it could be done secretly.

Again he wiped his forehead. Was there not? Suppose.

His eyes took on a look of horror as his idea took shape, developed, and grew with dreadful rapidity from a vague nebulous conception to a feasible plan, increasingly clear-cut in its details. Yes, he now believed that Clarence could be murdered and with complete safety, provided only that there was nothing to suggest the identity of the murderer, because once the police were really suspicious they pried and nosed till they got their proof. Thank heaven, in his case there was something to suggest it. Bellissa's legacy would be like a hand pointing unmistakably to himself. An attempt would mean certain conviction. He dared not risk it.

Unless he had an alibi.

THE INCREDULITY OF FATHER BROWN

G. K. Chesterton

Father Brown, at one period of his life, found it difficult to hang his hat on a hat peg without repressing a slight shudder. The origin of this idiosyncrasy was indeed a mere detail in much more complicated events; but it was perhaps the only detail that remained to him in his busy life to remind him of the whole business. Its remote origin was to be found in the facts which led Dr Boyne, the medical officer attached to the police force, to send for the priest on a particular frosty morning in December.

Dr Boyne was a big dark Irishman, one of those rather baffling Irishmen to be found all over the world, who will talk scientific scepticism, materialism and cynicism at length and at large, but who never dream of referring anything touching the ritual of religion to anything except the traditional religion of their native land. It would be hard to say whether their creed is a very superficial varnish or a very fundamental substratum; but most probably it is both, with a mass of materialism in between. Anyhow, when he thought that matters of that sort might be involved, he asked Father Brown to call, though he made no pretence of preference for that aspect of them.

"I'm not sure I want you, you know," was his greeting. "I'm not sure about anything yet. I'm hanged if I can make out whether it's a case for a doctor, or a policeman, or a priest."

"Well," said Father Brown with a smile, "as I suppose you're both a policeman and a doctor, I seem to be rather in a minority."

"I admit you're what politicians call an instructed minority," replied the doctor. "I mean I know you've had to do a little in our line as well as your own. But it's precious hard to say whether this business is in your line or ours, or merely in the line of the Commissioners in Lunacy. We've just had a message from a man living near here, in that white house on the hill, asking for protection against a murderous persecution. We've gone into the facts as far as we could, and perhaps I'd better tell you the story as it is supposed to have happened, from the beginning.

"It seems that a man named Aylmer, who was a wealthy landowner in the West Country, married rather late in life and had three sons, Philip, Stephen and Arnold. But in his bachelor days, when he thought he would have no heir, he had adopted a boy whom he thought very brilliant and promising, who went by the name of John Strake. His origin seems to be vague; they say he was a foundling; some say he was a gipsy. I think the last notion is mixed up with the fact that Aylmer in his old age dabbled in all sorts of dingy occultism, including palmistry and astrology, and his three sons say that Strake encouraged him in it. But they said a great many other things besides that. They said Strake was an amazing scoundrel, and especially an amazing liar; a genius in inventing lies on the spur of the moment and telling them so as to deceive a detective. But that might very well be a natural prejudice, in the light of what happened. Perhaps you can more or less imagine what happened. The old man left practically everything to the adopted son; and when he died the three real sons disputed the will. They said their father had been frightened into surrender and, not to put too fine a point on it, into gibbering idiocy. They said Strake had the strangest and most cunning ways of getting at him, in spite of the nurses and the family, and terrorizing him on his death bed. Anyhow, they seemed to have proved something about the dead man's mental condition, for the courts set aside the will and the sons inherited. Strake is said to have broken out in the most dreadful fashion, and sworn he would kill all three of them, one after another, and that nothing could hide them from his vengeance. It is the third or last of the brothers, Arnold Aylmer, who is asking for police protection."

"Third and last," said the priest, looking at him gravely.

"Yes," said Boyne. "The other two are dead."

There was a silence before he continued. "That is where the doubt comes in. There is no proof they were murdered, but they might possibly have been. The eldest, who took up his position as squire, was supposed to have committed suicide in his garden. The second, who went into trade as a manufacturer, was knocked on the head by the machinery in his factory; he might very well have taken a false step and fallen. But if Strake did kill them, he is certainly very cunning in his way of getting to work and getting away. On the other hand, it's more than likely that the whole thing is a mania of conspiracy founded on a coincidence. Look here, what I want is this: I want somebody of sense, who isn't an official, to go up and have a talk to this Mr Arnold Aylmer, and form an impression of him. You know what a man with a delusion is like, and how a man looks when he is telling the truth. I want you to be the advance guard, before we take the matter up."

"It seems rather odd," said Father Brown, "that you haven't had to take it up before. If there is anything in this business, it seems to have been going on for a good time. Is there any particular reason why he should send for you just now, any more than any other time?"

"That had occurred to me, as you may imagine," answered Dr Boyne. "He does give a reason, but I confess it is one of the things that make me wonder whether the whole thing isn't only the whim of some half-witted crank. He declares that all his servants have suddenly gone on strike and left him, so that he is obliged to call on the police to look after his house. And on making inquiries, I certainly do find that there has been a general exodus of servants from that house on the hill; and of course the town is full of tales, very one-sided tales I daresay. Their account of it seems to be that their employer had become quite impossible in his fidgets and fears and exactions;

that he wanted them to guard the house like sentries or sit up like night nurses in a hospital; that they could never be left alone because he must never be left alone. So they all announced in a loud voice that he was a lunatic, and left. Of course that does not prove he is a lunatic; but it seems rather rum nowadays for a man to expect his valet or his parlour-maid to act as an armed guard."

"And so," said the priest with a smile, "he wants a policeman to act as his parlour-maid because his parlour-maid won't act as a policeman."

"I thought that rather thick, too," agreed the doctor, "but I can't take the responsibility of a flat refusal till I've tried a compromise. You are the compromise."

"Very well," said Father Brown simply, "I'll go and call on him now if you like."

The rolling country round the little town was sealed and bound with frost, and the sky was as clear and cold as steel, except in the north-east, where clouds with lurid haloes were beginning to climb up the sky. It was against these darker and more sinister colours that the house on the hill gleamed with a row of pale pillars, forming a short colonnade of the classical sort. A winding road led up to it across the curve of the down, and plunged into a mass of dark bushes. Just before it reached the bushes the air seemed to grow colder and colder, as if he were approaching an ice-house or the North Pole. But he was a highly practical person, never entertaining such fancies except as fancies. And he merely cocked his eye at the great livid cloud crawling up over the house, and remarked cheerfully: "It's going to snow."

Through a low ornamental iron gateway of the Italianate pattern he entered a garden having something of that desolation which only belongs to the disorder of orderly things. Deep-green growths were grey with the faint powder of the frost, large weeds had fringed the fading pattern of the flower beds as if in a ragged frame; and the house stood as if waist-high in a stunted forest of shrubs and bushes. The vegetation consisted largely of evergreens or very hardy plants; and though it was thus thick and heavy, it was too northern to be called luxuriant. It might be described as an Arctic jungle. So it was in some sense with the house itself, which had a row of columns and a classical façade, which might have looked out on the Mediterranean; but which seemed now to be withering in the wind of the North Sea. Classical ornament here and there accentuated the contrast; caryatides and carved masks of comedy or tragedy looked down from corners of the building upon the grey confusion of the garden paths; but the faces seemed to be frostbitten. The very volutes of the capitals might have curled up with the cold.

Father Brown went up the grassy steps to a square porch flanked by big pillars and knocked at the door. About four minutes afterwards he knocked again. Then he stood still patiently waiting with his back to the door and looked out on the slowly darkening landscape. It was darkening under the shadow of that one great continent of cloud that had come flying out of the north; and even as he looked out beyond the pillars of the porch, which seemed huge and black above him in the twilight, he saw the opalescent crawling rim of the great cloud as it sailed over the roof and bowed over the porch like a canopy. The grey canopy with its faintly coloured fringes seemed to sink lower and lower upon the garden beyond, until what had recently been a clear and pale-hued winter sky was left in a few silver ribbons and rags like a sickly sunset. Father Brown waited; and there was no sound within.

Then he betook himself briskly down the steps and round the house to look for another entrance. He eventually found one, a side door in the flat wall; and on this also he hammered and outside this also he waited. Then he tried the handle and found the door apparently bolted or fastened in some fashion; and then he moved along that side of the house, musing on the possibilities of the position, and wondering whether the eccentric Mr Aylmer had barricaded himself too deep in the house to hear any kind of summons; or whether perhaps he would barricade himself all the more, on the assumption that any summons must be the challenge of the avenging Strake. It might be that the decamping servants had only unlocked one door when they left in the morning, and that their master had locked that; but whatever he might have done it was unlikely that they, in the mood of that moment, had looked so carefully to the defences. He continued his prowl round the place; it was not really a large place, though perhaps a little pretentious; and in a few moments he found he had made the complete circuit. A moment after he found what he suspected and sought. The French window of one room, curtained and shadowed with creeper stood open by a crack, doubtless accidentally left ajar, and he found himself in a central room, comfortably upholstered in a rather old-fashioned way with a staircase leading up from it on one side and a door leading out of it on the other. Immediately opposite him was another door, with red glass let into it, a little gaudily for later tastes; something that looked like a red-robed figure in cheap stained glass. On a round table to the right stood a sort of aquarium – a great bowl full of greenish water, in which fishes and similar things moved about as in a tank; and just opposite it a plant of the palm variety with very large green leaves. All this looked so very dusty and Early Victorian that the telephone, visible in the curtained alcove, was almost a surprise.

"Who is that?" a voice called out sharply and rather suspiciously from behind the stained glass door.

"Could I see Mr Aylmer?" asked the priest apologetically.

The door opened and a gentleman in a peacock green dressing gown came out with an inquiring look. His hair was rather rough and untidy, as if he had been in bed or lived in a state of slowly getting up, but his eyes were not only awake but alert, and some would have said alarmed. Father Brown knew that the contradiction was likely enough in a man who had rather run to seed, under the shadow either of a delusion or a danger. He had a fine aquiline face when seen in profile, but when seen full face the first impression was of the untidiness and even the wilderness of his loose brown beard.

"I am Mr Aylmer," he said, "but I have got out of the way of expecting visitors."

Something about Mr Aylmer's unrestful eye prompted the priest to go straight to the point. If the man's persecution was only a monomania, he would be the less likely to resent it.

"I was wondering," said Father Brown softly, "whether it is quite true that you never expect visitors."

"You are right," replied his host steadily, "I always expect one visitor, And he may be the last."

"I hope not," said Father Brown, "but at least I am relieved to infer that I do not look very like him."

Mr Aylmer shook himself with a sort of savage laugh. "You certainly do not," he said.

"Mr Aylmer," said Father Brown frankly, "I apologize for the liberty, but some friends of mine have told me about your trouble, and asked me to see if I could do anything for you. The truth is, I have some little experience in affairs like this."

"There are no affairs like this," said Aylmer.

"You mean," observed Father Brown, "that the tragedies in your unfortunate family were not normal deaths?"

"I mean they were not even normal murders," answered the other. "The man who is hounding us all to death is a hell-hound, and his power is from hell."

"All evil has one origin," said the priest gravely. "But how do you know they were not normal murders?"

Aylmer answered with a gesture which offered his guest a chair; then he seated himself slowly in another, frowning, with his hands on his knees; but when he looked up his expression had grown milder and more thoughtful, and his voice was quite cordial and composed.

"Sir," he said, "I don't want you to imagine that I'm in the least an unreasonable person. I have come to these conclusions by reason, because unfortunately reason really leads there. I have read a great deal on these subjects; for I was the only one who inherited my father's scholarship in somewhat obscure matters, and I have since inherited his library. But what I tell you does not rest on what I have read but on what I have seen."

Father Brown nodded, and the other proceeded, as if picking his words: "In my elder brother's case I was not certain at first. There were no marks or footprints where he was found shot, and the pistol was left beside him. But he had just received a threatening letter, certainly from our enemy, for it was marked with a sign like a winged dagger, which was one of his infernal cabalistic tricks. And a servant said she had seen something moving along the garden wall in the twilight that was much too large to be a cat. I leave it there; all I can say is that if the murderer came, he managed to leave no traces of his coming. But when my brother Stephen died it was different; and since then I have known. A machine was working in an open scaffolding under the factory tower; I scaled the platform a moment after he had fallen under the iron hammer that struck him; I did not see anything else strike him, but I saw what I saw.

"A great drift of factory smoke was rolling between me and the factory tower; but through a rift of it I saw on the top of it a dark human figure wrapped in what looked like a black cloak. Then the sulphurous smoke drove between us again; and when it cleared I looked up at the distant chimney – there was nobody there. I am a rational man, and I will ask all rational men how he had reached that dizzy unapproachable turret, and how he left it."

He stared across at the priest with a sphinx-like challenge; then after a silence he said abruptly: "My brother's brains were knocked out, but his body was not much damaged. And in his pocket we found one of those warning messages dated the day before and stamped with the flying dagger."

"I am sure," he went on gravely, "that the symbol of the winged dagger is not merely arbitrary or accidental. Nothing about that abominable man is accidental. He is all design; though it is indeed a most dark and intricate design. His mind is woven not only out of elaborate schemes but out of all sorts of secret languages and signs and dumb signals and wordless pictures which are the names of nameless things. He is the worst sort of man that the world knows; he is the wicked mystic. Now, I don't pretend to penetrate all that is conveyed by this symbol; but it seems surely that it must have a relation to all that was most remarkable, or even incredible, in his movements as he had hovered round my unfortunate family. Is there no connection between the idea of a winged weapon and the mystery by which Philip was struck dead on his own lawn without the lightest touch of any footprint having disturbed the dust or grass? Is there no connection between the plumed poignard flying like a feathered arrow and that figure which hung on the far top of the toppling chimney, clad in a cloak for pinions?"

"You mean," said Father Brown thoughtfully, "that he is in a perpetual state of levitation."

"Simon Magus did it," replied Aylmer, "and it was one of the commonest predictions of the Dark Ages that Antichrist would be able to fly. Anyhow, there was the flying dagger on the document; and whether or not it could fly, it could certainly strike."

"Did you notice what sort of paper it was on?" asked Father Brown. "Common paper?"

The sphinx-like face broke abruptly into a harsh laugh.

"You can see what they're like," said Aylmer grimly, "for I got one myself this morning."

He was leaning back in his chair now, with his long legs thrust out from under the green dressing gown, which was a little short for him, and his bearded chin pillowed on his chest. Without moving otherwise, he thrust his hand deep in the dressing-gown pocket and held out a fluttering scrap of paper at the end of a rigid arm. His whole attitude was suggestive of a sort of paralysis, that was both rigidity and collapse. But the next remark of the priest had a curious effect of rousing him.

Father Brown was blinking in his shortsighted way at the paper presented to him. It was a singular sort of paper, rough without being common, as from an artist's sketch book; and on it was drawn boldly in red ink a dagger decorated with wings like the rod of Hermes, with the written words, "Death comes the day after this, as it came to your brothers."

Father Brown tossed the paper on the floor and sat bolt upright in his chair.

"You mustn't let that sort of stuff stupefy you," he said sharply. "These devils always try to make us helpless by making us hopeless."

Rather to his surprise, an awakening wave went over the prostrate figure, which sprang from its chair as if startled out of a dream.

"You're right, you're right!" cried Aylmer with a rather uncanny animation, "and the devils shall find I'm not so hopeless after all, nor so helpless either. Perhaps I have more hope and better help than you fancy."

He stood with his hands in his pockets,

frowning down at the priest, who had a momentary doubt, during that strained silence, about whether the man's long peril had not touched the man's brain. But when he spoke it was quite soberly.

"I believe my unfortunate brothers failed because they used the wrong weapons. Philip carried a revolver, and that was how his death came to be called suicide. Stephen had police protection, but he also had a sense of what made him ridiculous; and he could not allow a policeman to climb up a ladder after him to a scaffolding where he stood only a moment. They were both scoffers, reacting into scepticism from the strange mysticism of my father's last days. But I always knew there was more in my father than they understood. It is true that by studying magic he fell at last under the blight of black magic; the black magic of this scoundrel Strake. But my brothers were wrong about the antidote. The antidote to black magic is not brute materialism or worldly wisdom. The antidote to black magic is white magic."

"It rather depends," said Father Brown, "what you mean by white magic."

"I mean silver magic," said the other, in a low voice, like one speaking of a secret revelation. Then after a silence he said, "Do you know what I mean by silver magic? Excuse me a moment."

He turned and opened the central door with the red glass and went into a passage beyond it. The house had less depth than Brown had supposed; instead of the door opening into interior rooms, the corridor it revealed ended in another door on the garden. The door of one room was on one side of the passage; doubtless, the priest told himself, the proprietor's bedroom whence he had rushed out in his dressing gown. There was nothing else on that side but an ordinary hatstand with the ordinary dingy cluster of old hats and overcoats; but on the other side was something more interesting; a very dark old oak sideboard laid out with some old silver, and overhung by a trophy or ornament of old weapons. It was by this that Arnold Aylmer halted, looking up at a long antiquated pistol with a bell-shaped mouth.

The door at the end of the passage was barely open; and through the crack came a streak of white daylight. The priest had very quick instincts about natural things; and something in the unusual brilliancy of that white line told him what had happened outside. It was indeed what he had prophesied when he was approaching the house. He ran past his rather startled host and opened the door; to face something that was at once a blank and a blaze. What he had seen shining through the crack was not only the more negative whiteness of daylight but the positive whiteness of snow. All round, the sweeping fall of the country was covered with that shining pallor that seems at once hoary and innocent.

"Here is white magic anyhow," said Father Brown in his cheerful voice. Then as he turned back into the hall he murmured, "And silver magic too, I suppose," for the white lustre touched the silver with splendour and lit up the old steel here and there in the darkling armoury. The shaggy head of the brooding Aylmer seemed to have a halo of silver fire, as he turned with his face in shadow and the outlandish pistol in his hand.

"Do you know why I choose this sort of old blunderbuss?" he asked. "Because I can load it with this sort of bullet."

He had picked up a small apostle spoon from the sideboard, and by sheer violence broke off the small figure at the top. "Let us go back into the other room," he added.

"Did you ever read about the death of Dundee?" he asked when they had reseated themselves. He had recovered from his momentary annoyance at the priest's restlessness. "Graham of Claverhouse, you know, who persecuted the Covenanters and had a black horse that could ride straight up a precipice. Don't you know he could only be shot with a silver bullet, because he had sold himself to the Devil? That's one comfort about you; at least you know enough to believe in the Devil."

"Oh, yes," replied Father Brown, "I believe in the Devil. What I don't believe in is the Dundee. I mean the Dundee of Covenanting legends, with his nightmare of a horse. John Graham was simply a seventeenth-century professional soldier, rather better than most. If he dragooned them it was because he was a dragoon, but not a dragon. Now my experience is that it's not that sort of swaggering blade who sells himself to the Devil. The devil worshippers I've known were quite different. Not to mention names, which might cause a social flutter, I'll take a man in Dundee's own day. Have you ever heard of Dalrymple of Stair?"

"No," replied the other gruffly.

"You've heard of what he did," said Father Brown, "and it was worse than anything Dundee ever did; yet he escapes the infamy by oblivion. He was the man who made the Massacre of Glencoe. He was a very learned man and lucid lawyer, a statesman with very serious and enlarged ideas of statesmanship, a quiet man with a very refined and intellectual face. That's the sort of man who sells himself to the Devil."

Aylmer half started from his chair with an enthusiasm of eager assent.

"By God! you are right," he cried. "A refined intellectual face! That is the face of John Strake."

Then he raised himself and stood looking at the priest with a curious concentration. "If you will wait here a little while," he said, "I will show you something."

He went back through the central door, closing it after him; going, the priest presumed, to the old sideboard or possibly to his bedroom. Father Brown remained seated, gazing abstractedly at the carpet, where a faint red glimmer shone from the glass in the doorway. Once it seemed to brighten like a ruby and then darkened again, as if the sun of that stormy day had passed from cloud to cloud. Nothing moved except the aquatic creatures which floated to and fro in the dim green bowl. Father Brown was thinking hard.

A minute or two afterwards he got up and slipped quietly to the alcove of the telephone, where he rang up his friend Dr Boyne, at the official headquarters.

"I wanted to tell you about Aylmer and his affairs," he said quietly. "It's a queer story, but I rather think there's something in it. If I were you I'd send some men up here straight away; four or five men, I think, and surround the house. If anything does happen there'll probably be something startling in the way of an escape."

Then he went back and sat down again, staring at the dark carpet, which again glowed blood red with the light from the glass door. Something in that filtered light set his mind drifting on certain borderlands of thought, with the first white daybreak before the coming of colour, and all that mystery which is alternately veiled and revealed in the symbol of windows and of doors.

An inhuman howl in a human voice came from beyond the closed doors; almost simultaneously with the noise of firing. Before the echoes of the shot had died away the door was violently flung open and his host staggered into the room, the dressing gown half torn from his shoulder and the long pistol smoking in his hand. He seemed to be shaking in every limb, yet he was shaken in part with an unnatural laughter.

"Glory be to the White Magic!" he cried, "Glory be to the silver bullet! The hell-hound has hunted once too often, and my brothers are avenged at last."

He sank into a chair and the pistol slid from his hand and fell on the floor. Father Brown darted past him, slipped through the glass door and went down the passage. As he did so he put his hand on the handle of the bedroom door, as if half intending to enter; then he stooped a moment, as if examining something; and then he ran to the outer door and opened it.

On the field of snow, which had been so blank a little while before, lay one black object. At the first glance it looked a little like an enormous bat. A second glance showed that it was, after all, a human figure; fallen on its face, the whole head covered by a broad black hat having something of a Latin-American look; while the appearance of black wings came from the two flaps or loose sleeves of a very vast black cloak spread out, perhaps by accident, to their utmost length on either side. Both the hands were hidden, though Father Brown thought he could detect the position of one of them, and saw close to it, under the edge of the cloak, the glimmer of some metallic weapon. The main effect, however, was curiously like that of the simple extravagances of heraldry; like a black eagle displayed on a white ground. But by walking round it and peering under the hat the priest got a glimpse of the face, which was indeed what his host had called refined and intellectual; even sceptical and austere: the face of John Strake.

"Well, I'm jiggered," muttered Father Brown. "It really does look like some vast vampire that has swooped down like a bird."

"How else could he have come?" came a voice from the doorway; and Father Brown looked up to see Aylmer once more standing there.

"Couldn't he have walked?" replied Father Brown evasively.

Aylmer stretched out his arm and swept the white landscape with a gesture.

"Look at the snow," he said in a deep voice that had a sort of roll and thrill in it. "Is not the snow unspotted – pure as the white magic you yourself called it? Is there a speck on it for miles, save that one foul black blot that has fallen there? There are no footprints, but a few of yours and mine; there are none approaching the house from anywhere."

Then he looked at the little priest for a moment with a concentrated and curious expression, and said: "I will tell you something else. That cloak he flies with is too long to walk with. He was not a very tall man; and it would trail behind him like a royal train. Stretch it out over his body, if you like, and see."

"What happened to you both?" asked Father Brown abruptly.

"It was too swift to describe," answered

Aylmer. "I had looked out of the door and was turning back when there came a kind of rushing of wind all around me, as if I were being buffeted by a wheel revolving in mid-air. I spun round somehow and fired blindly; and then I saw nothing but what you see now. But I am mortally certain you wouldn't see it, if I had not had a silver shot in my gun. It would have been a different body lying there in the snow."

"By the way," remarked Father Brown, "shall we leave it lying there in the snow? Or would you like it taken into your room – I suppose that's your bedroom in the passage?"

"No, no," replied Aylmer hastily, "we must leave it there till the police have seen it. Besides, I've had as much of such things as I can stand for the moment. Whatever else happens, I'm going to have a drink. After that, they can hang me if they like."

Inside the central apartment, between the palm plant and the bowl of fishes, Aylmer tumbled into a chair. He had nearly knocked the bowl over as he lurched into the room, but he had managed to find the decanter of brandy after plunging his hand rather blindly into several cupboards and corners. He did not at any time look like a methodical person; but at this moment his distraction must have been extreme. He drank with a long gulp and began to talk rather feverishly, as if to fill up a silence.

"I see you are still doubtful," he said, "though you have seen the thing with your own eyes. Believe me, there was something more behind the quarrel between the spirit of Strake and the spirit of the house of Aylmer. Besides, you have no business to be an unbeliever. You ought to stand for all the things these stupid people call superstitions. Come now, don't you think there's a lot in those old wives' tales about luck and charms and so on, silver bullets included? What do you say about them as a Catholic?"

"I say I'm an agnostic," replied Father Brown, smiling.

"Nonsense," said Aylmer impatiently. "It's your business to believe things."

"Well, I do believe some things, of course," conceded Father Brown; "and therefore, of course, I don't believe other things."

Aylmer was leaning forward, and looking at him with a strange intensity that was almost like that of a mesmerist.

"You do believe it," he said. "You do believe everything. We all believe everything, even when we deny everything. The deniers believe. The unbelievers believe. Don't you feel in your heart that these contradictions do not really contradict; that there is a cosmos that contains them all? The soul goes round upon a wheel of stars and all things return; perhaps Strake and I have striven in many shapes, beast against beast and bird against bird, and perhaps we shall strive forever. But since we seek and need each other, even that eternal hatred is an eternal love. Good and evil go round in a wheel that is one thing and not many. Do you not realize in your heart, do you not believe behind all your beliefs, that there is but one reality and we are its shadows; and that all things are but aspects of one thing: a centre where men melt into Man and Man into God?"

"No," said Father Brown.

Outside, twilight had begun to fall, in that phase of such a snow-laden evening when the land looks brighter than the sky. In the porch of the main entrance visible through a half-curtained window, Father Brown could dimly see a bulky figure standing. He glanced casually at the French windows through which he had originally entered, and saw they were darkened with two equally motionless figures. The inner door with the coloured glass stood slightly ajar; and he could see in the short corridor beyond, the ends of two long shadows, exaggerated and distorted by the level light of evening, but still like grey caricatures of the figures of men. Dr Boyne had already obeyed his telephone message. The house was surrounded.

"What is the good of saying no," insisted his host, still with the same hypnotic stare. "You have seen part of that eternal drama with your own eyes. You have seen the threat of John Strake to slay Arnold Aylmer by black magic. You have seen Arnold Aylmer slay John Strake by white magic. You see Arnold Aylmer alive and talking to you now. And yet you do not believe it."

"No, I do not believe it," said Father Brown, and rose from his chair like one terminating a visit.

"Why not?" asked the other.

The priest only lifted his voice a little, but it sounded in every corner of the room like a bell.

"Because you are not Arnold Aylmer," he said. "I know who you are. Your name is John Strake; and you have murdered the last of the brothers, who is lying outside in the snow."

A ring of white showed round the iris of the other man's eyes; he seemed to be making, with bursting eyeballs, a last effort to mesmerize and master his companion. Then he made a sudden movement sideways; and even as he did so the door behind him opened and a big detective in plain clothes put one hand quietly on his shoulder. The other hand hung down, but it held a revolver. The man looked wildly round, and saw plain-clothes men in all corners of the quiet room.

That evening Father Brown had another and longer conversation with Dr Boyne about the tragedy of the Aylmer family. By that time there was no longer any doubt of the central fact of the case, for John Strake had confessed his identity and even confessed his crimes; only it would be truer to say that he boasted of his victories. Compared to the fact that he had rounded off his life's work with the last Aylmer lying dead, everything else, including existence itself, seemed to be indifferent to him.

"The man is a sort of monomaniac," said Father Brown. "He is not interested in any other matter; not even in any other murder. I owe him something for that; for I had to comfort myself with the reflection a good many times this afternoon. As has doubtless occurred to you, instead of weaving all that wild but ingenious romance about winged vampires and silver bullets, he might have put an ordinary leaden bullet into me, and walked out of the house. I assure you it occurred quite frequently to me."

"I wonder why he didn't," observed Boyne. "I don't understand it; but I don't understand anything yet. How on earth did you discover it, and what in the world did you discover?"

"Oh, you provided me with very valuable information," replied Father Brown modestly, "especially the one piece of information that really counted. I mean the statement that Strake was a very inventive and imaginative liar, with great presence of mind in producing his lies. This afternoon he needed it; but he rose to the occasion. Perhaps his only mistake was in choosing a preternatural story; he had the notion that because I am a clergyman I should believe anything. Many people have little notions of that kind."

"But I can't make head or tail of it," said the doctor. "You must really begin at the beginning."

"The beginning of it was a dressing gown," said Father Brown simply. "It was the one really good disguise I've ever known. When you meet a man in a house with a dressing gown on, you assume quite automatically that he's in his own house. I assumed it myself; but afterwards queer little things began to happen. When he took the pistol down he clicked it at arm's length, as a man does to make sure a strange weapon isn't loaded; of course he would know whether the pistols in his own hall were loaded or not. I didn't like the way he looked for the brandy, or the way he nearly barged into the bowl of fishes. For a man who has a fragile thing of that sort as a fixture in his rooms gets a quite mechanical habit of avoiding it. But these things might possibly have been fancies; the first real point was this. He came out from the little passage between the two doors; and in that passage there's only one other door leading to a room; so I assumed it was the bedroom he had just come from. I tried the handle; but it was locked. I thought this odd; and looked through the keyhole. It was an utterly bare room, obviously deserted; no bed, no anything. Therefore he had not come from inside any room, but from outside the house. And when I saw that, I think I saw the whole picture.

"Poor Arnold Aylmer doubtless slept and perhaps lived upstairs, and came down in his dressing gown and passed through the red glass door. At the end of the passage, black against the winter daylight, he saw the enemy of his house. He saw a tall bearded man in a broad-brimmed black hat and a large flapping black cloak. He did not see much more in this world. Strake sprang on him, throttling or stabbing him; we cannot be sure till the inquest. Then Strake, standing in the narrow passage between the hat-stand and the old sideboard, and looking down in triumph on the last of his foes, heard something he had not expected. He heard footsteps in the parlour beyond. It was myself entering by the French windows.

"His masquerade was a miracle of promptitude. It involved not only a disguise but a romance; an impromptu romance. He took off his big black hat and cloak and put on the dead man's dressing gown. Then he did a rather grisly thing; at least a thing that affects my fancy as more grisly than the rest. He hung the corpse like a coat on one of the hat pegs. He draped it in his own long cloak, and found it hung well below the heels; he covered the head entirely with his own wide hat. It was the only possible way of hiding it in that little passage with the locked door; but it was really a very clever one. I myself walked past the hatstand once without knowing it was anything but a hatstand. I think that in consciousness of mine will always give me a shiver.

"He might perhaps have left it at that; but I might have discovered the corpse at any minute; and, hung where it was, it was a corpse calling for what you might call an explanation. He adopted the bolder stroke of discovering it himself and explaining it himself.

"Then there dawned on this strange and frightfully fertile mind the conception of a story of substitution; the reversal of the parts. He had already assumed the part of Arnold Aylmer. Why should not his dead enemy assume the part of John Strake? There must have been something in that topsy-turveydom to take the fancy of that darkly fanciful man. It was like some frightful fancy dress ball to which the two mortal enemies were to go dressed up as each other. Only, the fancy dress ball was to be a dance of death; and one of the dancers would be dead. That is why I can imagine that man putting it in his own mind; and I can imagine him smiling."

Father Brown was gazing into vacancy with his large grey eyes, which, when not blurred by his trick of blinking, were the one notable thing in his face. He went on speaking simply and seriously: "All things are from God; and above all reason and imagination and the great gifts of the mind. They are good in themselves; and we must not altogether forget their origin even in their perversion. Now this man had in him a very noble power to be perverted; the power of telling stories. He was a great novelist; only he had twisted his fictive power to practical and to evil ends; to deceiving men with false fact instead of with true fiction. It began with his deceiving old Aylmer with elaborate excuses and ingeniously detailed lies; but even that may have been, at the beginning, little more than the tall stories and tarradiddles of the child who may say equally he has seen the King of England or the King of the Fairies. It grew strong in him through the vice that perpetuates all vices, pride; he grew more and more vain of his promptitude in producing stories, of his originality and subtlety in developing them. That is what the young Aylmers meant by saying that he could always cast a spell over their father; and it was true. It was the sort of spell that the storyteller cast over the tyrant in the Arabian Nights. And to the last he walked the world with the pride of a poet; and with the false yet unfathomable courage of a great liar. He could always produce more Arabian Nights if ever his neck was in danger. And today his neck was in danger.

"But I am sure, as I say, that he enjoyed it as a fantasy as well as a conspiracy. He set about the task of telling the true story the wrong way round; of treating the dead man as living and the live man as dead. He had already got into Aylmer's dressing gown; he proceeded to get into Aylmer's body and soul. He looked at the corpse as if it were his own corpse lying cold in the snow. Then he spread-eagled it in that strange fashion to suggest the sweeping descent of a bird of prey, and decked it out not only in his own dark and flying garments but in a whole dark fairy tale about the black bird that could only fall by the silver bullet. I do not know whether it was the silver glittering on the sideboard or the snow shining beyond the door that suggested to his intensely artistic temperament the theme of white magic and the white metal used against magicians. But whatever its origin, he made it his own like a poet; and did it very promptly, like a practical man. He completed the exchange and reversal of parts by flinging the corpse out on to the snow as the corpse of Strake. He did his best to work up a creepy conception of Strake as something hovering in the air everywhere, a harpy with wings of speed and claws of death; to explain the absence of footprints and other things. For one piece of artistic impudence I hugely admire him. He actually turned one of the contradictions in his case into an argument for it; and said that the man's cloak being too long for him proved that he never walked on the ground like an ordinary mortal. But he looked at me very hard while he said that; and something told me that he was at that moment trying a very big bluff."

Dr Boyne looked thoughtful. "Had you discovered the truth by then?" he asked. "There is something very queer and close to the nerves, I think, about notions affecting identity. I don't know whether it would be more weird to get a guess like that swiftly or slowly. I wonder when you suspected and when you were sure."

"I think I really suspected when I telephoned to you," replied his friend. "And it was nothing more than the red light from the closed door brightening and darkening on the carpet. It looked like a splash of blood that grew vivid as it cried for vengeance. Why should it change like that? I knew the sun had not come out; it could only be because the second door behind it had been opened and shut on the garden. But if he had gone out and seen his enemy then, he would have raised the alarm then; and it was some time afterwards that the fracas occurred. I began to feel he had gone out to do something...to prepare something...but as to when I was certain, that is a different matter. I knew that right at the end he was trying to hypnotize me, to master me by the black art of eyes like talismans and a voice like an incantation. That's what he used to do with old Aylmer, no doubt. But it wasn't only the way he said it, it was what he said. It was the religion and philosophy of it."

"I'm afraid I'm a practical man," said the doctor with gruff humour, "and I don't bother much about religion and philosophy."

"You'll never be a practical man till you do," said Father Brown. "Look here, doctor; you know me pretty well; I think you know I'm not a bigot. You know I know there are all sorts in all religions; good men in bad ones and bad men in good ones. But there's just one little fact I've learned simply as a practical man, an entirely practical point, that I've picked up by experience, like the tricks of an animal or the trademark of a good wine. I've scarcely ever met a criminal who philosophised at all, who didn't philosophise along those lines of orientalism and recurrence and reincarnation, and the wheel of destiny and the serpent biting its own tail. I have found merely in practice that there is a curse on the servants of that serpent; on their belly shall they go and the dust shall they eat; and there was never a blackguard or a profligate born who could not talk that sort of spirituality. It may not be like that in its real religious origins; but here in our working world it is the religion of rascals; and I knew it was a rascal who was speaking."

"Why," said Boyne, "I should have thought that a rascal could pretty well profess any religion he chose."

"Yes," assented the other, "he could profess any religion; that is he could pretend to any religion, if it was all a pretence. If it was mere mechanical hypocrisy and nothing else, no doubt it could be done by a mere mechanical hypocrite. Any sort of mask can be put on any sort of face. Anybody can learn certain phrases or state verbally that he holds certain views. I can go out into the street and state that I am a Wesleyan Methodist or a Sandemanian, though I fear in no very convincing accent. But we are talking about an artist; and for the enjoyment of the artist the mask must be to some extent moulded on the face. What he makes outside him must correspond to something inside him; he can only make his effects out of some of the materials of his soul. I suppose he could have said he was a Wesleyan Methodist; but he could never be an eloquent Methodist as he can be an eloquent mystic and fatalist. I am talking of the sort of ideal such a man thinks of if he really tries to be idealistic. It was his whole game with me to be as idealistic as possible; and whenever that is attempted by that sort of man, you will generally find it is that sort of ideal. That sort of man may be dripping with gore; but he will always be able to tell you quite sincerely that Buddhism is better than Christianity. Nay, he will tell you quite sincerely that Buddhism is more Christian than Christianity. That alone is enough to throw a hideous and ghastly ray of light on his notion of Christianity."

"Upon my soul," said the doctor, laughing, "I can't make out whether you're denouncing or defending him."

"It isn't defending a man to say he is a genius," said Father Brown. "Far from it. And it is simply a psychological fact that an artist will betray himself by some sort of sincerity. Leonardo da Vinci cannot draw as if he couldn't draw. Even if he tried, it will always be a strong parody of a weak thing. This man would have made something much too fearful and wonderful out of the Wesleyan Methodist."

When the priest went forth again and set his face homeward, the cold had grown more intense and yet was somehow intoxicating. The trees stood up like silver candelabra of some incredible cold candlemas of purification. It was a piercing cold, like that silver sword of pure pain that once pierced the very heart of purity. But it was not a killing cold, save in the sense of seeming to kill all the mortal obstructions to our immortal and immeasurable vitality. The pale green sky of twilight, with one star like the star of Bethlehem, seemed by some strange contradiction to be a cavern of clarity. It was as if there could be a green furnace of cold which wakened all things to life like warmth, and that the deeper they went into those cold crystalline colours the more were they light like winged creatures and clear like coloured glass. It tingled with truth and it divided truth from error with a blade like ice; but all that was left had never felt so much alive. It was as if all joy were a jewel in the heart of an iceberg. The priest hardly understood his own mood as he advanced deeper and deeper into the green gloaming, drinking deeper and deeper draughts of that virginal vivacity of the air. Some forgotten muddle and morbidity seemed to be left behind, or wiped out as the snow had painted out the footprints of the man of blood. As he shuffled homewards through the snow, he muttered to himself, "And yet he is right enough about there being a white magic, if he only knows where to look for it."

CATH STAINCLIFFE

Cath Staincliffe was brought up in Bradford and graduated from Birmingham University with a drama degree. She moved to Manchester to work in community arts and spent the next eight years carrying out projects all over the north-west in partnership with community groups. She also set up Dance Train with a few friends: running discos for fundraisers and parties. After the birth of her first child she started going to writing workshops, following which she published poetry and short stories then moved onto longer fiction.

Looking For Trouble won the Commonword North West novel writing competition. Her single parent, private eye Sal Kilkenny works a double shift; stalking the mean streets of Manchester when she's not busy keeping home and hearth together. *Looking For Trouble* was short listed for the CWA John Creasey award and serialised on BBC Women's Hour. Since then Cath has written three further Sal Kilkenny mysteries and has had two more children.

Cath has been involved as a CWA member in developing Dead on Deansgate. She has recently completed *Wounded*, a multi-voiced story that is both police procedural and psychological thriller. She

is now writing the fifth Sal Kilkenny mystery and reviews for the Manchester Evening News and Tangled Web.

Bibliography

Looking For Trouble (Crocus, 1994)
Go Not Gently (Headline, 1997)
Dead Wrong (Headline, 1998)
The City Life Book of Manchester: Short Stories [contributor] (Penguin, 1999)

CAMPBELL ARMSTRONG

I was inspired to write my first book *Assassins & Victims* because I was kept awake all night long by a dog barking next door, and basically I wanted to murder it, and so it gave me the notion of an assassin who says he's a specialist in killing dogs, but he's lying. I wanted a gruesome end, and that's what I got. The second novel was a mystery I wanted to write because it had no real resolution – an experiment. It won a Scottish Arts Council Award anyway. Then I wrote *Death's Head* after I researched the death-camps of Nazism and discovered how some people managed to survive them. After that I wrote a couple of thrillers before I came to the Frank Pagan sequence, which began with *Jig*, then was followed by *Mazurka*, *Mambo*, *Jigsaw* and *Heat*. Then I retired Frank Pagan and wrote *Agents of Darkness* and *Concert of Ghosts* – both concerned with American politics and the nature of American democracy. Then I concentrated on some short noir-type thrillers; *Silencer, Blackout*, and *Deadline* – which are dark in their way. I moved away from fiction for one book, a memoir of my first wife and her long-lost daughter, *All That Really Matters*, a story that demanded to be told. And now I'm back working on a long suspense story set in Glasgow – my home city – about which I've never written before.

Bibliography

As Campbell Armstrong:

Jig (Hodder, 1987)
Mazurka (Hodder, 1988)
Mambo (Hodder, 1989)
Agents of Darkness (Hodder, 1991)
Concert of Ghosts (Hodder, 1992)
Jigsaw (Doubleday, 1993)
Heat (Doubleday, 1994)
Silencer (Doubleday, 1996)
Blackout (Doubleday, 1997)
Deadline (Doubleday, 1998)

As Campbell Black:

Assassins & Victims (Macmillan, 1968)
The Punctual Rape (Macmillan, 1969)
Death's Head (Collins, 1971)
Brainfire (Michael Joseph, 1980)
Letters From the Dead (Villard, 1982)
The Piper (Pocket Books, 1983)
Dressed To Kill (1984)
Raiders of the Lost Ark (1985)
The Wanting (Mandarin / Putnam, 1988)
The Homing [with Jeffrey Caine] (Putnam, 1989)
The Trader's Wife (Simon & Schuster, 1998)
The Surgeon's Daughter (Simon & Schuster, 1999)

As Thomas Altman

Kiss Daddy Goodbye (Corgi, 1982)
The True Bride (Corgi, 1983)
Black Christmas (Corgi, 1984)
The Intruder (Corgi, 1985)

Non-fiction

All That Really Matters (Little, Brown, 2000)
I Hope You Have a Good Life [US edition of above title] (Crown Books, 2000)

ANNE CLEEVES

Ann Cleeves grew up in North Devon. She has worked as bird observatory cook, women's refuge worker, probation officer and auxiliary coastguard. She started writing when her ornithologist husband was warden of Hilbre, an otherwise uninhabited island in the Dee Estuary. Ann has worked as reader in residence in libraries in the north of England, and is involved in setting up readers' groups in prisons. She is a member of the Murder Squad. Her short film, *Catching Birds*, won a Television Society Award.

She has written two distinct series. In the first an elderly naturalist solves conservation crime. These books are presently being reprinted in paperback by Allison and Busby. The second features Inspector Ramsay and is set in Northumberland. *A Lesson in Dying* was serialised on Radio Four. Her most recent novel, *The Crow Trap* (Macmillan), is set in Northumberland too, but is quite a different book. A psychological thriller, it has three women narrators.

Bibliography

A Bird in the Hand (Century/Arrow, 1986)

Come Death and High Water (Century/Arrow, 1987)

Murder in Paradise (Century/Arrow, 1988)

A Prey to Murder (Century/Arrow, 1989)

A Lesson in Dying (Century/Arrow/Allison & Busby, 1990)

Murder in my Backyard (Century/Arrow/Allison & Busby, 1991)

Another Man's Poison (Macmillan/Allison & Busby, 1992)

A Day in the Death of Dorothea Cassidy (Macmillan/Allison & Busby, 1992)

Sea Fever (Macmillan/Allison & Busby, 1993)

Killjoy (Macmillan/Allison & Busby, 1993)

The Mill on the Shore (Macmillan/Allison & Busby, 1994)

The Healers (Macmillan/Allison & Busby, 1995)

High Island Blues (Macmillan/Allison & Busby, 1996)

The Babysnatcher (Macmillan/Allison & Busby, 1997)

The Crow Trap (Macmillan, 1999/Pan, 2001)

Good books should
never go out of print.
The Four Just Men
The Four Just Men
£6.99 ISBN 1-84232-683-X
Bones
Bones
£6.99 ISBN 1-84232-663-5
G K CHESTERTON
The Innocence of Father Brown
'One of the greatest of all great detective figures'
– Kingsley Amis
The Innocence of Father Brown
£6.99 ISBN 1-84232-991-X
G K CHESTERTON
The Scandal of Father Brown
'One of the greatest of all great detective figures'
– Kingsley Amis
The Scandal of Father Brown
£6.99 ISBN 0-7551-0026-3
HOUSE OF STRATUS
www.houseofstratus.com

THE BIG NOVEL

CT prides itself on the number of top crime writers who are happy to write for these pages – and here's ***Natasha Cooper*** *(aka Clare Layton), regularly to be found as reviewee at the back of CT for her HarperCollins Trish Maguire crime treats, talking about the crime writer's life…*

Coming back to London after Heffers' excellent crime evening in Cambridge this year, I was reminded of an earlier version of the same occasion, when a couple of fellow crime writers and I were discussing the latest best-selling detective novel. "It's certainly a *long* book," one said, "but I'm not at all sure that it's a Big Book."

At the time I hardly thought about the proposition because I agreed with the assessment of that particular novel. Now, like the sensation of pain travelling slowly from a diplodocus's tail to its pea-sized brain, the question has arrived at the front of my mind, and it's beginning to obsess me. What exactly is it that makes a book 'big' rather than simply 'long' or indeed 'good'? Some writers have always produced big books, some achieve bigness half-way through their career and some write wonderful (and best-selling) small books. Others, in attempting to make their work bigger, succeed only in making it longer, and often bury its merits in wordiness and unnecessary digressions. I've asked various editors and critics what they think makes a book big and have received a variety of answers. Nearly everyone agrees that shifting points of view and complex story lines are essential. A wide geographical spread helps, as do parallel narratives set in different historical periods, and important political themes. The last can, of course, be dangerous. I have been disappointed in several promising novels, as their inadequately absorbed political theorising and lack of involving personal stories have turned them into tracts. But then my consciousness was raised in the sixties and for me the personal *is* political.

Reginald Hill's *On Beulah Height* manages to be a big book without moving geographically beyond a limited – if ravishing – area of the Yorkshire Dales, and it deals with the murder of small children by a paedophile known to them and their families. Its bigness comes partly from its very undomestic preoccupation with the exploitation of human beings for financial as well as emotional profit, and partly from the wide range of characters, all of whose stories are woven into the main narrative.

Of the current crop of political crime novels, Mike Phillips' *A Shadow of Myself* (HarperCollins, £16.99) is an obvious candidate for big-book status. It tackles racism, fractured families, and the struggle between the ideologies of East and West Europe. For me, it would have been bigger still if there had been some humour in it, as a counterpoint to the seriousness of the narrative, and if the relationships had been more fully realised – and warmer – than I found them. But it's an impressive and interesting piece of work.

There have been many critics who complain that American writing is so much more significant than British because there are no British writers producing state-of-the-nation novels these days. There may be few specifically literary novelists who are, although I can think of some, but Phillips is only one of several crime writers who are tackling just those sort of themes. Ian Rankin is another. Since he involved Rebus in crimes with political overtones, his books have become a great deal bigger than the early titles were. There are, of course, readers who prefer the early Rebus, but that's another question. For some commentators the quality that makes a crime novel big seems to be that it should be set outside England – for others, it is explicit violence. Regular readers of *Crime Time* will know my views on that, so I won't bang on about it now. Suffice it to say that the idea of realistically described torture adding importance to a writer's work horrifies me.

Most critical judgements have at least an element of solipsism in them, and it is quite likely that we accord big-book status only to works that happen to involve some of our own preoccupations – or that fire our own imagination. Into that category, I would definitely put Leslie Forbes's second novel, *Fish, Blood and Bone*. Forbes's main character is Claire Fleetwood, a forensic photographer with a dysfunctional family background that has left her to educate herself and find stability wherever she can. She has all the autodictat's characteristic enjoyment of facts, words, and the most recondite research, some of which occasionally threatens to drown the narrative. Claire inherits a property in East London from a relative she never knew she had and is soon suckered into a dangerous quest for a rare Tibetan poppy that may or may not exist. Her physical and emotional journey brings her into confrontation with her family's past, the drugs trade, the rape of the Third World's botanical heritage, a possible lost cure for cancer, and a feasible answer to the Jack-the-Ripper mystery. The novel moves between London, India and Tibet, crossing the cultural divide between the arts and sciences with ease, going backwards and forwards in time, building always towards the climax. Several mysteries are solved in the process, but the biggest discovery Claire makes is that however far you travel you end up looking at your own self. And that is perhaps why I find the novel so satisfactory, since my own interest in crime fiction (both in the writing and the reading) is to accompany characters I care about on their own pilgrim's progress towards enlightenment.

That is certainly why I find *The Dark Room* both the most interesting and the 'biggest' of Minette Walters's best-selling novels. She plays a lot of games with the reader's perception of her heroine, Jinx, and some have felt irritably manipulated, but I was hooked. First encountered in a nursing home, after an horrific car crash, Jinx has lost her memory. She and the reader gradually discover her past, her possible guilt of an appalling crime, her desperate fear, and ultimately her retaking of control of her own destiny.

Big or small, novels that work for me have characters I care about struggling to understand, facing dilemmas that seem overwhelming and yet are conquerable. If they show me a world I've never known or reveal aspects of familiar worlds I've never properly understood, then they are as big as I could possibly want.

THE BLOCK NEWSLETTER

***Lawrence Block** takes time out from chronicling Matt Scudder's life and times to write to us…*

First of all, *Hit List* should be bound and printed and in your favourite bookstores by now. *Hit Man*, Keller's first appearance, was either an episodic novel or a collection of short stories – or, as I saw it, both. *Hit List* is a more traditional novel, with Keller in the unaccustomed role of somebody else's target. The early reviews have been very generous, and I hope you like it.

If you're on-line, you can preview the first chapter of *Hit List* on my web site: www.lawrenceblock.com. Click on 'Books', click on 'Keller', scroll down to *Hit List*, and click on 'preview first chapter'. Read, enjoy, get hooked… and buy the book.

More big news – my web site, I'm happy to report, is up and running, and I'm just delighted with the job the webmeisters (meistresses actually) have done with it. The URL is http://www.lawrenceblock.com/index_flash.htm and I hope you'll hurry to check it out. I've tucked in a fair amount of content. All the books are included, with series listed in order, and some bibliographical data which should be useful. A page to bookmark is one headed PSSSST!!!, which provides updated information, along with my travel and appear-

ance schedule. I'll continue to send out the newsletter, but I doubt the printed version will get out more often than once a year.

The site also contains an order page, with an annotated list of what I've got for sale – mostly autographed books, but some audio tapes as well. There's a secure server, so you can fill out an order blank right there and – click! – send it right to me.

While *Hit List* is my only recent novel, here are some other books that might be of interest:

The Scoreless Thai

This book, fourth in the Evan Tanner series, first saw the light of print in the late 1960s as a Gold Medal paperback entitled, Lord help us, *Two for Tanner*. Subterranean Press has just brought out a handsome hardcover first edition with a new afterword and a great Phil Parks cover. You can order the book from the publisher (www.subterraneanpress.com) or from specialist stores or on-line booksellers – but why not buy it from me, autographed? (I took my compensation in copies, so I've got them to sell. Price is $30. If you can use five or more, they're just $18 apiece.)

Master's Choice Two

The premise seemed good to me – top mystery writers present two stories apiece, a favourite of their own and a favourite drawn from their reading. Readers and reviewers liked the idea, too, and volume one of *Master's Choice*, published last fall, was well received. (It's coming out soon as a Berkley paperback.) A second volume is just out in hardcover from Berkley, and I think it's a stronger book than the first, with stories by Evan Hunter, Clark Howard, Ian Rankin, Joyce Carol Oates, Joe Gores, Stuart Kaminsky, Reginald Hill, and many more. (My own pick's a favourite by Fredric Brown.) Great writers, interesting choices, and fine stories throughout.

Opening Shots

Another premise I'm proud of: nineteen top crime writers present their first published stories and tell how they came to write them – and how it changed their lives. Participants include Max Allan Collins, Donald E. Westlake, David Morrell, Margaret Maron, John Harvey, Loren Estleman, Sara Paretsky and a dozen more. If you picked up *Death Cruise*, you know what a good-looking and well-produced book the folks at Cumberland House turn out. They've done it again, and I hope it's the first of a series.

Murder Among Friends

As some of you know, once a month I have dinner with a group of writers. We call ourselves the Adams Round Table, although the table's rectangular and there's nobody around named Adams. (Don't ask.) Several anthologies of original stories have grown out of this association, and this latest is just out from Berkley Prime Crime. The usual suspects are on hand – Mary Higgins Clark, Peter Straub, Mickey Friedman, Judith Kelman, Warren Murphy, Susan Isaacs, Stanley Cohen, Whitley Stieber, Dorothy Salisbury Davis, and Justin Scott, who wrote the introduction. My contribution's a new Matthew Scudder story, set in the days when he was still a detective with the NYPD.

I've been writing more short stories

lately, perhaps encouraged by the reception of Orion's *Collected Mystery Stories*. The book has received strong reviews on both sides of the ocean, and has gone into a second printing. (You should be able to get it, in hardcover or trade paperback, at mystery booksellers in the States; if you care strongly about first editions, I can still supply hardcover firsts for $70.) Since the book came out, I've been surprisingly productive, and an American collection, which HarperCollins will publish this year under the title *Long Story Short*, will include ten or a dozen new stories. A really nasty one called *Sweet Little Hands* will appear in *Flesh & Blood*, edited by Max Allan Collins, a baseball story (*Almost Perfect*) is in Playboy, and five are set for various anthologies Otto Penzler is editing for New Millenium. A longer story will kick off another project, a series of anthologies on each of the Seven Deadly Sins I'm editing for Cumberland House. The first book is *Speaking Of Lust*, and my personal contribution is the 20,000-word title novella. It's an old-fashioned frame story, with four guys (The Priest, The Soldier, The Doctor and The Policeman) sitting at a card table and spinning yarns. I had great fun with this one, and I'll have more to say about it when the book's scheduled.

Some of you may have seen an enormous colour photo of me, wearing a beret and glowering balefully, in Barnes & Noble stores all over the US. (If you haven't seen the poster, you can see the photograph in question, by the estimable John Pinderhughes, on the back of *Hit List*.) I somehow became the poster boy for Universe, the print-on-demand outfit with whom I'm republishing *Random Walk*. You may have tried to order the book, and you may have failed in the attempt. The company has had growing pains, and the book got delayed. It's out now in a handsome trade paperback edition. This is a rather special book for me, unlike anything else I've done, and it failed to find its audience the first time around. Most booksellers can order it for you, and some B&N stores have it in stock – or check it out on-line at www.iUniverse.com.

Listen Up! As you may know, I've recorded audios for most of the Burglar books, but they've been severely abridged; while I've enjoyed narrating them, I've hesitated to urge them upon anyone. The *Hit List* audio is also abridged, but its running time is twice as long as the Burglar audios. I had fun recording it, and can recommend it for those of you who enjoy reading with your ears. I've also just finished recording *Telling Lies for Fun and Profit*, my most popular book for writers. It has never been available in audio, a form which seems to be particularly suited to self-help books, so I'm biting the bullet and publishing it myself. It's complete and unabridged, and will retail for around $40. I don't know how broad distribution will be, but you'll certainly be able to order it directly from me, through the newsletter or the website. I'll keep you posted...

Lynne and I have been travelling recently, and at the end of 2000 returned from a trip to Kaliningrad, the Baltics, Moscow, Belarus, Ukraine, Moldova, and Romania. Our country count stands at eighty-seven – and I hate to admit it but we're getting tired of running around. Tired or not, the publication of *Hit List* means it's book tour time...

TO THE MAX

His own books have earned him the sobriquet King of the Erotic Thriller; he's one of the genre's premier editors... Mr ***Maxim Jakubowski****.*

With *Demolition Angel* (Orion, £12.99), Robert Crais is shooting squarely for the big time with all guns and bombs blazing. A veteran scriptwriter who worked on *LA.Law* and *Hill Street Blues*, Crais is responsible for eight delightful Elvis Cole novels to date, a witty, inventive series featuring a hipper than hip Californian private eye which last year reached a marked crescendo in the moving *LA Requiem*. He has now taken a leaf from his friend Michael Connelly and consciously set aside his trademark series and penned a big thriller by numbers in a conscious attempt to conquer the best-seller lists. Carol Starkey used to be the queen of the bomb disposal squad until an explosion that scarred her badly and killed her partner and lover. She is now on the sidelines in a police conspiracy squad, bitter and lonely, when an innocuous bomb call turns into a charred murder scene. The modus operandi brings her past rushing back in fifth gear and the chase for the master criminal involved also involves Carol's redemption, alongside a breathless cat and mouse chase. The plot functions like clockwork, with every ingredient carefully dosed: the master criminal, the inevitable McGuffin, the heroine's alcoholism and lack of love life, the fascinating technical details about bomb making and defusing, the FBI computer know-how, but the book lacks soul in its relentless move forward.

Now on his third novel, Jerry Raine is a British author who prospers within the thin ranks of domestic miserabilism noir, if there is such a sub-genre. *Slaphead Chameleon* (Gollancz, £9.99) combines the quiet small-time desperation of his first books with a glimpse into the shadowy borderlines of folk singing and the music business. This is suburban crime at its quietest and most unassuming and packs a mean punch as its unshowy virtues accumulate. Raine has a gift for recreating the ordinariness of daily crime and much empathy for his collection of losers. More cheerful, if not totally manic is Marc Blake's *24 Carat Schmooze* (Flame, £12.00), like a British Carl Hiaasen where every London character is eminently dodgy and mired in a snake pit of intrigue and painful belly laughs. This is a sidesplitting romp of a thriller with all the charm of an alligator, as it follows a band of Dickensian modern geezers through a web of deceit and extortion. Guaranteed to cheer you up and worry you no end as you ponder the world you and Blake's characters somehow share. Instigator and eminence grise of Tart Noir, a breakaway group of female crime writers with attitude to spare (see their hilarious website on www.tartcity.com), Lauren Henderson is an endearing cross between Raymond Chandler and Betty Boop and her heroine, sculptress Sam Jones, has a knack for being in the wrong place at the wrong time, and usually in the wrong outfit. Her latest caper *Chained* (Hutchinson, £16.99/£10.00) is another racy set of misadventures in medialand as our involuntary sleuth gets beaten up, handcuffed and touched up, and that's only the beginning of her problems. Forget the angst and enjoy the ride. Equally lightweight but gossamer fun is another Tart Noir alumni, Sparkle Hayter's effervescent TV newswoman Robin Hudson in *The Chelsea Girl Murders* (No Exit Press, £14.99/£6.99). A fire forces this New York version of Bridget Jones with added spunk and wit to vacate her apartment and move into the legendary Chelsea Hotel. Needless to say, the unlikely-named Sparkle, ex-TV reporter and Canadian of this parish, has also lived in the bohemian hotel for some years and knows all its nooks and crannies, which proves useful as chaos soon ensues with a literal plague of bodies littering the rooms and stairways. Will Robin solve the fiendish crimes? Will Robin get the bad guy? The good guy? Both? A fun ride with enough jokes to fill a hotel room and a splendid cast of frenetic New Yorkers, which confirms Miss Hayter as the comic queen of all she surveys.

The next American crime offerings are in a lighter vein but no less entertaining for that. *Sick Puppy* by Carl Hiaasen (Macmillan, £9.99) sees the Miami eco-humourist in a marked return to form, raging against the despoliation of his native state with all fictional guns roaring and dark and bizarre mayhem littering the sunny landscape. Twilly Spree, who has become rich on the dirty money inherited from his real estate developer father, wishes to salve his conscience and embarks on a war against all sorts of environmental pirates who are spoiling the beauty of the land. The villains are more villainous and ridiculous than ever, the situations quite absurd and cartoonish, and the gleefully over-the-top action, spoils, chases and sundry scams and scandals will delight all Hiaasen's many diehard fans and convert anyone who has not yet been enchanted by his sardonic take on the sunny hell that is Florida. For further tropical mayhem, why not sample Tim Dorsey's *Hammerhead Ranch Motel* (HarperCollins, £6.99) in which the genial homicidal maniac Serge Storms races around Florida in pursuit of five million dollars hidden in the boot of the wrong car. This takes the Hiaasen formula and adds Tarantino-laced amphetamine to the mix and the ensuing mayhem is raucous, body-strewn and both sinister and hilarious. How can you not investigate a novel in which a troupe of dancing Chihuahuas are dressed up to predict the weather, followed by a phalanx of skydiving Hemingways. Makes British crime fiction look so parochial! And if you thought such sardonic humour was a male prerogative, the female criminal of the species can be equally subversive. Elizabeth Peters' *Thunder in the Sky* (Robinson, £6.99), twelfth instalment of the adventures of suffragette, sleuth and archaeologist Amelia Peabody, brings our doughty heroine to 1914 and a Cairo full of spies, plots, counterplots and dastardly deeds. When an artefact uncovered at a Giza dig, an exquisite sculpture found where it ought not to be, confirms to Amelia that her arch-nemesis, Sethos the Master Criminal is afoot and her son Ramses is in danger, our heroine, a cross between Miss Marple and Indiana Jones, is soon wielding a mean brolly to great effect. Endearing, exotic and with tongue in cheek delights to spare.

Denise Mina's debut novel *Garnethill* won the Crime Writers' Association John Creasey Award for best first crime novel, and introduced a striking new, bleak but realistic voice alongside Ian Rankin and Christopher Brookmyre's in the fertile hinterland of Scottish noir. *Exile* (Bantam Press, £9.99) is an assured follow-up which confirms Mina's place in the premier division with brutal but compassionate assurance. Maureen O'Donnell, a Glasgow care worker, travels to London to escape her own inner demons and investigate the last days there of a battered woman who had come to her for help and whose body has now been found in the Thames. Alone in a strange city, Maureen pieces the contradictory mystery together under severe pressure as the case trawls up worrying connections with her own friends and family. Atmospheric, intense and full of the disturbing flavour of inner city low-life, this is a novel which reminds me strongly of the deeply-felt empathy for the folk forgotten by society the late Derek Raymond imbued his London novels with. Exciting and moving stuff. *Sleeping Partner* by James Humphreys, a 10 Downing Street senior civil servant (Macmillan, £16.99) is equally gripping and a slick debut but never quite convinces. Narrated in the first person by a young woman accused of the murder of her cad of a property developer boyfriend as her trial begins, the ongoing courtroom drama is undermined by the fact she suffered amnesia following a car crash and is herself uncertain whether she committed the shotgun crime or not. This hoary plot device allows for the flowering of many red herrings and installs the shy Clarissa as a spectator in her own story. However, despite evocative glimpses into her Suffolk country childhood and flashbacks a go-go, she never comes to life as a realistic character and the final deus ex machina that reveals her fate and what genuinely happened comes about as both perfunctory and contrived. E for effort.

His publishers are heralding John Williams as a Welsh version of Irvine Welsh or Nick Hornby, but he deserves better accolades. *Cardiff Dead* (Bloomsbury, £9.99) is a wicked dip into the shady side of the Welsh city and a veritable wonderful gallery of bizarre, endearing, disturbing and colourful characters going about their lives of love, crime and drinking in the shadow of the new giant Millennium Stadium. Williams had covered the same ground in his collection of stories *Five Pubs, Two Bars and a Nightclub*, but his Cardiff Bay patch comes to life with even more depth here, smells, riff raff and all, as a musician returns to his native city on the occasion of the funeral of Charlie Unger, a black boxer and conga player with the Wurriyas ska group. How the survivors cope with the aftermath and the changes that have swept the boxing gyms and surfer beaches is a tale and a half, funny, touching and flirting with the borders of darkness. Also taking a walk on the wild and gritty side of life is Natasha Cooper's *Prey To All* (Simon & Schuster, £16.99), a powerful contrast to her entertaining but more lightweight Willow King series. London barrister Trish Maguire visits a woman in a prison cell serving a life sentence for her father's murder and is soon determined to right the unjust situation. A classic whodunit situation but handled with stark realism and a strong sense of interpersonal relationships within families and the legal profession. A big step forward for the always reliable Natasha Cooper.

Noir Fiction by Paul Duncan (Pocket Essentials, £2.99) is a breezy survey of a complex field in under one hundred pages. It's an impossible task, not made easier by Duncan's idiosyncratic approach which insists on devoting pages to Dostoevsky, Conrad, Camus and even Nathanael West! His insights into neglected pioneers like Gerald Kersh, William Lindsay Gresham, Shane Stevens, David Karp or Derek Raymond prove useful, but again there is so much more to say on the subject of many modern masters like Ellroy, Willeford, Goodis, Thompson, etc… Too recent to be included in Duncan's pantheon of darkness are two newer American authors, both on great form. *The Big Thaw* by Donald Harstad (Fourth Estate, £9.99) sees the return of Deputy Sheriff Carl Houseman in another case set in the dead of winter in a Fargo-like mid West. American procedural writing at its best, detailed, atmospheric and with a pace that never rests. At the other end of the temperature gauge is David Lozell Martin's *Pelikan* (No Exit Press, £6.99), a rollicking tale of scams and bad deeds set in New Orleans, a city that attracts as much crime as Miami. Featuring confidence artists, thieving nuns, crazy Creole doctors and oddball characters by the dozen, this is the flip side of the world evoked by *A Confederacy of Dunces* but no less comic. A guilty pleasure.

Take a body. Take a room that is hermetically sealed from the inside, doors, windows and all. Whodunit? Howdunit? The locked room mystery has always been one of the most fascinating exercises generations of mystery writers have practised their baffling skills to construct. *The Mammoth Book of Locked Room Mysteries and Impossible Crimes*, edited by Mike Ashley (Robinson, £6.99) offers another thirty-six brilliant conundrums and brain twisters that would confound Sherlock Holmes or Jonathan Creek. Led by a classic reprint from John Dickson Carr, who made the genre his own, this bumper collection presents brand new mystifications by some of today's most elegant practitioners of crime as puzzle, including Peter Lovesey, Bill Pronzini, Lawrence Block, H. R. F. Keating and others. This is entertainment at its mind-bending best, including the solutions to how a man can be strangled in a car in which he was alone in the middle of a traffic jam or how an unaccompanied male can be murdered in an empty all-glass lift! All tales delicious and perverse in the best possible manner.

MARK TIMLIN: A PERSONAL VIEW

The creator of Nick Sharman (and crime reviewer for The Independent on Sunday) *gives CT the unvarnished truth (if he can just remember what happened last night)… (and check out www.nicksharman.co.uk)*

One of my greatest pleasures upon receiving a new edition of *Crime Time* is going to The Verdict section and finding a review by Gerald Houghton. Not of one of my books, I hasten to add. As it goes, I've specifically asked our esteemed editor never to let Mr Houghton within a mile of one, because I can imagine exactly what would happen. Tears before bedtime, that's what. I've never met Gerald. We've never shared a glass of tea. In fact I wouldn't know him if he jumped up and bit my leg. And by the quality of the reviews I've read by him, I'm quite sure he's capable of biting a whole lot more than that. But I do see him in my mind's eye. And how do I picture him? Either as an elderly gentleman fallen on hard times, living in the turret of a Gothic pile somewhere like Crouch End, armed only with a quill and an inkwell loaded with vitriol, or else as a reconstructed punk rocker in a council squat in Croydon with scratchy vinyl copies of *God Save The Queen* and *New Rose* on his stereo, grubby X-Ray Spex and Adam & The Ants posters on the wall, picking at his spots, dressed in bondage strides and a grubby Sex Pistols T-shirt. In fact, he's probably neither of these, and something tells me I'll find out after this is printed. But Momma, those reviews! Good Lord above! Vicious but fair hardly sums them up. He pulls absolutely no punches and I love them. But why use only one per issue Mr Forshaw? As far as I'm concerned he could write the whole review section on his own. As long as I don't have anything published around about that time of course. In the last edition he decimated a book called *Tin Kickers* by Bill Murphy. As a matter of fact I read it myself and quite enjoyed it, if only because, for the first couple of dozen pages I was convinced it was called *Tin Knickers*. It was an inoffensive volume as far as I could see, but Houghton cut it off at the knees, filleted it with a sharp knife, and cooked it over an open fire.

Which brings me neatly to the whole question of reviews and reviewers. Particularly when they're bad reviews. Now, since I was first published thirteen years ago my books have been reviewed hundreds of times in various newspapers and magazines, and I've been very lucky. On the whole the mentions have been favourable. As a matter of fact, only a very few have been bad. When my latest book *All The Empty Places* came out last year I got several

reviews as usual, mostly good, in fact mostly excellent, except for one in *The Times*. Really it wasn't that bad a review at all. The geezer who did it just didn't get what I was doing and came across (to me at least) as a bit dim. No-one I met had ever heard of him and I get the impression he's a failed novelist who, when anyone gets a publishing deal, wants to open his veins. But what annoyed me was that everyone I knew saw the damned thing. No-one seemed to see the good reviews in *The Guardian* and the *Daily Mirror* for instance. And everyone was very vocal in telling me they saw it. Eventually I grabbed one pal of mine and asked why. "Because your reviews are always so good," he replied, "that it seemed strange." There's no answer to that I suppose. But reviews are very strange animals. I know of authors who say they never read them. To that I reply, "Liar, liar, pants on fire." Unless of course they don't read any publication that carries a review section. And they're few and far between, especially ones that literary types might subscribe to. Because, if I'm reading a paper and my name is mentioned, it jumps out of the page and smacks me between the eyes and I can't resist reading on. But authors, like any other creative artists trying to earn money from their creations, are in a difficult position. In this life, if you raise your head above the parapet you're asking for it to be shot off.

Consider this: if your missus has a baby and you dress the little nipper up nice, plonk it in its pram and go for a promenade down the high street, do people come up to you, peer inside and say, "Blimey, that's the ugliest little bastard I've ever seen in all my life." Do they buggery. Even if it *is* the ugliest bastard they've ever seen in their lives, they go, "Cootchie, cootchie coo, what a little sweetie." So why then, after writing a novel, after all those months of gestation and cries of, "Push, push", when it finally sits there, all new and fresh in its crisp little jacket, does some bleeder think he's got the right to jump all over it in his hobnailed boots? And why do we read other authors' reviews and enjoy them so much when they're bad? The Germans have a word for it: *Schadenfreude* – the malicious enjoyment of others' misfortunes. That's why.

As you might know, I do an occasional column for the *Independent on Sunday* reviewing crime novels. Not criticising, I hasten to add. Well, not often, but more of that later. *Reviewing* is what I do. Finding stuff that appeals to those of a like mind and telling them about something they might otherwise have missed. I don't like bad reviews of my work as you've probably gathered, and I don't like giving them. However bad I think a novel may be, someone's sweated blood over it, and far be it from me to rubbish it out of hand. Besides, if I don't like a book I don't read it. Simple.

But there are exceptions. Sometimes a novel or novelist is so annoying that I have to have a go. Usually a favourite of mine who I think has let me down by not doing as good a job as he or she might. But not always. Sometimes it's just because I think the writer is an absolute shit. So if that geezer who reviewed my book in *The Times* ever publishes a crime novel, by Christ I'll be waiting. Or better still, maybe Gerald Houghton will give it a shot. Then *Schadenfreude* will be mine.

TIMLIN'S TOP TIPS

John Connolly – *The Killing Kind*, Hodder & Stoughton

Michael Connelly – *A Darkness More Than Night*, Orion

Christopher Cook – *Robbers*, No Exit Press

Steve Hamilton – *A Cold Day in Paradise*, Orion

Scott Phillips – *The Ice Harvest*, Picador

Mark Powell – *Snap*, Weidenfeld & Nicholson

Jenny Siler – *Iced*, Orion

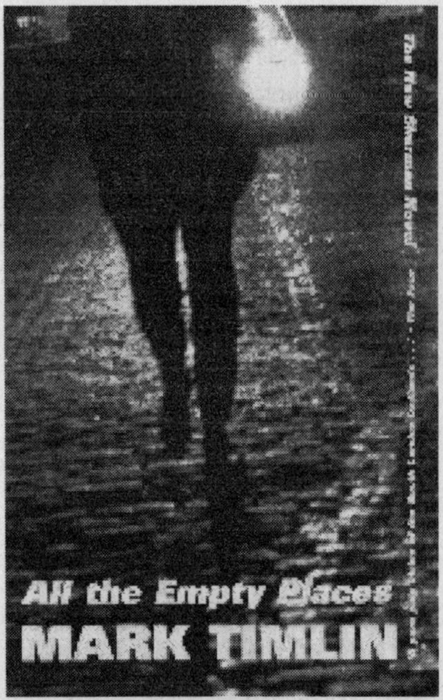

AUDIOCRIME

Brian Ritterspak

Robert Wilson's work is a natural for the audiobook medium, such is his considerable narrative grasp. With the right reader, his tales would seem perfect for the medium, and so it proves with Sean Barrett's reading of *A Small Death in Lisbon* (Isis). As Inspector Coelho is put in charge of the investigation of a young girl's murder in Lisbon, he opens up the dark secrets of Portuguese banks founded on the back of Nazi wartime deals. Wilson presents us with a rich panoply of characters, all creatively characterised by Barrett. Isis specialises in totally unabridged readings, and the total playing time of this audiobook is over seventeen hours. It goes without saying that the reader would not take that time to work his way through a novel as compulsive as this, but the experience here is rewarding and unique, with the cool and measured narrative voice sounding exactly the right note.

Isis remains an audiobook publisher firmly committed to the crime genre, and three new complete readings demonstrate the possibilities of the medium. With Faye Kellerman's *Jupiter's Bones*, we have one of the author's most inventive tales. Emil Ganz walked out of his family at the age of forty. For the next twenty years, his wife and children spend a great deal of time and money trying to locate Ganz, a noted physicist who specialised in the night sky. More than a decade after he disappears, Ganz returns, now calling himself Jupiter. He is now the guru of a New Age cult, preaching Armageddon. But as soon as he reappears, he is dead. Lieutenant Peter Decker is an expert on cults and refuses to believe that this is suicide. William Roberts' reading catches all the nuances and tension of one of Kellerman's most striking tales.

With *Deep Fall* by Bill Knox, we are presented with a more concise experience. Read by James Bryce, this is another compelling conundrum for the noted detective duo of Thane and Moss from the city of Glasgow police force, dealing with the bizarre events following the horrible death of an employee of an enamelling factory. This is a first-rate police procedural, even if the reading at times seems rather impersonal.

Back to the Kellerman family. Jonathan Kellerman's *Monster* was one of his most controversial Alex Delaware books, but this grisly and absorbing piece (while unlikely to win Kellerman any new readers) will be meat and drink to the true aficionado. John Moraitis is the reader, and his New York inflexions are perfectly apposite. As so often with the audiobook medium, listening seems to take considerably longer than any reading could. But if you're open to the experience, this is an exemplar of how it should be done.

Isis tapes are available by mail order from Isis Publishing on Freephone ***0800 731 5637*** *or from Soundings on* ***0191 253 4155****.*

BULLETS

Adrian Muller

Cartier Diamond Dagger

This year's recipient of the prestigious Crime Writers' Association's Diamond Dagger Award for lifetime contribution to crime fiction, sponsored by jewellers Cartier, goes to Lionel Davidson. Davidson is the only author to have received the Gold Dagger for best crime novel three times: *The Night of Wenceslas*, *A Long Way to Shiloh* (US title *The Menorah Men*), and *The Chelsea Murders* (US title *Murder Games*). By receiving this award Davidson joins past winners such as Colin Dexter, Reginald Hill, P D James and Ruth Rendell. *The Night of Wenceslas*, the author's first novel, was turned into the successful comedy *Hot Enough for June*, starring Dirk Bogarde. All of Lionel Davidson's crime novels are in the process of being reprinted by Arrow.

Crime on Television

ITV has recently commissioned Robson Green's production company to adapt Val McDermid's *The Wire in the Blood* for television. *Wire* was the follow up to McDermid's award winning crime novel *The Mermaids Singing*, which introduced criminal profiler Tony Hill and policewoman Carol Jordan. Green, last seen in *Touching Evil* will play Hill. No word yet on who will play Carol Jordan.

After rumours that Hugh Grant would play Elizabeth George's aristocrat Detective Inspector Thomas Lynley, the role has now been taken by Nathaniel Parker, one of the leads in the BBC's production of *Vanity Fair*. The Beeb is also responsible for *A Great Deliverance*, which has Parker teaming up with Sharon '*Glasgow Kiss*' Small as DS Barbara Havers.

Unusual Suspects

The authors who teamed up as the Murder Squad (John Baker, Chaz Brenchley, Ann Cleeves, Martin Edwards, Margaret Murphy, Stuart Pawson and Cath Staincliffe) to promote their work may have set a trend. Now banding together as the Unusual Suspects are Natasha Cooper, Leslie Forbes, Manda Scott, Michelle Spring, Andrew Taylor and Laura Wilson. Individually or in a group of varying size they provide readings and library talks, events in bookshops, after dinner speakers, and much more. The group held their highly successful St Valentine's Day Massacre launch at Crime in Store in February this year. For more info email info@unusualsuspects.co.uk

Conventions

Enter the following UK conventions in your diaries:

Crime Scene 2001

July 12-15, National Film Theatre,
South Bank, London SE1 8XT
Tel: 020 7815 1327
Email: brian.robinson@bfi.org.uk
Website: www.bfi.org.uk

St Hilda's Crime and Mystery Weekend: Scene of the Crime

August 17-19, St Hilda's College,
Crime and Mystery Weekend,
Cowley Place, Oxford OX4 1DY
Tel: 01865 276828
Email: eileen.roberts@st-hildas.oxford.ac.uk
(PLEASE INCLUDE POSTAL ADDRESS IN YOUR EMAIL)

Dead on Deansgate 2001:

Britain's biggest crime fiction convention
October 19-21, Renaissance Hotel, Manchester
For info contact: Waterstone's Booksellers,
91 Deansgate, Manchester M3 2BW
Tel: 0161 837 3000
Website: www.waterstones.co.uk/dod

Reprints

As the new British crime titles (tries to) list only first time crime publications, readers might be interested to know that Robert Hale is reprinting *The Law at Randado*, one of Elmore Leonard's western novels, and Ross Macdonald's second Lew Archer PI novel, *The Drowning Pool* is republished by Canongate.

NEW BRITISH CRIME TITLES

(Author – *Title* (Series), Publisher, Price)

January

Peter Abrahams – *Crying Wolf,* Michael Joseph, £5.99

Brigitte Aubert – *Death from the Woods,* Hodder & Stoughton, £17.99

Simon Brett – *Death of the Downs* (Fethering mystery), Macmillan, £16.99

Alys Clare – *The Tavern in the Morning* (Hawkenlye mystery), Hodder & Stoughton, £17.99

Michael Connelly – *A Darkness More Than Night* (Bosch & McCaleb), Orion, £16.99

Elaine Feinstein – *A Dark Inheritance,* The Women's Press, £9.99

Margaret Frazer – *The Reeve's Tale,* Robert Hale, £17.99

Pat Frieder – *Privileged Communications,* Robert Hale, £17.99

Steve Hamilton – *A Cold Day in Paradise* (Alex McKnight), Orion, £9.99/£16.99

Gerald Hammond – *Illegal Tender* (Three Oaks mystery), Macmillan, £16.99

George V. Higgins – *At the End of the Day,* Robinson, £17.99

Donald James – *Vadim* (Inspector Vadim), Century, £10.00

Russell Celyn Jones – *Surface Tension,* Abacus, £9.99

Morag Joss – *Fruitful Bodies* (Sara Selkirk), Hodder & Stoughton, £16.99

John le Carré – *The Constant Gardner,* Hodder & Stoughton, £16.99

Hector Macdonald – *The Mind Game* (debut crime novel), Michael Joseph, £10.00

David Ralph Martin – *Dead Man's Slaughter,* William Heineman, £16.99

Brad Meltzer – *The First Council,* Hodder & Stoughton, £12.99

David Michie – *Pure Deception,* Little, Brown, £10.00

Peter Millar – *Bleak Midwinter,* Bloomsbury, £9.99

Des Morley – *The House at Hungry Mountain,* Robert Hale, £16.99

Barbara Nadel – *Arabesk,* Headline, £17.99

Richard North Patterson – *Protect and Defend,* Hutchinson, £10.00

Jefferson Parker – *Red Light* (Merci Rayborn), HarperCollins, £9.99

Barrie Roberts – *Sherlock and the Crosby Murder* (Sherlock Holmes), Constable, £16.99

David Roberts – *Sweet Poison* (new series), Constable, £16.99

Christina Schwarz – *Drowning Ruth* (debut crime novel), Headline, £9.99

Nancy Taylor Rosenberg – *Buried Evidence,* Orion, £9.99/£16.99

Aline Templeton – *Shades of Death.* Hodder & Stoughton, £17.99

Kate Wilhelm – *No Defence,* Robert Hale, £17.99

Elizabeth Woodcraft – *Good Bad Woman,* HarperCollins, £9.99

February

Hilary Bonner – *A Kind of Wild Justice,* William Heineman, £10.00

Stuart Browne – *Dangerous Parking* (debut crime novel), Bloomsbury, £6.99

Clare Curzon – *The Colour of Blood,* Severn House, £17.99

Jeffery Deaver – *Manhattan Is My Beat* (Rune series), Hodder & Stoughton, £17.99

Frank Delaney – *At Ruby's* (Nicholas Newman), HarperCollins, £16.99

Eileen Dewhurst – *Closing Stages,* Severn House, £17.99

Peter Dickinson – *Some Deaths Before Dying,* Severn House, £17.99

Paul Eddy – *Flint,* Headline, £10.00

J M Gregson – *The Lancashire Leopard,* Severn House, £17.99

Martha Grimes – *Cold Flat Junction,* Headline, £17.99

John Grisham – *A Painted House,* Century, £16.99

Janis Harrison – *Murder Sets Seed* (Bretta Solomon), Robert Hale, £17.99

Daniel Hecht – *The Babel Effect,* Macmillan, £16.99

Jack Higgins – *Edge of Danger* (Sean Dillon), HarperCollins, £16.99

Hazel Holt – *Delay of Execution,* Macmillan, £16.99

Jon A Jackson – *Dead Folks* (Fang Mulheisen), Canongate, £9.99

J Robert Janes – *Beekeeper* (St-Cyr & Kohler), Gollancz, £9.99/£16.99

Iris Johansen – *The Search,* Hodder & Stoughton, £17.99

Danny King – *The Burlar Diaries,* Serpent's Tail, £6.99

Bernard Knight – *The Tinner's Corpse* (Crowner John), Simon & Schuster, £16.99

Sheila Kohler – *Cracks,* Bloomsbury, £14.99

Jose Latour – *Outcast,* HarperCollins, £9.99

Roy Lewis – *Dead Secret* (Arnold Landon), Constable, £16.99

Joan Lock – *Death in Perspective,* Robert Hale, £16.99

E A Macdonald – *The Keeper,* Pocket Books, £6.99

Jill McGown – *Scene of the Crime* (Lloyd & Hill), Macmillan, £16.99

Chris Niles – *Hell's Kitchen,* Pan, £5.99

James Pattinson – *Old Pals Act,* Robert Hale, £16.99

George Pelecanos – *Right as Rain* (new trilogy), Gollancz, £9.99/£16.99

Otto Penzler (editor) – *Murder and Obsession* (short stories), Orion, £9.99

Anne Perry – *The Whitechapel Conspiracy* (the Pitts), Headline, £17.99

Elizabeth Peters – *Lion in the Valley* (Amelia Peabody), Robinson, £6.99

Lynda Robinson – *Murder in the Place of Anubis,* Allison & Busby, £6.99

Betty Rowlands – *Touch Me Not* (Sukey Reynolds), Severn House, £17.99

Sally Spencer – *The Dark Lady* (CI Woodend), Severn House, £17.99

Robert K Tanenbaum – *Tue Justice* (Karp & Ciampi), Simon & Schuster, £10.00

Scarlett Thomas – *Bright Young Things,* Flame, £10.99

George Tiffin – *Mercy Alexander,* Picador, £12.00

Peter Turnbull – *Perils and Dangers* (Hennessey & Yellich), Severn House, £17.99

Stella Whitelaw – *Pray and Die* (PI Jordan Lacey-new series), Severn House, £17.99

Gerard Williams – *Dr Mortimer and the Barking Man* (Dr Mortimer), Constable, £16.99

Robert Wilson – *The Company of Strangers,* HarperCollins, £12.99

Valerie Wilson Wesley – *The Devil Riding,* Robert Hale, £17.99

March

Vivien Armstrong – *Rewind,* Severn House, £17.99

Andrea Badenoch – *Blink,* Macmillan, £10.00

Janie Bolitho – *Plotted in Cornwall* (Rose Trevelyan), Constable, £16.99

Dougie Brimson – *Top Dog,* Headline, £9.99

Marshall Browne – *The Wooden Leg of Inspector Anders* (new series), Pocket Books, £5.99

Paul Carson – *Final Duty,* William Heineman, £10.00

Caroline Carver – *Blood Junction,* Orion, £9.99

Tom Clancy & Steve Pieczenik – *Point of Impact* (Net Force), Headline, £6.99

John Connolly – *The Killing Kind,* Hodder & Stoughton, £12.99

Jeffery Deaver – *Death of a Blue Movie Star* (Rune series), Hodder & Stoughton, £17.99

Humphrey Hawksley – *Red Spirit,* Headline, £17.99

Lynne Heitmann – *Hard Landing,* Little, Brown, £9.99

Lynn Hightower – *Borderline,* Hodder & Stoughton, £17.99

Evan Hunter & Ed McBain – *Candyland,* Gollancz, £16.99

P D James – *Death in Holy Orders* (Commander Dalgliesh), Faber & Faber, £10.99/£17.99

Quintin Jardine – *Autographs in the Rain* (Bob Skinner), Headline, £9.99/£17.99

John Lawton – *Riptide* (Frederick Troy), Weidenfeld & Nicholson, £9.99/£16.99

Frank Lean – *Above Suspicion* (Dave Cunane), William Heineman, £16.99

Domenic Martell – *Gitana,* Gollancz, £9.99/£16.99

Priscilla Masters – *Winding up the Serpent* (Joanna Piercy), Allison & Busby, £6.99

Priscilla Masters – *Scaring Crows* (Joanna Piercy), Allison & Busby, £6.99

Scott McBain – *The Coins of Judas,* HarperCollins, £9.99/£16.99

Nigel McCrery – *Faceless Stranger* (Sam Ryan), Simon & Schuster, £5.99/£16.99

Margaret Meek – *If You Go Down to the Woods,* Severn House, £17.99

Chris Mooney – *Deviant Ways* (debut crime novel), Simon & Schuster, £10.00

Bill Murphy – *Fractions of Zero,* Hodder & Stoughton, £17.99

Michael Palmer – *Side Effects,*Century, £16.99

Anne Perry – *Resurrection Row* (the Pitts), HarperCollins, £5.99

Richard Pitman – *Joseph's Mansions,* HarperCollins, £9.99/£16.99

Ian Rankin – *The Falls* (Inspector Rebus), Orion, £16.99

Mike Ripley – *Lights, Camera, Angel* (Roy Angel), Constable, £16.99

Roberta Rogow – *The Problem of the Evil Editor* (Lewis Carroll and Conan Doyle), Robert Hale, £17.99

Betty Rowlands – *The Fourth Suspect* (Melissa Craig), Hodder & Stoughton, £17.99

Steven Saylor – *Honour the Dead* (non-Gordianus), Robinson, £16.99

C J Songer – *Hook,* Robert Hale, £17.99

Cath Staincliffe – *Stone Cold Red Hot* (Sal Kilkenny), Allison & Busby, £16.99

James Sturz – *Sasso* (debut crime novel), Century, £10.00

Alison Taylor – *Child's Play,* William Heineman, £15.99

Simon Temprell – *Previous Convictions,* Macmillan, £9.99

Andrew Vachss – *Choice of Evil* (Burke), Canongate, £9.99

April

Marian Babson – *Deadly Deceit,* Constable, £16.99

Nick Barclay – *Hooky Gear,* Sceptre, £10.99

Colin Bateman – *Shooting Sean* (Dan Starkey), HarperCollins, £6.99

Harry Bingham – *Sweet Talking Money,* HarperCollins, £5.99

Stephen Booth – *Dancing with the Virgins* (E Division), HarperCollins, £9.99

Carole Anne Davis – *Women Who Kill* (true crime), Allison & Busby, £16.99

Jeffery Deaver – *Hard News* (Rune series), Hodder & Stoughton, £17.99

Joolz Denby – *Corazon,* HarperCollins, £9.99

Paul Doherty – *Corpse Candle* (Hugh Corbett), Headline, £9.99/£17.99

Juliet Hebden – *Pel and the Butchers' Blade* (Commissaire Pel), Constable, £16.99

Mary Higgens Clarke – *Before I Say Goodbye,* Pocket Books, £6.99

Reginald Hill – *Dialogues of the Dead* (Dalziel & Pascoe), HarperCollins, £16.99

Jane Jakeman – *Death in the South of France,* Allison & Busby, £16.99

Gareth Joseph – *Homegrown* (debut crime novel), Headline, £5.99

Donna Leon – *A Sea of Troubles* (Commissario Brunetti series), William Heineman, £15.99

Jim Lusby – *A Waste of Shame,* Gollancz, £9.99/£16.99

Henning Mankell – *The Fifth Woman* (Kurt Wallander),Harvill Press, £9.99/£16.99

Viviane Moore – *The Darkest Red* (Chevalier Galeran), Gollancz, £9.99

Jonathan Nasaw – *The Girls he Adored,* Simon & Schuster, £10.00

Gilda O'Neill – *Getting There,* William Heineman, £16.99

Julie Parsons – *Eager to Please,* Macmillan, £10.00

James Patterson – *1st to Die* (new series), Headline, £16.99

Bill Pronzini – *Blue Lonesome,* Canongate, £9.99

Jim Williams – *Recherche*, Scribner, £6.99

Jim Williams – *The Strange Death of a Romantic,* Scribner, £7.99

May

Russell Andrews – *Icarus,* Little, Brown, £10.00

Campbell Armstrong – *The Bad Fire,* HarperCollins, £9.99

Jake Arnott – *He Kills Coppers,* Sceptre, £10.99

John Baker – *Shooting in the Dark* (Sam Turner), Gollancz, £9.99/£16.99

Maria Barrett – *The Dream Catcher,* Little, Brown, £9.99

Raymond Benson – *Never Dream of Dying* (James Bond), Hodder & Stoughton, £17.99

John Case – *Trance State,* Century, £10.00

Mia Couto – *Under the Frangipani,* Serpent's Tail, £10.00

Jeffery Deaver – *The Blue Nowhere*, Hodder & Stoughton, £14.99

Sally Emerson – *Broken Bodies*, Little, Brown, £15.99

Lisa Gardner – *The Third Schoolboy*, Orion, £9.99/£16.99

Patricia Hall – *Skeleton at the Feast* (Michael Thackery), Allison & Busby, £6.99

David Hewson – *Lucifer's Shadow*, HarperCollins, £16.99

Kathy Hogan Trocheck – *Irish Eyes* (Callahan Garrity), Robert Hale, £17.99

Bill James – *Pay Days* (Harpur & Iles), Constable, £16.99

Laurie King – *Folly*. HarperCollins, £9.99

Steve Martini – *The Jury*, Headline, £17.99

Priscilla Masters – *Embroidering Shrouds* (Joanna Piercy), Macmillan, £16.99

John Matthews – *The Last Witness*, Michael Joseph, £9.99

Jane Morell – *The Reckoning*, Robert Hale, £17.99

David Pirie – *Murder Rooms: The Patient's Eyes* (Sherlock Holmes), Century, £10.00

Robert T Price – *Big Deal* (Kenny Madigan). Robert Hale, £17.99

Malcolm Pryce – *Aberystwyth Mon Amour* (debut crime novel), Bloomsbury, £9.99

Julian Rathbone – *Homage*, Allison & Busby, £16.99

Peter Rawlinson – *The Richmond Diary*, Constable, £16.99

Robert Reuland – *Hollowpoint*, Jonathan Cape, £15.99

Peter Robinson – *Cold is the Grave* (Alan Banks), Macmillan, £12.99

Rob Ryan – *Trans Am*, Headline, £9.99

Manda Scott – *No Good Deed*, Headline, £10.00

Sarah Smith – *A Citizen of the Country*, Arrow, £5.99

Jose Carlos Somoza – *The Cave of Ideas*, Abacus, £9.99

Michelle Spring – *In the Midnight Hour* (Laura Princepal), Orion, £9.99/£16.99

Jane Stevenson – *London Bridges*, Vintage, £6.99

Boris Vian – *I Spit on Your Graves*, Canongate, £5.99

Kevin Wignall – *People Die* (debut crime novel), Hodder & Stoughton, £10.00

James Wilson – *The Dark Clue*, Faber & Faber, £9.99

June

Jane Adams – *Like Angels Falling*, Macmillan, £16.99

Rennie Airth – *The Blood-Dimmed Tide* (John Madden), Macmillan, £12.99

Ace Atkins – *Crossroad Blues* (Nick Travers), Robinson, £6.99

Pauline Bell – *Reasonable Death* (DI Mitchell), Constable, £16.99

Robin Cook – *Shock*, Macmillan, £16.99

Denise Danks – *Soft Target* (Georgina Powers), Gollancz, £9.99/£16.99

Lindsey Davis – *A Body in the Bathhouse* (Marcus Didius Falco), Century, £15.99

Paul Doherty – *The House of Death* (Alexander the Great), Robinson, £16.99

James Ellroy – *The Cold Six Thousand*, Century, £15.99

Penelope Evans – *First Fruits*, Allison & Busby, £17.99

Robert M Eversz – *Killing Paparazz*, Macmillan, £9.99

John Fusco – *Paradise Salvage*, Scribner, £10/£16.99

Jonathan Gash – *Every Last Cent* (Lovejoy), Macmillan, £16.99

Alan Glynn – *The Dark Fields*, Little, Brown, £10.99

Sue Grafton – *P is for Peril* (Kinsey Millhone), Macmillan, £9.99

Susanna Gregory – *An Order for Death* (Matthew Bartholomew), Little, Brown, £12.99

James Hall – *Kill Switch* (Rafferty & Thorn), HarperCollins, £9.99

Steve Hamilton – *Winter of the Wolf Moon* (Alex McKnight), Orion, £9.99/£16.99

Sylvian Hamilton – *The Pendragon Banner* (Sir Richard Straccan), Orion, £9.99

James Harland – *The Month of the Leopard,* Simon & Schuster, £10.00

Ellen Hart – *The Merchant of Venus* (Jane Lawless), The Women's Press, £6.99

Alan Jacobson – *The Hunted,* Hodder & Stoughton, £17.99

Anita Janda – *The Secret Diary of Dr. Watson* (Holmes & Watson), Allison & Busby, £17.99

Paul Johnston – *The House of Dust* (Quint Dalrymple), Hodder & Stoughton, £17.99

Max Kinnings – *Fixer,* Flame, £10.99

Richard Littlejohn – *Reasonable Force,* HarperCollins, £5.99

Sam Llewellyn – *The Malpas Legacy,* Headline, £9.99/£17.99

Marianne Macdonald – *Blood Lies* (Dido Hoare), Hodder & Stoughton, £17.99

Sharyn McCrumb – *The Song Catcher* (Ballad series), Hodder & Stoughton, £17.99

Michael McGarrity – *The Judas Judge* (Kevin Kerney), Robert Hale, £17.99

Gwen Moffatt – *Quicksand,* Constable, £16.99

Peter Moore Smith – *Strange Bliss,* Hutchinson, £10.00

Natasha Mostert – *The Other Side of Silence,* Hodder & Stoughton, £17.99

Chris Paling – *Newton's Swing,* Vintage, £6.99

Eliot Pattison – *Water Touching Stone,* Century, £10.00

Daniel Pennac – *Passion Fruit* (Belleville Quarter), Harvill Press, £9.99/£16.99

Danuta Reah – *The Butcher's Birdsong* (Lynne Jordan), HarperCollins, £9.99

Nicholas Rhea – *The Sniper* (Pemberton), Constable, £16.99

Kevin Sampson – *Outlaws,* Jonathan Cape, £10.00

Andrew Taylor – *Death's Own Door* (Lydmouth), Hodder & Stoughton, £17.99

For further information on the above titles, or to order books, contact:

Crime in Store

14 Bedford Street, Covent Garden, London WC2E 9HE

Tel: +44 (0)20 7379 3795, fax: +44 (0)20 7379 8988

Email: CrimeBks@aol.com Website: http://www.crimeinstore.co.uk

Murder One

71-73 Charing Cross Road, London WC2H 0AA

Tel: +44 (0)20 7734 3483, fax: +44 (0)20 7734 3429

Email: 106562.2021@compuserve.com Website: http://www.murderone.co.uk

Post Mortem Books

58 Stanford Avenue, Hassocks, Sussex BN6 8JH

Tel: +44 (0)1273 843066, fax: +44 (0)1273 845090

Email: ralph@pmbooks.demon.co.uk Website: http://www.postmortembooks.co.uk

THE CRIME TIME PANEL

*CT's editor **Barry Forshaw** chooses to disagree (over Chianti and Fava beans) with three of the magazine's key reviewers (all-rounder **Eve Tan Gee**, classic crime lover **Judith Gray** and hard-boiled **Brian Ritterspak**) on just about every crime novel that the quartet have jointly read. Whose side are you on?*

Barry Forshaw: Under pressure from you all, I agreed to give this column a miss in the last issue. Your excuse then was too many books, too little time. Has anything changed?

Brian Ritterspak: No, not really – there are far too many books being published, particularly in the crime genre. How the hell can anyone keep track of them all?

Eve Tan Gee: Absolutely. But, come on Brian, we're all guided by word of mouth, and fellow crime readers and writers point us to the books that we really should read, right?

Judith Gray: You're not influenced by publishers' blurbs on books you pick up?

Forshaw: They can act as a kind of guide, but after you've been promised the Second Coming for the twenty-seventh time, a certain cynicism sets in, doesn't it?

Gray: I'd put it more strongly than cynicism – more a total refusal to believe anything on the blurb of a book written by the publisher... unless the quote is from an unimpeachable source like Crime Time, of course.

Ritterspak: Well, that's pretty doctrinaire, isn't it? You have to use the blurbs as some kind of a guide.

Forshaw: Am I right in thinking this is a first – we've all read all the books?

Gray: You must be joking!

Ritterspak: Try us.

Forshaw: Okay, let's begin with *The Man Who Became Sherlock Holmes*, a biography of Jeremy Brett from Virgin. Rather unfortunately subtitled *The Tortured Mind of Jeremy Brett*, I found this fascinating – and moving.

Gray: I agree. I know you like Basil Rathbone's Holmes, but there you have to put up with Nigel Bruce's Watson. Jeremy Brett has Edward Hardwicke – and Brett, for me, was the definitive incarnation. Although I had some notion of how difficult his life was, Terry Manners lays it out unflinchingly.

Ritterspak: Yes – before we all knew that something was seriously wrong, those last two episodes in which he is bloated and nervy hinted that something had happened to the actor.

Tan Gee: It was worse than that: the restraint and perfectly etched touches of the early episodes had become full-blown mannerisms. I must say I found Terry Manners' book rather penny-plain in style, but it told the tale.

Gray: I liked *Manslaughter* by David Ralph Martin (Heinemann) – Bristol lends itself to a smack city narrative such as this – the city fathers wouldn't like it, but it's an atmospheric piece.

Ritterspak: For me, the key book in the latest batch was the new George Pelecanos, *Shame the Devil*. Not really a thriller – just a superbly written novel.

Tan Gee: This is solid Pelecanos – powerfully written, but somewhat on autopilot, don't you think?

Gray: No, I felt it was vintage stuff.

Forshaw: Okay, what about Deon Meyer's *Dead at Daybreak* (Hodder) and Judith Cutler's *Dying by Degrees* (Headline)? I found both very diverting.

Tan Gee: Yes, I enjoyed both. I've not liked every one of Cutler's Sophie Rivers books, but this was a real find for me.

Ritterspak: *Dead at Daybreak* was sufficiently blood-boltered for me – nothing genteel about this one.

Gray: Well, that's more your style than mine. But *Dead at Daybreak* is a very professional piece of work. I was really impressed by Russell James' *Painting in the Dark* (Do Not Press). This is a very ambitious book with its large panoply, and I like the way James tackled the British and German American views of the Nazis.

Forshaw: Yes, he's handled all that in a totally responsible way whilst delivering the goods in a nicely labyrinthine plot.

Ritterspak: It wasn't the best thing I've read by Russell James, but at times it was a salutary reminder of just how good he is.

Tan Gee: Speaking of how good people really are, who around this table really liked Derek Raymond?

Forshaw: I guess we're onto *The Crust on its Uppers* (Serpent's Tail), right? You know, Eve, I think I'm right in saying that this is your first Derek Raymond novel, and you shouldn't judge him on that.

Tan Gee: Why not?

Ritterspak: Yes, why not? I still think it's a wonderful piece. Very mannered, of course.

Forshaw: Exactly – and as such, perhaps not the best approach to Raymond. He wrote much finer books...

Tan Gee: Well, I've long thought that I should read him, but I must say that this one, with its overblown, recherché style didn't inspire me to pick up another book by him.

Gray: I really liked Gillian Linscott's *The Perfect Daughter* (Virago), although I don't think Nell Gray is sufficiently differentiated from the million other female crime novel protagonists we are confronted with.

Tan Gee: I thought this is the best Nell Gray yet, written with real energy and intelligence.

Forshaw: I know we all read *The Raymond Chandler Papers* (Viking). I take it this has a universal thumbs up – or does it?

Tan Gee: Up to a point, Lord Copper. Wonderful stuff here, but it is a cannibalised version of previous books isn't it?

Ritterspak: I didn't realise that at first, but I can't say it really mattered, even though some of the material was familiar.

Gray: I had real pleasure from three very disparate books: Gareth Creer's *Big Sky* (Doubleday), Vicki Hendrick's *Voluntary Madness* (Serpent's Tail) and Jefferson Parker's *Red Light* (HarperCollins). In their very different ways, these all represent crime writing of a rare order.

Tan Gee: I'm in accord with you on that, I enjoyed all three, although the Hendricks did the most for me.

Forshaw: This is the time I bring up Agatha Christie...

Ritterspak: Must you?

Tan Gee: There you go again, Brian! I suppose we're going to get the usual facile dismissal, but you can't argue with the fact that she remains one of the most influential crime writers of all time.

Gray: Absolutely! And there's a curious thing about her work: because there is so much of it, and because the plots sometimes slip away, you can read them again with renewed pleasure.

Ritterspak: Well, I think that says it all, doesn't it? The plots "sometimes slip away"?

Gray: I can see there's no use trying to convince you, Brian. Anyway, I thought that the two Christie *Murder by the Box* volumes (four novels each, HarperCollins) were great fun, and I reread every novel virtually in succession.

Ritterspak: My God!

Tan Gee: I dipped into the box, and I had a good time.

Forshaw: Okay: in the Pan Classic Crime series, how about *My Name is Michael Sibley* by John Bingham?

Ritterspak: Now this really *is* classic crime. The characterisation here is a million times more sophisticated than Dame Agatha.

Forshaw: Okay Brian, your antipathy is registered. Judith?

Gray: Yes, I thought the Bingham a highly unusual piece of writing, with the psychological realism utterly plausible.

Tan Gee: Didn't you say, Barry, that you liked Colin Harrison's *Afterburn* (Bloomsbury)?

Forshaw: Yes: not much subtlety, but a pungently written thriller that didn't allow you pause to ask inconvenient questions.

Gray: I enjoyed that one, although I feel a little more subtlety of characterisation might have been shoehorned in without any serious damage to the pace.

Forshaw: Thanks everyone – I think that's it. I don't think you've yet seen D. R. Macdonald's wonderful *Cape Breton Road* (Chatto), and it's good to see Arcadia books bring out its new Eurocrime series with reissues of such Nicholas Freeling gems as *Because of Cats* and *Some Day Tomorrow,* although I think they're a little pricey at £10.99, however attractive the format is. You've all got your bags of books and eight weeks before our next panel. You must admit these shebangs are better when we've all read the books.

THE OTHER BIG SLEEP

Michael Carlson

Howard Hawks shot *The Big Sleep* in late 1944, going well over schedule and finishing in January 1945. The film was not released until August 1946, and not until there had been re-shooting and substantial re-editing of the original version. It was often assumed that this re-shooting was necessary because the story was incoherent: the famous anecdote that no-one could figure out who had committed one of the murders or why, and when Chandler himself was called in, neither could he! The discovery and restoration of the original 1945 cut of the film by the UCLA Film Archives helps us put that myth to rest. But just for the record, there are six killings committed during the film, and they all make sense, more or less.

The first is the pornographer and blackmailer Geiger, who is killed by the Sternwood's chauffeur, Owen Taylor, in order to save Carmen Sternwood. Taylor steals the film of Carmen, and is chased from the scene (two cars roar away as Marlowe approaches the house). Taylor is killed by Joe Brody, who takes the film from him. Brody is shot by Carol Lundgren, Geiger's 'chauffeur', who thinks, mistakenly, that Brody killed Geiger. These three killings conclude the first part of the story, the Carmen blackmail plot.

The other half of the story is the Eddie Mars/Sean Regan plot. Mars' enforcer, Canino, kills Harry Jones, who is attempting to peddle information about Mars on behalf of Agnes, Joe Brody's girl. Canino, of course, is killed by Marlowe, and then Eddie Mars is shot accidentally by his own hoods, falling into the trap he set for Marlowe. The death of Sean Regan, the murder which hangs over the entire story, is usually attributed to Carmen, as it was in the novel, but the film's suggestion is actually that Mars did it himself (or ordered it done) and blackmailed Carmen, who was too high to know whether or not she'd done it herself. Mars' failure to recognise Carmen when she's with Marlowe is the crux of that argument; it convinces both Marlowe and me (although Mars certainly should have recognised Vivian's wild society bimbo younger sister anyway).

In his excellent monograph on *The Big Sleep* (BFI 1997), David Thompson deals with the changes as part of Howard Hawks' appropriation of the Bogart / Bacall characters, turning them into himself and his wife, Slim. Thompson's feeling is that Hawks, having modelled Bacall's image after his wife's, then lost interest in her, presumably because she wouldn't 'play ball', as it were. He quotes a letter from Raymond Chandler which says the 1945 version was 'nonsense' because it had been cut to edit out Martha Vickers' performance, which had stolen the film from Bacall. Whether that is true or not, it's not a huge leap to assume that Hawks may have been more than interested in Vickers, whose performance is one of the very best in all crime films, and, as Thompson points out, Hawks' seems to take great care in his lighting of her. And since the principal photography over-ran so badly in 1944-45, it's also not unreasonable to assume that some of the changes many of the people involved in the film refer to may have arisen from other considerations than just the script. But there is no doubt that the principal motivation for the re-shooting for the 1946 version was to make Bacall look better, and try to grab some of the electricity between her and Bogart which had made *To Have and Have Not* crackle. After that success, Bacall had played in *The Confidential Agent*, with Charles Boyer, and it was a flopperoo. Thompson mentions that her agent, Charles Feldman, wrote to Jack Warner suggesting changes in *The Big Sleep* that would benefit Bacall. Feldman (who had 'stolen' his wife, Jean Howard, from the clutches of Louis B. Mayer himself) wrote a detailed proposal to Warner, who agreed with his ideas, and ordered the re-shoot. Turner Film Classics now broadcasts the 1945 version (not colorised and not speeded up a couple of frames per second to squeeze in more commercials) along with a thirty minute postscript narrated by Bob Gitt of the UCLA Film Archive, detailing and explaining the major changes. A quick run-through of the major changes is instructive.

The 1945 version details Marlowe's search of Geiger's house, which establishes both that someone broke into the house via the kitchen window, and that someone in the house uses perfumed handkerchiefs (we've already had our hints that Geiger is gay). In the 1946 version, there's a dissolve straight to Marlowe discovering Geiger's client book.

Marlowe drives the passed-out Carmen home, which includes a lovely shot of Martha Vickers reflected in the rear-view mirror. When he reaches the Sternwood place, he gives Carmen to the butler, with instructions. In the 1946 version, they cut directly to a new scene, with Carmen being deposited in bed and Vivian at the bedside. Sparks fly, as Marlowe makes some suggestions about Sean Regan, and Bacall says, "You go too far".

In the 1945 version there was a scene in which Marlowe explains to Vivian the things he's now already explained in the bedroom, so the scene was re-dubbed, with dialogue that is visibly out of synch.

In the 1945 version, Marlowe hands over Carol to Bernie Olds, and they go to explain things to cop Cronjager (James Flavin) and DA Wilde (Thomas Jackson).

Marlowe explains the story so far to the

DA (and to the audience). After leaving the DA's office, Marlowe and Olds discuss the link between Regan and Eddie Mars. This leads to:

Vivian (wearing a veil) waiting in Marlowe's office. She pays Marlowe $500,and says the case is closed. Marlowe brings up Regan, we get a great line ("My brandy's just as good as his"), and then, after Vivian leaves...

Marlowe calls Mars at his club (long distance) while burning the photo of Carmen in his ashtray.

In the 1946 version, Marlowe hands over Carol (4) and then we cut straight to Vivian (in a shiny suit) meeting Marlowe in a bar (6). The entire expository scene disappears. The bar is the setting for the famous 'horse race' scene between Bogart and Bacall, one added to facilitate Feldman's suggestion of more suggestion between the two. She again pays Marlowe off, they go through their 'in the saddle' metaphors, and then, with no hint of brandies in the offing, Marlowe asks, "Who told you to sugar me off the case, Eddie Mars?" They then dissolve to Marlowe calling Eddie Mars (again long distance) at his club (7), but this time from the pay phone in the bar.

When Marlowe beats up the would-be 'robber' in the parking lot of Mars' joint, a cut away of Bacall is added in the 1946 version.

The next new scene may well have been shot in 1944 for the original version, but left out of the edit. In it, Marlowe returns from Mars' casino to discover Carmen in his apartment. Between biting him, she tells Marlowe that Sean Regan didn't like her, and that Mars calls Vivian. He kicks Carmen out and we dissolve to his being awakened by a call from Olds.

In the 1945 version, Olds meets Marlowe in his office and tells him to 'lay off' because Vivian has changed the DA's mind. In the 1946 version, we don't know who changed the DA's mind, and Marlowe has an extra line, "I know you just work here". He then starts explaining things to Olds, in a futile attempt to make up for the cutting of (5) above.

In the 1945 version, Marlowe is KO'd by Canino, and wakes to find to find Vivian and Mrs Eddie Mars (played by a platinum blonde Pat Clark). In the new version, shot to give Bacall better close-ups and more flattering angles, the role of Mrs Mars is played by Peggy Knudsen, who is more self-assured, somewhat sultrier, and more of a Hawks' type woman than Clark. Knudsen fits in better with the other Hawks' type dames in the cast: Martha Vickers, Dorothy Malone, Carole Douglas, Joy Barlowe, Lorraine Miller, and Shelby Payne, although she's the only one of the bunch who doesn't appear to fall for Marlowe immediately!

Having seen the revised cut, Jack Warner cabled his New York executives that "the new version, with new scenes protecting Bacall, comes off great". And it does. David Thomson is probably right to think that some marvellous stuff with Martha Vickers was lost along the way, and that Hawks may have rebelled against losing Bacall as his Galatea. But for whatever reason, the second cut adds pace and sizzle to the thriller, and if a little coherence is lost (which I still see as an arguable point), who cares? As an exercise in the mechanics of novel into film scriptwriting, in the essential differences between stories in print and on film, in the workings of the studio system and on the wonder of the collective art of filmmaking, the TCM comparison of the two versions repays every minute of watching. It may not be what Bacall meant when she tells Bogart, "It's nothing you can't fix", but the line rings true anyway.

LONDON FILM FESTIVAL: WHERE THE ELITE MEET IN SEATS

Michael Carlson

Once again, under Adrian Wootton's programming, a wide selection of crime films were at the centre of the London Film Festival: a very mixed bag, but one filled with some fascinating material. If overall the crime portion didn't match up to the Festival in general, that might be because the overall quality was so high. As usual, the one big problem with London is its size: there simply is no way to see everything you want to, and with press showings restricted to daytimes, it leaves you feeling distinctly sunlight-deprived after two weeks.

The big star was the man who wasn't there, James Caan, whose Guardian Lecture (which surely would have been one of the Festival highlights) had to be cancelled at the last minute when Caan's schedule wouldn't allow him to attend. Which was a shame, not only because he's a great actor, and starred in one of the seminal crime movies of all time, but because his personal take on the Festival's two films in which he acted would have been interesting. Neither *The Yards* nor *The Way of the Gun* is a fully satisfying movie, but Caan's role in the latter is more interesting. There's a poster up for *Way* which quotes some idiot's review saying, "At last, Hollywood does have a brain". It's bad enough this ditz dismisses so much out of hand, but as Benicio del Toro says to Caan at one point, "This isn't a brains kind of operation". What it is is a film that takes a thoughtful and potentially riveting script and buries it under a mountain of styling, profiling, and sub Walter Hill homage to Peckinpah type gore. Dumbo partners del Toro and Ryan Phillippe open the movie getting beat up by a bunch of suburban discoers, and then morph into SAS-type weapons experts with an arsenal big enough to take on

Guatemala next time their soccer team decides to go to war.

Del Toro plays Longbaugh (as in the Sundance Kid) and Phillippe is Parker (as in if Richard Stark were a person and alive he'd be turning over in his grave) while Caan (remember him?) plays the bag man for the millionaire (Geoffrey Lewis) whose unborn baby (inside surrogate mother Juliette Lewis – nice choice of genes) they kidnap. Caan gets to do some nice things with the old man role, old and wise in the ways of the criminal world, and it's his performance that is really the centre of the film. It doesn't have to be, in fact, it probably shouldn't be, because the script actually sets up some nice conflicts and twists, particularly in the relation between Lewis and his younger wife (Kristin Lehman) who doesn't want to spoil her looks with a baby. She's also having an affair with... well, there are overtones of Titus Andronicus here, but let's not give too much away. As the plot weaves thicker, it starts to rely a bit too much on synchronicity, but just at the point the story starts to get interesting, director / writer Christopher McQuarrie resolves every ambiguity by shooting the shit out of it. He's a talent, and working with lensman Dick Pope he's made a film full of atmospheric shots and narrow corridors that force the characters down paths which offer no alternatives. At the end of every path, sadly, is nothing more than a shootout.

If *Way* is about surrogate families, *The Yards,* like James Gray's first film, *Little Odessa*, is about real families under pressure, and particularly about the mother / son relationship. In this case the son is Mark Wahlberg, who is just out of prison, and the mother is Ellen Burstyn, high-strung and vulnerable. Her sister, played by Faye Dunaway, is married to a big-time public transportation contractor (James Caan) and Wahlberg is given a job which of course turns out to be firmly mired in a criminal world of bribery to get contracts and sabotage to eliminate the competition. Further complicating things is Wahlberg's buddy, Joaquin Phoenix, who benefitted from Marky's doing the right thing once, and who now is dating Dunaway's daughter, Charlize Theron. And what makes it even better is that Marky Mark and Charlize got caught doing it just before he was sent away. In fact, we're left with the suspicion that he should've been imprisoned for incest, rather than car theft. Like *Little Odessa, Yards* is rather too slowly paced to be able to take advantage of the classic situation in which Wahlberg finds himself trapped. Thus the resolution becomes a damp squib, and the resolution of the romantic dilemma is laced in melodrama in extremis. Caan, here playing a mini-Godfather, doesn't really get much of a chance to move within the corrupt world of city politics, and the film would probably be stronger if it gave us more of that side of the equation, and less of the West Side Story stuff. Burstyn and Dunaway are rivetting, if never wholly convincing, as the queens of Queens, but they're more convincing than Charlize in her black wig. Harris Savides' photography is wonderfully grimy and dark, all 1970s New York, but Howard Shore's music sounds like Carmine Coppolla through a synthesizer.

James Caan is slightly too old to play Bill Clinton, but Clintonian allegories were another sub-genre of the festival (and in that category we could see *Quills*, though admittedly it was aimed more at the Jesse Helms anti-NEA faction of Congress than against Kenneth Starr's chambers... though President Bubba as De Sade is an interesting conceit). *The Con-*

tender is the more obvious – and successful – of the two. Written and directed by Rod Lurie, it traces the efforts of a right-wing Senator (Gary Oldman) to block the nomination of a female Senator (Joan Allen) as Vice President. In order to do this he releases photos of her, in her college days, gang-banging a fraternity. There's a subplot involving another Senator (William Peterson) which, although clever, is also telegraphed and provides a sort of non-political way in which to resolve the dilemma. But in the end, everything rides on the broad shoulders of a very Clinton-like Jeff Bridges, a President full of easy charm and ready, winning wit.

Lurie has made the closest thing to a Frank Capra movie we've seen in years, and if that is praise it is also criticism, because the impassioned speech from one man is not really going to overturn the ingrained corruption of a political system, as we have just seen in the US Presidential elections. Capra's films always uphold the system by placing someone in opposition to it – the system which is celebrated at the end is shown to be nothing but venal, yet we're supposed to believe in it because the occasional superman makes it work. Call me a child of the 1960s, but it doesn't work for me, and didn't in the 1950s! But it does provide feel-good moments, and Lurie's feel-goods are as powerful as Capra's. Allen, who is arguably our finest actress, provides some excellent nobility, and Bridges, arguably our most underrated actor, is as convincing as the Prez as he was as the Big Lebowski (Lurie insists that the Big Guy *is* Jeff's real personality), but Oldman gets to steal the show in a performance of sheer melodramatic evil that is just fun to watch.

Nick Nolte gets to give his melodramatic turn as a corrupt state politician in Alan Rudolph's *Trixie,* a strange hybrid of screwball comedy and Monicagate allegory which never really works as either. Emily Watson plays the eponymous heroine, who uses a Gracie Allen (the Burns and Allen one) accent to speak in malapropisms, a trait that begins to grate quickly, in part because some of the phrases are old-hat and over familiar. Hired as a security guard at a lakeside casino, Watson soon finds herself drawn into the shady doings surrounding land-dealing, and then into murder, when the developer's drug-addled temptress, Lesley Ann Warren, is killed. Rudolph builds everything to a denouement of Nolte, the corrupt politician, and a wonderful encounter between him and Watson which is like a thespian duel at three paces. Nolte, playing the role with cigarette holder to remind us, perhaps, that Frank D. Roosevelt himself had a few sexual secrets but wasn't such a bad President, finally confesses to sexual shenanigans but nothing else. And, in a strange twist of fate, the Monica Lewinsky character turns out to be the killer. This one's really too slight and confused to win audiences over; it's Rudolph being clever, but without the heart that cuts the cleverness and informs his best films. I get the feeling he sensed that too, because when in doubt he lets the camera linger on close-ups of Emily Watson, and though audiences can lose themselves for ages in those wonderful eyes, it's not exactly what they want from movies. Though it might do for a few hours or more.

It would probably do for Gabriel Arcand, who plays a withdrawn, blues-addicted, morgue attendant in Louis Belanger's strangely undisturbing *Post Mortem.* Arcand has a literally life-affirming encounter with Sylvie Moreau, who arrives as one of his clients. She is a single mother who makes her living being picked up by men and then

knocking them out and robbing them. It's an interesting take on French-Canadian respectability, made more so by her born-again Catholic mother. Moreau wants to get enough money together to get herself and her daughter out of Montreal and to the country. Eventually, however, she messes up, and is choked to death, so it seems, by what we might call a disgruntled client. The client, of course, is American, and you know how Yankees are when they don't get what they pay for. Hence her progress to the morgue. From a crime movie point of view the assumption must be that, Kathy Reichs notwithstanding, Montreal is the place to commit a crime, since the police don't even appear to have searched the body in situ before it arrives in the morgue. Be that as it may, what makes this film work is the structure, told in a series of flashbacks which serve to reveal the nature of the characters as much as the details of the plot, and outstanding performances by the two leads (it was the first film role for Moreau). Belanger has a nice touch with revealing characters through details of scene and background; the film ends with Moreau having made it to the country, where, dressed in a L'il Abner Daisy Mae-type get-up, she's pumping gas! Born again, indeed.

Another resurrection of sorts takes place in *Animal Factory*, Steve Buscemi's film based on Ed Bunker's prison novel. This has all kinds of street cred for Buscemi, especially as Bunker himself plays in the movie, but it also has some serious problems, mainly that it's impossible to believe that Ed Furlong would last, oh, twenty minutes in this prison, and it's even harder to believe that Willem Dafoe would keep his hands off Furlong's ass for even half that time. This romanticism doesn't sit easily with the supposedly hard nature of the prison film; in fact, it seems downright old fashioned. There are lots of things to like about the film, including John Lurie's score, and an incredible performance by Mickey Rourke as Furlong's transvestite cellmate, but where, for example, *Trees Lounge* had a sense of reality about it, *Animal Factory*, ostensibly gritty and authentic, smacks of romanticism.

Romanticism was present in abundance in the work of Eric von Stroheim, and the LFF featured Bill Schmidlin's magnificent reconstruction for Turner Classic Movies of *Greed,* now running at four hours (Stroheim's original cut ran eight!). The missing footage has been added using the original production stills, taken for continuity purposes, which are given the same live-action camera treatment as the Ken Burns *Civil War* documentary. Schmidlin worked from Stroheim's final shooting script to make the inserts, and it all works amazingly well. Interestingly, despite the basically static nature of the still photos, the cutting of those sections is actually paced faster than the original film. It may be something purists will argue over, but it presents something closer to Stroheim's original, and makes it accessible to modern audiences, and for that we should be grateful.

One of the highlights of the non-crime portion of the Festival was another of Schmidlin's projects, the re-cutting of *Elvis: The Way It Is,* a 1970 documentary of Elvis at the International Hotel in Vegas, originally directed by Denis Sanders. Schmidlin went back to the original footage, removed most of the sidebars involving the celebrity audience, and gives us a remarkable record of the King at his height, including rehearsals and relationships with the 'Memphis Mafia'. There is a moment when, in the scripted back and forth between Elvis and his (black) backup singers when he surprises one of them, and she almost literally melts under his attention. I would have scoffed at the King in 1970: thirty years later I was blown away.

My favourite of the films I saw was *Joe Gould's Secret,* Stanley Tucci's magnificent adaptation of the New Yorker articles by Joseph Mitchell, with Tucci as Mitchell and Ian Holm as Joe Gould in the performance of a lifetime. Ang Lee's *Crouching Tiger, Hidden Dragon* was fun, and has justifiably garnered much attention, but it's a shame films like *Peking Opera Blues, Fong Sai Yuk,* or *Once Upon a Time in China* never received mainstream attention. Of course, they didn't have Chow Yun-Fat, Michelle Yeoh, or the new Gong Li, Zhang Zi Yi, starring in them.

But the finest film in the Festival was another reissue, Budd Boetticher's *Seven Men From Now,* the first of his Randolph Scott westerns, and, although I was doubting Clyde Jeavons' evaluation of it, the best (even better than *Ride Lonesome).* This restoration from the UCLA film archive shows off William Clothier's brilliant Eastmancolour photography, and the relation between Scott's hero and Gail Russell's marvellous frontier wife adds a dimension to Scott's usual lonesome, obsessed hero. I could've watched it again immediately after it finished.

One I couldn't have watched again was the latest British designer gangster epic, *Sexy Beast,* with Ben Kingsley auditioning to be this generation's Bob Hoskins, but more on that next issue.

BOOKS ON FILM

Michael Carlson

Night of the Hunter – Simon Callow (BFI Film Classics, ISBN 0-85170-822-6)
The Searchers – Edward Buscombe (BFI Film Classics, ISBN 0-85170-820-X)
Back in the Saddle Again – edited by Edward Buscombe & Roberta F. Pearson (BFI Publishing, ISBN 0-85170-661-4)
Slasher Movies – Mark Whitehead (Pocket Essentials, £3.99, ISBN 1-903047-27-7)
David Cronenberg – John Costello (Pocket Essentials, £3.99, ISBN 1-903047-26-9)
Philip K Dick – Andrew M. Butler (Pocket Essentials, £3.99, ISBN 1-903047-29-3)
Cyberpunk – Andrew M. Butler (Pocket Essentials, £3.99, ISBN 1-903047-285)
Marilyn Monroe – Paul Donnelly (Pocket Essentials, £3.99, ISBN 1-903067-315)
High Concept – Charles Fleming (Bloomsbury, £7.99, ISBN 0747542627)

Simon Callow has already written a biography of Charles Laughton, but this study of Laughton's only film as director was well worth the extra effort. And effort there was: prompted by an angry letter which followed an extract from the biography in *Sight and Sound,* Callow did further research regarding authorship of the film's screenplay. The resulting product is part of an analysis of a classic film which proceeds in a very precise and workmanlike manner, but transcends that mundane because of Callow's own feeling for the film and its director, and also because the film lends itself so well to this sort of discussion. That is

because it is both a work of individual creative integrity and a perfect illustration of the collaborative process of film working at its best. Not for this study the horror stories of fights between director and studio, of temper tantrums by actors, grubby competition for credit between writers and director. Everything is so, well, gentlemanly that you wonder whether the creative tension on which so many seem to feed is really necessary.

As it happens, I had seen *Night of the Hunter* quite recently, in the wonderful little Action Cinema on the Rue des Ecoles in Paris, and with its images fresh in my mind I was surprised at how vividly Callow was able to, bit by bit, reconstruct the film from its parts, including recognising those moments where it perhaps goes over the top. I think there is a point about Pearl, the daughter, which needs to be considered: since Pearl is the name given to the perfect child of the adulterous union between Hester Prynne and the reverend Dimmesdale in *The Scarlet Letter*; this reflects on the nature of Bob and Willa's relationship. I was also struck by the evident influence of Tennessee Williams; Davis Grubb's story *The Gentleman Friend* reminds one of *The Glass Menagerie* done as noir.

Edward Buscombe's study of *The Searchers*, while no less effective or complete, lacks the spark of Callow's, but this is probably because the film itself is one of the most studied and commented on in all cinema, and the relatively new tack which Buscombe takes is to see it as a commentary on race. Buscombe is particularly good on the myth of captivity narratives on which the film draws. He also finds for himself a small problem, namely Ford's handling of Martin's (Jeffrey Hunter) 'marriage' to Look, the Indian he inadvertently buys as a wife. Buscombe thinks this is the

film's only weak point, but I'm not sure I agree. I find the brawling scenes between Hunter and Ken Curtis tedious and overdone, while in Look's character I find both sympathy and a foreshadowing of the entire moral of the story. Martin (and Ethan) misinterpret Look's devotion, and only understand it when it is too late. It is a mistake Martin, at least, will not make again. Yes, I know it's not a crime movie, and I've never had it at the very top of my own personal John Ford list, but it's a film you need to see, and this is a study that fully justifies a classic film. If I sound critical of it, it may be only in comparison with Buscombe's even better volume on *Stagecoach*, in the same series. If you are interested in westerns, you might also be interested *Back in the Saddle Again,* a collection which Buscombe has co-edited and also provided one of the best essays included, on photographing Indians. It's an off-beat collection; with a fine piece by Noel Carroll, "The Professional Western South of the Border", and a fascinating one by William Boddy on the boom period of the TV western in the 1950s.

Mark Whitehead's *Slasher Movies* is my favourite among all the Pocket Essentials series so far. I can't pretend to be an expert on the subject, but what he says about the genre makes sense, and if you knew nothing about it going in, you would have a good grounding for approaching the films he analyses, and a good guide as to which ones are worth approaching. This is what the Pocket Essentials set out to do, and Whitehead does it with a surprisingly casual humour that belies the very serious nature of his writing. I happened to read this at the same time I saw the documentary *American Nightmare*, and his book stands in refreshing contrast to the overly aca-

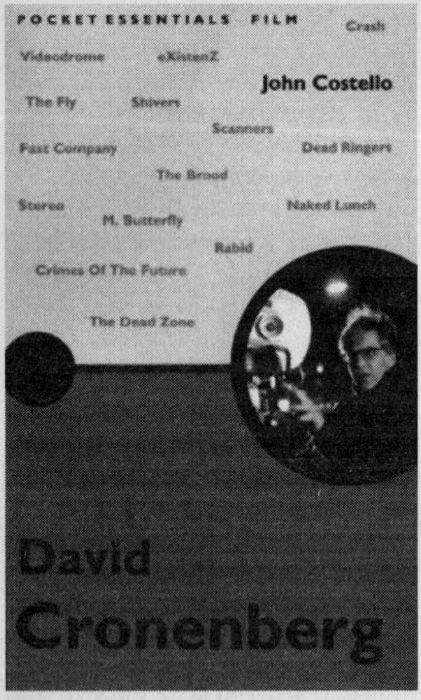

demic approach of the film.

In *David Cronenberg,* John Costello has a subject who would seem to encourage academic analysis, but he avoids that, and the resulting essential will still fit in your pocket. Although it's only peripheral to the genre, I'd rate *Dead Ringers* as one of the best crime films of the 1980s, indeed one of the best films. Again, I wouldn't feel competent to comment on all the details Costello has included, which I enjoyed, but I did notice that he locates Montreal's Ile des Soeurs (Nuns Island) to Toronto: I only mention that because I was living in Montreal when the film came out. Costello is very convincing on why Cronenberg will go down in film history as a major iconoclastic figure of filmmaking: I believe he will be remembered as one of the best artists in any genre to tackle the nature of humanity in an age of techno / bio change.

Cronenberg adapted Burroughs and Ballard to the screen, and that was a major concern of theirs. I'm surprised he's never turned to Philip K Dick, whose concerns were parallel to his. Instead Dick on film has been left (in the mainstream) to Ridley Scott's *Blade Runner*, which stylistically was one of the most influential films of the past quarter-century, including a major influence on the crime genre (it received a number of votes in Crime Time's Millennial Top Crime Movies poll) and Paul Verhoeven's *Total Recall*, arguably the most interesting of 'Arnolt's' films. Like Cronenberg, Dick is a figure whose analysis could fill whole libraries, so anyone working in a limited space, as Andrew Butler does, can only give you an outline. Butler's outline is fine, and he covers the main issues surrounding Dick's life and work, which

are becoming increasing inseparable as the critical mass grows. Dick has already transcended cult status, and you should seek out this book if you've never been exposed to Dick before.

Dick also is one of the sources of 'cyberpunk' fiction, the genre for which the film version of *Blade Runner* serves as a template, and which is also heavily influenced by the style of film noir and hard-boiled fiction. Andrew Butler has also produced the Pocket Essential guide to cyberpunk, and though it seems solid enough on the leading cyberpunk authors, I think he gives the detective influence rather short-shrift, and crucially omits any mention of Richard Paul Russo's very interesting trilogy of cyberpunk hard-boiled novels featuring detective Frank Carlucci. Butler is better on the films, from *Blade Runner* to *Matrix*, and I'm sure as a consumer guide to the literature he's accurate enough (it's significant that as he analyses the genre's works they appear to get progressively less interesting: what is the half-life of a genre these days?)

What is the half-life of Marilyn Monroe? About a millennium, I'd guess. What is most interesting about Paul Donnelly's brief survey of her life and career is the relatively few top class films she made. *Some Like It Hot* is an acknowledged classic, *Seven Year Itch* is perhaps close, and of course she has marvellous small parts in *The Asphalt Jungle* and *All About Eve,* but most of her other best roles establish her as a talented comedienne in films that transcend their era mostly in her performance (the beauty of *Gentlemen Prefer Blondes* is seeing her 1950s glamour contrasted with Jane Russell's 1940s va va va voom). Her last film, *The Drifters,* might have signalled a career change for her, but it was a cursed production, and also can be seen as a last gasp for a dying era (Clark Gable and Montgomery Clift as well as Marilyn). Donnelly doesn't get sidetracked too far into the mystery of Marilyn's death, which would probably be enough for a separate volume. While I find the idea she was murdered compelling, the evidence is still less than compelling (my favourite theory was Matthew Smith's that the fatal dose of nembutal was administered in an enema – I reviewed that volume for Crime Time under the headline The Enema Within). James Ellroy, who discounts all tales of Marilyn, the Kennedys, Lawford and murder, posits, in *American Tabloid*, a Monroe who puts out for virtually everyone except JFK, but FBI agents fudge the evidence on their tapes in order to appease J Edgar Hoover, who gets what he wants to hear. So should we all.

Or she may have just been a victim of Hollywood excess, like Don Simpson. *High Concept* is subtitled *Don Simpson and the Hollywood Culture of Excess* but, interestingly, the book is actually stronger on the actual filmmaking part of Hollywood than it is on the excess. Fleming doesn't have the verbal flair nor the salacious eye for detail to really capture the culture he writes about, the way, say *Easy Riders, Raging*

Bulls did, but this book would be well read as a companion piece to that one, because Don Simpson was, as Fleming accurately notes, the end product of that excessive generation. The follies of the wannabe auteurs chronicled in the latter book opened the door for producer-driven, high-concept movies, and may have relegated 'auteurs' to the relative onanism of Sundance and the Independent Film Channel circuit forever. Fleming's writing is best when he's dealing direct with his sources on the production of the various Simpson / Bruckheimer films, which is a valuable piece on analysis. And since his sources appear to be largely disgruntled writers or other low-level personnel, we get a unique insight into the Hollywood dynamic on the personal level. He's less insightful on the topic of Simpson himself, almost as if the almost insane levels of self-abuse and self-aggrandisement in which Simpson indulged are too much to be able to explain or justify. But you read for a couple of hundred pages about Simpson's constant efforts to reshape his body before Fleming drops in passing the fact that Big Don was five foot seven inches tall! Hollywood is an epicentre of the world's most serious outbreak of Little Man Disease, and Don had it bad.

Hollywood does showcase the American dream in its most blatant form, and a lot of that depends on self-invention, or re-invention. When Fitzgerald said there were no second acts in American lives he had something quite different in mind. Fleming is good on the fake biographies (ever notice how all actors were once professional quality sports stars, but injury or fate conspired to drive them into acting instead?), on the fake bodies (Simpson had so many cosmetic surgeries at one point his friends didn't recognise him – another Hollywood cliché is the publicist denying the

obvious surgery) and even the fake personalities (Simpson would make abusive phone calls to show off for guests, with no-one on the other line; he once described himself as the "kind of guy who'd put a million of his own money into a film he believed in" but really was the kind of guy who would charge his drugs to the budget of a film someone else was paying for). You can see it's easy to fall into the cataloguing trap, and Fleming at one point virtually abandons Simpson to give us lists of various Hollywood types and their drug problems, their insane demands for star treatment, their sex lives. He also loses touch with Simpson's pictures, but then, Simpson did that too.

Don Simpson died on the toilet, reading a biography of Oliver Stone. Greek playwrights could've done that one better. I wonder if Stone dared take this book into the loo with him?

DIGITAL DICKS AND CYBER COPS

Charles Waring

Love it or loathe it, the Internet is here to stay. Once the elite plaything of suited corporate business types and nerdy cyber-geeks, the personal computer is now almost an integral fixture of every home throughout the Western world. If you're not on-line, you're liable to be regarded as something of a Luddite and ostracised by your fellow human beings simply because of your inability to understand the challenging dialect of the brave new cyber world – if expressions like 'logging on', 'downloading' and 'surfing the net' leave you bamboozled and reaching for a dictionary, then you'll be seen as much more than out of step with the times: you'll be as out of place as Hercule Poirot in an episode of *NYPD Blue*.

Of course, there will be those who courageously resist the hard-sell tactics of computer companies and the 'information age' zeal of the current government, but I'll warrant that even the most obdurate of technophobes will capitulate to the digital revolution in the end: resistance is futile, earthling! Ultimately, like television, the web will trap us all (especially if the government has its way and monitors all e-mails!). But before Big Brother's virtual spider eats us up, we at CT thought it was about time (seeing that most people can access the internet these days) that we reviewed some of the websites devoted to TV's supersleuths and cult coppers.

There are literally hundreds to choose from out there in the vast, sprawling virtual galaxy that is the worldwide web. They range from the stunning and exceptional to the yawningly average and those which seem like they were cobbled together in a couple of minutes with bits of sticky-back plastic. Some have eye-catching visual effects and a host of intriguing features while others just consist of a single page of badly typed copy. But don't make the mistake of assuming that the official fan sites are automatically the best – often, more thought and effort is injected into the unofficial sites created by enthusiastic amateurs. So, after many nights of typing the names of TV shows past and present into search engine boxes and separating the grain from the chaff, so to speak, here is CT's assessment of a just a few of the myriad cop and detective websites currently in operation.

The Sweeney

Personally, I can't abide John Thaw's stilted, overly mannered portrayal of Colin Dexter's snobbish, opera-loving detective, Inspector Morse in the eponymous TV show. For me, Thaw will always be Jack Regan of *The Sweeney*, an uncouth, sartorially challenged, working class copper who calls everyone 'sunshine' and who stops blaggers in their tracks when he yells, "Shut it!" Of all the websites I visited to research this article, the official *Sweeney* site (www.thesweeney.com) gave me the greatest sense of pleasure. It's an imaginative, fun-packed site that's both informative and entertaining. Along with all the usual features (a history of the show, a detailed episode guide, the obligatory photo gallery and profiles of the main characters), it includes a hilarious 'style guide', which gives you the opportunity to explore Regan's dingy-looking front room with your mouse and get the low-down on naff 70s fashions. Don't you just love brown and orange colour schemes? Visitors to the site can also indulge in a rather primitive 70s video game called 'pong' (as once played by Regan and Carter in the programme during a pub scene), access video and sound clips from the show (including a section called 'swearing', which in the 70s meant nothing more potent than 'bastard' or 'sod'!), consult a rhyming slang lexicon to assist decipher quaint cockney expressions like 'doing a Royal' and find out more information on those gas-guzzling motors driven in the series. If you're a boy who likes his toys, then a visit to this site should be a priority. The Guv'nor of cop show sites.

The Professionals

The Professionals was probably the dumbest British-made cop show of the 1970s. But it was also energetic and, for impressionable teenagers, that meant it was bloody exciting – every episode reverberating with seismic explosions, squealing car tyres and the staccato crackle of gunfire. More boys with their toys, I'm afraid! At the centre of this apocalyptic melee were two cerebrally challenged cops, Bodie and Doyle. They worked for CI5 (Criminal Intelligence 5, though there was no intended irony there) under the supervision of their gammy-legged superior, Gordon Jackson (previously seen as the butler, Jackson, in *Upstairs Downstairs*, a role which, for me, undermined his authority in *The Professionals*). Bodie (played by Lewis Collins) was mean, moody and taciturn, communicating by means of grunts, clenched fists and pulling the trigger on his handgun (a modern equivalent of Neanderthal man then) while his partner, Doyle, had a similar hard-man image but one which was somewhat negated by his girly mop of permed corkscrew curls (Kevin Keegan, eat your heart out!). As far as IQs went, CI5 made *The Sweeney* look like candidates for *University Challenge*.

In homage to *The Professionals* is a very fine website (www.personal.u-net.com/~carnfort/Professionals/) created by Dave Matthews, whose devotion to the 70s series has resulted in a visually arresting site. Although not labelled with an official tag, Matthews' efforts have not gone unnoticed by some of the production team responsible for the original programme. As a result, Matthews' site is 'authorised' by *The Professionals'* creators. Like the Sweeney site, with its attention focused on macho-action, cars and guns, this site is more likely to generate interest in the male section of the population.

Dempsey And Makepeace

In the wake of *The Sweeney* and *The Professionals* came the unlikely *Dempsey and Makepeace*, a far-fetched series that paired a tough magnum-toting New York cop (James Dempsey played by Michael Brandon) with a posh British undercover policewoman who was also a member of the aristocracy (Harriet Makepeace played by Glynis Barber). Running for only three seasons (1985 to 1986), this daft show garnered a substantial fan base which, bizarrely, persists even today, going on the evidence of the series website (www.jamesbond.simplenet.com/demspeymakepeace). This is an average site with all the bog standard features (history, biog, FAQs, etc) but does boast a rather weird section called Fan Fiction. Believe it or not, there are people out there in cyberspace who are such zealous fans of *Dempsey and Makepeace* that they are prompted to write short stories about the two cops. The phrase 'get a life' springs to mind.

Hawaii Five-O

Who can forget the lantern-jawed profile of Detective Steve McGarrett (played by the imperious Jack Lord) sporting a quiff the shape and size of the breaking surf on Hawaii's golden beaches? McGarrett's sober, mirthless demeanour made even the most miserable of TV detectives, such as Inspector Morse and Jack Frost, seem like jovial party animals by comparison. McGarrett's immortal catchphrase was, of course, "Book 'em, Danno", which he customarily uttered at the end of each show to his sidekick, Danny Williams. Boasting one of the most memorable of opening title sequences for any cop show (including that stirring theme tune accompanying images of shaking hula-girl hips and big flowery guys in canoes), *Hawaii Five-O* bore the distinction of being the longest running police drama on American TV (it ran for twelve years, from 1968 to 1980). The series proved immensely popular with audiences on both sides of the Atlantic and there is even rumour of a new series and a possible Hollywood movie. However, speculation aside, if you're a devotee of this classic cop drama and require instant gratification, the show's website (www.mjq.net/fiveo) is bound to satisfy the most insatiable of cravings. Packed with fascinating background facts, loads of trivia (including the present location of McGarrett's Ford Mercury – and it's for sale!), startling revelations (apparently the FBI attempted to influence the production of the programme after they were depicted in a somewhat less than flattering light) and sound clips of McGarrett enunciating his three favourite little words, this comprehensive site should administer a nirvana-inducing fix for Five-O addicts. Of course, if you've truly lost your marbles you might consider attending some of the *Hawaii Five-O* conventions held in the States (which are advertised on the site). By the way, amongst the merchandise you can purchase is a T-shirt inscribed with the words 'Praise The Lord'. Hallelujah to that, Danno!

Kojak

Like Steve McGarrett, the chrome-domed, lollipop-sucking Big Apple detective, Lieutenant Theo Kojak (played by Telly Savalas) had a memorable catchphrase in "Who loves ya, baby!" The savvy, street-wise cop, who customarily wore a three-piece suit, donned a trilby and called everyone 'pussycat' is celebrated at www.Desilu.com/TVLand/Kojak. In truth, it's not a spectacular site and is characterised by all the usual features: episode guides, a sound directory (which includes the memorable theme tune) and a photo gallery. But perhaps the most interesting feature can be found if you click on the 'links' section, where you'll discover a rather macabre site called 'Find a Grave' (I kid you not!). Here, you can actually locate Telly Savalas's current sub-terranean residence, complete with a picture depicting its headstone. In fact, if tracking down the final resting place of film stars and entertainers satisfies your morbid curiosity, then 'Find a Grave' could be the website you've been looking for! As they say: only in America!

The Rockford Files

Until I watched the American private eye series, *The Rockford Files*, in the late 70s, like most Brits at the time, I had absolutely no idea what that new-fangled gadget called an answer machine was. Indeed, one of the most fascinating aspects of this particular show was the cryptic message that ex-con turned sleuth for hire, Jim Rockford (played with characteristic aplomb by James Garner), received on his answer machine every week. Almost all of those weird and often humorous messages can be found transcribed at www.tvparty.com.recrock, an informative site devoted to the TV show that made a hero (albeit a reluctant one) out of a yellow-bellied coward. Thankfully, there are no ghoulish surprises at a site that includes all the standard features, none of which surpass its entertaining list of answer phone messages. Here's a taster from the fifth season episode, *Rosendahl and Gilda Stern Are Dead*: "Hello? You the guy who lost his wallet in the Park Theater? Well, I'm kinda like into leather. So, I'll be returning the money, but I'm going to keep the wallet."

Starsky and Hutch

Another classic American 70s cop show which boasts an excellent website is *Starsky and Hutch* (www.spe.sony.com/tv/shows/sgn/sh). The dynamic west coast crime fighting duo and their jive-talking, turkey-necked ghetto buddy, Huggy Bear, are the focus of a colourful site that in addition to the standard list of episodes and background info offers a couple of unique extras – you can actually help the guys crack a case by using video evidence (a feature called 'Eye Witness') and can 'accessorize' Huggy Bear by assisting him with his choice of wardrobe! Some features of this fun site take time to load but it's definitely worth the wait.

The Bill

ITV's long running police soap, *The Bill*, also has a strong website. Located at www.thebill.com, this well-appointed site includes the novel feature of a virtual tour of the ground and first floors of the Sun Hill nick (though you have to download and install a special 'plug' to gain access). You can keep up to date with synopses of current episodes as well as accessing an archive that includes all the previous cast of the series (filed under 'the Old Bill'). There's also a useful dictionary page to keep you up to date with police parlance, especially if you want to know what a 'black rat' is. In the 'Interview Room', members of the cast are interrogated but it's hardly the third degree. However, anoraks will appreciate an interview with a long-serving minor character referred to as 'Trev' (an acronym for Totally Reliable Extra Veteran) – Trev is an expert at cameo parts (usually non-speaking, but occasionally he gets the odd line or two). Played by Vic Gallucci, our Trev has made in excess of 800 appearances on the show since his walk-on debut back in 1989. If this kind of trivia takes your fancy, then the Bill's website could be right up your street.

Inspector Morse

God, he's a miserable bastard. No, not God: I mean, Morse, the crusty Oxford Inspector who finally bit the dust in the episode, *A Remorseful Day*. I for one didn't mourn – a coffin is the best place for the cantankerous old git in my estimation. At least the old duffer's out of his misery now. But you won't find the opera-loving curmudgeon resident at 'Find a Grave'... yet. In the meantime, Morse continues to live on at his official website, www.inspectormorse.co.uk. Not really a very inspiring website, this. Functionally, it's OK, but nothing out of the ordinary here, although I admit to being very confused when a plot synopsis I was reading of the concluding episode described the story as 'explosive'. Of all the epithets I could think of to describe Morse, explosive is unequivocally not one of them! Also included are interviews with Morse's creator, Colin Dexter and the late Malcolm Bradbury (who dramatised *The Wench Is Dead* episode). Like many 'official' websites, this one may follow our illustrious Jag-driving bobby to the grave by the time you read this. About as inspiring as quaffing a pint of flat real ale.

Columbo

Just one more thing.... One of the most popular TV detectives could be mistaken for a down and out – scruffily attired in a cheap, dirty brown raincoat, Lieutenant Columbo (his first name was concealed) was the most unlikely of goggle box supersleuths. The quizzical, apologetic, cigar-chomping LAPD man who was undoubtedly smarter than the clothes he wore is celebrated at a splendid website (www.columbo-site.freeuk.com) that has pages devoted to Columbo's dog (a loppy-eared Bassett hound), his mysterious wife who was never seen, the beat up Peugeot he drove in addition to all the usual website features. An impressive site.

Here's a list of other sites you may want to explore:

Hill Street Blues: www.net-hlp.com/hsb/
NYPD Blue:
 www.stwing.upenn.edu/~sepinwal/nypd
Brooklyn South:
 http://home.akos.net/~kamalu/bk-south.htm
Charlie's Angels: www.charliesangels.com
Cagney and Lacey:
 http://w3.one.net/~voyager/candl.html
Moonlighting: http://people.ne.mediaone.net/
 dianedemelo/moonlighting
Magnum, P.I.:
 http://pro-or-contra.com/magnum/html
The Saint: www.saint.org

MUSIC

Charles Waring

Bullitt: Lalo Schifrin
(Aleph Records 018)

If you read my article on Lalo Schifrin in CT 21, you'll no doubt be aware that the original 1968 Warner version of the *Bullitt* soundtrack differs substantially from the music that actually appears in the film. In particular, the omission of the longer movie version of the main theme has perplexed both Schifrin zealots and even the casual soundtrack buyer, many of whom must have been disappointed to find that the version of the track used in the Ford Puma advert is commercially unavailable. Thankfully, Schifrin himself has remedied the situation by digitally re-recording the entire soundtrack, including the elusive, slightly slower movie version of the main theme. Issued on the Aleph label, a company run by his wife, Donna, and devoted entirely to recordings of Schifrin's music, this new version of *Bullitt* was recorded in Germany with the composer conducting the WDR Big Band. In addition to new recordings of the material featured on the Warner CD, Schifrin includes previously unreleased movie versions of *Ice Pick Mike* and *Room 26* along with music cues that failed to make the final cut of the film (namely *Just Coffee* and *The Architect's Building*). The sound quality is superb and the WDR Big Band attack Schifrin's stylish, jazz-inflected score with enormous verve and dynamism. Another attractive feature is the stylish packaging, which includes an insightful essay by Nick Redman accompanied by photographic stills of Steve McQueen from the film. If you purchase this direct from Schifrin's own web site (www.schifrin.com) you'll receive an added bonus in the shape of an autographed photo of the composer.

Buddism: Roy Budd
(Cinephile CMOCD016)

Like Lalo Schifrin, British movie composer Roy Budd was recently a recipient of CT's Musical Mugshots series. This new compilation is an intriguing project masterminded by Paul Fishman, son of Jack Fishman who was Budd's manager, occasional musical collaborator and the producer of the *Get Carter* soundtrack. *Buddism* is in essence an assemblage of remixes that injects the Budd sound with a contemporary edge to attract a new, younger audience. This anthology draws from Budd's cinematic soundtrack canon, including music culled mainly from crime thrillers like *Get Carter* (the original version of the theme tune), *Black Windmill*, *The Marseille Contract*, *Stone Killer* and *Fear is the Key* (including the famous tyre-screeching car chase sequence featuring Tubby Hayes's blistering sax solo over a propulsive jazz-funk groove). The remixes mostly enhance rather than disfigure Budd's music – in the main, they are subtle and sympathetic to Budd's original ideas, though the robotic house mix of the main theme to *The Marseille Contract* does, I feel, take things a tad too far. I've no doubt that some purists and soundtrack anoraks will probably deplore what they perceive as an adulteration of Budd's original movie scores, but to my ears *Buddism* is an imaginative project that works extremely well. If it introduces Budd's music to a new generation of listeners, then all the better! An excellent release.

Get Carter: Roy Budd
(Cinephile CMED0017)

Yes, I know what you're thinking – hasn't *Get Carter* both the movie and soundtrack, been featured in CT before? Well, yes it has, but this is a newly remastered version housed in an attractive gatefold sleeve featuring a bonus CD packed with dance remixes of the popular main theme. According to Paul Fishman in the copious liner notes (which also include pertinent observations from Jonathan Ross and the film's director, Mike Hodges, amongst others), the original master tapes to *Get Carter* were in a parlous state but have been lovingly and assiduously restored for this definitive reissue. Indeed, the improved sound quality is immediately striking, particularly in relation to the memorable fragments of movie dialogue that intersperse the music tracks, which range from the jazz-funk minimalism of the classic main theme with its haunting harpsichord motif to the psychedelic easy listening ambience of *Getting Nowhere in a Hurry*. The additional CD with its myriad dance remixes of the haunting title tune did little for me – however, if it succeeds in winning Roy Budd some new fans, then who am I argue? A classic soundtrack that should be in every film buff's CD collection.

The Italian Job: Original Soundtrack
(MCA 60074/112488-2)

The famous 1969 caper movie about a bunch of British crooks busting four million dollars worth of gold bullion from a security van in Turin during an international football match seems to occupy a special place in the nation's cinematic psyche. Starring a laddish Michael Caine alongside an imperious Noel Coward, with Benny Hill as a buffoonish boffin accompanied by a veritable legion of airborne Mini Coopers (the real stars of the film!), it's a movie that seems as quintessentially English as fish and chips. Paradoxically, the film's soundtrack wasn't even composed by an Englishman, although lyricist Don Black (famous for his collaborations with John Barry) contributed the words to the opening song, a dreamy easy-listening ballad called *On Days Like These,* sung by the ex-bus driver turned smooth crooner, Matt Munro. The entire score was actually composed by the legendary African-American jazz musician and record producer, Quincy Jones. Jones's ebullient score effectively captures the essence of what this sceptred isle's patriotic football fans would probably call the 'bulldog spirit'. This is particularly evident on the boisterous football terrace anthem, *Getta Bloomin' Move On! The Self Preservation Society*, the undoubted highpoint of this hugely enjoyable reissue. However, with a running time of a somewhat parsimonious twenty-eight minutes, this reissue would have benefited immensely from the inclusion of some choice morsels from the film's dialogue (for instance the memorable, "You're only supposed to blow the bloody doors off!"). This minor grumble aside, *The Italian Job* soundtrack is a must for any movie aficionado.

Ghost Dog: The Way of the Samurai: The Album
(Sony Music Soundtrax 496146 2)

One of the striking features of this movie (an engaging tale starring Forest Whitaker as a Mafia hitman who lives by the warrior code of the Japanese Samurai) is Wu-Tang Clan member Rza's incidental music (for those CT readers not au fait with rap or hip-hop music, the Wu-Tang Clan is regarded as one of rap's pioneering groups). However, the widely available official soundtrack album features not a single note of Rza's evocative instrumental score but opts to concentrate on some of the more overtly commercial hip-hop songs that appear at brief intervals throughout the film. I have to confess I was profoundly disappointed when I discovered this fact, although I believe that Rza's original score is available (at some considerable expense) as a Japanese import. However, despite my obvious chagrin at the shortcomings of *Ghost Dog: The Album*, it features some strong hip-hop cuts, namely *Cakes* by veteran old-school rapper, Kool G Rap, a hefty slice of fat-butt funk, and the bluesy, southern-fried soul-rap of *Strange Eyes* by Sunz of Man, 12 0'Clock and Blue Raspberry. Rza himself produces all the cuts on offer, guesting as an emcee on a couple of tracks and also appearing as a solo artist with the abrasive, mystical *Samurai Showdown*. Actor Forest Whitaker supplies pertinent dialogue from the film that is interspersed at irregular intervals between the music tracks. Not bad, and seriously worth checking out if you're a CT reader who's into the rap scene (if such a creature exists!). But if you've seen the movie you'll probably share my disappointment at the omission of Rza's superbly atmospheric score.

Third World Man: Original Motion Picture Soundtrack
(Palm Pictures PALMCD-23042)

This is the soundtrack to a Jamaican cops 'n' robbers film bankrolled by none other than former Island Records mogul Chris Blackwell (he now runs Palm Pictures). Blackwell's investment has paid off handsomely so far – to date, this hi-tech action flick has already become Jamaica's largest grossing movie of all time. But whether the world at large will respond in the same way remains to be seen. Not having seen the film, I can't comment on its quality, however, what I can say with certainty is that the movie soundtrack is a sparkling showcase for some of the Caribbean island's most dynamic performers. Jamaica's most famous musical duo, Sly and Robbie, are the musical fulcrum upon which *Third World Cop* hinges – the groovesome twosome are present in the capacity of both artists and producers. As the former, they contribute the film's taut drum and bass theme tune (*Capone's Theme*) and a couple of atmospheric reggaefied dub instrumentals. As producers, the duo mastermind the lion's share of the album, including cuts by Beenie Man, Red Dragon and two songs from the Innocent Crew, *Papers* and *Mambo Jambo*, the latter a delightful melange of Latin and Jamaican rhythms. The Marley Brothers contribute *Call the Police* featuring the Ghetto Youths Crew, while the dreadlocked male singer, Luciano, revisits Junior Marvin's reggae classic *Police and Thieves*. With its mixture of reggae, dancehall, raggamuffin, hip-hop, r'n'b and drum and bass flavours, *Third World Cop* proves an intoxicating tropical brew that will enliven any party.

Music From and Inspired By Shaft
(LaFace 73008 26081 2)

It's somewhat ironic that John Shaft – undoubtedly one of the most iconic of

African-American cinema characters – began life as a white private investigator. Bizarre but true, I'm afraid. Hollywood moguls aiming to cash in on the box office success of Melvin Van Peebles' seminal *Sweet Sweetback's Baad Asss Song* persuaded *Shaft* creator Ernest Tidyman to transform his vanilla-coated Philip Marlowe clone into a bad mutha of a brother and thus a legend was born. To be fair, *Shaft* was no classic – indeed, Isaac Hayes' compelling score was the real star of the show, and while most people have forgotten the movie, the South Park star's theme tune remains an evergreen. So much so in fact, that it must have posed a dilemma for director John Singleton on his updated version of the film starring Samuel L. Jackson as a Shaft for the new millennium (Jackson plays Shaft's nephew, while Richard Roundtree makes a cameo appearance as the original Shaft character). In a sensible move, Singleton has retained Hayes' classic theme tune, though the chrome-domed Black Moses provides a new recording which faithfully adheres to his original arrangement. In fact, the best thing about this soundtrack is the opening wah-wah driven theme tune. As for the remainder of music featured, it's the usual farrago of contemporary r'n'b and hip-hop, omitting David Arnold's incidental mood music. Truth to tell, *Shaft* the soundtrack is a bit of a yawn-fest apart from a couple of decent R. Kelly numbers *(Bad Man* and *Up and Outta Here*) and Donell Jones's *Do What I Gotta Do*. With a few exceptions, it's mostly average fare and not in the same league as Hayes' original Oscar winning 1971 score (it's also doubtful whether all the tracks featured here actually appear in the film!). Not bad, but definitely not a bad mutha!

Charlie's Angels: Music from the Motion Picture
(Columbia 4984782)

They're back! Well, sort of, if you know what I mean. Somewhat surprisingly, the movie version of the 70s TV show *Charlie's Angels* has garnered appreciative reviews from both the tabloid newspapers and broadsheets (though this may have something to do with the gratuitous display of Cameron Diaz's shapely derriere throughout the film!). Indeed, as an action movie that doesn't take itself too seriously, *Charlie's Angels* is a lot of fun. It also boasts an engaging though camp soundtrack that is a somewhat bizarre mixture of new American r'n'b tracks (by the sassy girl group, Destiny's Child) and some 70s and 80s tunes, ranging from disco anthems by Tavares, Leo Sayer (yes indeed!) and Marvin Gaye to pop oddities like The Vapors' *Turning Japanese* and Spandau Ballet's nauseating ballad *True*. It's an eclectic, entertaining collection enhanced by Apollo Four Forty's boisterous remake of *Charlie's Angels'* original theme tune.

John Carpenter's The Fog (Silva Screen Records FILMCD 342)
John Carpenter's Escape From New York (Silva Screen Records FILMCD 327)

"Movies are pieces of film stuck together in a certain rhythm, an absolute beat, like a musical composition. The rhythm you create affects the audience." This intriguing analogy, uttered a few years ago by the American filmmaker John Carpenter, is an apposite one considering his musical involvement in many of his own films. Apparently, Carpenter (who has no formal music training despite the fact that his father was in charge of the music department at the University of Kentucky) began writing his own scores because it was a cheaper option than hiring someone else to do it for him. Using mainly synthesisers, Carpenter patented a distinctive, minimalist style which often beautifully complimented movies such as the cult favourites *Dark Star*, *Assault on Precinct 13* and, of course, *Halloween*. Just released on CD are the haunting scores Carpenter composed for two of his most popular films: *The Fog* (1979) and *Escape From New York* (1981). *The Fog* is a horror story narrated by veteran actor, John Houseman, about a small Californian coastal community haunted by a marauding band of ghostly nineteenth century pirates seeking revenge for the treasure they were cheated out of. Needless to say, a pall of fog always accompanies the seamen's appearance. Included on the CD is Houseman's opening monologue, establishing the spooky atmosphere for Carpenter's chilling, ambient score. The main theme begins with some dramatic blasts of gothic organ before evolving into a gently undulating, mesmeric piece based around the repetition of a musical motif played on an acoustic piano which is then echoed by a harpsichord-like synthesiser part. The whole thing, in fact, sounds reminiscent of Bach invention. Even more effective is *Matthew Ghost Story*, where low, sustained synthesiser notes underpin delicate filigrees of ghostly acoustic piano. *Reel 9* with its tense, throbbing bass rhythms and ethereal sound effects works particularly well in mirroring the movie's grisly denouement. Also included are four bonus tracks and a radio interview with the film's star, Jamie Lee Curtis, along with informative sleeve notes from Carpenter himself.

In direct contrast, Carpenter's score to the futuristic action thriller, *Escape From New York* starring Kurt Russell as the moody, taciturn cycloptic anti-hero, Snake Plissken, is a triumph of electro-minimalism. This newly expanded, remixed and

remastered version of Carpenter's original soundtrack features fragments of dialogue from the film and several previously unavailable music cues that were cut from the final edit. In many ways, *Escape From New York* is a quintessential Carpenter soundtrack, denoted by the omnipresence of pulsing bass rhythms, martial drum patterns, looped cyborg synthesiser sequences and big, bold washes of metallic electronic keyboard. Carpenter's brooding soundscapes ably convey the movie's depiction of America as a violent dystopia. As both these memorable, groundbreaking scores testify, John Carpenter's musical ideas evince a simplicity and directness that is stunningly effective and which are as potent, in their own way, as the film music composed by greats like Bernard Herrmann and Ennio Morricone. Highly recommended.

Walkabout: John Barry
(Silva Screen Records FILMCD 339)

Alright, so Nick Roeg's dazzling 1970 movie *Walkabout*, depicting the adventures of two children abandoned by their suicidal father in the Australian outback, is patently not a crime movie. However, John Barry wrote a wonderful, evocative score for the film which has never been commercially available until now. Recorded in Dolby Surround Sound with Nic Raine conducting the City of Prague Philharmonic Orchestra and the Crouch End Festival Chorus, Silva Screen Records should be roundly applauded for bringing Barry's magical score to CD. The superb sound quality is only surpassed by Raine's musical direction of the orchestra. The film's main theme with its delicate ripples of harpsichord accompanying an elegant melody played by the string section is arguably Barry's most evocative piece (at least that's my opinion), conjuring images of wonderment, adventure and a sense of childhood innocence. The main theme is reprised for *Back To Nature*, that memorable scene in the film where Jenny Agutter sheds her clothing for a skinny dip in a lake (Agutter, incidentally, contributes to the CD sleeve notes). The nine cues comprising the *Walkabout* score are majestic symphonic pieces that stylistically anticipated Barry's movement away from jazz-inflected James Bond style scores towards the more mature, grandiose orchestral sound that characterised films like *Out of Africa* and *Dances With Wolves* later on in his career. Also featured on this excellent CD are excerpts from seven other Barry scores, including *Séance on a Wet Afternoon*, *The Betsy* and *The Chase* (the 1967 escaped convict thriller starring Robert Redford and Marlon Brando). This is a must-have item, not only for John Barry fans but also for any devoted film soundtrack enthusiast.

VIDEOCRIME

Barry Forshaw

How long will it last? The current liberalisation of film censorship is very welcome, and who could argue if fewer restrictions for adults mean a few more for children? The new climate has inspired one distributor, Tartan Video, to initiate a unique offer: they are planning to replace censored copies of the films at half price. Welcoming the BBFC's move to liberalise classification standards for 18-category films, they applaud that fact that over eighteens will finally be treated as responsible adults with free choice over what they want to watch. But as Tartan are a company with a real knowledge of the products they sell, they are keen to be able to offer films in versions the director intended. To this end, they have asked the BBFC to reclassify all their previously censored films. Under more realistic guidelines, the uncut versions will be available for the first time ever in the UK. Owners of previously censored Tartan video films will be able to send the tapes to the company's offices and receive the new uncut versions for half price, as they become available. The returned tapes will be donated to charities promoting civil liberties. We'll report in this column when the offer begins. Pessimist that I am, though, I'm sure a politician wishing to make a name for him- or herself will soon step into the arena and plead for greater censorship. After all, neither of the main political parties has shown anything but a nannyish attitude to what adults may watch.

It's a cause for genuine regret that the Warner animated series of Batman has never been treated with any kind of respect in this country. Chopped up and shown in braindead kiddie TV shows, it's clear that no producer has ever looked at how adult and intelligent these episodes are (far more, for instance, than the last Batman live-action movie), and only the Cartoon Network has shown many of the episodes uncut. The follow-up series, *Batman of the Future* (Warner) lacks the dark and brooding quality of the earlier series (which clearly showed the influence of the grim Tim Burton movie vision, even reusing Danny Elfman's pounding symphonic theme from the first film), but this series is still well worthwhile. Featuring a young protege of Bruce Wayne's in a superpowered suit (sans cape), the series is still rich with invention and wit. But quite its cleverest coup is featuring an ageing and crusty Bruce Wayne, directing his impetuous young follower electronically from the dark confines of Wayne mansion. The contrast between the old guru and the inexperienced acolyte (the latter inevitably inclined to screw things up) is always a safe theme in fiction, and so it proves here. The latest volume, *Spellbound*, features episodes of varying quality, but at its best, it is highly diverting, even if *Batman: The Animated Series* remains the finest achievement in this field.

While Carlton TV may not be exactly a byword for very best the medium has to offer, its video arm is a repository for some really interesting material. The new items (in their very different ways) demonstrate this fact: the simultaneous DVD and VHS release of *The Remorseful Day*, the final film in Colin Dexter's long-running (and highly successful) Inspector Morse series. This has all the authority and interest of the series at its very best (not to mention John Thaw's definitive portrayal of the morose, opera- loving cop), and, of course, there is something about it which makes it different from all other episodes in the series…and you all know what that is.

and James Schiff adds…

A company committed to some of the very best in crime movies in the DVD format is Universal Pictures Video, whose schedules lately have sported some real gems. The release of *Henry: Portrait of a Serial Killer* was exemplary, even though it regrettably had to be the trimmed version sanctioned by the BBFC, but such superb crime-related pieces as John Sayles' *City of Industry* were given the deluxe treatment, and lovers of crime movies are keenly awaiting the forthcoming DVD of John Carpenter's early classic *Assault on Precinct 13*, which remains a definitive picture of urban violence, all too prescient today. The company has also made it possible for us to take another look at a much-maligned movie, *Love, Honour and Obey*. This was the film in which the reaction against East End gangster movies really set in, and this uneven but beguiling piece took far more stick than it deserved. True, there is the occasional air of luvvies playing tough about some of the casting, but had it not arrived along with some truly bad crime movies, its reception would have been far more sympathetic. In this superb DVD transfer (with the customary crystal clear picture and sound,) it's definitely worth a second look - or a first, if you were put off by the initial set of reviews.

THE VERDICT

Epitaph for a Spy by Eric Ambler
Pan Classic Crime, £5.99
Pan has launched a series of reprints of crucial crime novels, and this is one of three Ambler novels included in the bunch. The books come complete with new introductions by modern authors, in this case by Robert Harris, though it is apparent that Harris has written one essay to be used for all three Ambler novels. This is a service, since Ambler had gone out of print, and should not have been allowed to do so. Harris identifies the important influence Ambler had on much work that followed. His novels may be read as period pieces, as Harris suggests, but they also feature a particularly modern kind of anti-hero, one who influenced figures as diverse as Hitchcock and John Franklin Bardin: *Epitaph* is a particularly revealing book in that sense. Although it features a typically unappealing Ambler anti-hero, it is more parlour mystery than existential thriller. Who is the spy who used the wrong camera? Colonel Mustard in the conservatory with the billiard cue perhaps? The lines of social strata had yet to be destroyed by the oncoming war, and thus their transgressions in ways more subtle than we are used to today reverberated far more deeply to Ambler's contemporary audience. Strangely, for one who is looked at as a stylistic innovator, Ambler's novels

read far better as proto-screenplays: plot in the service of character. It is useful indeed to see them back in print.

Michael Carlson

Fly in Amber *by Vivien Armstrong*
Severn House, £17.99, ISBN 0 7278 5562 X
Acclaimed cook Bryony Eastwood is coming to terms with the presumed death of her husband. She is offered a live-in contract by her agent at short notice and decides to accept it. Her new employer is an investigative TV reporter called Carey Barnes, married to a beautiful film star. Bryony discovers dark secrets behind the apparently happy facade: Carey is the target of hate mail, and his wife is an alcoholic. And when a corpse turns up in the wine cellar after a fancy dress party, Bryony soon find herself in a downward spiral of deceit and danger. Armstrong has a sharp year for the felicities and absurdities of dialogue, and a characterisation in this efficient thriller is always well honed.

Barry Forshaw

Hit List by Lawrence Block
Orion, £16.99, ISBN 0 75283 838 5
This is the second Keller novel (Keller being a professional hitman) and it falls onto the lighter, Bernie Rhodenbarr side of Block's crime-writing split personality. Like the Rhodenbarr books, this has what might be called a puzzle plot, and, like them, its lightness derives primarily from word play. When Keller does this it's funny (particularly when he tells a sales girl that he's glad the earplugs he's buying are stale, because otherwise they might reproduce!) but it starts to feel formulaic when other characters answer in kind: this has also been the nature of the Rhodenbarr books. Puzzle plots also have problems when one element doesn't seem to fit. In this one, where another hitman is stalking Keller, the unknown stalker goes to great lengths to identify Keller, getting a good look at him at an airport when he arrives for a job. When he kills the wrong person in the dark we can accept it, when he kills the wrong person in the rain it rings hollow, but when he comes face to face with Keller four or five times in the denouement, and never recognises him, it forces the reader to reengage his sense of disbelief. On the other hand, Keller's life in Manhattan is a psychotic Mr Goodbar in reverse. Faced with the problems of intimacy in the big city, women might beware of becoming too intimate with this guy. When he opens up, someone gets closed up! Block's New York often seems like a giant roach motel (a metaphor he uses, though not for the city itself); if so, I'm still wondering if Keller is just a killer (Keller / killer geddit?) roach or maybe more a human spray can of Raid.

Michael Carlson

Gone Bamboo by Anthony Bourdain
Canongate, £10, ISBN 0 86241 825 9
As well as being happily married, Henry and Frances are also trained assassins, and right now they're enjoying a peaceful existence of sun-bathing, drinking and drug-taking on Saint Martin, an idyllic Caribbean island. But Henry's immediate

past is about to catch up with him, with the result that there's another assassin after *him*. And pretty soon it looks like they may have to do the worst thing imaginable – leave the island. But Henry has other ideas... *Gone Bamboo* is peopled with colourful eccentrics. From the cross-dressing Mafioso boss James 'Jimmy Pazz' Calabrese to the curmudgeon with a colostomy bag, Charles 'Charlie Wagons' Iannello, the characterisation is never less than sparkling. Bourdain's skill lies in his low-key approach to what could so easily have become high farce, and his unrivalled ear for the nuances of gangster-speak is brilliant. In his introduction, the author invites us to take *Gone Bamboo* to the beach and get sand between its pages. And it's that sort of novel – the characters enjoying the sort of sun-drenched, hedonistic lifestyle you'd normally find in a Jackie Collins bonkbuster. But set against this backdrop of sun, sand and sex is the hard-edged pulse of Mafioso string-pulling, and the ever-present threat of a violent comeuppance for all concerned. A cross between *The Sopranos* and *Baywatch*, if you enjoyed Bourdain's debut novel *Bone in the Throat*, you'll love this one. Henry and Frances are the new Bonnie and Clyde – you'll be rooting for them all the way.

Mark Campbell

The Sleep of the Dead by Tom Bradby
Bantam, ISBN 0 59304 234 4
We seem to be enjoying a golden age of brilliantly written first novels: Tom Bradby's *Shadow Dancer* received a nosegay of rave reviews, all praising the assurance and skill of his writing. With *The Sleep of the Dead*, Bradby has overcome the inevitable second novel problem: this one is every bit as assured as its predecessor, and combines characterisation as astute as anything in literary fiction with the forcefully realised mechanics of the thriller novel. Julia Haviland has had a troubled childhood. And when her father, Colonel Mitchell Haviland, dies in the Falklands in a mystifying act of heroism, Julia finds that her return from fifteen years in China means that she must come to terms with the ghosts of the past. Living under the threat of an inquiry that will almost certainly end her career in military intelligence, Julia finds herself confronting the past again, with the image of her beloved father ever more present in her thoughts. Only by a painful and dangerous investigation, can she lay the ghosts of the past – and perhaps come to terms with the problems of the present. What makes this forcefully written piece such a commanding read is the multifaceted characterisation of Julia. But Bradby does not try to make us like her, and we're quickly involved with her plight as she tries to rend the veil of secrets that is destroying her life. This is a novel about the destructive effects of suspicion and betrayal on human existence (a superscription from Shakespeare makes this clear, although it is evident from the first chapter onwards), and the novel functions both as an exemplary psychological thriller and a novel of character.

Eve Tan Gee

Brief Notices

A Round-Up by Eve Tan Gee

The current selection of crime and thrillers has thrown up some cherishable items. Donald James' *Vadim* (Century) has the epic scope of his earlier Constantine Vadim books, and the picture of Moscow under siege (while owing something to Martin Cruz Smith) is as powerfully realised as ever.

Snakeskin by John McCabe (Doubleday) is an off-kilter, blackly comic tale of two people meeting 37,000 feet above the Atlantic and entering a bizarre relationship.

Jenny Siler enjoyed much approval for *Easy Money*, and a new book, *Iced* (Orion), is just as individual in its attention-grabbing narrative. Her protagonist, Megan, has spent time in a cosy cell in a New Mexico prison, and returns to a grim Montana in the grip of winter. But a job repossessing cars goes awry when she takes a jeep whose owner has been stabbed to death. Quite as impressive as Siler's debut novel.

Two new Kurt Wallender mysteries from the remarkable Henning Mankell, *Sidetracked* and (in paperback) *Faceless Killers* (Harvill) demonstrate the kind of adroit plotting and sense of locale that marked earlier outings. *Sidetracked* has already gleaned several awards, and a few pages of Mankell's astringent prose will show why.

Candace Robb's *A Trust Betrayed* (Heinemann) is a Scottish murder mystery in Robb's most assured style, with the usual clever accretion of historical detail seamlessly incorporated into a strong plot. This is by no means one of her best books, but it's still in the upper echelons of historical crime writing.

O Gentle Death by Janet Neel (Constable) is a journey into darkness delivered in the quiet and involving style we expect of this writer. Forget the uninspiring blurb (always a feature of Constable books): this is well worth the attention of the discerning crime buff.

Jarred Cade is an acknowledged expert on Christiana, and *Agatha Christie and the Eleven Missing Days* (Peter Owen) has already received much acclaim for its impressively detailed examination of the Queen of Crime's mysterious disappearance. Much has been written about this incident, but this book could be said to be the final word.

Spike by John Burns

Macmillan, £16.99

Max Shard is back, and it's a real pleasure to reacquaint ourselves with John Burns' cynical Fleet Street hack. As before, the authenticity of the writing makes the plots really leap off the page, and Max is the perfect guide through a dark and blackly comic world. Max Chard finds himself doing what a Chief Crime Correspondent is rarely expected to do: spy on a young woman through her bedroom window. But his editor has received a tabloid tip that a Labour MP (with a previously unblemished reputation) is enjoying a little extra-conjugal pleasure. Max is mentally composing his headline when he sees the MP leave the mews house in the early hours, and he spots a mysterious figure dressed in black also loitering. Soon Max has a whole suitcase of questions: why is his editor reluctant to run the scoop? Why is the MP's mistress reported missing the next day? And who is the figure in black? When the body of the young woman is found at the bottom of nearby cliffs in the MP's constituency, Max starts to realise that adultery is only one part of the story. Again, the impressive trick of marrying the investigative reporter detail with a solid crime narrative is brought off with aplomb. Of course, Max is more than a simple hack: questions of honour and commitment are subtly mixed into the murky brew here, but never at the expense of a powerful piece of storytelling. But the emphasis is always satisfyingly on the steadily unfolding revelations – and there are some choice ones on offer here.

Brian Ritterspak

Coffin's Ghost by Gwendoline Butler
HarperCollins, £5.99, ISBN 0 00 651361 1
Several decades ago an authority wrote

that a genuine police procedural listing every minute move by a police team would not only be inordinately long but as boring as a similar description of a stockbroker's office. Gwendoline Butler has always maintained that every writer – whether depicting Hamlet, Oliver Twist or a police detective – must be an entertainer, and this she has unerringly proved in each of her seventy books to date. She has developed the skill, displayed by the weaver, of artfully threading warp and woof to make up a colourful picture you only recognise when it is complete. She may introduce late a character or event that becomes vital. *Coffin's Ghost* starts with Coffin's casual affair with a journalist when he was lonely and missing his lovely wife Stella. Then the ominous scarlet threads begin to form patterns. Dismembered limbs found outside a refuge for battered women, once the house in which Coffin had lived. A French girl who had worked there suddenly reappears – and as suddenly disappears. Is she, or was she, the owner of the legs labelled 'J. C.'? Stella is working with two television personalities who by chance had both been married to the same woman – and their joint step-daughter disappears. A flood in the gun club leads to a missing gun. The governor of the local prison is attacked on Coffin's doorstep – was it intended for John? A cat's head is found in John and Stella's flat. A dealer in illegal frozen beef finds more than he bargained for in his coldroom. A woman's dead body leads Coffin to investigate a 'greasy spoon' café in the shattering finale as the missing step-daughter is found while corruption shows up in the police force itself. All these threads are woven so professionally by Mrs Butler that you realise the crime is no longer a simple murder, even with the subsequent killing of the usual vital witness, but that the crime spreads its tentacles in various directions simultaneously. Gwendoline Butler is the best plotter in crime fiction today. Coleridge wrote, "The willing suspension of disbelief for the moment, which constitutes poetic faith", and this certainly applies to a Gwendoline Butler novel.

Ken W. Ferris

Echo Burning by Lee Child
Bantam Press, 0 5930 4659 5
There was a time when a US-set crime novel by a British writer (such as James Hadley Chase's *No Orchids for Miss Blandish*) could get away with a certain carelessness in local detail. Not any more. Since the Englishman Lee Child began writing his superbly authentic thrillers (notably *Killing Floor*, *Die Trying* and *Tripwire*), few readers on either side of the Atlantic would accept anything other than the gritty authenticity of books such as Child's latest, *Echo Burning*. He prides himself on the plausibility of his settings and characters, and actually has a more striking sense of the American landscape that many native writers. He never allows the reader to forget just where his hero Jack Reacher is, what he's feeling, smelling, seeing. And Reacher has slowly but surely become one of the most fully-rounded protagonists in thriller fiction. It's hardly surprising that the novels have been optioned for filming; what is surprising is the fact that it hasn't happened before. Jack finds himself suffering the intense heat of a Texas summer, and (leaving behind a messy situation) hardly worries about the dangers of who will pick him up when he hitches a ride. But it's a beautiful young rich girl driving a Cadillac who gives Jack a lift. Carmen tells him she has a little girl who is being observed by unseen and sinister forces. And her brutal, abusive husband is in jail, more than likely ready to kill her when he gets out. It's obviously highly inadvisable for Jack to travel to Carmen's remote ranch in Echo County and become involved in her problems, but (needless to say) he does just that. And he's soon encountering lies, lust and prejudice, with untrustworthy cops and lawyers absolutely no help. Jack finally realises that there is only one way to resolve this lethal situation. As always with Child, the narrative rattles along with real élan, and the sultry characterisation keeps everything ruthlessly on track.

Eve Tan Gee

Angels Flight by Michael Connelly
Orion, £5.99

This is Connelly's sixth Harry Bosch novel, and it's somewhat a transitional work. The scale is greater, as Harry finds himself in the middle of a politically sensitive murder involving an attorney who bears more than a passing resemblance to the star of newsroom, courtroom and cable TV, Johnnie Cochrane, defender of the oppressed and OJ Simpson. As a former crime reporter, Connelly has said that the OJ trial was a nadir for him, and his disgust with the process, and the way it was covered in the media, prompted his desire to write about it. This requires a change of sorts for Bosch, whose troubles with authority have been a focal point of the previous novels. In those cases, however, the authority has been more immediate; here, Bosch is in danger of crossing the very heart of the city's police and political establishment. That Bosch's marriage starts to crumble while all this is going on is no surprise, given the circumstances of his relationship with Eleanor, the gambler who betrayed him in the first Bosch novel, *The Black Echo*. Her return to Las Vegas takes place mostly off-stage. At first this seems to be slighting Bosch's private life, but in the end the effect on the reader is exactly like the effect on Bosch: this is something beyond his (and our) abilities to change or to handle. It's a brave piece of writing by Connelly, which is in keeping with the rest of this novel. Although the cyber-crimes which lie at the heart of the killings could lend themselves to a gimmicky plot, they are kept subservient to the real issues, which are celebrity, money and power. And when Bosch comes face to face with that power, as he inevitably does, we may be disappointed that there isn't more of an explosion, but we aren't surprised. That's Connelly's city of angels, and the angels have indeed taken flight. Last year I called this the strongest crime series being written in America: I see no reason to change that opinion now.

Michael Carlson

The Oxford Book of Detective Stories
edited by Patricia Craig
Oxford University Press, £12.99

This anthology is subtitled "an international selection" but apart from the fact that it is a selection and it is international, there is nothing in particular to distinguish it, and one would have hoped for more from Oxford's first such collection since 1926. The international flavour is the strongest point; stories from many of the usual suspects but also from some writers rarely seen in English. Craig's avowed aim is to show the scope of the genre, but she actually restricts herself to a fairly narrow-gauge view of crime fiction, and a strangely limited set of suspects in her choices. Her major omissions are

Poe from the founding fathers, and most of the major English parlour mysteries from their 'golden age' in the early part of the last century. This is an odd choice, simply because Craig also feels it is her

duty to see women represented fairly (virtually half of the selections from more contemporary writers are women), so choices like Marsh or Allingham might have been thought relatively automatic. Craig is overtly and overly fond of the 'urbane puzzle' type story, but does Amanda Cross really add anything to our understanding of the genre? Likewise, Borges is an essential choice, but I wonder if writers other than the mainstream masters like Primo Levi might have been found within European literature. As it is, Craig winds up with a few people writings pastiches where the originals might have been far better and more enlightening. Sara Paretsky's softboiled detective is a worthwhile choice, but Ruth Dudley Edwards' Father Brown? If we're after better representation of women, what about those who worked in the pulp magazines? In fact, the pulps in general, and the digest-sized magazines that followed them are sadly underrepresented. Hammett, Chandler, and Erle Stanley Gardner are in (and the introduction chooses the strangest, least impressive quote of Chandler I would have thought possible) but where are the likes of Mickey Spillane or Mike Shayne, who set the tone for whole generations of writers? Where are the masters of the short story form who laboured in the pages of Ellery Queen or Alfred Hitchcock? Where are modern stylistic innovators like George Higgins or James Ellroy? I'm sure budgetary and rights considerations played their part, but I wonder. If the anthology could feature an original story, why would it come from James Banville? When one considers what is out, it makes one reconsider what is in.

Michael Carlson

Noise Abatement by Carol Anne Davis
Do Not Press, £7.50

Carol Anne Davis specialises in transforming the mundane into the macabre. Here, she trespasses further into Patricia Highsmith territory by subjecting her hero, Stephen Day, to a severe case of everyday irritation: the lads in the flat upstairs are driving him and his wife mad by their noise. Loud noise erupts at any time – the middle of the night, mid afternoon, whether the lads are home or not. The horrors are those of a bad dream rather than a nightmare. The lads upstairs are not monsters from hell. They apologise, turn down the noise for a few minutes, then carry on as before. Police and Environmental Health are too busy to do anything. Meanwhile, Stephen's work is suffering. His wife devel-

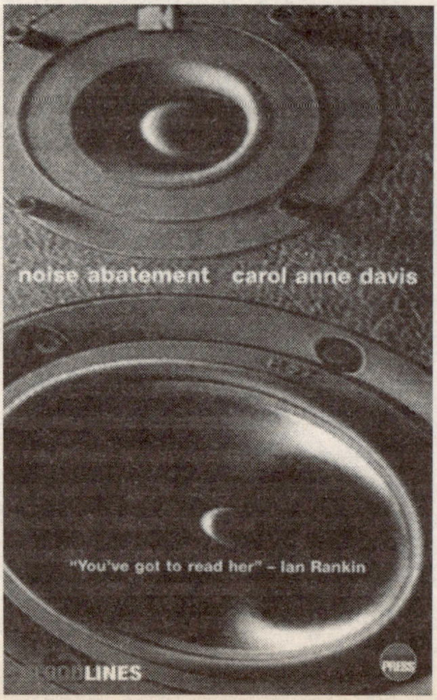

ops spastic colitis. Something must be done. But what? They can't sell the flat because every time someone calls, blasts of noise come from upstairs. They can't persuade the boys to stop. They can't force them. They have no way out. Many of us have fantasised about how we would deal with this situation – like Stephen, we'd like to kill the blighters. Unlike Stephen, we don't do it. *Noise Abatement* shows how easily – as if sleep-walking or staggering from loss of sleep – any one of us could cross into that world of living nightmare.

Russell James

Sidewalking by Nick Duerden
Flame, £6.99, ISBN 0 340 76620 4

It seems that there is no end to our appetite for gangster capers, and Nick Duerden's inventive and involving book is a worthy contribution to the genre. But what makes it strikingly different from other novels in this vein is its sympathy and humanity (characteristics hard to find in this hard-boiled universe). Duerden's protagonist, Jake, is one of life's losers who finds his life transformed when a relative dies and leaves him well provided for. But this is dirty money, proving that Jake's grandfather's frequent boasts about gangland connections have proved true. Improvidently, Jake enjoys his well-heeled new lifestyle, but his indiscretion results in him being chased by a ruthless girlfriend, the police and (most dangerously) a vicious veteran gangster. Utilising the blackly comic style of such films as *Lock, Stock and Two Smoking Barrels*, Duerden takes the reader on a helter-skelter trip from the more dangerous patches of London to the hectic streets of New York. And the lineage of the author's hero stretches back even further: the novel reads like a demented version of John Buchan's *39 Steps*, with a beleaguered hero pursued on all sides and unable to turn anywhere for help. The first person narrative is sharp and funny, and among the host of début novels clamouring for our attention, this is a particularly enjoyable outing.

Barry Forshaw

The Infiltrators by Philip Etiennne & Martin Maynard
Michael Joseph, £15.99

The phenomenal success of the Andy McNab books (in which the reader is taken into the secret world of the SAS by an authoritative narrator) has created a hungry market for similar insider-narrated exposés. This fascinating account is the first clandestine account of life with Scotland Yard's most secret undercover unit. The information that Etienne and Maynard vouchsafe us is cool and dispassionate, but the final effect of their book is like that of the best-written thrillers. After all, many of the most gripping genre titles

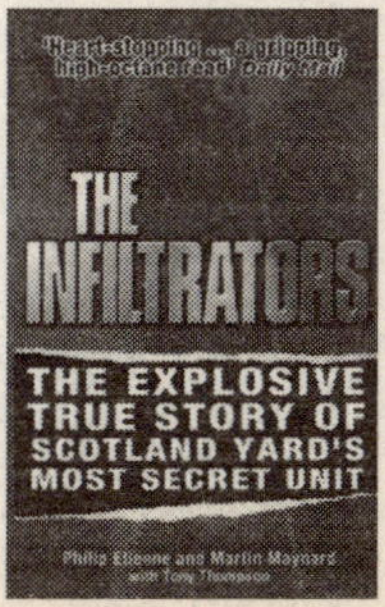

have the hero inside some dangerous criminal organisation, at great risk to life and limb if he is discovered. The difference is that the situations described here have all the palm-sweating authority of the real thing. The authors are two of London's most successful villains, with drug trading as their speciality. But as well as shifting massive amounts of cocaine, ecstasy, crack and cannabis, they still find time to deal in stolen cars, credit cards and whatever shady deal comes their way. Both have all the glittering prizes that crime can bring, and they are known to boast about their achievements. Other villains feel comfortable with them – which is precisely the idea, as these men are actually undercover police officers. As a study of Scotland Yard's covert operations, this is truly compelling stuff. And as a description of two lives permanently on the line, it has an authenticity all too rarely found in fiction.

Barry Forshaw

Transfer of Power by Vince Flynn
Pocket, £6.99, ISBN 0 671 02319 5
Vince Flynn's *Term Limits* was a novel and imaginative political thriller in the *Absolute Power* vein, and managed to marry its high-octane thriller plot to some extremely persuasive political detail. Flynn pulls off the trick again in *Transfer of Power*, while sacrificing something of the plausibility of the earlier book. This one has an intriguing plot idea: what if America's most powerful leader was also its prime target? In the heart of Washington, a group of terrorists has captured the White House, massacring dozens of innocent bystanders. While the Secret Service manages to evacuate the president to his underground bunker, they are not able to stop over a hundred hostages being taken. One man is sent in to break through the political agendas and knee-jerk responses: Mitch Rapp, a crack counter-terrorism operative. Moving through the now dangerous corridors and secret passageways of the presidential mansion, Mitch finds that the threat to the president comes not from the terrorists alone. Not for a second does any of Flynn's narrative seem likely, but that hardly matters when the adrenaline produced by the narrative kicks in. And there is no question that Flynn is cornering the market in action-packed political thrillers. Mitch is a convincing protagonist, and there will be some sweaty palms among readers caught up in his lethal dilemma.

Vic Buckner

I'll Be Watching You
by Richard Gallagher
Virgin, £16.99, ISBN 1 85227 931 1
As new legislation makes the crime of stalking (hopefully) easier for the police to deal with, it was inevitable that the phenomenon of stalkers and their victims would find its way into a book. Thankfully, Richard Gallagher's carefully researched collection of case histories is responsibly and intelligently handled, even though the sensational nature of the material makes for luridly compelling reading. As Gallagher repeatedly points out, it is not just celebrities who are the target of disturbed individuals (although the gunning down of John Lennon remains probably the most infamous example). And although the author deals with celebrated cases such as Lennon and Jodie Foster and her dangerous follower, he is equally in charge of his material when dealing with the lives of ordinary men and women who find their entire existence turned around when a pathological obsessive fixates upon them. Gallagher has inter-

viewed victims, the police and psychologists to create a rounded picture of a disturbing trend. Would more input from the stalkers themselves have granted more insight? Possibly - but Gallagher's book handles the subject as penetratingly as can be imagined.

Barry Forshaw

Even Steven by John Gilstrap
Michael Joseph, ISBN 0 7181 4440 6
Gilstrap has produced some highly authoritative thrillers in which characterisation that leaps off the page is seamlessly melded to plotting of machine-like precision. *At All Costs* was a breakthrough book for the author, and the sheer panache of that book is replicated in *Even Steven*, which modifies the kinetic movement of the action into something richer and more subtle, with human longing as a key theme. The Martins (Bobby and Susan) have one desire: to have a child of their own. While considering how their marriage could be consolidated by such a gift, the couple undertake a camping trip, little realising that this will utterly change their lives. An unkempt, dirty young boy, shivering with cold, appears at their campsite, and the Martins' parental urges are soon kicking in. But when the boy's kidnappers make a violent appearance, the couple find themselves caught up in the savage killing of a police officer. Soon they are outrunning a band of dangerous criminals, and while struggling to stay alive, dark emotions concerning their failed pregnancies add a disturbing spin to the situation. Gilstrap has pulled off two difficult tricks in his invigorating tale: the narrative itself is fresh and innovative (very welcome in these days when many thrillers are content to warm over exhausted plot devices); but he has also adopted and customised a device once very popular in the thriller genre – the action takes place over the course of twenty-four hours, and Gilstrap ensures that the ratcheting up of tension always has a ticking clock as its motor. Finally, of course, however assured a thriller is at dispensing action, it's the characterisation that really lays claim to a reader's attention. And the conflicted couple at the centre of *Even Steven* are so roundly drawn that few readers will be able to avoid empathising with them.

Vic Buckner

An Unsuitable Death by J. M. Gregson
Severn House, £17,99, ISBN 0 7278 5574 3
The body of a beautiful woman is found on the Lady Chapel altar in Hereford Cathedral, and the signs are that the bloody serial killer known as Sacristan has designed the death as part of one of his unholy tableaux. But all is not as it seems. The girl's killer was in a sexual liaison with a well-known MP, and a young actor had asked her to change her lifestyle and marry him. Then there is the abusive stepfather, now the sinister leader of a cult, and her drug world associates. Gregson's doughty protagonists Lambert and Hook have a considerable number of strands (perhaps too many in strictly logical terms) to separate in this divertingly plotted thriller, rich in atmosphere and nicely observed moments.

Judith Gray

A Cold Day in Paradise
by Steve Hamilton
Orion, £9.99
Alex McKnight leaves Detroit and retreats to Paradise after losing his partner and nearly being killed in a shooting. Paradise, in this case, is a small town in Michigan's Upper Peninsula. This is the country of Ernest Hemingway's short stories, closer to wilderness than to Motown. But it's not far enough for McKnight to escape the past. It returns to haunt him in two ways. First, he's called to help the scion of the local aristocracy, who arrives to meet his bookie and finds the man dead. Bodies mount up, and suspicion falls on McKnight himself, not least because the killer appears to be mimicking Rose, the man who shot McKnight and his partner. But Rose is behind bars. Or is he? The other ghost from the past is the gambling grandee's wife, with whom McKnight once had an affair. And not only has the husband called on him for help, he considers McKnight his best, indeed his only friend. Eventually, McKnight is forced to leave his cabin in the woods and re-enter the world of deception and violence, and Hamilton constructs a plot so clever it's actually something of a let down when it resolves itself without the full bloody closure. This book won an Edgar for best first novel in America, and you can see why. Hamilton writes well, with a particular ability at leaving things unsaid between people. His prose may not be lean or compelling like Hemingway's, but his use of those silences, of which there are so many up in Michigan, reminds us of him just a little.

Michael Carlson

Candyland by Evan Hunter / Ed McBain
Orion, £16.99, ISBN 0 5750 7252 0
As Ed McBain, he created the groundbreaking 87th Precinct series, whose innovations were much plundered by TV series such as *Hill Street Blues* and crime writers such as Patricia Cornwell. As Evan Hunter, he wrote such indelible fifties novels as *The Blackboard Jungle* and the screenplay for Hitchcock's *The Birds*, but with *Candyland*, the two writers (who are one and the same person) have both names on a novel for the first time to produce a compelling piece of work. Architect Benjamin Thorpe has an obsession: unknown to his family, he wanders the New York streets in the wee small hours looking for dangerous female companionship, and has a confrontation in a seedy brothel that will change his life. A teenage prostitute known as Heidi has crossed paths with him, but ends up strangled and viciously mutilated in an alleyway. Thorpe is the obvious suspect... but is he too obvious? McBain has stated that he felt many readers had forgotten who Evan Hunter was. However, he has decided to give this writing persona another spin, but the portmanteau writing credit is actually something of marketing ploy. This is a crime novel of some considerable psychological power, and actually reads like neither of the 'two' authors' previous books.

Barry Forshaw

Turnstone by Graham Hurley
Orion, £9.99, ISBN 0 75283 186 0
It might be too much to expect DI Joe Faraday to ask for, "Just the facts, ma'am", but as police procedurals go, this Portsmouth-set novel with its murder at sea could be described as a cross between Dragnet and

Fastnet. Flip as that may sound, there are a lot of things to like about Turnstone. The Portsmouth setting is gritty and convincing, the quick profiles of its lowlife making a dramatic background to Faraday's own depression. Throw in the usual internal wrangles of an over-stretched police force trying to move past the cowboy practices of its own past, and Hurley has given Faraday plenty of conflicts to consider. And that's before we get to his deaf-mute son. Hurley is best in his characterisations, just as convincing dealing with the petty egos of academics as the untrammelled ones of corrupt cops. His Portsmouth comes alive precisely because of that characterisation, through which Faraday moves neutrally enough to let us keep our perspective. If the case of murder that follows winds up being somewhat melodramatic and not necessarily the most convincing crime, its resolution works primarily because of the twist involving Faraday's own love life. It's a twist that Hurley bends for all its worth, to the point that Faraday appears to let the electricity he feels overcome what should be a detective's natural revulsion to duplicity or betrayal. One hopes he'll be back in another volume to learn his lesson.

Michael Carlson

Murder Through the Ages edited by Maxim Jakubowski
Headline, £12.99, ISBN 0 7472 7253 0
It isn't just the fact that Jakubowski graces these pages that prompts the thought that he is one of the best crime anthology editors in the genre (along with Mike Ashley, who – funnily enough – is also a CT contributor). This new collection, all bias aside, is a true delight: a smorgasbord of centuries-spanning historical mayhem that manages to include a pretty stellar selection of crime scribes: Lovesey, Keating, Lindsey Davis, Judith Cook, Carol Anne Davis and many others. The stories are new, and satisfaction is guaranteed – not all the tales are as compulsive as Manda Scott's, but there isn't a dud – and how many anthologies can that be said of?

Judith Gray

Surface Tension by Russell Celyn Jones
Abacus, £9.99, ISBN 0 349 11311 4
With *Surface Tension*, Russell Celyn Jones builds on the impressive intricacies of *The Eros Hunter* and renders a thriller that is as much a penetrating novel of character as it is packed with the requisite suspense. Brother and sister Mark and Geena have a relationship that is so intense, many of their

friends at the Dark Side of the Moon pub are given to fervent speculation as to just what goes on between them. When Natasha enters the scene and becomes a close friend of Geena, Mark begins to believe that her intention is to drive them apart. Geena already has problems: a neurologist cannot find a reason for the hallucinations she suffers. And when Geena starts digging and discovers a dark family secret, Jones' ambitious novel takes on questions of identity that move beyond the realm of the thriller. His canvas is wide: from the less salubrious areas of North London to the dangerous townships of South Africa, he takes his characters on a probing and relentless journey that always manages to remain thought-provoking even as it draws the reader deeper and deeper into a net of malign human behaviour. But what particularly distinguishes the book is the carefully drawn sibling relationship at its centre: more overtly literary novels have not treated the subject as intelligently as this.

Ingrid Yornstrand

Breaking and Entering
by H. R. F. Keating

Macmillan, £16.99, ISBN 0 333 90279 3

It is amazing to think that Keating wrote his first inspector Ghote novel *The Perfect Murder* in 1964. Here we are in the twenty-first century, and Keating is still delighting us with such expertly turned tales of Bombay-set mayhem as *Breaking and Entering*. The city is alive with the news of local bigwig Ajmani's savage murder, and the police force is unable to solve the mystery of how he could be stabbed in his heavily guarded mansion. Ghote has been given the less prestigious task of tracking down a cat burglar who bears the nickname Yeshwant. With the dubious help of his old friend Axel Svensson, Ghote is on the point of revealing the cat burglar's true identity, and (needless to say) his investigation looks likely to throw light on the murder of Ajmani… What has made this series so beguiling is Keating's effortless conjuring up of the sultry Indian locales, along with the perfectly anatomised jealousies and infighting of the local police force. Ghote remains one of the most individual sleuths in crime fiction, and he owes little to other classic models (except, perhaps, Holmes – but which literary sleuth doesn't?). This novel has some of the smoothest and most ingenious plotting of the series, and there are no signs that Keating has lost the freshness and inspiration that characterised his very first Ghote book.

Vic Buckner

The Constant Gardener by John le Carré
ISBN 0 340 73337 3(hb) / 0 340 73338 1(pb)

There were those who feared that the end of the Cold War would deal a fatal blow to the creativity of many first-rate thriller writers who specialised in this territory. In the case of John le Carré, this would have meant the loss of not only Britain's finest thriller writer, but a serious novelist of quite as much literary gravitas as any of his mainstream contemporaries. Certainly, *The*

Spy Who Came in from the Cold remains as utterly compelling today as when it was written, whereas post-Cold War le Carré themes such as financial double-dealing seemed to inspire him less than the world of shifting identity he had dealt in so skilfully. But with *The Constant Gardener*, we have the author once again firing on all cylinders. The characterisation is as elegant and expressive as ever, the prose as limpid and forceful. But, most of all, le Carré has found a theme quite as pregnant as any he has handled in the past: the malign, deceptively ameliorative world of global pharmaceuticals. In the new novel, the customary themes of betrayal and danger are explored in a narrative that exerts a total grip throughout its considerable length. His protagonist, Justin Quayle, is an unreflective British diplomat whose job in the British High Commission in Nairobi suggests one of Graham Greene's dispossessed protagonists trying to survive in the sultry corruption of foreign climates. President Arap Moi's Kenya is a country in the grip of AIDS, while political machinations maintain a deadly status quo. When Quayle's wife (who has taken more interest in what is happening around her than her husband) is killed, his investigation of her murder leads him into a murky web of exploitation involving Kenyan greed and a major pharmaceutical company eager to promote its 'wonder cure' for tuberculosis. As Quayle looks deeper into the company his wife had been investigating, all he has carefully built around him begins to crumble. The steady accumulation of tension and rigorous delineation of character is emblematic of le Carré at his finest, and it is a tremendous pleasure to find the author so resolutely back on form, fired with a real sense of anger at the duplicity of the modern world.

Vic Buckner

Mystic River by Dennis Lehane
Bantam, ISBN 0 593 04750 8
When word of mouth on thriller writers among aficionados is particularly good for a certain author, that's a reason to pay attention. But when similar acclaim comes from fellow practitioners, readers really need to mark their cards. Dennis Lehane has become a must-read novelist on the strength of such gritty and forceful thrillers as *Darkness, Take my Hand* and *Gone, Baby, Gone*. Praised for his taut, carefully orchestrated story lines and expressively drawn, vulnerable characters, Lehane is the kind of writer who has achieved his position by stealth rather than massive advertising campaigns. The

new book, *Mystic River,* confirms his status as one of the most vigorous and skilful American talents in years. Childhood friends, Sean, Jimmy and Dave have their lives changed when a strange car turns up in their street. After one boy gets into the car and two not, a terrible event happens which terminates their friendship and changes their lives. Twenty-five years later, Sean is a homicide detective, while Jimmy has taken a criminal route. When Jimmy's daughter is found savagely killed, Sean is assigned to the case. And with his own personal relationships in deep trouble, he finds he is obliged to go back to the life he thought he had left behind, coming to terms with his ex-friends and a confrontation with a human monster. As psychological thrillers go, this one is non-pareil, and has to be read.

Barry Forshaw

A Sea of Troubles by Donna Leon
Heinemann, £15.99, ISBN 0 434 00974 1
It's not necessary for an author to live in a particular locale to render his or her settings authentic, but Donna Leon's vivid recreation of Venice for her inspector Brunetti mysteries would seem to owe something to her intimate knowledge of the city. As much as the beleaguered Brunetti, Venice is a powerful protagonist in these elegantly constructed tales, and this latest is evidence of a deepening and refinement of Leon's art. Two fishermen have been killed on the island of Pellestrina, south of the Lido on the Venetian lagoon. Commissario Brunetti finds it difficult to penetrate the close-knit community, locked behind a code of loyalty and an insularity that the Mafia would be proud of. But solving the murders is not his only problem: when the Questore's secretary, Signorina Elettra, volunteers to come to the island, Brunetti finds himself obliged to protect her – and, furthermore, deal with the confused feelings he has for her. Perhaps this isn't the best place for those new to Leon to start, as the style is more clipped and elusive than usual. But for aficionados, the delights are many (not least Brunetti's emotional involvement), and the set pieces are orchestrated as richly as ever.
Eve Tan Gee

Pagan Babies by Elmore Leonard
Viking, £16.99, ISBN 0 670 88504 5
He smokes dope, has a taste for Johnnie Walker whisky and once smuggled a truckload of cigarettes over a state border for the Mob. But what confirms that Father Terry Dunn is not your average Catholic

priest is when he walks into a Rwandan bar and calmly shoots four men. Dunn is one of the central characters in the latest madcap opus from veteran crime writer, Elmore Leonard, an offbeat caper about a priest who leaves his mission in Africa and heads home ostensibly to attend his mother's funeral. Dunn finds a friend in Debbie Dewey, an aspiring comedienne who's just spent the last three years in a women's prison for aggravated assault (she ran over her former boyfriend in a revenge attack for his robbing her of her savings). Dunn and Dewey make an unlikely couple and set out to take the Mob for a ride to the tune of $250,000 with a children's charity scam. Along the way, Leonard's customary assortment of vividly drawn scumbags adds extra spice to the tale. Both witty and possessing a natural fluidity, Leonard's adroit use of dialogue accelerates character development and greases the wheels of a wholly unpredictable plot. First class entertainment.

Charles Waring

The Colour of Night by David Lindsey
Warner Books, £6.99, ISBN 0 7515 2889 7
In such thrillers as *In the Lake of the Moon* and *Requiem for a Glass Heart*, David Lindsey has shown himself to be a writer with a punchy yet elegantly textured style. He is strikingly good at torpedoing the clichés that accrue to the thriller protagonist, and in this new book Harry Strand is a particularly felicitous creation. Harry is trying to forget his career in American intelligence and struggling to come to terms with the tragic death of his wife in a car crash. He has reinvented himself as a successful art dealer, but his new life is ruptured when the seductive Mara Song comes to him with a beguiling

proposition – to act as broker for her astonishing portfolio of sketches by modern masters. It's an offer he can't refuse, but when he discovers a video cassette at Mara's home that shows his wife's final moments of life as her car is forced off the road, he realises that the only thing that matters in his life is finding her killer – now within his grasp. By engaging us in Strand's problems so irresistibly, Lindsey is able to ensure that the mechanics of his plot move with relentless precision as his hero gets nearer and nearer to his wife's murderer.

Barry Forshaw

Motherless Brooklyn by Jonathan Lethem
Faber, £9.99, ISBN 0 571 19797 3
His publishers have launched Jonathan Lethem's irresistible thriller in this country with the Newsweek plaudits he had gar-

nered: the author was named as one of the '100 People for the New Century'. To that they can now add the prestigious Crime Writers Association Award the book has picked up. If this means that readers will take up a writer new to them, that's all to the good, for this is a truly unique and flinty novel, shot through with sardonic humour and extremely quirky characterisation. Lionel Essrog, aka The Human Freakshow, is a victim of Tourette's Syndrome (the uncontrollable impulse to declaim nonsense, touch all surfaces and other disturbing symptoms). And when a local tough guy and fixer, Frank Minna, adopts the adolescent protagonist (along with three other orphans from the St Vincent Home for Boys) and educates them to become members of his close-to-the-edge detective agency, Lionel's life is changed irrevocably. But when Minna (known as the Secret Prince of Brooklyn) is savagely killed, Lionel find himself obliged to become a real detective, and is soon up to his neck in the murky world in which Minna moved. It became a cliché for television detectives to be disabled in some fashion (blind, heavily overweight, wheelchair-bound, etc.), but any suspicions that Lethem will be going down that familiar path are soon ruthlessly expunged. This treatment of the protagonist's condition is both responsible and compelling, lending his narrative a hard-edged realism.

Judith Gray

Crazy Man Michael by Jim Lusby
Gollancz, £9.99, ISBN 0 575 07056 0
DI Carl McCadden is being tipped to head up a new unit: the Murder Squad, which the Irish Minister for Justice is planning to form. The unit will have exclusive responsibility for tackling homicide throughout the Irish state, and the first assignment will be to investigate a group of unsolved murders of women. But as McCadden readies himself for this high-powered job, he encounters an undercover policeman called Wallace who has a strange story to tell – and, what's more, is being pursued by Special Branch. McCadden realises that it would be far more sensible to avoid the trouble that Wallace brings with him, but, inevitably, he is soon deep in a very dark business that threatens everything he has worked for. Jim Lusby has been steadily building his McCadden character through three previous thrillers, all rich in atmosphere and crammed with the kind of assured plotting that is found too rarely these days. *Making the Cut* was a powerful début that the author succeeded in building upon, and this latest outing is probably the most complex yet. By dividing his hero's sympathies, Lusby presents him (and the reader) with a host of difficult moral decisions that give a keen edge to the

plot. Some of the revelations (including corruption in high places) are familiar, but it is more and more difficult for authors to avoid treading these familiar waters. The point is:

can Lusby ring enough changes to make his novel stand out from the crowd? And on that score, there is some room for debate.

Barry Forshaw

The Devil's Highway by Hannah March
Headline, £5.99, ISBN 0 7472 6013 3
It's 1761, and amateur sleuth Robert Fairfax is shocked to discover that the Stamford to London stagecoach has been attacked by a highwayman. Three victims lie dead, and a fourth has mysteriously vanished. Employed by the local JP, Fairfax goes on the trail of the killer – but his path becomes ever more tangled, and as the possible assailants mount up, it's clear that his task is far from easy... It takes a prodigious talent to make such a promising scenario flat and lifeless. Hannah March achieves it. Largely incident-free, the bulk of the narrative concerns itself with endless cross-examinations of suspects. Characters are clichéd and under-described, preferring long, drawn-out speeches to real conversations. Period detail is scarce, whilst dialogue is rarely more than two-dimensional – the odd 'twixt' and 'misdoubt' remind the reader that the speaker hails from a previous age. Fairfax himself is little more than a cipher – a generic detective with no discernible features of interest. The solution to the stagecoach assault is admittedly satisfying, but comes too late to make the novel anything other than immensely dull. Much of the preceding content – dialogue, mainly – is padding; and unexciting padding at that. Historical colour seems almost non-existent, as does humour, excitement or pacing. Everything that happens is described in the most listless terms imaginable, and in avoiding the obvious possibilities of the setting, March consistently pulls her punches, providing us with, ultimately, a book that doesn't even approach the dizzying heights of a pot-boiler.

Mark Campbell

A Distinction of Blood by Hannah March
Headline, £5.99, ISBN 0 7472 6014 1
Writing period tales of sleuthing, to use an older term than detection, involves more than the occasional fashionable word or phrase. The lack of scientific aids and knowledge of modern psychology, and the reliance on protracted means of communication are more abstruse than, say, *A Yankee at the Court of King Arthur*. Hannah March used to quote scenes and persons in the eighteenth century for her hero, Robert Fairfax, but her (or is it his?) present story relies less on names and events. The description of a fat lady at the begin-

ning of chapter five reads like that of one of the cruel woodcuts and caricatures of that time. Covent Garden's many abodes of vice are little mentioned: the Hellfire Club dismissed as relatively harmless. Fairfax is first engaged to check the lifestyle of the new son-in-law, Baron Mortlock (a significantly ambiguous name) only to find him murdered. His death occurs in the next room to his wife's levee, her circle of sycophants all having good reasons for loathing Mortlock. Fairfax catches the killer and solves the ancillary mysteries, although we wonder at the end what happens to most of the cast. There is a curious error when the musician suspect admits to meeting a girl at the inquest for the first time, when he had already had a long talk with her at the levee earlier. The story reads smoothly and rhythmically, and could apply to other periods with ease. The title provides a neat ambiguous clue to the crime.

Ken W. Ferris

Firewall by Andy McNab
Bantam, £16.99, ISBN 0 5930 4616 1
Let's face it – we all thought that Andy McNab was set to become a one-book-wonder, parleying his experiences in the SAS into a single, (highly readable) book, *Bravo Two Zero*. But with such impressive books as *Crisis Four, Immediate Action* and *Remote Four*, he has established a striking body of work, more sophisticated than his first outing, but with all the brute force and kinetic action we want from him. The new book is a streamlined thriller in which Nick Stone (ex-SAS, now working for British Intelligence on 'deniable operations') is handed the freelance job of snatching a Mafia warlord and taking him to St Petersburg – lucrative, but highly dangerous work. Stone is soon deep in the lethal underworld of Estonia, caught between a Russian initiative to hijack cyber-espionage operations, and American and British agents out to thwart them. Not to mention the bloody interventions of the Mafia... The first-person narrative has some of the wry charm of Len Deighton's earliest (and best) espionage novels, with the bolshy protagonist sharply drawn, and the action has the seamless skill that we expect from McNab. But what marks this one out as an advance on his earlier work is the new level of ingenuity in the plotting: we're pretty familiar with the Russian Mafia by now (not least from James Bond movies), but McNab builds some exhilarating narrative twists into his treatment of the theme that ensures a lively ride for the reader.

Brian Ritterspak

Dying Embers by Margaret Murphy
Macmillan, £16.99, ISBN 0 333 90327 7
In *Dying Embers*, we are reminded that evil festers in places other than the mean streets of noir fiction. By drawing us into the apparent safety of a well-run school, Margaret Murphy lulls us into a false sense of security. She then destroys that security by portraying a world in which drug-related violence is endemic. Geri Simpson is a teacher at St Michael's Secondary School. One of her sixth form pupils, Ryan Connelly, has gone missing, and when his body surfaces, it is burnt beyond recognition. The authorities believe that Ryan accidentally immolated himself whilst experimenting with drugs. Geri knows better, because

Geri knew Ryan, and the circumstances in which he is assumed to have died simply don't fit with what she knew of him. A multi-layered novel, exceptionally well written, and disconcerting. I, for one, will be reading this writer's backlist.

J. Wallis Martin

Arabesk by Barbara Nadel
Headline, £17.99, ISBN 0 7472 2348 3
Barbara Nadel continues to go from strength to strength with her atmospheric and idiosyncratic Istanbul-set thrillers featuring the unorthodox Inspector Ikmen as the protagonist. The third book, *Arabesk*, bears the strapline, "The Donna Leon of Istanbul", but Nadel needs no comparisons with other authors: she is very much an individual talent in her own right. The scion of one of Turkey's most aristocratic families, Inspector Suleyman, is unfamiliar with the downmarket, noisy world of Arabesk music. And when the peasant wife of one of its star performers is killed in a sumptuous Istanbul apartment, he finds himself unable to cope with the case. Needless to say, Suleyman's mentor, Inspector Ikmen, is persuaded to become involved (despite being on sick leave), and both are plunged into a world that hides depths of menace beneath its beguiling exterior. As before, Nadel presents a gallery of richly created characters, along with the non pareil scene-setting we expect from her. If at first it seems that a certain freshness is lacking from this third outing for Ikmen, that's probably due to the fact that Nadel has now made us thoroughly familiar with his world. Nevertheless, this remains one of the most original crime series currently in progress.

Barry Forshaw

The Mandala of Sherlock Holmes by Jamyang Norbu
John Murray, £16.99, ISBN 0 7195 5640 6
They began very shortly after Conan Doyle wrote his last Sherlock Holmes short story, and the honourable tradition of the Holmes pastiche has continued (with widely varying success) ever since. Some of the attempts to create new adventures for the Great Detective have been worthy but dull, fatally lacking the fire and invention of the wonderful originals. Others (such as Nicholas Meyer with *The Seven Per Cent Solution*) have spun wonderful variations on the basic premise. Norbu's ingenious and delightful tale is definitely among the more beguiling additions to the genre. For the first time, we are treated to the amazing events of Holmes' time in Tibet, when the world believed him dead after the fatal struggle with Professor Moriarty at the Reichenbach Falls. There is a particularly clever juggling act going on here: not only is the ventriloquism by which Doyle's ascetic hero is recreated quite faultless, the sense of locale is brilliantly conjured, with the medieval splendour of Lhasa particularly well brought off. Also (without giving too much away), the author has created a splendidly nasty master criminal for Holmes to duel with. There is a problem created by this highly diverting book: all subsequent new adventures for Baker Street's most famous resident have quite a lot to live up to if they are to top this one.

Barry Forshaw

The Deposition of Father McGreevy by Brian O'Doherty
Arcadia, £11.99, ISBN 1 900850 48 6
The 1950s. William Maginn is drinking in a

London pub, when he hears of the strange demise of an isolated mountain village in County Kerry – in fact, the place where he was born. Returning to Kerry, Maginn realises that there is an astonishing story to be told: the sad destruction of a town that encapsulated Ireland's ancient traditions and mystery. All the women in the village have mysteriously died, with a priest, Father McCready left to sort out the chaos. In the outer world, war rages as Maginn attempts to save what is left of the parish and deal with the distrust and superstition of the townsfolk. Brian O'Doherty is a writer with a very individual gift, and this fascinating tale is couched in language that is both poetic and allusive. The central narrative is handled with all the authority and power one could wish for (with the editor hero Maginn sympathetically and richly drawn). But it is the elegant prose, involving the reader deeper and deeper in the strange, unreal situation that truly mesmerises. Whether read as a penetrating vision of a small village under threat from tensions within, or as a magical and atmospheric piece of fine writing, O'Doherty's unusual book convinces on all levels.

Ingrid Yornstrand

Survivor by Chuck Palahniuk
Vintage, £6.99
"Every generation reinvents Christ", says Tender Branson, survivor of the Creedish religious cult's mass suicide. Tender has emerged from the isolation and discipline of a closed community into the headlight glare of the twenty-first century and he is reinventing as he goes. As one cult is extinguished, another begins. A surviving church member is hunting down and killing those who opted out of 'the reckoning' and the trail is leading to Tender. A ravenous media, sensing blood, begins to prowl and Tender finds himself signed by agents and repackaged as a messianic guru. His life of domestic servility and emotional repression is turned into a global marketing empire. Tender, pumped full of steroids and image-makeover drugs, becomes a walking loaded gun with the safety off. In the media age if something doesn't happen in front of a camera or a microphone then, like the tree in the forest, it doesn't happen at all. Tired of this intrusion but intent on a confession, Tender decides to tell his story into the black box recorder of a hijacked jumbo jet with no crew and no passengers, cruising at 30,000 feet on autopilot, waiting for engine burn-out and terminal velocity. His suicide letter is a countdown. In the sixties the novelist's response to the growing consumer culture and horror of war was with a bitter irony (Kurt Vonnegut), surreal twist (Thomas Pynchon) or gleeful cheer (Terry Southern). How do you react to a new century where the facade has been torn down? Chuck Palahniuk responds with a beaten nihilism. His voice is that of a Holden Caulfield off the antidepressants. Like *Fight Club* before it, an outsider opts out taking the world down with him. Instead of a guerrilla faction of street-brawling consumer terrorists, *Survivor*'s opt-out is fundamentalist religion. With the black humour bile of Bill Hicks and the sardonic staccato of Vonnegut, Palahniuk wearily rails against the trivial horror of modern life; Stair-Masters, mini vacuum-packed peanuts, TV movie biopics, fake evangelists, product placement, etiquette

guides. Taking all these elements he puts them through a mincer, multiplying the anger and adding a *Life's Little Instruction Book* twist of anti-homilies in bite-sized form. With one of the most startling openings of recent fiction *Survivor* grabs you, not letting go until the pages have counted backwards descending, like the crashing plane, in an inevitable momentum. After *Survivor*, most books will be mere join-the-dots.

Mike Paterson

Hush Money by Robert B. Parker

The Spenser novels have moved into their own postmodernism, going beyond self-parody to a place where they exist in a framework which renders almost everything irrelevant except the way the big guy, his black alter ego, his new age Guinevere, Susan, and a few other characters act out their scenes: the point is not so much where you get as how you get there. *Hush Money* reminds me in many ways of Donald Barthelme's *Snow White* in that it has removed virtually all the conventions of traditional detective stories (as Barthelme did for fairy tales) and replaced them with the conventions of Spenser. Or maybe he's just Quentin Tarantino with a set of references that go back beyond movies and TV from the 1960s. I'm not complaining about this, necessarily, because *Hush Money* is one of the most entertaining of the series, with the straight-men for Spenser's ironic turns coming mostly from academe. They may be targets far too easy for Parker to take pleasure in the pot shots he doles out; in Harvard Yard Spenser and Hawk are like comic piranhas in a fish tank full of doped-up carp. But it works, and that's when you realise that the focus of the book has moved away from crime and into faculty politics (and Parker refers to the old adage about faculty politics being so vicious because the stakes are so small). Of course long time readers (going back to *The Godwulf Manuscript*) will remember that Parker himself came out of academia, discovered, as it were, by George V. Higgins. If this may be seen as a return to his roots, well, it is done in style. The tenure battle which sparks Parker's investigation revolves around a gay 'outing' activist linked to the rejected professor. The activist is found dead, an apparent suicide, and the professor's father, a boxing trainer who was Hawk's mentor, asks Hawk to get involved. Hawk turns to the great white father, which prompts a rare moment of introspection between our two heroes, one which includes Hawk pointing out rhetorically 'you my friend' and Parker replying 'embarrassing, but true'. A parallel story, involving a friend of Susan's who thinks her ex-husband is stalking her, also gives Spenser a chance to riff on relationships. What could be happier? Throw in Pearl the wonder dog and a macho gourmet recipe for those busy days when a detective just has nothing on the shelves, and what could be better. And there's a white supremacist militia out there in the woods of Maine who blow up Spenser's car for good measure. If the plot has a major hole, it is in delineating exactly how the story's crucial odd couple ever managed to get together in the first place – a not unimportant point whose importance will be clearer once you've read the book, as you surely will, and enjoy it, in spite of that large and crucial unanswered question.

Michael Carlson

Red Light by Jefferson Parker
HarperCollins, £9.99, ISBN 0 00 710194 5
At the end of Parker's last novel, *Blue Hour*, ambitious Orange County detective Merci Rayborn has caused the death of her partner, Tim Hess, an older cop with cancer with whom she has a single night's affair. She's left with Hess' baby, however, and now, in *Red Light*, Rayborn is trying to cope with her loss, not only of Hess but perhaps also of her priorities for her police career. She is seeing a police colleague, Mike McNally, like her a second generation cop, but the shadow of Hess hangs over the relationship. Soon, even more hangs over it. Nineteen year old hooker Aubrey Whitaker was being turned in a sting operation by McNally's vice unit, and when she is murdered it soon becomes evident McNally's relationship with her had gone over the bounds of the purely professional. At the same time, in a clear-out of unsolved cases, Merci is handed the murder of another hooker, this one from thirty years before, and as she investigates she soon begins to uncover secrets which seem to reverberate in the present power structure of her own department. With all the clues in the Whitaker killing pointing to McNally, Merci finds herself put in a position where every move seems to involve some sort of betrayal. This is one of Parker's best, his Orange County *Chinatown*, although he's more interested in the individual emotions of his characters than in the analysis of bigger social issues. It's also like George Higgins seen from the other side. The older cops inhabit a Higgins-type world, where the favour bank is always open. Merci might have a baby out of wedlock, but she'd like to think she wouldn't abuse the law, even for a friend. Parker writes convincingly, getting past the potential dangers of too much coincidence. I just wish the publisher would decide if he's Jefferson Parker (title pages) or T. Jefferson Parker (page headers). Personally, I thought TJ was a pretty good name. Why lose it?

Michael Carlson

1st to Die by James Patterson
Headline, £9.99, ISBN 0 7472 7437 1
Great detective series invariably have the death-watch beetle chewing away at the central concept, so that authors from Conan Doyle to Colin Dexter have tried to kill off their sleuth (Dexter succeeded, Doyle didn't). James Patterson's diverting Alex Cross series was definitely showing signs of slipping into auto-pilot, perhaps because Patterson set himself the task of maintaining a protagonist who wasn't a recovering alcoholic or dealing with a broken marriage (the two principal clichés of the genre). This first novel in a new, non-Cross series has clearly had a galvanising effect on the author, with Lindsay Boxer, the only woman homicide inspector in San Francisco, making for a well-rounded and engaging heroine. When a psychotic killer begins savagely murdering newlywed couples on their wedding nights, Lindsay inaugurates the Women's Murder Club with coroner Claire, journalist Cindy and attorney Jill as her partners. While the basic concept isn't really plausible, Patterson's too professional a writer not to make the most of his new set up, and in his trademark brief chapters manages to guarantee reader interest until the satisfying finale. Perhaps not all of his multiple heroines are as well characterised as Lindsay, but few will complain when Patterson delivers the requisite tension.

Eve Tan Gee

Roses are Red by James Patterson
Headline, £16.99, ISBN 0 7472 6346 9
If you have a formula that is working well, why change it? This is clearly James Patterson's thinking, and his series of Alex Cross thrillers have gone from strength to strength utilising a novel but basic premise. While Patterson is clearly a stylish and original writer who could afford to take his time without losing the reader, he ensures that his chapters are absolutely the shortest in the business: often, only one or two pages long. As Patterson has frequently said, this ensures that his readers simply cannot put his books down: after all (they reason), that next chapter is so short I may as well read it. But this is not to say that Patterson's books, such as this latest, are simply express train rides. Alex Cross is a particularly well drawn protagonist, and Patterson has set himself a difficult task with his hero by avoiding the clichés of most thriller writers: Alex is not an alcoholic, is not in constant conflict with his superiors, and doesn't have a messy private life. It is a tribute to Patterson's skill that his detective still remains an extremely engaging character. *Roses are Red* centres on a series of meticulously planned bank robberies, with Alex up against a grimly sadistic master criminal organising the heists. As always, Patterson brings off his psychopathic villain with real skill. We've been here before, but few will complain of over familiarity when the author's sure-fire tactics have us turning those pages with ever increasing speed.

Eve Tan Gee

Half Moon Street by Anne Perry
Headline, £6.99, ISBN 0 7472 6232 2
Anne Perry continues to weave her beguiling spell, combining an adroitly plotted murder mystery and a lamentable social evil. Her Victorian mysteries have all the requisite scene-setting atmosphere and even a leavening of Dickens' social conscience. In this one, a bizarre murder has Inspector Thomas Pitt thrown into London's Bohemia, with playwrights battling against censorship and the new art of photography being born in the back streets. With his wife Charlotte on holiday in Paris, Pitt is aided by her mother, now married to an actor. And in the booksellers and tobacconists of Half Moon Street, Pitt discovers a sinister side of the photographers' art. Perry at her accomplished best.

Ingrid Yornstrand

Bad Night Is Falling by Gary Phillips
No Exit Press, £6.99
The tangled history of urban Los Angeles has been the basis for some excellent fiction, particularly in James Ellroy's novels and in films like *Chinatown* or *Roger Rabbit.* As a case study in the corruption of growth, LA shines as a beacon in the swamps, somewhere just below sea level. The strongest parts of Gary Phillips' novel featuring the black detective Ivan Monk deal with the history of LA, in particular the way the police functioned as part of a right wing cabal dedicated to using the anti-Communist hysteria of the post-war era to enable them to proceed unfettered with profitable land development schemes. Phillips weaves this background into the story well. The story itself, however, is less well woven. It meanders and drags, and seems to sputter out at just the points it should be picking up speed. It's full of logical inconsistencies: Monk's girlfriend is a judge(!) who finds herself coming under intense public and media pressure for her decisions. Yet when her boyfriend is arrested and charged with manslaughter, rather than intensify the media frenzy against her, it all seems to go quiet. This is not the Los Angeles of OJ Simpson and Rodney King. This overall sloppiness is reflected time and again in small errors that are littered throughout the book. If you're detective is named Monk, and you're going to eulogise Lester Young within your story, you damn well ought to know that Young played the tenor sax, not the trumpet. If Monk is going to wear a Negro League baseball cap, you ought to know the Monarchs and Grays were two different teams. Chicken hawks are the guys who cruise for young male prostitutes, not the hooker boys themselves. I could go on and do the Spanish ones too. And if you're going to describe meal after meal that characters eat, you need to find another adjective besides tasty. Food is the key to my favourite passage from the novel. Monk has just mentioned the Daisy Dinosaur chain, and his girlfriend 'scrunches her features': "'What? The children's playland with those loud kill-the-slobbering-alien video games, singing dinosaur waiters and waitresses, comic book panels for wallpaper, and jumping pits full of sticky, gummy rubber balls?' The mention of the facility, with the attendant carousing children, seemed to bring her up short." Does anyone *you* know really talk like that? We should all be brought up so short! Or at least maybe Ivan Monk could be.

Michael Carlson

Tom Clancy's Powerplays: Bio-Strike
by Jerome Preisler
Penguin, £5.99, ISBN 0 1402 7926 1
When an author achieves the upper echelons of bestsellerdom, his very name can sell a book – even if it's just the writer's basic premise worked into a novel by other hands. Most of Arthur C. Clarke's work falls into this category these days, and this fast-moving thriller is similarly a collaboration between mega-seller Tom Clancy and the lesser-known Preisler. What really counts, though, is just how well the goods are delivered, and Clancy's well known way with an ever-accelerating narrative is very capably duplicated by his co-author. The most dangerous weapon of the century has been deployed by a man who can threaten

the very existence of the human race. Criminal genius Harlan DeVane has created and unleashed a lethal genetically engineered superbug that is resistant to all cures. DeVane plans to auction the bug but his first plan is to destroy his nemesis, Roger Gordian, another master of technology. As Gordian is infected with the disease, his search for a cure will mean not only his own survival but possibly that of millions of others. DeVane is a criminal monster out of the Fleming school: larger than life, utterly ruthless, but still handled with great plausibility. The battle between the two protagonists is dispatched with palm-sweating skill.

Brian Ritterspak

Temple by Matthew Reilly

Macmillan, £9.99

In the jungles of Peru, an astonishing race is underway to locate a legendary Inca idol which may be used as the basis for formidable new weapons. This is high adventure of a rare order, an inventive tale shot through with imagination and flair. Reilly is clearly concerned with maintaining a killing pace (which can, in the wrong hands, be a touch unrelenting – but not so here). At over 600 pages, *Temple* is a lengthy read – but the time passes very quickly. The fact that Hollywood is beckoning Reilly comes as no surprise.

Barry Forshaw

A Trust Betrayed by Candace Robb

ISBN 0 434 00932 6

Not so long ago, historical crime novels were a rare breed. In the dizzying profusion of such titles at present (with anywhere from ancient Rome to Renaissance Italy a fit locale for dark deeds and pre-Holmes detectives), a certain panache is needed to make a new entry rise above the crop. Candace Robb has demonstrated in such novels as *The Apothecary Rose* and *The King's Bishop* that her Owen Archer mysteries are worthy successors to the groundbreaking medieval novels of Ellis Peters, full of satisfyingly convoluted plotting. *A Trust Betrayed* inaugurates a new series of mysteries set in Scotland at the time of Robert the Bruce. In the spring of 1297, Margaret Kerr is afraid that her merchant husband Roger has been caught up in the pending rebellion against the English. Her husband's cousin and factor, Jack Sinclair, agrees to try to locate Roger in the dangerous city of Edinburgh. When he is found murdered, Margaret undertakes to solve the mystery herself, but she quickly discovers that Scotland at war is a very dangerous place for a

woman alone. Apart from the effortless conjuring up of historical detail (a sine qua non of the genre), Robb is particularly acute at dealing with issues such as the place of women in this troubled society: without ever making Margaret a proto-feminist, she cannily examines attitudes to gender in the distant past while never forgetting the imperatives of a rattling yarn.

Noirotica edited by Thomas S. Roche
Black Books, ISBN 1 892723 03 4
Noir fiction and the erotic – natural bedfellows, right? Simile, of course, intended. Interestingly, the number of anthologies that make the connection explicit are few and far between – but this is one of the most provocative. Contributors include Brian Hodge, Lucy Taylor and Bill Brent, and sharp entries are cheek-by-jowl with some distinctly non-libidinous tales. Not so Maxim Jakubowski's *Phantom Lover*, which is (unsurprisingly) the most compelling – and disturbing.

Eve Tan Gee

No Good Deed by Manda Scott
Headline, £10, ISBN 0 7472 7345 6
This is a deeply atmospheric thriller, dark to the point of opacity, which establishes its bleak tone from the start. A child (who is he?) awakes in a filthy darkened room, littered with bottles and syringes. He hears a woman (who is she?) whispering urgently through the blackness that the men (who are they?) will soon come back and hurt them again. Nothing is explained – either to the child or to the reader. It is quite deliberate. Manda Scott has created an atmosphere of absolute darkness. At first the reader is like the boy, a mute observer with almost no idea of what is happening, to whom and why. As early chapters unfurl, a threatening dawn starts to emerge. The woman and the rescuers are an undercover unit in Special Branch. Their quarry is a Glasgow drug baron who has ruthlessly eliminated the competition. In keeping with the 'cat in a coal cellar' atmosphere of this book, practically no-one has ever seen him. No-one knows where he came from or who he might be. There also seems to be a mole in either Special Branch or the police – and soon, of course, we realise that the mole must be one of the central characters.

Russell James

Final Appeal by Lisa Scottoline
HarperCollins, £5.99, ISBN 0 00 710489 8
Philadelphia Lawyer Grace Rossi is rebuilding her life after a divorce, and finds herself holding down a part-time job with a federal appeals court. But she's given a hot potato: a significant death penalty appeal. And then an apparent suicide in bizarre circumstances leads Grace to become involved in a murder investigation. Scottoline balances some forceful plotting with a strongly realised protagonist and highly plausible background detail.

Barry Forshaw

Storm by Boris Starling
HarperCollins, £5.99, ISBN 0 00 651205 4
Boris Starling's debut novel *Messiah* won much critical acclaim. But this former Mastermind contestant (specialist subject: the novels of Dick Francis) has turned in a less than impressive follow-up. *Storm* is three books in one, and each is clearly derivative. First there is a ferry capsizing (*Titanic*), followed by a hunt for a serial killer necessitating the help of a dangerous criminal (*Silence of the*

Lambs), resulting in a climax straight out of *The X Files*. The central character, Kate Beauchamp, is a half-formed set of responses searching for a personality. She begins as an actress, transmogrifies into a Detective Chief Inspector, and finally descends into the sort of gibbering female beloved of tacky horror films – an unlikely avoidance of safety at the end left me shaking my head in frustration. That she would turn up for work mere hours after surviving a horrendous ferry disaster seems unlikely, as is her fear of bathroom sinks and the refusal to allow her boyfriend (another ferry survivor) any form of counselling. A de rigueur subplot concerning her estranged father is ultimately unrewarding. But once you have got past Starling's obtrusive info-dumping and melodramatic writing style (often using strange half sentences in a bid to increase tension), then it's not all bad news. The investigation itself is often tense, and the plot becomes more pleasingly labyrinthine as it reaches its conclusion. Overall, though, the far fetched leaps of logic and the clichéd subject matter leave a lot to be desired.

Mark Campbell

Umbrella Man by Doug J. Swanson
No Exit Press, £5.99
I suppose it was just a matter of time before Jack Flippo, Dallas' most entertaining failed lawyer turned detective, bumped into the JFK assassination, still the most interesting thing to come out of his backyard (unless you're one of those born-again droolers who find the Dallas Cowboy cheerleaders sexy).

But like a conspiracy theorist whose flow charts have become overloaded, Swanson manages to bury his basic premise in a book which seems to want to do too many things at once. Flippo's forte is humour, which basically gets him fired from his law practice, and back into his sleazy private eye office. But here the laughs come mostly from Jack's avant-garde artist girlfriend Lola, who is strangely excited by thoughts of middle America, and by the sons-in-law of professional hit man Weldon, whose bumbling redneck antics do strike a resonant Texan chord. The bubba brothers get all the good lines, apart from the clerk in a small-town 7-11 who allows how it's OK for him to call his cousin Budlie at two in the morning because "he ain't been able to sleep since his fiancée run off with the exterminator". The interface of those characters with Eddie Nickles, ex-cop turned Grassy Knoll conman, is where this story takes off, or doesn't, because the other serious crime here (besides the assassination) involves Nickles' past. Jack is presented with an erstwhile partner: bail-bondswoman Treena Watts, who seems likely to reappear as a permanent fixture. Swanson's good at keeping things moving, and the way each conspiratorial aspect of the JFK killing is eventually debunked leads one to believe that as a columnist on the local paper he's probably more tired of hearing about Dealey Plaza than Carl Hiaasen is about *Miami Vice.* This may explain the twists and turns, and why things just seem to stop. Perhaps I was expecting too much. It may not be the best intro to Flippo, but still, this ride is more fun than one in an open-topped limo through Dealey Plaza. Lone crazed assassin my butt.

Michael Carlson

Bloggs 19 by Tony Thompson
Warner Books, £6.99, ISBN 0 7515 2241 4
The Protected Witness Unit (PWU) is designed to hold prisoners who are giving evidence of assistance to the police in cases of serious crime. All inmates are known to staff simply as Bloggs, followed by a number. The timing of this utterly involving tale of brutal crime (with a protected witness at the centre) could not be better, as we are all gripped by ever more unlikely cinematic tales of East End villains. This is the real thing, however, and makes for tough, unvarnished reading. In Christmas 1995 the corpses of three men were found in a Range Rover in a secluded country lane near the Essex village of Rettendon. All three were notorious villains, and each had been dispatched by a bullet in the head from a shotgun at point-blank range. A break-

through for police came when one of the gang involved decided to break ranks. Initially this story seemed too outrageous to be believed, but as the evidence started to come together, the bizarre motives behind the killings coalesced. Thompson's narrative involves everything from Irish terrorists and European smugglers to prostitution and police corruption. As Crime Correspondent of the Observer, he has precisely the kind of cool command of his facts that makes this the best kind of true crime writing.

Barry Forshaw

Deathtrap by Peter Turnbull
Severn House, £17.99, ISBN 0 7278 5597 2
Turnbull has had a lengthy career as a reliable and adroit practitioner of the crime and mystery novel, with such titles as *Condition Purple* and *The Killing Floor*, among his most beguiling work. This new thriller comfortably accommodates his familiar tropes, and will while away a happy hour or two. George Hennessy, detective Chief Inspector at Micklegate Bar police station in York is enjoying his work until the body of an ambitious journalist is discovered. Suicide or murder? While no new innovations are inaugurated in Turnbull's narrative, it is a highly professional and well-turned piece of work.

Judith Gray

The Third Messiah by Christopher West
Allison & Busby, £16.99, ISBN 0 7490 0485 1
Christopher West's Chinese novels such as *Death of a Blue Lantern* have marked him out as a crime writer with a rare gift for evocation of place and atmosphere. The comparisons with Martin Cruz Smith's use of Russia as a setting in *Gorky Park* were inevitable, but West's sharply plotted novels more than stand comparison. A mysterious new sect in Beijing is attracting disenchanted young people. But does the cult hide a sinister secret? And what will be the fate of the acolytes? Few readers will be in suspense long about whether or not any cult is sinister – and it's not long before bloody mayhem is let loose at the farm where the cult resides. But China's notorious security forces make no inroads, so it's up to West's protagonists Wang Anzhuang and Rosina Lin to penetrate the veil – and the sinister secrets they uncover have them in mortal danger before an apocalyptic menace. West's knowledge of the country garnishes his strikingly written piece with highly plausible detail, and his heroes quickly win the reader's sympathy. Perhaps not as impressive as the author's earlier *Red Mandarin*, this is nevertheless an authoritatively handled thriller.

TO READ – OR REALLY NOT TO READ...

John Kennedy Melling

One of Sir Noel Coward's brilliantly satiric songs was titled *Why Do the Wrong People Travel? And the Right People Stay at Home?* This could apply to audiences at events in libraries and bookshops! Why do the usually sparse audiences turn up? To buy a signed copy? But most shops in England and America keep a supply of them. To look at the author, see how he dresses, or work out where she buys her clothes? When Bette Davies signed copies of her book at Hatchards, the police had to put up crash barriers to control the crowds. For a free glass of wine? Some bookshops stop that by charging an admission fee, refundable against purchases that night. It must be either to hear an author read, or to learn if he has something helpful and interesting to say.

Some writers seem constitutionally incapable of reading properly, monotonous and inaudible. Reading is a good let out if the author doesn't have anything useful to say about the genre or its history, or helpful advice to would-be writers in the audience. My esteemed colleague Gwendoline Butler is an excellent public speaker and broadcaster – she read History at Oxford and lectured there, and has made a special study of the genre of crime fiction, contributing to leading reference books here and in the USA. A year or two ago, we tried the experiment of my reading short excerpts at relevant points in her lecture: as an editor, I edited the excerpts to make the maximum impact (as opposed to what the late Professor Tovey called 'bleeding hunks' torn from the corpus of a work). But it didn't succeed – it distracted from the flow of her lecture, and subtracted time better employed in direct discourse – so we dropped the idea. This augmented the advice she always gives to embryo writers, not only those present but those who took the trouble to write to her afterwards. So, literally, a good time was had by all!

I have written more than once about the excellent crime library in Paris, the Bibliothèque des Literatures Policières. Recently I travelled to Paris by the Eurotunnel and spent an afternoon there. I had been corresponding with the Chief Librarian, Madame Catherine Chauchard, from whom a fax was already awaiting me at the Hotel Normandy on arrival. I went by taxi the first day to the library, situated in the rue du Cardinal-Lemoine, in the Fifth Arrondissement on the South Bank near the Boul' Mich. Madame Chauchard handed me over to Madame Michele Witta, who explained her grandparents were translators from the French, as was she and her own daughter. The building is newly built (save for one ancient wall) and was created by a former mayor of Paris to form part of the Direction des Affaires Culturelles. In the reference library are five thousand volumes – including my own *Murder Done to Death*. This French library is the only one in the world covering every language – the two others in Sweden and Finland deal only with their own language.

In an issue in 1999 of *Le Nouveau Detective* magazine, I saw a 1953 reference to The Great Carrington, a world famous conjuror I had seen in the Casino at Le Touquet as a boy. One minute to find the 1999 issue, another for the 1953 issue, and two minutes for a photocopy. It has since become an article for a leading English conjuring journal. Crime comics? In the next air-conditioned gallery were drawers full of them in every tongue – Dick Tracy, Fantomas, the lot. Was I aware of the French pulps? No, I only possess a few American and British issues. Drawer after drawer of these fascinating small books, similar to the British Sexton Blake Library or the pocket-size Dixon Hawke books. (Walking back along the Left Bank I managed to buy a French pulp at one of the many stalls.) Magazines next, including our own ***Crime Time*** – again, every language was represented. Books – starting with a complete run of the excellent series *Le Masque*, and *The Murder of Roger Ackroyd* (with its original jacket) conservatively valued at £1,200. Michele stated categorically that the term 'noir' is derived from the Series Noir, started in 1945 by Gallimard, not from film directors filming scenes in darkness or fog to cut down on scenery building costs! A support for this may perhaps lie in one French writer's contention that the French used 'noir' as a meaning of the original English Gothic or suspense novel.

I had submitted an article for *Gibbons Stamp Monthly* on stamps featuring famous fictional detectives, of which I have most specimens. Had I included their French series? She presented me with the six first day cover postcards of 1996, most of the designs from their collection. She also gave me the year's annual, which records every translation of foreign crime novels into French.

There is a Leo Malet lecture theatre. The two exhibitions were about the 813 Magazine and Frédéric Dard, who had just died. He should have received the CWA Diamond Dagger. Dard wrote conventional detective novels, as Hélène de Monaghan explained. Many of his nearly 200 books featured San-Antonio, a best-selling creation dating from 1952 and published by Fleuve Noir. There is an element of parody in his books. San-Antonio's cases affected the French espionage novel and owes much to Aldous Huxley. Dard wrote *Les Pensées de San-Antonio*, a hilarious collection of witty one-liners, and the *Dictionnaire San-Antonio,* a massive 630 pages with a complete bibliography, full dictionary of the hundreds of words he invented, and a centre section listing the terms he invented for amorous activities, women's anatomy and men's thoughts.